P9-BIK-137

Six Ways to Write a Love Letter

JACKSON PEARCE

sourcebooks
casablanca

Copyright © 2022 by Jackson Pearce
Cover and internal design © 2022 by Sourcebooks
Cover illustration by Liza Rusalskaya/The Drawing Arm Australia

Sourcebooks and the colophon are registered trademarks of Sourcebooks.

All rights reserved. No part of this book may be reproduced in any form or by
any electronic or mechanical means including information storage and retrieval
systems—except in the case of brief quotations embodied in critical articles or
reviews—without permission in writing from its publisher, Sourcebooks.

The characters and events portrayed in this book are fictitious or
are used fictitiously. Any similarity to real persons, living or dead,
is purely coincidental and not intended by the author.

All brand names and product names used in this book are trademarks,
registered trademarks, or trade names of their respective holders.
Sourcebooks is not associated with any product or vendor in this book.

Published by Sourcebooks Casablanca, an imprint of Sourcebooks
P.O. Box 4410, Naperville, Illinois 60567-4410
(630) 961-3900
sourcebooks.com

Cataloging-in-Publication Data is on file with the Library of Congress.

Printed and bound in Canada.
MBP 10 9 8 7 6 5 4 3 2 1

To Dale, Kyle, Gwen, and Michael
for the most metal verse in the Bible.

Vivi Swan Band Member
Not-So-Sweet Skateboarding Slip

Vivi Swan, the pop princess whose sold-out Sweethearts world tour starts in nine days, is finding herself in the midst of a disaster that for once has nothing to do with broken hearts! Her tour drummer, Jason Diamond, broke both his elbows in a skateboarding accident over the weekend. He's out for at least two months, leaving the Swan team rushing to find a replacement. Insider sources tell us Remy Young, an LA-based session drummer and former Quiet Coyote band member, is being tapped for the job. Pro tip, Remy: stay away from skateboards.

Comments: 56
Author: Bianca Treble

Chapter One

It was midmorning when Remy woke up. Or at least it was probably morning. It was hard to tell sometimes in Venice Beach—the area had that yawning, cheerful sense of dawn late into the day. The sun was always fresh and white-gold, the shadows always gentle and beckoning, the scent of hibiscus and sand and salt always bright in the air. He turned to look at the fig tree rasping against the screen of his open window—it looked like the leaves were dry, which was disappointing. It'd rained last night for the first time in ages, but in the daylight, it felt like he'd only dreamed the storm. It'd felt so magical last night, the water falling from darkness.

Remy rolled over and off the side of his mattress, which was situated on the floor—what is the actual purpose of a bed frame? Floorboards creaked under his feet and reflected the sunshine back at him every bit as brightly as a mirror would. Remy liked California. *Loved* California? No, not quite. Here, it was hard to shake the perpetual feeling of being on vacation. The pale-peach signs, the ten-for-a-dollar avocados, the fact so many people *were* on vacation… California felt like an incomplete dream, and while that was lovely, he always had the sense he needed to wake up, get a move on with things.

He changed into a T-shirt and pulled a button-down over it, rolling the sleeves up to his elbows. In the living room, Val was already awake, watching television absently—though there was a decent chance Val had simply never gone to sleep at all. Val's girlfriend was curled up under his arm on the sofa bed that was always bed, never sofa. Technically, this was a one-bedroom carriage house—all they could afford to purchase in this area—but with a little bedroom negotiating, the three of them had managed to live in it for nearly a year now. Besides, Remy and Val had always shared small spaces—a bedroom, a van, a studio. They'd grown into each other, vines and fruits overlapping, until you could hardly tell whose roots were whose.

"Coffee?" Remy called to Val and Celeste as he shimmied through the space between the TV set and the edge of the sofa bed.

"Yeah," Val said, looking disappointed that Remy was up. Remy's presence indicated the day had to begin, and Val was on a personal quest to become an owl or vampire or sentient night-blooming flower.

"Me too—I'll help," Celeste said, unwinding herself from Val's arms. She looked so lifelike next to him—tanned and dark-haired and curvy and the kind of person whose warmth you felt from across a room. Val was gaunt, the tattoos running across his chest and down his arms making him look more so, like you could cut yourself on his collarbones or elbows. Celeste slid sweatpants on over her underwear—Remy had long gotten over any particular thrill of seeing her underwear—and joined him in the kitchen, land of mauve appliances and laminate countertops. He ground coffee beans while she rooted out sprouted-grain bread to toast. In California, even the discount food was health food.

"What're you doing today?" Val called out to Remy from the living room.

"Studio. Do you need me before the gig?" Remy answered, pouring the coffee into the filter.

Val appeared in the kitchen door, wearing black jeans, last week's eyeliner, and an expression too warm for either. "No. Just asking. Who's in the studio?" There was a forbidden curiosity in his voice—there always was when it came to Remy working on music with strangers. Val wanted to know but also didn't want to know.

"No one," Remy said. When it was *someone* in the studio, there was no telling how long he'd be stuck there. *Someones* had the time to play around. To send runners out for sushi or weed or cupcakes while the studio musicians hung out, waiting till they were needed next. He was paid by the hour, so it wasn't necessarily a waste of time, but it meant he cleared his evening schedule when *someone* was in the studio. But the *no ones* of the world couldn't afford to rent the studio and musicians on a lark, not even the *no ones* signed to labels. *No one* got in, laid down their tracks, and got out.

Celeste's toast popped up; she layered it with butter and sliced figs then made her way to the dining room, which—like the living room—didn't fulfill its intended purpose. It was her office, where she managed her celebrity-culture websites the way Remy imagined naval captains managed ships. Celeste was the sort of person you knew named herself president of clubs and CEO of lemonade stands in her youth. She didn't have problems, she had opportunities, and she didn't have arguments, she had wars. It was a natural skill set, which meant she had quickly turned blogs that started out discussing topics like celebrity camel toes into a very legitimate business venture.

Val stole the first cup of coffee then slunk past Remy to the patio, walking absently the way he often did. Val's mind never stopped, never paused, never relaxed; back in Florida, when they shared a bedroom, Remy would wake in the night to find Val staring at the ceiling, wide awake. Not unable to sleep, but unwilling—it was like Val thought sleeping would derail his mind entirely, like it was easier to just keep it tearing along, racing into the dawn. Problematically, Val wasn't wrong. He was at his most poignant, most musical, most artistic, most moving, most creative when he allowed his mind to run ceaselessly. More problematically, he'd found a variety of substances to keep it running when his body asked it to sleep.

Those substances were a thing of the past—but Remy was always watching for the warning signs he'd missed the first time around. Celeste too, of course, but Remy couldn't help but feel she was the backup plan while he was the first line of defense. He was keenly aware Val hadn't written a song in almost two years, and Remy always wondered if his brother would break, would use again if only to draw another song up from the depths of his soul.

"I thought he had a melody last week," Celeste said thoughtfully from over Remy's shoulder. He turned to face her, and she shook her head at his expression. "Stop it—I'd tell you if I thought he was on something. It was a nice one, but then he stopped humming it. Maybe it's the little seed sprouting though, you know?"

"Maybe," Remy said. "I didn't hear him humming anything new. Do you remember how it went?" He didn't like the tinge of jealousy he felt over Celeste hearing something new from Val—however short it was—when he didn't.

"It was definitely new, but he was working through it mostly at night, after you were in bed," Celeste said quickly.

"Sure. That makes sense," he said, even though he wasn't entirely sure it did.

Village Studios was on a corner in Downtown LA that wasn't too far from Venice Beach, but given that it was LA, it was a nearly two-hour commute. Remy ditched the bus a single stop early so they didn't see him getting off it. No one rode the bus in this town, which was a pity since public transport wasn't terrible, but Remy's options were limited. There was the old touring van that he and Val drove from the Florida panhandle to Nashville and then on to LA three years later—but it didn't have air-conditioning or power steering. There was also Celeste's old BMW, vintage cool and painted a bright lemongrass color—but Celeste was forever needing it to rush over to some celeb hot spot or another, so it wasn't handy to borrow. Thus, Remy was left to the bus. It wasn't that Remy was worried about people judging him for taking public transit; it was just that he didn't feel like explaining why he defied the city's unspoken three-cars-per-person rule.

Village was an old, famous recording studio with big windows and a beautifully decorated lobby. The exposed brick walls were lined with photos of musicians who had recorded there—B.B. King, Nat King Cole, John Mayer, Coldplay, Madonna. The receptionist smiled at him through flawless makeup, the kind she'd applied so deftly that a younger Remy wouldn't have even realized she was wearing it. Oh, simple, stupid, younger Remy.

"Studio A," she said. "You're the first one, though."

Of course he was. *Someones* could be late, *no ones* had to be on time; Remy was neither, so he had to be early.

Remy walked past the photographed eyes of wealthier musicians, down a green-carpeted hallway, then through the heavy door into Studio A. The control room walls and adjacent lounge were covered in mahogany paneling, the mixing boards and computer monitors set up in such a way that it looked like an altar to a technology god. Soft light from expensive, paper-covered lanterns lit his way through the leather-filled lounge area and into the live room. Oriental rugs covered the floor, and the back wall was draped in thick red curtains. A row of candles were lined up on the windowsill between the live and control rooms, and the room smelled clean but not like cleaner—a bright, citrusy incense sort of smell. This was a great studio for a *no one* to get. It must be the sort of *no one* a label was excited about.

Remy's drum set—well, the studio's drum set, since it probably cost about seven grand and ha ha ha to the idea of Remy owning that—was already set up, as was a keyboard. He selected a few drumsticks and spun them between his fingers then paused to crack each of his knuckles. He liked being in the studio, liked the simplicity of it. He had one job in here: play the drums. There was no one to watch over, no anger to quell, no longing to fulfill. Just play the drums, get the job done, and move along. People often spoke about following their passions but rarely spoke about the value of good old-fashioned busy work or its meditative qualities. No, it wasn't fulfilling, but that meant it wasn't dangerous. You couldn't break your heart on busy work.

One by one the other studio musicians filtered in. They were older than him, for the most part, sporting beards and slight bellies, their bright eyes and faces aged by the California sun and smoking. They greeted him politely and then went to work tuning or answering emails on their phones. Like Remy, they all wore dress shirts over T-shirts, the sleeves rolled up. Professional, but not boring-adult professional. A flicker of movement in the control room, and one of Village's producers appeared, his voice booming into the live room a moment later.

"Alright, folks, we've got about five minutes. Just a scratch demo, music's on the way," he said, and at that moment, a harried-looking assistant came in, handing out sheet music. Everyone flipped through it absently, the first guitarist being the only one who took the time to pick out the parts. Pop music was, for the most part, painfully easy to play, especially the drum parts—Remy could've done them live, with the music scrolling past him like real life Guitar Hero. Still, he rustled through the papers once, then a second time, then set them up on his music stand.

"Hey, Remy, can you come in here for a second?" the producer's voice called back through the speaker a few moments later.

Remy nodded and rose, mildly concerned—getting called into the boss's office was nerve-spiking no matter how good you were at your job. He rounded the corner into the control room and leaned against the door. The producer spun around in one of the four ergonomic office chairs lined up at the control desk. He—his name was Skipper, but Remy refused to think of an adult man by that name on principle—was older, and his silvery hair was always trimmed flawlessly, like he stopped at the barbershop every morning to get the angles lined up (which he very well might have).

"What's up?" Remy asked.

"I have a job for you, if you want it," the producer said, looking pleased with himself.

"Always," Remy said and slid into another one of the chairs.

"You know Vivi Swan?"

"I don't *know* her," Remy said, because this was LA and the producer might have meant the question literally. "I recorded on her last album, though. I never met her. We did everything separate." He remembered the album well enough—though admittedly, he had a good memory. It was a series of breakup songs. Angry ones, sad ones, excited ones, dreamy ones. One breakup song after another.

"Oh, right, right," the producer said. "She recorded the vocals in, like, Japan, right? Anyway, she's doing a world tour, and her tour drummer just fell off a skateboard and fractured his elbow." As he said this, he lifted his phone to show Remy a gossip site article on the incident, like Remy had asked for hard proof. "They leave in two weeks and need a replacement. I know Walter Cunningham, the tour manager, and told him you might want it. Interested?"

Remy lifted his eyebrows for two reasons:

One, because he couldn't for the life of him figure out why a drummer experienced and talented enough to be a tour musician would risk being on a skateboard, a machine known for smashing bones.

Two, because this was a big job. Vivi Swan wasn't a musician so much as a pop culture icon. A frequent fixture on Celeste's websites, a tabloid staple, blond and tall and leggy and undeniably beautiful but also undeniably inhuman, in that way all megastars were. They were all over LA, these creatures from movies and music and reality shows, and in person they were always thinner, shorter, and stranger. They didn't look like they belonged here; they looked like they were only pretending to be human, not made of carbon but perhaps neon or gold. Playing for someone like Vivi Swan wasn't just a gig—it was a résumé throne.

"They'd need you about six weeks of the North American leg. You know the music already, it'll be easy money," the producer went on, and his voice sounded a little strained—Remy could tell he'd already told Vivi Swan's people that Remy was a sure thing. "What's your holdup?"

"Just short notice, that's all," Remy said. "Six weeks?"

"Yep," the producer said. "Not too long. You went on longer tours than that with Quiet Coyote, didn't you?"

"Eight months," Remy said, nodding, even though he suspected a Vivi Swan tour bore little resemblance to him and Val touring in the Van, which they'd hastily graffitied QUIET COYOTE on the side of the night they signed with their label. Of course, Remy and Val had been *together* for that tour, which was perhaps the biggest difference of all. To go off on his own like this, to just say yes and leave Val alone for the first time in…well, *ever*—

The producer cleared his throat. "Look, Remy—I'll be honest, I told them you were in. You never turn down jobs. I figured you'd jump at this."

"I never turn down *local* jobs. I just—I've got some other engagements. I mean, don't we have the next three weeks booked here?"

"I can find another studio drummer, man," the producer said, starting to sound desperate. "I can't believe you're not freaking out. This is Vivi Swan. This will be killer for your résumé. You've said you want to do more producing—well, having Vivi Swan on your résumé, even if you were just her tour drummer, will open some serious doors."

The producer wasn't wrong—Remy knew breaking in as a producer in LA was every bit as difficult as breaking in as an actor or singer or photographer or whatever. It required schmoozing, required wrapping your arms around young starlets, required sunglasses and fedoras. Remy was not good at those things. This might be a chance, the only chance, and it was just six weeks, right?

Celeste could keep an eye on Val for six weeks. It'd be fine.

Remy took a deep breath, and that California feeling, that perpetual dream sensation, rattled around in his lungs, fighting expulsion.

"Yeah. Okay. I'm in," Remy said briskly. His chest tightened with something not quite excitement and not quite fear.

The producer hurried to give Remy a list of phone numbers, oblivious to the fact Remy was fairly certain he was experiencing an existential crisis.

The *no one*—the *talent* was the real term—they were expecting showed up a few moments later, sporting artistically unkempt hair and skinny jeans, with his own producer and girlfriend in tow. Skipper was a good producer, but no one used the studio's producer anymore—not the way they used the studio's musicians. The talent's producer was marginal at best. He sat behind the controls, a forty nestled between his legs, and moved the controls up and down, accomplishing very little by way of changing the sound despite his claims that he was "getting a feel for the heart of the piece."

They finished the track, then another, then waited while someone ran out to get the producer another bottle of beer. The talent was young, probably eighteen or so, though he'd already lined his arms with tattoos. He didn't look tired or worn.

"Is this your first album?" Remy asked as they waited for the runner to return. The other musicians were on their phones or talking idly; Remy could tell the talent was only pretending to go over the notes on his music stand. That was something Remy'd always done when Val wasn't in the studio to start a conversation or instigate a random jam or suggest a cash-prize relay race through the studio halls.

The talent shrugged, trying to look like he wasn't excited, wasn't worried, wasn't just another music-loving teenager desperate to become something greater. "Did a demo last year. Did pretty well in my home region."

"Which region?"

"Maine," the talent said without blushing, which Remy appreciated. He respected people who weren't ashamed of where they came from, no matter how small or how far away from Nashville or LA or New York. "We're working on a second song," he added.

Ah, the second song. People thought breaking into the music industry was difficult, but they were wrong. Breaking in with one song was *hard* but not really difficult. But getting a foothold, getting a second song? That was the real test. The steepest step of all. The word *difficult* didn't do it justice.

"This could be it, man. Sounds great," Remy said and smiled. He didn't believe this, really, but he'd been wrong before. And besides, if the label realized the producer was crap and made a few changes, it really could be a totally serviceable pop song. Remy dared to entertain the idea that perhaps, after the Vivi Swan tour, he'd get recommended to produce the piece.

The talent nodded in appreciation, a glimpse of a grin on his face. The kid was only two or three years younger than Remy, but in music industry years, that was a decade. Remy fought the urge to give him advice: Save your money. Don't get too excited. Having a backup plan isn't the same as failing. Let someone else buy the drinks. Remember there are more of you. There are always more of you.

Remy didn't tell him any of this, though, because he knew the talent wouldn't listen. He'd been the talent once, after all, and he hadn't listened when a handful of seasoned musicians had tried to tell him the same thing. Why listen to some downers in the recording studio when you could listen to the label, the press, the producers screaming YES in your ears?

Then

"What do you want to play?" the music teacher had asked. She was smiling and sweet-faced, with pale lips and wearing a high turtleneck. The woman wasn't wearing makeup—Remy's parents would never have allowed the kids to take class with her if she had been. Her cheeks were nonetheless rosy, and her slightly crooked teeth were bright white from a diet void of coffee and soda.

The room was filled with secondhand instruments, brought via a volunteer's pickup truck. Until now, the monthly "extra" lesson was art or sometimes gymnastics; getting a music class put into rotation had been a very big deal. When church services had ended, and the congregation had kissed the pads of their three middle fingers then held them to the sky—their traditional farewell to one another and the Lord—the children had rushed from the chapel to the activities room, ruffly skirts and shiny shoes roaring into the tiny space.

Val had gone wild. He picked up every instrument, playing with each one for a few moments. A tambourine, a guitar, the drumsticks, a ukulele, and a marimba missing the top few resonators. He crashed through the music room the same way he'd crashed through kickball and choir and each and every church bake sale. Val wasn't afraid of breaking things.

Remy, on the other hand, had merely watched his brother for the first few moments. The other students were showing off the handful of hymns they already knew how to plunk out on the piano, or strumming an out-of-tune guitar, or giggling as they tried (in vain) to produce a decent sound on a weathered trumpet. It wasn't that Remy couldn't decide which to play; it was just that the instruments merely looked like different ways to make noise. He failed to see the point.

Finally, at the music teacher's prodding, he wandered to a snare drum that had been recently abandoned by twin girls one year his senior. He tapped the drum gently with his fingertips, creating a quiet sound, like rain on a nice roof.

"Ah, yes. The drums are very important, you know," the music teacher, who'd followed him over, said wisely. She had picked up the drumsticks from where they'd been discarded on the floor. The sticks were beaten and grayed with age, but Remy liked them all the more for that. They felt storied, hitting him with the same sense of displaced nostalgia he'd had when he and Val snuck TV and saw R2-D2 in *Star Wars*. Dusty and beaten. That robot and these drumsticks had tales.

Remy hit the little snare drum lightly, grinning at the rattling sound that rose from it. The teacher smiled back.

"The drummer is the heartbeat of the band," she had said. "Without the drummer, everything falls apart."

Chapter Two

To say that playing music at live shows was different from playing music in the studio was like saying a wild tiger was different from a stuffed one or that a man with a real gun was different from a child with a water pistol. The pieces were the same—band, drums, music, listeners—but the result was impossibly different.

In the studio, everything was controlled.

The music could be stopped, taken back, perfected. You could tweak bits and pieces on the computer, you could finesse and change, and you never worried too much about the amount of sweat accumulating on your brow because it wasn't like anyone was taking pictures of you. Music there felt like an art or math project, something that could be broken down into notes and melodies and strings.

Live music, however, was *alive*. There was no fixing a mistake, no going back, no stopping to tell the bassist he was rushing into the bridge. Live music moved like an animal, twisting through the crowd, driven by the musicians but rarely owned by them. The crowd added to the noise, their shouts and cell phone sounds and glasses clinking together or shattering on the ground. It was different every time because living things are never the same twice.

Plenty of musicians preferred it this way. They liked riding atop the creature that was a live show, being bucked and thrown and sweating and trying to survive it all. Val was one of those musicians. When he played live, he didn't look like a musician playing a song; he looked like a wild thing in its habitat. He commanded the eye not with his sound or his look or his voice but with his entire being.

Remy did not.

There was a time when the high of live shows pulled him along, but now, that high came with the frustration of being unable to correct mistakes, the memories of Val at his worst, the reminder of how the label had snuffed them out like they were stompable insects. He and Val would kiss the pads of their middle three fingers then wave to the crowd—a Quiet Coyote tradition—and then the venue would close, the people would leave, the stuff would need to be loaded up, and they'd return to the hotel or motel or friend-of-a-friend's couch, struck by how silent the world was compared to how loud it'd been just hours before. And they'd make five hundred dollars or so for it all.

The irony that Remy was bemoaning his way to this particular live show, which he would attend bearing the news that he'd just signed on to do two months' worth of live shows with a pop star, was not lost on him. He finished in the studio early, killed time at a coffee shop on Abbot Kinney for an hour, then made his way over to the venue—a place called SALT (in all caps—*always* in all caps, or the owner got pissed). He cut around to the back, where the van was parked. Val had a cigarette propped in his mouth and was diligently unloading equipment with the bassist.

Val tilted his head up in greeting as Remy approached. Unloading was one of the few times of day when his brother was all business, and

Remy knew better than to meddle in it with conversations or hellos or news that he'd be leaving town for six weeks. He ducked into the front seat of the van, where he found Celeste on her laptop.

"Is merch already out?" he asked.

"It's in the dressing room. We got here early. Val wanted to make sure the lights were right."

"He what?"

Celeste looked up at him. "Something about the house lights flashing? Or...I don't know. The lights were wrong." She smiled, and there was a hint of humor in it—of quiet acknowledgment that sometimes what was Very Wrong to Val wasn't necessarily what someone else might consider Very Wrong.

Remy shrugged. "It's hard to play with lights distracting you," he said.

Celeste's face fell a little, and Remy felt a twinge of remorse—she wasn't wrong for her exasperation, after all. Val was the sort that would suddenly decide the fifteen-minute sound check wasn't good enough and spend another thirty saying, "Yeah, yeah, YEAH," into the mic at varying pitches, pushing dials and running back and forth across the stage, all of which made no discernible difference. Rather than being the problem child, though, Val was usually viewed as some sort of genius, a delicate and exotic plant that needed just the right conditions to grow, and what the hell is wrong with you that you can't encourage and understand that?

But that didn't mean that, sometimes, you couldn't roll your eyes at him or at least *want* to roll your eyes at him. Remy did—often, actually. Celeste did too. But doing so together? That still felt like a betrayal, even after all this time—a betrayal Remy might have overlooked had he not just agreed to leave his brother for six weeks without warning.

Remy made his way through the loading dock and into the

backstage maze. SALT smelled like old wood and ocean water and spilled beer, and it was excellent. The place made you want to create something, or do something, or run away from home. It wasn't the nicest club in LA, obviously. It wasn't even a nice club, period. But Remy and Val had been playing here since before Celeste, before they bought the carriage house, before even Remy had accepted the fact they weren't likely to grace the Billboard charts again anytime soon. SALT was home base in the same way that Val was home base, which made it all the more worrisome that they were playing here less and less these days. He couldn't blame the club—after all, Quiet Coyote hadn't created any new music in two years. How long could you play the same set, tossing in a cover now and again, before people got bored of it?

Remy walked down to the dressing room—the small one, since SALT never wanted to open the large, fancy one for them, opting to save it for special occasions like Remy's mother saved her wedding china. The small one had a few fat chairs with worn leather, each more comfortable than the last. Fluorescent lights, a table, an abstract mural that had been signed by various musicians over the years, and a cabinet which was, as Remy always requested, stocked only with water. Alcohol had never really been Val's vice, but the news that Remy was going to leave for six weeks with someone like Vivi Swan… well. It was the sort of thing that might set him off.

Remy cracked open a bottle of water and sat back, playing with his phone until Val appeared, then the keyboardist and bassist, and finally Celeste, who was still pecking at her laptop even as she walked.

"Lights fixed?" Remy asked Val.

"Yeah. They switched to those ones that flicker. I can't stand those. I changed them all back," Val said, sounding annoyed. He slumped back in another chair and kicked his feet up on the table.

"I could make a million dollars teaching girls how to get out of cars in short dresses. You know they're going to take crotch pictures, honey. It's not fair, but you know they'll do it, so *put your purse over your vag*," Celeste said under her breath, though the room was quiet enough that she might have shouted it.

"And *then* go into the market selling specialty crotch-blocking purses," Val suggested.

"Brilliant," Celeste said and shut her laptop. "Though, honestly, I should go back to running the sorts of sites that cover cellulite and sex tapes. Maybe the 'celebs without makeup' stuff. That's where the money is."

"People are idiots," Val responded, shaking his head.

"Yeah, well, money from idiots spends the same, especially multiplied by five. We could get a new TV if I did an article on Tuesday Rivers's butt pads," Celeste said, sighing. Celeste had worked out early on that the key to success wasn't pumping up a single website's reputation but rather running multiple websites at once, linking them to one another, sharing information across the void. She had one that was more vulgar than the others, one that focused on teen audiences, one that focused on musicians, another on actors, another on female starlets. They were all run under different names, so when Celeste shared information across the lot, it looked like a story was blowing up—even if it was truly something small and inconsequential.

It was pretty damn genius.

"Well, good news for Tuesday Rivers's butt pads, then—I can cover the TV," Remy broke in casually. "I took a gig today."

"New studio? Pass me a water," Val said as Celeste leaned back in her chair absentmindedly.

Remy shook his head and grabbed a bottle. "Not a studio. Touring. I'll be gone for six weeks."

Then he tossed his brother the bottle of water, which Val almost missed despite his eyes being particularly wide at the moment.

Remy hadn't meant for the words to clunk from his mouth like that. He'd meant to get through the show tonight, to perform big and proud and go home, then tell Val in the morning, which was the responsible and adult thing to do. The show, however, was such a damn convenient distraction—it meant Val wouldn't have all that long to rage about the news, since they had to be onstage in ten.

It also was a pretty cowardly thing to do, and Remy knew it. He ducked his head, pretending to be distracted by the broken zipper on his jacket.

"Six weeks? Did you just say six weeks?" Val said. His voice was even, but in a dangerous sort of way—the steady drone of a growling dog before lunging.

"Yeah. It's a last-minute thing, the other guy broke his arm on a skateboard," Remy said, trying to make his voice bouncy and light. *Oh, I had no idea this would be a problem! I have no idea why you're angry, Val! I'm just the drummer!*

"What kind of punk-ass idiot gets on a skateboard before a tour?" the keyboardist said, and it was a real question and a much-needed one—the keyboardist *didn't* know just how angry Val was, which meant his question carved out at least a few layers of tension.

"I know, right?" Remy answered. "Dumbass."

"Six weeks," Val said again, flatly. "Six weeks, seriously? You just take a tour for six weeks without even talking to me? You're in our band, dumbass. How am I supposed to replace you on such short notice?"

"I have a buddy who drums—" the keyboardist began then stopped when he saw the fire in Val's eyes. The keyboardist looked like he had many regrets, including but not limited to: speaking, meeting Val, and being born.

Remy lowered his voice. "It's just a pretty great opportunity, Val. I'm sure we can find a drummer who can play our stuff. I'll even head up the search if you need me to."

"I don't want *a drummer*, Remy. You're my brother, you're the producer, and you're one of the original members. I want *you* playing with me. I know I can find *a drummer*," Val said, shaking his head. "You aren't available. We have gigs lined up. And besides, what's the point? Why go on tour to play drums when you can play drums here?"

Remy opened his mouth to respond—though, even at this point, he hadn't worked out what exactly he would say—but Celeste jumped in, diffusing as best she could. "Who's the tour with?" she asked.

"Vivi Swan. I played on her album, so I already know the songs."

The room went still. Then the keyboardist snorted and shook his head in something between jealousy and wonder. Celeste's mouth curled into a smile. "Okay! Finally you know! It all got announced online this morning, but I couldn't tell you since *you* didn't know about the job yet."

"Wait, what?" Remy said.

"Everyone in pop culture knew you were getting offered the job. That producer Skipper leaks like a sieve, Remy."

"Huh. He did say he'd already told Vivi's people I'd take it," Remy said thoughtfully.

"Can we focus? Who the fuck is Vivi Swan?" Val asked. "Do we know her?"

"You know her. Everyone knows her," Celeste said and immediately opened her laptop. She typed at the speed of light then began to rattle off the names of Vivi Swan's exes—musicians and actors and models and sons of politicians who had populated her screen. There were more people than Remy had dated, period.

"That girl has *problems*, you hear me? Daddy issues," the keyboardist said.

"Her parents are great. They live in Tennessee. One's a dentist," Celeste challenged.

"How do you know they're great? Have you *met* them?" the keyboardist answered.

"I'm just saying that you can't claim *daddy issues* just because someone dates lots of guys. And then writes songs about them. That make her insanely popular. Look—my money comes from gossip articles, and I know it. Her money comes from breakup songs, and she knows it. I can respect that. She's ridden the breakup song thing into platinum records and commercials and a freaking traveling Grammy Museum exhibit. She's dating Noel Reid right now, and I am *so excited* to hear whatever breakup song she writes about him."

Val looked disgusted, like Remy had told him he was taking a part-time job as a sewage inspector. He peered at the photos Celeste had pulled up. "Six weeks of *that*? Look at the stage in those concert pictures. What the hell is that?"

"She had a candy-themed set in her last show," Celeste said and narrowed the search field to include only concert photos. Dozens of photos of Vivi Swan appeared, leggy and blond, with pointed eyeliner and cherry-red lipstick. She was posing amid brightly colored palm trees and lollipops and sunshines with faces. It looked like she'd been dropped into an animated painting. Behind her, dancers wore giant, goofy smiles. And behind *them* was the band, including the drummer Remy suspected he was replacing, who was playing a kit with neon pink-and-yellow swirl covers.

Val busted out laughing, but it was cold. "It looks like he's playing on a drum set made out of an acid trip. You're better than this shit, man. Come on. This isn't an opportunity, it's a punishment." If he couldn't get Remy to quit with guilt, he'd try basic shaming.

"Val. She's playing an arena of sixty thousand," the keyboardist said, pointing to the shot of Vivi Swan taken from behind her so that rather than the stage, you saw the audience—a dark stadium with a billion tiny lights from cell phones and cameras and glow sticks. Vivi Swan looked like she was about to be swallowed by them but had her shoulders back and head up like it wouldn't hurt, or maybe like it would but she didn't care.

Val rolled his eyes. "Fine. Whatever, man. It's not just that I hate pop music—it's that she's not even a musician. She's a product." He was right, of course. Vivi Swan had a perfume line and a deal with Diet Coke, and Remy was pretty sure she'd been in some CoverGirl commercials at some point. She was manufactured in a way Quiet Coyote had never been—which was, perhaps, why she'd outlasted Quiet Coyote. She was custom-made; they were a happy accident.

"Seriously though, Remy, tell me what she's like," Celeste said, sounding hungry. "If there's any insider information…"

"I'm sure they'll make me sign a nondisclosure," Remy said. "And besides, given who she is, I bet I'll talk to her twice, tops."

"Yeah, but still. I'm good at my job. I'll make sure it never leads back to you," Celeste said.

"Stop it, both of you. Are you serious right now?" Val said, looking astounded that Remy and Celeste were talking with such certainty about the gig. "Why are you doing this? Is it about the money? Fuck the money. Right now, Remy, I could make fifteen thousand dollars if I changed the lyrics of 'Everything but the World' to 'Everything but Colleen' and played some Grammy exec's wife's tennis party—"

"Wait, what?" Celeste said. "What's a tennis party?"

"I don't know, she's into me and tennis or something. My point is,

I'm not doing it, because that's not who I am. This kind of tour is not who you are. Unless you have some deep need to be a bubblegum tour drummer that I didn't know about?"

Remy took a breath. He wasn't ready to tell Val just how much he wanted to produce for others, how this was a chance to network, to meet people, to get his name out. So he simplified it into a summary that would make Val angry but wouldn't make him explosive. "I just want to do it, brother."

Less than thirty seconds later—just long enough for Val to delve back into stony, furious silence—a runner came to retrieve them. They played the show as they'd played it hundreds of times before, and for the first time in ages Remy liked each and every song again. His stomach clenched. What the hell had he done? Traded the danger he knew for the danger of a candy-themed stage set?

"Thank you, beautiful people," Val panted into the microphone just before they launched into their last song—always better to say your farewells to the crowd before they mill away at the end of the set. "We're Quiet Coyote, and we'll be back in six weeks. Get your asses back here and see us again."

He glanced back at Remy as he said this, a burning sort of expression in his eyes. Remy lifted the sticks high, rattled off the lick that sent Val into the first verse. Like he always did, like he'd always done, like they'd always been. Like they wouldn't be at all, for six weeks.

Remy played on, because despite the worry spreading in his chest like a sickness, he didn't know how to do anything else.

Chapter Three

"There's a stylist who picks out my clothes. They'll be delivered at the rehearsals," Remy said when Celeste lifted an eyebrow at his largely empty bag. There was one pair of jeans, two T-shirts, boxer shorts, undershirts, and a handful of store-brand toiletries.

"They pick your *clothes*?" Val said, shaking his head. "For fuck's sake. Are they going to dress you like a piece of Laffy Taffy to match the set?"

"I don't think so," Remy said, but he didn't really know. They weren't going to literally dress him like a piece of candy, he figured, but they could very well want him in some sort of bright-pink tank top or banana-yellow shorts or whatever. He involuntarily grimaced at the thought. His sense of self wasn't as tied to shades of black as Val's was, but banana-yellow still wasn't exactly his vibe.

"You're going to regret this," Val said, sighing—he'd traded in anger for parental-brand disappointment. He smiled sardonically. "At least I'll get a picture of you dressed as a piece of candy as a souvenir, though."

"I'll buy the frame as repayment for springing it all on you," Remy offered and grinned. It was an attempt at a truce, and it seemed to work—a little, anyhow. Val nodded and looked around, like he was thinking of where he'd hang the candy photo.

"If you need any information on stuff in my name, it's in my room. Red folder," Remy said, more to Celeste than Val. She nodded, understanding that Remy meant more than old copies of power bills—he meant information on Val. The therapist, the counselor, the people at the treatment facility Val had been at for a few weeks, all details he'd taken her through last night.

"We're taking your room while you're gone, cool?" Celeste cut in.

"Yeah, fine," Remy said. "Don't smoke in my bed."

"How're you gonna stop us?" Val answered and grinned wickedly.

Remy sighed. "Whatever. I need to head out," he said, stooping to swing his bag—an old orange camping backpack—over his shoulder. Remy danced around the word *leaving*. He was *heading out*. He was *going to work*. He was *taking a gig*. Taking a gig was something easily understood, something that made sense, something temporary, dictated by contracts and signatures rather than emotions and music. *Leaving* was something else entirely. They'd left before, six years ago, when they crossed the Florida state line and made a vow to never look—or write, or call—back, the van seeping with cigarette smoke and the scent of sweat and hunger and *freedom*.

This wasn't leaving. Leaving meant never coming back. This was just a vacation, not a split, not a break, not forever. They could do this.

"Right. Later," Val said then reached for Remy's shoulder and pulled him close into a hug that, had it lasted one moment less, would have been little more than a clap on the back. As soon as Val released Remy, Celeste swooped in, hugging him tightly in a way that made him certain she was hugged as a child. She was stronger than she looked, and up close she smelled like coconut and lemongrass.

She pulled back and left her hands on his shoulders, looking him square in the eye. "And remember—being an anonymous source pays well. I won't stiff you just because you're basically my brother-in-law, okay? You'll get the five grand like everyone else."

"How generous," Remy said, smirking.

A half hour later, he'd arrived at the arena loading docks, which were largely empty save for two semitrucks, both of which had already been wrapped with giant pictures of Vivi Swan's face peering at him over big sunglasses. VIVI SWAN—SWEETHEARTS WORLD TOUR was splashed across it in a cheery, neon-pink font. Maybe Val was right, Remy thought, and he *would* be dressed as a giant piece of Laffy Taffy.

"Hey, man," Remy said, tilting his chin at a man sitting in a lawn chair flicking at his phone aimlessly. "I'm Remy Young. I play the drums."

"You got clearance?" the guy—Phil, according to the name tag on his beaten Microsoft Theater polo shirt—asked, lifting his eyebrows.

"I've got nothing. They just told me to be here at nine," Remy explained. He still had fifteen minutes, which was less time than he liked, given that he didn't know if Vivi Swan was the "where the hell is everyone, we're supposed to start at nine" sort or the "wait, we had rehearsal at nine?" sort.

Phil eyed Remy, then his camping backpack, then sighed and grabbed for a walkie. In a few moments, a sunny guy with movie-star slick hair and an enormous coffee stuck his head out one of the side doors, balancing to keep it open with his foot.

"Come on in!" the guy—this *had* to be Walter, the tour manager he'd talked to on the phone—called. Remy thanked Phil, who didn't respond, then hurried to the door.

"Hey, Walter Cunningham?" Remy said, smiling and offering his hand.

"Nope. I'm his assistant," the guy said. He shook Remy's hand briefly then turned and started down the hallway, neat leather shoes clicking on the concrete floor as Remy struggled to keep up. "Walter's on the phone and probably will be all morning, but I can get you started. Did you get a copy of all the music?"

"Got everything printed out in the bag," Remy said.

"Perfect. She likes to do covers every now and then, but it's usually nothing difficult, especially for the drummer," Walter's assistant said. "We try to get music out, but you probably want to make sure your tablet is always charged in case we can't get a printer." Remy opted not to mention that he didn't own a tablet.

The hallways were labyrinthine, bare save for the occasional piece of neon paper labeled *To Stage* or *To Talent Dressing* or *Crew*. Walter's assistant sipped his coffee loudly and sped up, moving so fast that Remy was both amazed the guy could walk so quickly and struggling not to pant as he hurried behind.

"You need coffee? Water? Anything? Say so now, since they're about to start," Walter's assistant called over his shoulder.

"I'm set," Remy said, and they finally reached the hall that circled the bottom floor of the arena. Tunnels popped up every dozen yards or so, giving Remy a few moments to glimpse inside. The seats roared to the ceiling, ghostly for their vacancy. The musicians already onstage were tuning, plucking, and sound checking, while a handful of people wearing headsets were scurrying back and forth, dodging dancers as they did so. Walter's assistant finally turned right, down one of the tunnels, and the arena unfolded above Remy's head.

"Toss your bag anywhere for now, it'll be safe. I'll get your paper-work," Walter's assistant said, motioning to the area on the edge of the stage, already messy with water bottles and sweatshirts and cell phones. Remy obeyed, ran a hand through his hair, then took a deep breath. It was time to drop the worry over leaving Val on his own for so long, the wariness over knotting himself to someone like Vivi Swan. It was time to work, and Remy had always, always been a professional.

"Alright, so, here's all the basics," Walter's assistant said when he returned, the pen between his teeth muddling his words. He had yet another clipboard now and pushed it into Remy's hands. There were highlighter marks at all the places Remy needed to initial, sign, or fill in information. It was standard—length of contract, expectations, the whole shebang. There was, of course, the nondisclosure, just as Remy had told Celeste there would be. Along with this there was a place for Remy to fill in information on any "close friends or family significantly involved" in the entertainment business, along with the names of their bands or shows or websites or YouTube pages, presumably so Vivi Swan's people could scour them for anything potentially damaging to the Vivi Swan machine.

Remy wrote in Val and Quiet Coyote's name but didn't bother with Celeste's—because he didn't know the names of her various gossip websites anyhow. This was by design: Celeste kept the names of her sites a secret from everyone, Remy and Val included. The fewer people who knew where she was on the internet, the fewer people could stop up the leaks she subsisted on. Plus it wouldn't do her any good if her friends didn't get hired by the rich and famous because they named her websites on their nondisclosure agreements. She needed those friends to keep on cleaning celebrity bathrooms or going to celebrity gyms or PA-ing on film sets.

Celeste really was a genius.

When Remy was finished signing his life away, Walter's assistant introduced him to the rest of the band—Michael and David, middle-aged men on guitar and keyboard. The second guitar player, Parish—who apparently also played the banjo and fiddle for some songs—was the closest to Remy's age, except for the backup singers, a collection of pretty young and (probably intentionally) ethnically diverse women. Remy committed all the musicians' names to memory—he wanted to know them and for them to *like* him and remember him and later go to him to produce their solo albums.

"Let me know if you need anything," David, the keyboardist, said. "Or Michael. We've been touring with Vivi since her first North American tour three—no, wait, *five* years ago. God. When did I get old?" he said jovially, the lines in his freshly shaven face crinkling. "Anyway—"

A voice boomed over a speaker, cutting David off. It had to be Walter talking, though Remy couldn't see where he was. "Okay, so, new guy's here—Remy Young on drums, everyone," he said. All eyes turned to Remy, each face glowing with the halo of the stage lights. Remy smiled and waved a little as he slid into the seat behind the drum set.

"And Ms. Swan has also arrived, so go ahead and set up from 'Stay,' folks. We'll be marking first, but all in," Walter-the-disembodied continued.

The dancers instantly arranged themselves; Parish, Michael, and David moved back across the stage. Remy licked his lips, tried not to reveal the twist in his stomach over not getting so much as a practice run-through before Vivi Swan—his boss—arrived. The show was ready—or at least, it was for everyone else. Remy had missed the music rehearsals, the tweaks, the lighting changes, the testing of a dozen different clothes under lights to make sure all the black pants stayed black rather than looking ruddy brown under a million watts of electricity. A roadie brought him a music stand with sheet music, which Remy didn't need but appreciated all the same. He was hurriedly picking his way through it when—

"You're the new guy!" a voice said cheerfully.

Remy turned, face expressionless, mind still a frenzy of triplets, and saw her. The real her, not the one on the magazine covers or Celeste's computer screen. The actual Vivi Swan. She was wearing tall shoes and high-waisted pants, hair in a perfectly messy ponytail. She smiled, cherry-red lipstick revealing bright white teeth. She glowed—maybe from the lights behind her, maybe from something within her. It was hard to tell.

He'd never been starstruck before—not once, not even when he and Val were new to the music scene. They had no idea who celebrities were, after all, since most things pop culture were banned throughout their youth, and once they had a hit, they were too keenly aware of how fleeting and fragile celebrity was to be impressed by it.

But at that moment, Remy felt struck—maybe not starstruck but struck by *something*.

He shook it off immediately, regaining the decorum he'd been hired for. "That's me. Remy Young. Thanks for the opportunity," Remy said, rising and extending a hand over the drum set. Her handshake was strong, but her fingers small—they, like every part of her body, were long and willowy.

"Thanks for jumping in with us," Vivi answered, voice still cheery. It felt trained, as intentional as her hair and makeup and clothing.

"No problem. Happy to help," Remy said. "And I promise to stay off any skateboards."

At this, Vivi laughed—too loudly, given the quality of the joke—and drew the eyes of the rest of the stage toward her. They applauded her arrival; she moved on and hugged the other band members briefly (Remy remembered that they'd known her far longer than he had) then was given a mic and a few last-minute directions from the choreographer. Orders called out, chatter on headsets, a few mic checks and squeals, then—

"Let's go from 'Be Mine.' After the cross and transition—all good?" Walter asked over the speaker. Vivi gave him a thumbs-up, because the question was aimed solely at her—Remy's entrance was old news now.

But this was what he was good at. Being the professional. Being the guy who'd studied the music, who knew it by heart, who knew exactly the way it sounded on the album.

The rest of the band turned toward Remy, waiting for a curt nod, a sign he was ready; Michael picked out three notes on the bass and *crash*, they were playing the song. The band kept their heads toward him, guiding, waiting, maintaining eye contact without words or explanation; it was the perfect blend of the emotionless busywork of the studio and the excitement of playing music live. The notes became ropes that spun 'round their wrists and hands and heads, holding them together, tugging each along if anyone started to slide off the beat. Vivi's voice joined in, but Remy focused on his hands, on watching the other musicians, on the beat.

He was here, and he was playing the drums, and he was doing it without his brother out front—and, so far as he could tell, nothing was falling apart just yet.

Chapter Four

Two days from the first show, and Remy was finally used to the lights. The dancers. The moving sets, the number where he—and the rest of the band—moved under the stage via the hydraulics and Vivi performed an acoustic song on the guitar. She was a fair player— nothing wildly impressive—and Remy never heard much of the song anyhow, since she didn't play the entire thing until the dress rehearsal. The usually quiet backstage area he'd been hydraulicked into was a noisy chaos of costume changes and set changes, aerialists hooking themselves to rigs and stagehands passing out bottles of water. Michael switched to the banjo for the next number; David cracked his knuckles and produced a towel to wipe the sweat off his brow. Around them, dancers ripped off costumes; David laughed when Remy tried a little too hard to avoid staring at their high, small breasts.

The dress rehearsal proved just how well-oiled a machine it all was. It felt a little odd being on a tour where nothing—*nothing*—was duct-taped together. The road manager came around during every break, writing down everything from the band's dietary preferences to what sort of drumsticks Remy would prefer to use. ("The other guy liked what's in the bag, Innovatives, I think, but we can order whatever. Just let me know.")

It was during the dress rehearsal that Remy noticed a guy he didn't recognize. He didn't know everyone's name yet, not by a long shot, but he knew all the faces at this point and enough names that he no longer felt or was treated like "the new guy." This new guy, however, was wearing a white T-shirt and jeans. He had a beanie on and the sort of scraggly five o'clock shadow that made Remy certain he was someone from the industry—a musician, maybe an actor. His face was too intentional to be an accident and too casual to be someone who had a regular job. The stranger lingered in the seats near the assistants and task rabbits, drinking something in a glass bottle, though Remy couldn't work out what it was from the distance.

They were on the back end of the show—the last five songs of the twenty-song set, not including any covers Vivi Swan wanted to play—when Remy recognized who the stranger was, in part because he saw Vivi wink at him. Vivi's set was so streamlined, each head nod, each arm wave, each hair flip so choreographed that this small change caught Remy's attention.

It was Noel Reid—the wink triggered his name and the memory of Celeste saying Noel and Vivi were an item. Remy knew his face, of course—much like Vivi's face, you couldn't *not* recognize Noel Reid given the sheer volume of tabloids he appeared on. He was a musician, a guitar-playing, doe-eyed sort of guy whose songs were covered on college campus quads everywhere. It wasn't Remy's type of music, frankly, but given the number of platinum albums the guy had, it was clearly *someone's* type of music.

Noel saw Vivi wink and smiled in response before looking back to his phone, an act that Remy couldn't help but be offended by. This was a huge fucking production, with moving sets and dancers and aerialists who were about to drop down from the ceiling, and this guy was looking at his phone? It was one thing for someone who'd seen it a million times to be disinterested, but to ignore it right off the bat?

They rounded to the last song, pausing so Vivi could say some canned things to the audience—something about accepting yourself, and ignoring bullies, or whatnot; it was all so scripted that Remy could practically hear Val laughing at it. When she finished her speech, he cued the next song, the last song, and as it was full dress, an onslaught of gold glitter confetti began to rain from the ceiling. The song reached its height; Vivi, in a long, sparkly ballgown, stepped onto a platform that floated over the empty audience. The screens on the wall flashed, a soundtrack of riotous applause roared over the speakers, the dancers ran out, and Vivi Swan skipped off the platform as it returned to the stage like a princess off for a lark around the castle.

It was the finale; Michael and Parish walked toward the front of the stage, playing loud and complicated solos one after another while the dancers bowed. Vivi Swan was racing around the staircase that arced over Remy's head; once there, she motioned toward him, and he looked out toward the fake audience and grinned in gratitude; she repeated the act with David, whose keyboards were set up on the opposite side of the staircase. Finally, Vivi herself skipped toward the front of the stage, where she took the hands of her backup singers and bowed with them, then once on her own. The music peaked, the lights went brighter to the sun, and then *pow*—it was done.

"Nice work, everyone." Walter's voice cut off the canned applause so abruptly that it startled Remy. There were purple waves in front of his eyes from the sudden darkness, and he heard the others sniffling and shuffling around, trying to pick the guide lights out from the strips of glitter confetti.

"No big problems from here, you good, Vivi?" Walter asked. A click, then Vivi Swan's mic went live. The house lights came up, dull and gentle compared to the stage lights.

"I'm set, some costuming problems, not much else. Oh, and that section at the end of 'Let's Go Hide,' where I'm in the audience, can we extend that? I don't think it'll be long enough for me to make a full loop. And I was thinking about maybe playing a little longer once I'm out at the tree," she said then turned to look at the rest of the stage, hunting for another problem to remedy. "Looks good from back there?"

"As good as they're going to look from the nosebleeds," Walter said jokingly.

"Wait, they don't?" Vivi answered immediately, eyes widening.

"No, doll, it's great. It's all great. Nice show, everyone! My assistant will give everyone their call time. Very important: make sure your personal stuff gets loaded! Roadies are only loading what's on the stage and backstage right now. Anything you need with you, you need to take with you, yes?"

The dancers headed backstage, already unhooking clasps; the rest of the band began unplugging and helping coil up cords. Remy followed suit, reorganizing the stick bag as he'd found it. Vivi Swan's security team—four large guys with faces that Remy wouldn't mess with—was helping her down from the stage. Noel rose, sticking his phone in his back pocket, and opened his arms. She ran into them enthusiastically, hitting him hard enough that he had no choice but to pick her up.

"Remy?" a voice said. Remy spun around to see two roadies waiting to take apart the drum set.

"Sorry, sorry—here, I can help," Remy said.

"We've got it," one of the roadies said kindly. "Seriously, man. You did your job—go rest so we can do ours, right?"

"Sure—thanks, man," Remy said, shaking the roadie's hand. He headed backstage just as Vivi Swan pulled Noel toward the stage, their conversation coming within earshot thanks to the space's acoustics.

"I just need to change, and we can go."

"Okay, okay," Noel said, sounding annoyed. "You already have makeup on though, right?"

"Yes, but I need to have them do street makeup. This is too much for dinner," Vivi said, as if this were the most obvious thing in the world. "It won't take long," she added.

"It takes at least an hour," he said, exasperated. Remy walked faster to get away from the conversation.

"That's for hair *and* makeup. I can keep this hair," she answered plainly, like a teacher explaining a simple concept to a student.

"It's just dinner," Noel said—Vivi was also walking quickly, like she was trying to get away from the conversation just as much as Remy was. "Can't you skip the airbrush makeup and everything?"

"You know there will be paparazzi there."

Remy arrived at the open door to the musicians' dressing room. The others weren't there, so Remy sat and busied himself with his phone, trying to ignore Vivi and Noel's conversation—but they were loud, and their voices grew ever closer as they made their way down the hall.

"Yeah, the paparazzi will be there because your managers are going to call them," Noel muttered. "Whatever. I'm going to go smoke."

"What? You told me you'd stop smoking."

"I told you I'd stop smoking *in front of you*," Noel answered as he passed the band's dressing room door.

"You know what I meant—" Vivi went on, and now she was in the doorway. Unlike Noel, though, she stopped and looked inside, eyes falling to Remy. There was no pretending he hadn't overheard the conversation. "You all signed a nondisclosure agreement," Vivi said stiffly, though her lips were curved into a forced smile.

"Sorry?" Remy asked.

"A nondisclosure. Everyone signed it. I don't want to see anything about my and Noel's discussion online, alright?" Vivi said, voice becoming lighter, as if she were saying something kind rather than something threatening.

"I'm just here to play the drums," Remy said reassuringly, burying the desire to scoff deep within his chest. Vivi gave him a curt nod then vanished back down the hall.

They moved from the arena hotel into the tour buses that evening after a lengthy lecture on bus etiquette from Walter's assistant: "Always wear a seat belt while sleeping unless you want to go flying at every pothole. No fish in the microwave. If you snore, find a solution, now. The drivers will tidy up, but they're not disposing of any biological hazards." Despite the warnings, Remy struggled not to look awed by the bus he'd be sharing with Michael, David, and Parish—the bus slept six but wasn't packed out as tightly as it could be.

"You two are stuck with us old-timers," Michael said to Parish and Remy. Parish laughed a bit but didn't seem to think it was all that funny; he looked a little longingly out the window at one of the coed dancer buses.

"This one is a nicer bus, kid. Tour long enough with Vivi and you get some perks," David said wisely. "Theirs is a twelve-sleeper. Which is ironic, given that they never actually sleep. Party all the time on the dancer bus."

"*Twelve*?" Remy said, impressed, wondering what the bunk configuration was.

"Yep. And trust me, not one of those kids will follow the no-solids rule," Michael said, jerking his finger toward the bathroom.

"True," Parish said. "Last tour I did, everyone was on the same bus, save the talent."

"Whose tour?" Remy asked, curious. Probably some neo-rock outfit, given that Parish was styled more like a rock star than anyone else, with jet-black spiked hair and thick eyeliner. Remy would never have said it aloud, of course, but Parish looked like the intentional version of what Val was naturally.

"Nick Maddon," Parish said, rolling his eyes.

"*Oh,*" Remy said. You couldn't be in music without knowing at least one horror story about Nick Maddon. He was a former child star, having melted twelve-year-old hearts everywhere on a show called *Lunch Bunch*. He aged and, as many a child star did, wanted to make sure the world noticed: full sleeves of tattoos, a weirdly affected tough attitude, and a series of DUIs and drug arrests and vandalism charges. And a record contract, of course—like all child stars, he landed a record contract.

"Yeah," Parish went on. "I like to party as much as the next person, but that guy...he just...damn. He made everyone drink or smoke or whatever with him, always, which was fine, but when the cops showed up, he wasn't going to pay for everyone's lawyers, you know? After fines I basically ended that tour right where I started, as far as my bank account goes."

"There's a reason he burns through bands," David said, nodding. "If the talent's reputation has gotten shitty enough that even the gossip sites know they're the worst, it's not worth taking the gig no matter what the pay is. Take that advice to the bank, kids," he added, looking pointedly at Parish and Remy.

"Noted," Remy said then jutted his chin toward the bunks. "Whose is whose?"

He waited as the others chose their beds; it didn't need to be said aloud that being the new guy, he'd need to pick last, and thus he wound up stuck in a top bunk. It was, however, a nicer mattress than the one he had at home. *Everything* about the bus was nicer than he had at home. There were hardwood floors and buttery-leather couches in a living area, a small kitchen with a sink and a refrigerator stocked with sparkling and still water. The windows were covered by wooden blinds, and there were two small granite-topped tables sticking out from the sides. The bus gained even more space when parked—the living area could be extended, an additional couch folded up from the floor, and a sunshade extended on the opposite side so they could sit out with lawn chairs and beers, if so inclined.

An hour before they started off, Walter's assistant was rushing between the buses, handing large coffees to the drivers. David was asleep, Michael was smoking, and Parish, for all his talk of the pressures and pitfalls of drinking, was on the dancer bus, seemingly enjoying strong cocktails just as much as the rest of them, if the sound of laughter was any indication.

Remy wandered outside and leaned against the bus. The sun was setting, the air warm and gentle, lavender streaks making their way across the sky. After so many days in the arena, he'd become disoriented—where was Venice Beach? Toward his right, the east, he thought, though he wasn't certain. If it weren't for the scent of sweet olives and salt in the air, he might have even been convinced he was no longer in LA at all. He turned his phone around a few times in his hands. Celeste and Val would probably be headed to watch someone's gig, and he didn't have anyone else to call.

A black SUV pulled up to the curb on the other side of the sidewalk then slowly went up and over it—no one said anything, which was how Remy knew it had to be Vivi returning from her dinner with Noel Reid. She got out of the car, lipstick still flawlessly red, tailed by one of her security guys. There was no one here to ward against, but he kept his eyes sharp, passing over Remy with a cool confidence that told him he'd memorized the tour crew and already knew Remy's face.

"How was dinner?" Walter's assistant's voice rang out from between buses.

"Perfect," Vivi said brightly, with the simplicity of someone answering an interview question. "Are we all set?" She came to a stop by Walter's assistant and surveyed the buses, one hand still clutching the designer purse slung over her shoulder. With her heels, she was taller than him—probably taller than Remy too.

"We're good to go," Walter's assistant said, looking pleased.

"I'll go settle in, then. I want to fall asleep before we start moving. If I can. First leg still makes me nervous," she said, and to Remy's surprise, it looked like she really meant it.

"You could just meet us in Seattle," Walter's assistant said in a singsong voice that implied they'd had this conversation before.

"It's tradition," Vivi said playfully and knocked his shoulder before starting toward her bus—which would take her past Remy. Her heels clacked softly on the pavement, a confident tempo despite their height. When she saw Remy, she smiled again in that practiced way.

"Hey! Thanks again for joining us so late. You're all ready to go?" she asked, as if she hadn't snapped at him about a nondisclosure just a few hours ago.

"Yep. I'm looking forward to it," he said, lowering his phone and turning the screen off.

"Awesome," she said and grinned even wider. "Have a nice night with the guys on the bus! Let David know I had the galley stocked with Nutter Butters just for him. If he hasn't found them already."

She was gone nearly as soon as she'd appeared, a whirl of vanilla-scented lotion and blond hair, imaginary and artificial as a fairy-tale princess.

Chapter Five

Thirty thousand people screaming didn't sound like people at all. They sounded like a lion, or a thunderstorm, or an earthquake: something alive and infinitely powerful and beautiful and dangerous.

Seattle, opening night of an arena tour, and a thirty-thousand-person-strong hurricane was roaring. Remy was seated at his drum set, which was below the stage—hydraulics would lift him up moments before the first song began. Up onstage, videos played of Vivi Swan writing music, of her talking to the camera about her process.

The ground beneath him shifted and he ascended, feeling a little too much like that tethered goat in *Jurassic Park* going up into the T. rex pen. The single thing that was thirty thousand individual things came into view. A clear plastic panel in front of Remy's drum set made it feel even more like he was watching the crowd through a two-way mirror—he saw them, but in the black, they didn't realize he was there. He forced himself to breathe evenly, to move slowly and deliberately so as not to startle them and cause an attack—

The lights surged; Remy jumped, his eyes went wide, a moment of utter panic flashed through him, fight and flight and nausea, and then *go.* He kicked into action, spurred—thank god—by muscle memory from the rehearsals. He tapped off a beat, and David joined him on guitar. The crowd screamed a deafening pitch—Quiet Coyote's audience hadn't been so largely female, and he somehow hadn't realized the sound of a crowd of women screaming would be so wildly different from the sound of a crowd of mixed genders screaming.

The dancers slid onto the stage, the song began, time till the first verse growing smaller and smaller and smaller, and then, with a ripple from the keyboards, Vivi herself was launched from underneath the stage, dress bubbling around her like Marilyn's.

The screaming peaked, and Vivi began to sing, her voice the final brick in a wall holding the thirty-thousand-person creature back from swallowing the rest of them whole. This wasn't at all like playing music live with Val; with him, there was always an element of the unexpected, a crazy, potentially disastrous feeling that something could go wrong—and Val liked it that way. Here, however, there was all the danger but none of the unexpected; the crowd was a lion with teeth and claws, but Vivi was a sleek and confident lion tamer who had a whip but rarely used it.

Three songs in, the music quieted so Vivi could address the crowd with a canned speech. She walked to the front of the catwalk and put a hand to her eyes, trying to see beyond the blinding lights.

"Hello, Seattle!" she said. They screamed—Remy was pretty certain they'd have screamed even if she'd gotten the city wrong. She grinned, an expression he caught via the giant screens that were zoomed in so close on her face that if she'd had a fleck of mascara on her eyelids, they'd have caught it. Of course, Vivi Swan didn't have out-of-place makeup. She didn't have out-of-place anything, curated as she was.

"You guys are amazing. Thanks so much for coming to our first show!" she said, and they screamed again. "When I say *thank you*, though, I want you to understand how much I mean it. I want you to understand how much I appreciate you all coming to see the show. I see you guys, way in the back, with the STRONGER sign—you made it light up and everything! It must have taken ages."

They screamed again. Whenever she paused, they screamed. Remy looked toward the back of the arena and, sure enough, he could faintly make out a sign that had the word *stronger* lit up in something like Christmas lights—it was the name of one of Vivi's singles. She kept talking; he knew her words had to be rehearsed, yet they felt undeniably personal.

"So many of you have amazing shirts that you made. I was look-ing at the audience earlier, and I thought, wow, you guys understand me because we're all…we're all just alike. We all know what it's like to be excited. Or in love. Or to be heartbroken. Don't we?"

They screamed again, again, again. Remy couldn't help but remember the thing Val had said about Vivi back when all this began—that she wasn't a musician, she was a product. Remy had agreed with Val then, but now he understood the product wasn't beauty or lip gloss or perfection. Vivi's product was empathy, and she peddled it so flawlessly that not one of the thirty thousand people knew it was a product at all.

During intermission, the band huddled in the dressing room, mopping their brows and blinking hard against the still-there glare of the stage lights. Halfway through, one of the backup singers—her name was Laurel, if Remy's memory was accurate—poked her head into the dressing room, all smiles and makeup that went shiny instead of melting under the stage lights.

"How's the first show going, Remy?" she asked, stepping inside. Laurel was wearing a wedding dress; the second half of the show opened with a song about interrupting a wedding. Laurel played the moody bride.

"Going great," Remy said, smiling at her then nodding a hello as the other singers, Ro and Destiny, walked inside (wearing bridesmaids dresses, because sure).

"We're trying to get everyone together after the show—all the musicians, I mean, singers and band. We'll be on Bus Three. Want to come?" Laurel asked the room.

"Absolutely," David said, nodding; Parish and Michael did the same.

"Yeah," Remy added. "That'd be great."

The bell chimed, the signal for everyone to get into their places. They left the room in a rustle of crinolines and hype-yourself-up-now deep breaths. One of the stagehands gave Laurel a bright-pink bouquet that matched the bridesmaids' dresses as she moved to her position; the dancers hustled around all the musicians, far more eager to slide into their spot at the absolute last second than the rest of the cast.

The first number was heavily choreographed—the bridesmaids danced around Vivi as she pretended to interrupt Laurel's wedding and steal away with the groom, who'd always loved Vivi and had somehow found himself engaged to the terrible, shrill, horrible Laurel character. During rehearsals, Remy had thought on how he'd flip the song and turn it into one from Laurel's point of view—realizing the man you're marrying is running away with his first love, a tall, blond, leggy thing that looks as unlike you as possible.

Reimagined, it still sounded like a Vivi Swan song. That was the thing about her music: no matter how you turned it, flipped it, mirrored it, flattened it, each song was all about her own heartbreak.

When the show ended—eighteen songs in all, including the acoustic numbers Vivi played solo—there wasn't a wild amount of celebrating backstage. Everyone was too exhausted, too busy analyzing their performances, trying to avoid the light or stagehands who would tell them they'd missed a mark or a cue or an entrance. Vivi Swan herself had a meet and greet with fans in a back room; her team hurriedly reapplied her makeup and tidied her costume then yanked her away while everyone else slumped toward the arena showers. ("This venue's got better ones than the bus, but that's not always the way," Michael said.) They had to be at the next show— Portland—the following evening; the crew would pack overnight, and buses would pull out as soon as everyone was loaded up.

Freshly showered, Remy went looking for Bus Three. The buses weren't parked in order and were all painted identically—it took a few tries before he found the right one.

"Hey, Remy's here!" a woman's voice called loud enough that he heard it before opening the door. When he did open it, there was a light round of cheering, and Laurel welcomed him. She was wearing sweatpants and a T-shirt, as was most everyone else.

"Have a seat, have a seat. Do you want anything to drink?" she asked warmly.

"I'm set, thanks," Remy said, nodding a greeting at Parish before he sat down beside him on one of the galley couches. The bus was almost identical to the band's bus, but it smelled like hairspray and tea. Ro and Laurel were sitting across from each other at the kitchen table, while David was talking on his phone quietly, light beer in hand.

"Alright, Remy. First show. What'd you think?" Parish asked. It was a weighted question, and from the way Laurel and Parish watched him, Remy knew the answer was going to tell them something important about him.

So he hedged his bets and simply shrugged, saying, "It was a good show."

"Boo!" Laurel said, laughing.

"Don't be an asshole," Parish said and grinned. "That crowd. It's fucking crazy, isn't it?"

Remy laughed back at them. "Yeah, yeah, I'll give you that. I've never played to a crowd like that."

"*It was a good show*," Laurel mocked him. "Pyro! Lights! Screens! Dancers! It's like a circus on steroids."

"No one with a heart condition should attend," Remy agreed then dared to add, "I've never felt like so many people would be fucked if I messed something up. The dancers and the talent and you guys… Christ. Drummers shouldn't be given that kind of power."

"And trust me, Vivi Swan'll know if you mess something up," Laurel said, with a little bit of an eye roll.

"Yeah?" Remy asked.

"Oh, yeah. I did her last tour with her, and she lost her shit when one of the other singers screamed after some maniac jumped onstage," Ro called over.

"Seriously?"

Ro nodded. "Because it was a part where the backup vocals are piped in—the mix is better when it sounds like a chorus, so they doubled our voices, and we just lip-synched the chorus. So there were all these videos of the freak jumping onstage and Charlotte screaming and no sound coming through the mic."

"And that was worthy of her losing her shit?" Remy asked.

"Yep. She's psycho," Laurel said.

"Hey, careful now. What if Remy's her spy?" David interrupted. He'd ended his call and come in on the conversation.

"Her spy?" Remy said.

David went on, brows knitted in faux intensity, "Vivi always has a plant somewhere in the group—someone to watch us, make sure we aren't selling her secrets. Could be you."

Remy laughed. "I'm definitely not the spy."

"Exactly what the spy would say," David said, grinning. "Anyway, yes—the thing with the dude jumping onstage was worthy of her losing her shit because it made people think if the backup singers were lip-synching, she was too."

"Ah," Remy said, nodding. Everyone lip-synched at some point, but it was like trying to look cool—it was expected you do it but also that you never, ever get caught doing it.

"But she also might be a little psycho," David said, giving Laurel an amused look. She shook her head in exasperation at him.

"Good to know. I'll do my best not to get caught faking the drums," Remy said, and the room tittered.

"Alright, everyone has a drink, right? Or water? Or something?" David asked. Destiny reached into the fridge and tossed a can of ginger ale to Remy, who barely caught it. With a beverage now in everyone's hand, David lifted his beer into the air. "To the first show."

"To popping Remy's cherry," Laurel seconded.

"What are you, thirteen?" Ro said.

"To Seattle," Michael said.

"To psychos," Ro said.

"To the psycho who's paying us to be here," David said but laughed as they clinked cans and plastic cups and bottles then downed their drinks.

Then

"I wrote something," Val had said, holding up a piece of paper.

"A poem?" Remy asked. They were in their tiny bedroom, which despite its size wasn't particularly cluttered by toys or books or clothes.

There were beds, drawers, and matching nightstands with matching Bibles on them. Val flicked the light over his own Bible on and shoved the piece of paper across the space between the beds, where Remy could reach it.

"No, a song," he said as Remy plucked it from his fingers.

It was short and written in pencil on paper torn from one of their spiral notebooks, the edges frayed on the left side. Remy read through it once, then again, then looked at Val.

"This isn't a song," he said.

"Of course it is," Val said, giving Remy an annoyed look. "I can play it on guitar—it'll go like this." He hummed a few lines. "I'd write it in notes, but I don't know how to do that yet."

"That's not what I meant," Remy protested. "It's not a song. Not one we could play."

Val rolled his eyes. "Just because it's not holy doesn't mean we can't play it."

"Yes, it does," Remy argued. They'd been taking music lessons for five weeks and had so far learned to play a smattering of praise songs—songs their parents and friends and church elders knew the words to. Songs they approved of. It wasn't that Remy thought them incapable of playing anything else—it wasn't even that he worried it was wrong to play something else. It was that Val was suggesting something entirely foreign. He might as well be saying that he'd written a song in the language of minor surgical procedures or to the tune of the color green.

"Listen," Val said and picked up his guitar from the corner. He glanced at the door once before carefully, quietly, and very slowly picking his way across the strings, whisper-singing the words to the song. It was about driving cars fast—which was also a little ridiculous, seeing as how their family minivan went anything but, so it wasn't as if he had any experience with the sensation. The chorus—which was most of the song—went, "Then I shouted *accelerate!* Because I won't be *sedate!*"

"It's *sedated*," Remy said.

"You can say it however you want in songs," Val answered. "If you write them, I mean. You can write whatever you want because it's yours."

"Hey!" a thundering, deep voice shouted from down the hall. In a few swift, water-like moves, the light went off, the paper went under a pillow, the guitar disappeared to the far side of the bed. "I hear you talking! You'll wake up the baby! Go to sleep!"

"Or what?" Val whispered, defiance so quiet that even Remy could barely hear it.

When the homeschool music class ended to make way for classes in sewing (for the girls) and camping (for the boys), Val and Remy's parents allowed them to continue taking lessons privately. This was a very big deal, and both knew it was largely because their parents needed a place to stash them while they cared for baby Mercy.

Mercy was sick. She'd come too early and was tiny, with limbs that had the smooth, slick look of plastic. Her eyes were big and vein-blue under her lids, and when she cried, it was more like an animal's mew, tiny and frail. Nothing they did helped—not the pastor, or the elders, or the old ladies who had seen hundreds of births in their lifetimes.

"How's your little sister?" their music teacher asked. He was brown-eyed, with slightly receding hair and a well-kept beard. Everything about him was warm and modern and unlike anyone they'd ever met before. He wore shoes with neon laces and had a phone with programs he used to click a beat for them to play to. They'd met him in the music store, where he taught lessons, but going through the music store was too expensive. Now they met in his living room after he got home from work, while his pretty young wife made dinner in the kitchen.

"She's doing better," Val said, but his face told the real story—that she was still sick, that she was always sick and tiny, with expressionless, thin features that made her more wormlike than person.

The music teacher nodded. "I'm glad she's doing better at least. Does this mean she's taking some medicine, now? Has she been to see the doctor?"

Val was motionless, while Remy shook his head a tiny bit. Remy said, "Pastor Ryan said that it's like this, sometimes. That it will get worse before it gets better."

The music teacher swallowed and looked uneasy; his wife poked her head out of the kitchen, and they made quick, grim eye contact.

"She really is getting better. She gained a lot of weight already. So we just don't really need doctors. Our family heals really well," Val said quickly, shrugging it off like the music teacher's concerns were a little ridiculous.

"Yeah, yeah, I'm sure," the music teacher said brightly, and the boys grinned.

They went about their lessons, first individually then together, playing a simple rhythm on their instruments. Val then played one of the songs he'd written for the music teacher, singing along so quietly that his voice could barely be heard over the simple, twangy guitar.

"Hey, that's pretty good!" the music teacher said, and Val beamed. "You really wrote the entire thing by yourself?"

"Yep," Val said.

"What about you, Remy? Have you written any songs?" the music teacher said warmly.

Remy shook his head, trying to not feel ashamed. Val was the musician; Remy was just the drummer. Drummers didn't write songs, didn't dream in melodies the way guitarists did. The idea of writing a song was as foreign as the idea of painting a masterpiece or cooking a lobster or touching snow.

The music teacher moved on swiftly, saying, "Maybe you can collaborate on Val's songs with him. Almost all real musicians collaborate with another songwriter or producer." He lingered on the terms—*collaborate, songwriter, producer*—making them sound exotic and desirable. To prove his point, he slid a CD off a nearby shelf and pulled out the liner notes, holding them open so Val and Remy could look. "See?" he said, pointing. "Eight different people worked on this song."

"How?" Remy asked eagerly.

"Well, let's say you've got Val's song—can you play it again, Val? Only this time, just keep playing the guitar part over and over. We'll add the words in a minute." Val obliged, staring at his hands and hiccuping over fingerings every now and again. "Perfect. So, Remy," the music teacher said, speaking up a little, "what you add to the song might change the whole feel. So, if I play this"—he played a quick triplet tempo, one that overpowered the guitar—"it has a big, powerful feeling, right? But if I play this"—he tapped the cymbal gently, so the guitar took the lead—"it's quiet, right? Try it."

Remy picked up the second tempo, and when he was feeling risky, began hitting the cymbal a touch harder on every fourth note then every eighth; he and Val grinned at each other. The music was becoming a wild thing, something bouncing between them rather than a song that lived in Val's fingertips. The music teacher asked Val to start singing then harmonized with him.

"There you go," the music teacher said, grinning, as the song faded from the air, notes still lingering like the scent of something bright and citrus. He looked between them, eyes sparkling with pride. "That's the way real musicians do it. They help each other be better."

Chapter Six

Show two, Portland, was just a short hop down the coast, but Remy was asleep by the time they pulled in. When he finally rose the next morning, David and Michael were already awake, sipping coffee in the galley and talking about going out for lunch. Remy made himself a cup of coffee, while Michael rose and parted the blinds to peer outside. "Fucking hell, man."

"Huh?"

"Look," Michael said and stepped aside so Remy could look for himself. In the streaky predawn light, a thick row of teen girls and, Remy presumed, their mothers stood along the fence that separated the loading area from the Portland arena's parking lots. They had signs—VIVI I'M 15 TODAY, or ALL THE WAY FROM TEXAS—WORTH IT FOR VIVI, or just VIVI SWAN 4 LIFE. They even looked like her—sundresses with cardigans, long hair in side braids, a few with her trademark cherry-red lipstick.

"I can't believe they didn't wake you up when we pulled in," David told Remy. "They were screaming so loud, I thought it was the apocalypse. Every tour with her, they get bigger and louder. Last year they realized she couldn't have her name on her bus anymore—they used to swarm in front of it and chant, and it was a nightmare."

"Least it means she's selling?" Remy said.

Michael gave him a look. "Yeah, yeah, and you don't care about the gender of the baby as long as it's healthy, right?"

The show went well—so identical to the one the previous night that for a moment Remy felt turned around, unsure if they'd already performed a song or not. This never happened with Quiet Coyote; every show was different and alive and its own indigo child. He paid slightly more attention to her conversations with the audience this time, trying to pick out how they were different from the night before. The words all had the same shape, but there were different pauses, different laughs, hallmarks that her words were genuine. Things that made all fifty thousand people feel special, like she was a close friend rather than someone they'd paid dearly to see.

When it was over—there were fireworks that lit the sky at this show during the finale, since it was an open-top arena—the lights faded, the audience filed out, their voices hoarse and raspy from shouting lyrics. Unlike the previous show, though, security held the crew in their dressing rooms.

"What's the problem?" Parish asked as Remy made another turkey sandwich from the craft services table.

"Half the damn arena filed to those fences on the exterior to see her load up," one of the enormous security guys said. "We're trying to get her bus to the front so she doesn't have to walk by the fence."

Michael nodded, stretching his hands behind his head and stifling a few curse words. It was already two hours after the show; arena security, rather than just Vivi's team, was starting to file back and forth in the hallways on golf carts or Segways.

"I can just run. I'm capable of running." Remy heard Vivi's voice.

He rose and went to the doorway, along with the rest of the band. The dancers were all in hoodies and sweatpants, their faces scrubbed clean of makeup and hair knotted on top of their heads. They were clustered together; the five girls that made up the show's opening band looked more excited at the drama than weary.

"We'd really rather you not do that, Miss Swan," someone—a member of arena security—said. "They're not thinking straight right now. If the fence gives, we'll have injuries. Even if it doesn't give, we don't want anyone to get stepped on."

"It's not going to stop until I leave," Vivi said. "What if we just say I took a private car out earlier?"

"We've tried that. We're trying to scramble the buses so yours is in front. Probably something you want to do at future concerts," the security guy said rather pointedly to Walter's assistant.

"I'll just get on whatever bus is in front, and we'll switch somewhere, then," Vivi said.

"We can try, Vivi," Walter's assistant said as calmly as possible, "but it's eleven fifty. If the drivers stop after midnight, it constitutes a full day, and we'll have to either wait for them to sleep or wait for new drivers. Also, there's a load of paps out there too, most of them on motorcycles—you'll have to deal with them if you switch."

Vivi took a big breath then blew it out. Her makeup was still flawless—so much so that Remy suspected she'd had it touched up. She'd changed, not into overnight riding clothes like the rest of the group but into heels and shorts that made her look impossibly leggy.

"So we just wait…forever?"

"Give us some time," the security guy said.

But an hour later, the crowd was still there—smaller but still there—and now it was nearing 1:00 a.m. The busses had shuffled a bit, getting Vivi's as close to the door as possible. Walter's assistant stood on a chair and announced the order the buses were in.

"Get on them, don't turn on the lights, don't try to put anything underneath. Got it? We just need to clear out," he said. The crew, who by this point was exhausted, nodded. The opening band, Kitten Kitten, ran out first, then the dancers, who were instructed to keep their heads up lest the crowd mistake any of them for Vivi in disguise. They were spacing out the exits so there wasn't a sudden spike in insanity.

"Alright, band, move," a security member said. David, Michael, Parish, and Remy gathered, bags slung over their shoulders. They waited for a nod from one of Vivi's security team guys then pushed through the door.

It was like walking into a wall of soprano sound, which was really saying something given the show he'd just played. On the stage, though, there was some degree of space between him and the screaming; here, they were separated by the width of a bus and some chain link. The crowd started pounding on the fence, signs waving, eyes lit up in glints and bolts and sparkles, and Remy, for the first time in his entire career, found himself afraid of fans. They looked like they'd eat him whole before they even realized what they'd done.

The bus door swung open, and for a second, Remy thought it odd that the regular driver wasn't the one at the wheel. It wasn't until he'd filed on behind the other four that he realized why. Despite matching exteriors, this bus was very, very different—because it was Vivi's bus. They'd gotten on the wrong one, somehow. They'd been told to get on the wrong one; there must have been some mistake amid all the chaos. Remy spun around and took the stairs two at a time—their bus was probably the next one in line, a simple mistake. He winced under the noise of the crowd and ran to the other bus, leaping on board—yes! His normal driver was in the driver's seat, looking as overwhelmed as Remy felt.

"Where's the rest of them?" the driver asked. Remy turned to look behind him and realized the rest of the band hadn't followed him—they were on Vivi's bus, which was pulling away, through a tunnel of blue-jacketed security guards pressed against the fence. The door to the arena opened again, and the crowd grew somehow louder, and the fences pitched precariously forward. Remy watched as the people in the front—a position that had probably been hard-won—went from excited to frightened, as the weight of the people behind pushed them into the chain link. They were girls, probably Remy's little sister's age, and their eyes went wide with fear. Remy's stomach lurched—

"Wait, this isn't right!" a voice said—Vivi's voice. Remy spun to face her. She looked at him, then the driver, then shook her head. "Forget it, just go!"

"You sure, Miss Swan?"

"Go, hurry, before they crash the fence!" Vivi said frantically, pushing past Remy and dropping her purse into one of the galley seats. The driver nodded, closed the door, and urged the bus forward. Vivi lunged for a switch to turn the lights on and waved goodbye, smiling happily at the crowd as they passed. Her makeup was still perfect. There was no indication—not even a hair out of place—that gave away how anxious her voice had been moments before.

Chapter Seven

Vivi sat in one of the galley seats, which Remy was grateful to see the driver had cleaned while they were out to lunch. She flicked the overhead lights off so only the dim runners and table lights were on, more familiar with the bus than Remy himself was.

"I guess they're more or less all the same?" Remy asked out loud, when a few moments had gone by—Vivi staring out the window at the handful of paparazzi tailing the bus, while Remy continued to stand, unsure where, exactly, he should go.

"Hm?" Vivi asked, looking back at him. She smiled brightly, an expression he was starting to suspect had little to do with her emotions and more to do with her training.

"The buses. I just meant—you know where all the lights are," Remy said, shrugging and wondering why he chose this of all topics. He finally sat on the couch across from her because he felt a little creepy standing, looming.

"Ah, yeah," Vivi said and nodded. "It's actually that my bus is the same model, just a single sleeper. The galley is more or less the same, though."

"Oh?"

"Yeah. Mine has different counters."

Vivi turned back toward the window. Remy considered jumping off the bus entirely.

"They're still out there," she said, sighing. "They want to hear me say something about Noel. There's no point in chasing someone on a bus otherwise."

Remy had no idea what, exactly, she was talking about—if something specific had happened with Noel, or if they just wanted some general comments on Noel, or if they just wanted to hear her say his name—each of these seemed possible. He waited for a moment, wondering if she would explain it. When she didn't, Remy realized Vivi must simply *expect* him to know. As if everyone simply knew everything about her. He held in a snort of mild contempt.

"What?" Vivi asked.

Apparently he hadn't held in that snort as well as he'd thought. "Do you want anything in the meantime? Water? Diet Coke? Beer?" he covered for himself hurriedly, motioning toward the fridge.

Vivi checked the time on her phone and frowned. "Too late for caffeine—water? Thanks."

He handed her a bottle of water and took a soda—caffeine be damned—for himself. He sat down at the galley table and opened it, removed his phone from his pocket, and began to pick at it. He didn't want to sit across from her again, implying he expected them to have Family Hour since they were stuck on a bus together—both for her sake and for his. The last thing he wanted to do was get into a long conversation, since that was where he was most likely to say something stupid and get himself in trouble. Silence was golden.

"Sorry about this," Vivi said, finally turning away from the window. "Are the rest of the guys on my bus?"

Golden. Silence is golden. Silence is motherfucking golden, god-damn it. He smiled at her. "Yep—I was too. I ran for this one, and they stayed, I think."

Vivi smiled a little—not the bright one, but one that only involved her lips, one that looked a little more genuine despite the fact those lips were still—were always—cherry red. "Guess I'll take them over the dancers, huh? At least the band likes me."

Worried his expression would give away the fact that the band *didn't* especially like her (which made him wonder how the dancers felt), Remy hurriedly filled the space by saying, "Based on what I hear about the dancer bus, they'd be way more likely to raid your personal liquor cabinet."

"Ha, I'd like to see them try. On my bus, they'd find sparkling water and Diet Coke. Though, oh—David might go for that bottled sweet tea."

"Sweet tea, huh?"

"Nashville," she admitted.

"Florida," he replied.

She smiled again, larger this time. "Really? I didn't peg you for Florida."

"That's because most of my people wear jean shorts," Remy said, which was actually Val's go-to Florida insult line. It made Vivi laugh, though, so he was glad to have stolen it.

Remy went on, "I lived in Nashville for a little while though, a few years ago. My brother and I moved there to record our first album."

"It's a beautiful city," Vivi said.

"It is. And less country music than I thought."

"Hey now, I started in country music," Vivi said, feigning offense.

"I didn't say it was a bad thing," Remy said hurriedly, thinking that this was exactly the sort of thing he'd been worried about saying, damn it.

Vivi ignored his defense. "You should've given country music a shot, actually. You've got a country music name."

"Remy's a country music name?"

"No, Remember Young is a country music name. You'd have to sing something twangy. And do some covers of classics. And wear a cowboy hat."

Remy snorted and shook his head. "I don't think I can pull off a cowboy hat. And I don't think I want to start going by *Remember* again."

"It's a hell of a name," Vivi said, swinging her legs off the couch so she was facing him. "Is there a story behind it?"

Remy considered this—because the answer was there was a long, involved, and not-entirely-pleasant story behind his name. One that wasn't made for bus rides and definitely wasn't made for a girl like Vivi Swan. Then again, if she knew his real name, she might know *something* of his origin story, which meant an out-and-out lie wouldn't do him any good.

"It's a virtue," he said, opting for the shortest, plainest version of the truth. "So I'm Remember, my older brother is Valor, and my little sister is Mercy." Vivi's eyebrows lifted, and Remy grinned. "You can say it. My parents never gave us a chance."

"Valor?" she said warily.

"He goes by Val. Plus we were homeschooled, so there was minimal opportunity for kids to make name-themed jokes. Though one kid in our homeschool group used to punch me and yell, 'Remember *this*?' so I still got my fair share of teasing," Remy said thoughtfully.

"Seems fair. Everyone has to get teased for something."

"What'd you get teased for?" Remy asked before thinking better of it. He believed her, of course—everyone, no matter how famous or pretty or skinny—has a teasing story. But he was curious to know what asinine aspect her classmates had chosen. Hair? Teeth? Quiet Coyote had toured with a girl who'd been picked on for the size of her fingernail beds, so anything was possible.

"I had cornrows," Vivi said, lifting her eyebrows, a small smile playing with the corners of her mouth.

"Uh."

"Yep. Cornrows. Have you seen the picture? It's all over the internet," she said, waving a hand.

Still wide-eyed, Remy picked up his phone to look for it—

"You can't look it up!" Vivi said, looking horrified.

"You just said it's all over the internet!" he answered, though he dropped his phone immediately.

"I don't *want* it to be all over the internet! It just is. I'm not sharing it so everyone can gawk at the thing, it's just, it was in a yearbook, so someone found it and—"

"Oh my god," Remy said—because the picture had already been loading when he dropped his phone, and now it was beaming up at him from the table. Chubby-cheeked, and with tiny, almost piggy eyes, a young Vivi Swan looked at him dead on from his phone screen. She looked proud—she looked like she felt pretty. And she had cornrows. Dozens and dozens of cornrows, with little beads on the ends.

"We'd gone to Jamaica for a family trip, and I got them there," Vivi said when she realized it was too late, that the photo was pulled up.

"So you paid someone to appropriate the absolute hell out of Jamaican culture on your head?" he said, daring to walk the line between joking and professionalism.

"Your name's Remember!" she argued.

"Yeah, but someone did that to me before I was old enough to protest," Remy said. He then made a show of putting the phone down, proving he was no longer staring at the picture. Vivi didn't look particularly offended by the whole thing, which was a relief—in fact, she looked amused, if anything.

Vivi took a long drink of her water. She did so carefully, so there was no risk of her lipstick smudging. "I loved that Quiet Coyote record, by the way," she said as she screwed the cap back on.

"Thanks," Remy said. He meant it, specifically because she said *record* rather than song. Everyone knew "Everything but the World," their hit, but not many people knew the album. Val probably would have quizzed her, eager to make her prove she knew the entire record—and to be entirely honest, Remy would have liked to have seen that. But the word *record* alone was enough to make him feel a strange sense of release, like they were meeting in the middle of some sort of musical island.

"And you and your brother are still doing gigs, right?" Vivi said.

"We are," Remy said, lifting an eyebrow. "And if you can tell me my birthday and shoe size, this will get creepy."

Vivi flushed a little under all her makeup. "Sorry. I just like to know who's on tour with me. I always read the security briefings Walter draws up."

Remy nodded—this made sense, though it was, in fact, a little creepy. "It's fine. And yeah, we're still playing gigs. I'm trying to get more into producing, though," he said.

"Producing? That's great. Play me something you're working on," she commanded.

"Uh," Remy said, blinking. He was instantly ashamed of his hesitation. Wasn't this the justification for taking the tour? That it was a great resume builder for producing? This was Vivi Swan herself. If she liked what he played, it wouldn't be her name on his résumé, it'd be her *endorsement*.

But there was still something scattering about how she'd asked him to play something—how she'd said it in a way that made it clear *no* wasn't really an appropriate answer. Gathering himself as best he could, Remy rose, walked to the sound system, and plugged his phone in. He chose one of Quiet Coyote's songs—sort of. It was one of the last songs that Val wrote, just before the creative blocks wedged themselves into place. It was the second song, the one they'd been working on when the label dropped them. As such, it'd never been released and wasn't a part of their SALT set—it was just too depressing for Val to play.

"That's a hell of a hook," Vivi said, nodding along as the song played over the bus's impressive speakers. The hook had been all Remy's doing—an addition in the studio, synthesized brass instruments and the sound of hands clapping. The hook was what people remembered, was what kept people coming back and singing along and creating remixes and performing covers. The hook was what made their hit single a hit—which was perhaps why Val hated hooks now. He wanted his music to be a secret, special thing, rather than something the general population could pump their fists to.

Remy returned to the galley table and busied himself spinning his empty soda can around in his hands while he waited for the song to end. Vivi listened intently, appearing to pick out all the layers, to listen to the parts rather than the whole. When it was done, she grinned at him, and something in his core felt unlocked. Warmed.

"That was great."

"Thanks," he said, voice rockier than he'd anticipated—her smile was so different up close, in only the best way. He hurried to the sound system and unplugged his phone. In the silence that followed,

Vivi looked out the window again. "Are the paparazzi still there?" Remy asked.

"Yep," Vivi said. "They'll give up eventually, though. It's just that there's no one else to follow around here. When I was just starting out, my friend Tuesday and I used to have a system—if one of us was being chased, the other would call in and say we were going to dinner or shopping or sometimes something dramatic, so they'd turn around and come to us instead. It was usually Tuesday being chased, since she was more famous back then, but I thought it was so much fun. Times have changed."

She had to be talking about Tuesday Rivers—how many girls named Tuesday could there be in the world? She was one of those tragedy cases, a child star eager to prove to the world that she was a grown-up now; she seemed an odd choice for Vivi to call *friend*. Remy was about to say something—he wasn't entirely sure what, he just knew he needed to keep the conversation going—when Vivi's phone rang.

"Hey, Walter," she said when she answered. "No, it's fine. I'm on the band bus with Remy." His name sounded different when she said it; there was no weight in it, like there was when Val said it, and it wasn't the professional, nearly branded version of his name that he heard when colleagues at the studio said it. She said it the way someone like Celeste said it—someone who knew him, but not someone who attached a fat, loaded history to his name.

Of course, Vivi didn't know him, Remy reminded himself. Not really—not beyond this conversation and whatever she'd read in the stalker file her people had assembled. Yet still, he liked the way the word sounded in her voice and was pleased when she said it again.

"Remy and I are just talking. No, it's fine—let's try to outdrive the paps. They're not going to chase us forever, not if they think we're going to drive through the night. Hey, tell David I'm going to eat all his Nutter Butters."

There was a laugh on the other end of the line, loud enough that Vivi flinched and pulled the phone away. She went on, "Can Steve and Big John meet me when we change over though, just in case? Oh, no, tell them it's not their fault! I'm not mad. It's fine, really. Okay. Bye."

She hung up and tossed the phone beside her on the couch. "You can go to sleep."

Remy's lips parted at the simplicity of the command, delivered with the same confidence as her command he play her something had been. When was the last time he'd been ordered to bed? When he was eight? Nine, maybe? He felt his face twisting, pride battling with professionalism—

"I mean, don't feel like you've got to stay up and entertain me or something," Vivi said, shrugging.

Oh. She'd meant *can* as in *you're free to go to sleep* rather than an order. In retrospect, Remy couldn't quite tell—had he interpreted it as an order because of how she'd said it or because there was a lingering expectation of that sort of behavior from her?

It'd been too long since he'd spoken, so he let words tumble from his mouth, hoping at least some were the right ones. "I don't need to go to sleep yet. I'm fine."

"I'm fine too," Vivi answered and smiled a little. She smoothed her shirt, and Remy noticed she was still wearing her high heels. He considered telling her she could take them off, if she wanted, but it sounded weird even in his mind, so he refrained.

"Well," Vivi said. "Play another song?"

It wasn't a command—and now that Remy was thinking on it, he realized it hadn't been a command the first time either, not really. He took a breath and looked at his laptop. There were a handful of unfinished songs there, sure, but it seemed a little much to play a second or third or fourth. He hated those musicians who sat back and played their half-baked tracks or poetry-slam read you their lyrics, waiting for you to recognize their genius. He hated the prospect of accidentally being one even more. He looked back at Vivi. "I have some stuff from our last album?"

"But I've already heard that," she said. "It's less fun when they've all been polished up and sleek."

"That's when they're best! When they're *done*," Remy argued.

She shook her head. "No way. I like it when they're still little baby songs and are ugly and weird."

"I don't have baby songs. I produce, I don't write. When I've worked on a song, it's *done*."

"Seriously? You *never* write?"

"Nope, that's my brother. He carves, I polish." *Or he used to, anyway.*

Vivi looked skeptical. "Not *one* ugly baby song? Seriously? That's basically ninety percent of what I have."

"Well then, play me one of these beloved ugly and weird baby songs of yours," Remy said, lifting his eyebrows.

Vivi's lips parted into a perfect O, like she couldn't believe his audacity—and honestly, Remy couldn't believe his own audacity. He'd just forgotten for a moment that this wasn't another musician—this was Vivi Swan. She probably didn't even do nearly as much songwriting as she got credit for, despite her ability to play guitar. He was just about to backtrack when she closed her lips and gave him a smug look.

Vivi rose then slid down across from Remy at the galley table. "Alright. I'll bite."

Chapter Eight

Vivi pulled a notebook from her purse, a Moleskine with rubbed corners and wear-softened sides. It looked like nothing that would belong to Vivi—it was far too trashed and common. She held it such that only she could see the interior as she flipped to the back, finding the page she was after almost immediately. She laid the notebook on the table, where it flopped open easily; it was a page with graph paper lines, on which she'd written both music and a handful of lyrics in messy number charts.

"Okay, so, it should be this one..." she said, thumbing through her phone. She laid it beside the notebook; Remy saw her eyes bounce back to the sound system and knew she was confirming his phone was still over there—that there was no risk he'd record this and share it. Satisfied that he was leak-proof, Vivi hit Play on her phone screen. Guitar—bright and springy and very Vivi Swan—rose from the tiny speaker. Vivi took a breath and then began to sing along with it, voice low at first but rising with each line of lyrics she ran her finger across.

It was a breakup song, which was no huge surprise, though it felt oddly unspecific—it was more like a template, ready to be filled in with details when she finally had the heartbreak needed to finish it. Vivi only had a few lines here and there, opting to hum through bits that were incomplete, where a series of question marks were scribbled in the lyrics section of her notebook. The guitar part was good, and Remy felt a pull in his chest to add to it, that desire to polish the piece up. Without entirely meaning to, he began to tap out a beat on the table.

Vivi looked surprised then pleased, so he began to play it a bit louder and hum the counter melody along with her. It changed the tone of the piece—made the whole thing take on a cool, almost eighties feel. When the song ended, Vivi looked up and him and smiled then quieted her phone.

"See? The ugly baby song part is the best part. It's the part that's alive," she said. She fluttered her fingers against the edges of the notebook affectionately, like it was a cat; the resulting noise even sounded like a tiny purr.

"The part that's alive?" Remy answered, nodding. "That's something my brother would say. He never minded the studio, but he liked live shows better. He said the music was alive there but trapped when you put it on a record."

"Things in a zoo can still be alive, even if they're trapped," Vivi answered without hesitation.

Remy laughed once at Val's expense. "Tell my brother the song can be like an animal in a zoo, and he'll literally never record anything again and probably become a PETA activist," he countered, though he instantly felt guilty for this—Val was his brother, after all. Remy took a big breath. "But Val is just like that. He's different. But it's good—it keeps him focused on the music."

Vivi nodded and closed her notebook. "Oh. Yeah, sure—the music should always be the focus. I'm sure I'd still be playing guitar if

I'd never sold a record. I'd be a guitar-playing veterinarian or marine biologist."

"Marine biologist?" Remy asked.

"That's what I wanted to be in middle school," she said, and Remy realized middle school was likely the last time Vivi wanted to be anything other than herself—she became *the* Vivi Swan when she was fifteen, after all. "What about you? What'd you want to be other than a musician?" she asked.

"I…have no idea."

"What? How do you have no idea?" Vivi asked with a look that told him she suspected he was lying.

Remy frowned. "Val wanted to be a musician from the moment he started playing guitar. I always sort of went along with it, I guess."

"You never wanted to be something on your own? Seriously?" Vivi asked.

He shook his head. "Val's persuasive." That was the short version. The long version was that musician was the only job that didn't involve the church, or the Lake City government, or the pastor's son's pool-cleaning business. Remy might not have known what he wanted to be, but he knew he didn't want to be any of those things.

"What about now? Still want to be a musician?" Vivi asked, sounding genuinely curious.

Remy lifted his eyebrows a bit. "I guess it'd be nice to be both a musician and…I dunno. One of those people who teaches dogs to do unusual tricks? That seems fun."

Vivi snorted—straight up *snorted*, and Remy couldn't stop himself from laughing both with her and at her. She turned neon-red and tried to hide her face behind her hand, but it was no use—she was undeniably a mess of laughter.

"You laugh, but you'll be calling me when you need a dog that's trained to make the bed," Remy said, feeling weirdly accomplished at how hard he'd made her laugh. She wiped at her face, still snickering, then sighed.

"Okay, okay. Dog trainer. Fancy dog trainer. Got it. I'll let you know if I hear of any job openings," she said, almost sincerely.

He smiled and studied the way her angel-carved cheekbones stood out on her face. She had freckles on her nose and across her clavicles; small and scattered and nearly covered by makeup, but freckles, just like many other girls in the world who'd spent a moment of time in the sun.

"What?" she asked, bringing a hand to her face worriedly. She turned to look at her shadowy reflection in the window—

"Nothing, nothing," he said quickly, realizing that perhaps he'd been staring, not studying. "Sorry."

She met his eyes for a second, almost suspiciously, then slid her Moleskine notebook back into her purse. "Okay, look," she said, voice going weirdly hesitant for someone like her. "I'm going to ask you to do something with me that I don't normally ask. But it's sort of something I always do after shows."

He blinked. "Sure…"

"I need you to watch *House Hunters International* with me. Or at least not care that I'm about to watch it, because I'm sort of getting antsy over the fact that I haven't yet." The words tumbled from her throat nervously—hilariously nervously.

"*House Hunters International*?" he asked, failing to keep a smile from his face.

"It comes on at eleven and basically plays all night. And it's amazing. I mean, no, actually, it's the worst, but that's why it's amazing."

"I don't see how I could get between you and something as amazing as a show about house hunting. Internationally."

Vivi shook her head then made a sort of face at him, one that smudged her lipstick. "Don't tell anyone, okay?"

"Nondisclosure agreement," he reminded her.

She paused. "I didn't mean it like that."

"I won't tell anyone," Remy promised, finally understanding just how sincere the worry in her eyes was. It was just a ridiculous show, but it was *her* ridiculous show, and if it got out that she watched it, there'd be mentions in magazines and producers asking if she wanted to make an appearance, and it would become another brick in the Vivi Swan Wall of Things. "I promise," Remy added.

Vivi smiled as she rose, found the remote by the couch, and flipped the television on. She scanned the channels with expertise until she found what she was looking for.

Here was the "plot" of the show, so far as Remy could tell: People with a lot of money looked at houses then decided which one to buy. He had trouble understanding why anyone as poor as himself or as rich as Vivi would be interested—because for the two of them, the houses featured were out of the question. Still, he rose and sat on the opposite end of the couch from Vivi.

"Oh, I've seen this one. This couple sucks. They turn down the best house because of the paint color," she said eagerly.

"I'm sorry, are we watching an episode where you already know which house they'll choose?" Remy asked and smiled again, or maybe just didn't stop smiling.

"The point is to make fun of the couple. Come on, Remy, figure it out," Vivi said, and swung her legs onto the couch. Her feet were close to him—strangely close. Not touching; there was a nearly tangible distance between her feet and his legs, a no-fly zone that pressed him even closer into the arm of the couch. She inched her toes back, and it made Remy feel better that she seemed aware of the no-fly zone as well.

"Alright. I am making fun of…the fact that they are insisting on something with a new bathtub. Because that's stupid."

"Especially in Italy. Nothing's new over there," Vivi agreed. "Nice work, Remy."

They watched the episode, then the next, and the next, until Vivi was slumped down on the arm of the couch, hair fluffed by her head. It was the most imperfect he'd seen her, which made it hard not to stare. Her eyeliner was the tiniest bit smudged, and she still hadn't fixed her lipstick. If she were anyone else, he'd have offered her a T-shirt, since the glittery, fitted shirt she was wearing looked like it'd outstayed its comfort; she kept twisting and rearranging it, which revealed the angry red lines it left on her torso.

He forced himself to stop staring and turned back to the current episode—the fourth, so far. She wasn't kidding about them airing it all night. "That guy is a douchebag," Remy said. "And I think his mustache is drawn on. But seriously, he wants two offices? Who needs two offices in one house?"

"One's for drawing the mustache on. The other's for work," Vivi said, voice wispy. She was fighting to keep her eyes open.

"That's fair. I'd like to see a mustache-focused office," Remy said but lowered his voice. She smiled a little—very little, mostly with her cheeks, and then her eyes drifted once, twice…and she was out.

Which meant Remy really didn't know what to do. He was tired too—not as tired as she was, clearly, but tired enough. But it seemed wrong to leave her out here, unbuckled and alone. If the bus took a weird swerve, she'd hit the floor. There was a buckle on the seat, but he couldn't get it without digging around behind her, which seemed like a great way to get fired. Instead, he carefully grabbed his laptop then slid onto the floor in front of the couch, leaning against it. She'd hit him before the floor if the bus swerved. Plus, this meant he couldn't really see her anymore, which was probably for the best. He couldn't seem to stop staring, especially now that she was asleep. Sleeping Vivi Swan looked so unlike Stage Vivi Swan—more delicate and gentler and beautiful in an entirely different way.

The house hunters continued for another two episodes while Remy mostly ignored them, instead sliding his earphones on and reading music blogs. It was nearly four thirty when Vivi's phone rang, startling her awake and him out of the computer screen. He turned to look at her; she was rubbing her eyes, further smearing the eyeliner and clearly confused as to why she was on a couch. When she saw him, she startled—then seemed to remember why she was there.

"Where's my phone?" she said, voice a little gravelly.

"I think—here," he said, lunging for it and handing it to her. She cleared her throat before answering, turning her voice cheery and bright again. It was Walter's assistant—they were pulling over up ahead so everyone could shuffle buses.

"The paps are gone?" Remy asked.

Vivi put her feet back on the floor, blushing a little as she adjusted her skirt. "Looks that way. Thanks for letting me crash on your bus."

"Thanks for introducing me to the wonders of *House Hunters International*," he said.

"You can pretend you don't like it all you want, but I'm telling you, you'll watch it again. It's like a parasite. It gets in your skin," Vivi said with a cautious smile then stood. She avoided his eyes as she collected her shoes then disappeared into the bathroom with her purse. Remy silently wondered if the bathroom was clean and free of embarrassing lotions or creams or magazines until she emerged. Her lipstick was fixed, her eyeliner perfect, and her hair sleek and polished. She looked exactly like she had when she'd accidentally boarded the bus four hours before.

"I thought…aren't you just jumping on the other bus? Sans paparazzi?" Remy asked as she walked back out. She smelled like powder makeup and soap.

"Camera phones," Vivi said knowingly. "People with camera phones are everywhere."

Remy couldn't argue with that. The buses turned in to a bright, shining gas station, and one by one, everyone who'd jumped on the wrong bus disembarked. Vivi put her sunglasses on and stood in the stairwell, waiting for security to wave her onto her bus. The doors opened; Vivi looked back at him and smiled.

"Thanks for the company, Remy."

"Back at you," he said, which after the words left his mouth, he decided were the stupidest words he'd ever said in his life. "See you later," he added, attempting to recover.

And then she vanished, clipping down the steps in her heels and hurrying across the parking lot, head down, toward her own bus. Remy watched her go, knees on the couch, leaning over the back so he was nearly pressed against the window. He saw a few camera flashes— gas station patrons with camera phones, just like she'd worried about. She high-fived the other band members as she passed them (slightly awkwardly) then was swallowed up by her own bus. Her absence was so full, made the bus so empty, that for a moment Remy did nothing but blink and pick at his own fingers.

"Let me tell you, kid," David said as he crashed through the bus door, instantly occupying the space with strong, male energy so different from the delicate candy-floss feel that had been Vivi Swan. He went on, "Spend a few hours on Vivi's bus and you'll hate this one. You missed out. The floors are heated marble."

"Heated marble? You're kidding," Remy said, grinning and trying to sit casually, aware he was trying too hard. Why was it strange, watching them sling their bags into their bunks? Watching Parish root into the refrigerator and Michael yawn, mouth wide? This was their space, after all.

"Yep, heated marble," Parish said, rolling his eyes a little. "And she has Wi-Fi. Real satellite Wi-Fi, not just a phone tethered to a laptop—which, by the way, we were supposed to get for this tour, but that shit didn't happen. *And* there's an espresso machine that I don't think has ever been used."

"Not a bad place to spend an evening," Michael said, nodding. "I mean, once we got over the fear that this was all a setup to catch us fucking with her stuff."

"No kidding," David said. "It felt like I was back at church in Kentucky. Feet on the floor, hands folded." He crossed his arms and did an impression of a scolded little boy, and it made everyone laugh. "Anyway," David said, turning to Remy. "What'd you do all evening here with her?"

"Nothing, really," Remy said immediately, without a second thought. "She sat on her phone, and I sat on the computer."

"Well. You missed out on those heated floors," David said, flashing a grin before heading to his bunk.

Remy licked his lips. "Looks that way."

Chapter Nine

"Did you guys seriously get chased out of Portland?" Celeste asked excitedly over the phone. "You should have called me!"

"I didn't know that was newsworthy. Doesn't Vivi Swan essentially get chased everywhere?" Remy answered. His phone was smashed between his cheek and his shoulder as he sorted through the new sticks that had just come in—after two tour stops, he'd finally decided to ask for the brand he really wanted, more to see if Walter's assistant would come through on the offer than out of real need. Yet here they were, a brand-new box full of sticks and brushes and mallets. He was organizing them around the drum set in the hours before the show. They were in Grand Rapids, and the sun was blinding in the clear blue sky above them.

Celeste sighed. "I mean, sort of. But still. I would've liked to blog a play-by-play. Vivi Swan: The High-Speed Chase, live."

Remy snorted. "I couldn't have done that anyway. Seriously, Celeste, I can't give you anything for the site. She's pretty serious about the nondisclosure stuff. She even supposedly has a spy on staff to let her know what people are saying about her or to other people or whatever."

"Of course she does. Famous people don't want the peons of the world to know what they're actually like," Celeste said breezily.

Remy felt something in him rise to defend Vivi—to tell Celeste that they'd played songs together, that Vivi had a real laugh that was harder to coax out than that fake one, to tell her about *House Hunters*—but Celeste would want to blog about all of that. Even if he'd sworn her to secrecy, though, there was something pleasant about keeping that time with Vivi to himself. He felt like an insider, like he was more than just a—

He rolled his eyes at himself. This was exactly what Vivi sold, nightly, onstage—the illusion of friendship, of a relationship, that she was something *more* than a singer the fans paid to see. Empathy. He'd bought into it, just like they did, and this was monumentally embarrassing. How long had he been in this industry? Too long to fall for shit like this.

"Ugh, fine. Fine," Celeste said. "Hey, Val's working on a song!"

"What?" Remy said too sharply. "Is everything okay?"

"Chill, yes. He's fine. He moped around for a week and threatened to pull together a new band and name it *Burrito Armageddon*, but he got over it. Now he's working on something. It's been sticking around for a few weeks."

"Oh," Remy said. He couldn't decide if he was embarrassed about his reaction or desperate to press the issue. Was she *sure* he was fine? Really, *really* sure?

"Remy, he's writing music again. He's not using. It's a good thing," Celeste said, voice becoming uncharacteristically gentle. "You act like I'm telling you he said yes to that 'Everything but Colleen' gig. *That* would be something to worry about."

"Right. Yeah. Of course," Remy said.

Celeste went on. "Anyway—you got a birthday card from your

mom, complete with Bible verse and plea for you to ditch Val and come back to Jesus-slash-Florida. Do you want me to save it for you? Val is pissed about it, of course. That they asked you, not that they consider him a lost cause."

"Of course. Well, remind him that it doesn't matter if they know where we are. I'm not going anywhere without him."

***

During the show that evening, Remy watched the writhing, gleeful audience. Val was particularly good at working an audience. He'd pause to take a long breath before a song, and the people would take it with him, undirected, following their leader obediently. It felt like a kind of hypnosis, the way Val commanded them.

This was not the case with Vivi. She didn't command them; she simply moved along, and they followed, because every few moments she turned back to them and smiled and waved, and they trotted behind like eager puppies. During one of her acoustic breaks, after she'd wandered through the audience and touched hands and taken gifts of flowers and teddy bears (which her security team took immediately), she sat on the edge of her gazebo, playing a simple melody on a ukulele, of all things.

"I got this ukulele from a friend, ages ago," she said, pausing—the crowd filled the silence with a loud cheer, and she smiled, or smiled bigger, anyhow. "And I've always wanted to play it for you, but it's hard to find a song that really *works* on this instrument, you know?" They cheered, as if they each truly believed the *you* was them.

She went on, still strumming, still playing the melody. "So, a while ago, I thought I really needed to find a song. You know— enough excuses! Find something we can all sing along to." They cheered. Remy was in total darkness, at this point—most of the band was sitting, though Parish and Michael had both dashed backstage, probably to grab a drink. They were still twenty minutes away from the intermission, but some nights it felt like the lights leached all the energy from you, and a bottle of water consumed in fifteen seconds felt like life force. David was sitting just offstage, but Remy stayed put, slouching over on his stool, enjoying the darkness that felt like quiet even though it wasn't.

"And so, I wrote a song especially for the ukulele. The sort of song that makes me feel like I'm falling in love. Do you know what I mean?" She looked up at them each time she asked a question then parted her lips and grinned, admiring the size of the audience with wonder. "Anyway, I'd like to play it for you now, if that's okay. It's called 'Count on Me.'"

She didn't launch into the song—she waded into it, picking across notes carefully, the small instrument delicate in her hands. It was a song about love—the way love looks in movies and books, all sweet meet-cutes and perfect kisses in the rain. Not real love: perfect love, a difference Vivi noted in the lyrics. It was a pretty song, suited for both the ukulele and Vivi's voice—she didn't have the pipes for loud, belting songs. If he were being honest, Remy had heard plenty of better singers without record deals and world tours. Knowing this didn't make him like the song any less.

In the finale, Vivi wove around the band, as per usual, pointing them out so the audience could cheer. They went wildest for the dancers and backup singers—the people in the sparkliest costumes—but cheered nonetheless for the band on Vivi's command. The fireworks exploded, the lights clicked out, and the stage fell into a flurry of activity. Remy abandoned his drum set and went back to the band's green room, where Michael was already sitting, mopping his sweaty brow with the white, 100-percent-cotton hand towels that were on the band's tour rider for just this purpose. David lifted his eyes when he passed Remy on the way down the hall.

"Musician party tonight, friend," he said kindly. "Just for a few hours, before we pull out."

"Bus Three?" Remy asked, and David nodded.

As they packed, Remy slunk back to the bus and changed into riding clothes then slapped a ball cap on his head and went for Bus Three. He was nearly there when he heard the rushing sound of another bus door opening—

"Remy!" Vivi said—he knew it was her without looking at this point, as he spent so much time listening to her voice. She was darting down the bus stairs, still in heels and hair and makeup and the sleek blouse she always wore from the arena back to the bus. Her lipstick was, as always, perfect.

"Hey," Remy said, stopping short, unsure if he was supposed to call her Vivi or Miss Swan. It had to be Miss Swan. Right? Only her actual friends and fans who thought they were her friends would call her *Vivi*, and he was neither. How had he not sorted this out before now?

Vivi smiled a little but seemed a touch off-balance. "I saw you walking by—do you have a minute? I wanted to hear your thoughts on that song I played you when we were leaving Portland."

He hesitated longer than he meant to, unsure what, exactly, she was asking. Did she want to watch junk television with him, or did she really just want his thoughts on music? Something delicate in her eyes almost implied the former, but it seemed beyond presumptuous to assume Vivi Swan was looking for a regular *House Hunters International* partner.

"Or…were you headed somewhere?" she asked when he took too long to reply, looking from Remy to the direction he'd been walking in. At that moment, the Bus Three doors opened, and laughter poured out.

"Remy—oh, hey, Vivi," Laurel called across the lot to them, her voice changing entirely when she said Vivi's name. It became happier, shinier—more like Vivi's stage voice. She let the bus door shut behind her and started their way.

Remy cleared his throat and said to Vivi, "I do have plans—but I can cancel them if you want to work on something now. Or you can email whatever you've got to me, and I can give it a listen tonight?"

Laurel reached them, a grin stretched across her face. "Want to join us, Vivi? Just for a little bit?"

Vivi smiled instantly, the expression suddenly trained. "Not tonight, but thanks. Remy, maybe tomorrow sometime, to work on that song? I can fit you in somewhere in the early evening—I'm in New York in the morning, but I'm flying back private that afternoon."

"Working on a song? Very cool," Laurel said, still grinning. Remy thought, though he couldn't be certain, that Vivi hoped Laurel would spontaneously vanish just as badly as he did.

"That sounds good. Should I...come by...your bus?" Remy asked. Immediately, he realized that his words sounded a) stupid and b) a little lewd.

"Yes. I'll tell my security team," she said. Then, briskly, "It was nice to see you, Laurel—"

"You're sure you don't want to come hang out?" Laurel asked, jumping again.

"No, no, I'd ruin it. You'd all have to turn over your cell phones, and I know everyone hates that," Vivi said, smiling again and waving her hands, like this was such a silly problem, but hey, what're ya gonna do? "See you tomorrow, Remy!" She took a surefooted step back into her bus; the doors wheeled shut behind her.

"She could just *not* make us turn in our phones," Laurel grumbled as soon as Vivi was out of sight.

"Does she always make you, when she's around you guys?" Remy asked as, together, they started toward Bus Three.

"She's never around us. We're lepers once we're offstage. Except for *you*, apparently. How'd you swing that?" Laurel asked.

Remy shrugged. "It's just because we got stuck on the bus together. I played her one of my pieces, and she was into it. It's not like we're friends or anything."

"Ha, trust me, I know—Vivi Swan doesn't have friends. But whatever you are, hang on to it. It's career gold," Laurel said, sounding disheartened. "She wouldn't even tweet about my solo album. I asked her, and she gave me some line about not wanting to associate her brand with too many projects. But I'm like ninety percent sure it's just because it had a song about masturbating on it."

"Really?"

Laurel nodded. "It's a great song. But I guess the Vivi Swan Brand doesn't masturbate. No wonder she's always so pissy, right?" she said as they reached the Bus Three door. She turned to Remy, a laugh in her eyes, and it suddenly felt like returning the laugh was required in order to board the bus.

So Remy laughed, loudly, and followed her inside.

Noel Said WHAT!?
America's Playboy earns his title

Vivi Swan and Noel Reid have supposedly been headed to splitsville for a while now, but last night, sources tell us Noel Reid may have accelerated the trip. While at one of his favorite haunts—LA's swanky Reign club—he was caught by our cameras getting more than a little friendly with a handful of ladies. When asked about how Vivi would react to his dirty dancing, Noel grinned and said, "The heart wants what it wants."

Vivi is currently on the first leg of her world tour, and her tour buses were chased out of Portland two nights ago by aggressive paps (not ours). Fans finally got a few cell phone pictures of the starlet, and she doesn't *look* too torn up about the whole Noel thing. Then again, maybe her heart wants someone else these days anyhow? She's due for a new breakup— and frankly, we'd love to hear the song she'd write about Noel. Though, Vivi, let's be real—at this point, have you considered writing a song called "Maybe It's Me"?

Comments: 721

Author: Bianca Treble

Chapter Ten

They had an off day before the Phoenix show, which meant the four o'clock sound check they usually revolved around never happened, leaving everyone on the tour a little listless. Parish and Ro had rented a car to tool around the city and David had a phone call with his family, which left Remy, Laurel, and Michael to grab lunch together. Despite their best efforts to have a totally non-music-industry meal, the conversation fell into one about Auto-Tune and SoundCloud and the amount of talent coming out of New Zealand.

It was nearly five o'clock before Remy put on his best studio clothes and made his way over to Vivi's bus. He walked to the door and lifted his hand to knock, but almost immediately, it flung open. It wasn't Vivi Swan on the other side—it was a beefy security guard who stomped down the steps, one eyebrow raised threateningly.

"Um, I'm supposed to meet Miss Swan here? For a production session?" Remy said, picturing how his arms would look when this guy broke them in half. "I'm the drummer," he added, like this was some sort of supersecret passcode that would explain everything.

The security guy radioed someone else then nodded at Remy,

stepping aside so he could ascend into the bus. Remy stood in the doorway, confused, looking for Vivi, but the place was empty. It smelled a little like her—like sugar and hairspray—but other than that, there was no sign she'd ever been here, much less a sign she was here now.

"Wait, am I—she was supposed to meet me. Should I come back later?" Remy asked the security guy. The man shrugged, which, given the size of his shoulders, looked like two boulders rising.

"She said to let you in. We let you in. You want to go?"

"I—no," Remy said, frowning. He didn't have the pay grade to stomp out because she wasn't on time. "I guess I'll just…sit. Here. And wait."

The man nodded then put a hand to his ear, listening to something over the headset. "She says help yourself to anything in the fridge."

"Are you talking to her now?" Remy asked.

"No. I'm talking to head of security."

"And he's talking to her?"

"No."

Remy stared. The man stared back.

"Okay," Remy said, nodding and forcing a smile. "I'll just sit here. At the table."

"Right," the security guy said then turned and stepped off the bus.

Remy slid into his seat, wondering if there were cameras on him. That didn't seem totally out of character for Vivi Swan. Was she watching him now? Checking to see if he'd try to sneak into her bedroom or paw through cabinets? He became very aware of the line of his spine, trying to perfect a casual slouch as he surveyed the room.

The lounge—here, it was definitely a lounge rather than a galley—was wide and long, with cream-colored benches and two matching recliners. There was a ruby-red-and-navy oriental rug down the center of the room, and the area was lit by gentle strips of light glowing from the ceiling. He spotted the refrigerator—full size, of course—in the galley, where there was a large stainless steel sink and a stackable washer-dryer hidden behind a slightly adjacent pocket door. The bedroom was just beyond, in the back, though it was unsurprisingly closed off.

Remy opened his laptop and, to busy himself, drew up a standard collab contract for himself and Vivi to sign—he was surprised she hadn't brought up a collab contract, to be honest, but one of them needed to, now that they were actually having planned production meetings. Twenty minutes passed, then thirty. At forty-five, he rose and went to the refrigerator. It was full of bottled smoothies and iced teas, the drawers packed with hummus and vegetables and yogurt cups. He found a sparkling water in the door and took it, wondering how he'd look drinking on camera. He'd decided he was on camera. He had to be.

He sat back at his computer. He turned the text in the contract blue, then pink, then black again.

At fifty-three minutes, his phone rang. It was an unknown number with a New York area code. He answered the call, expecting to be asked to complete a survey he didn't want to complete or pay a forgotten bill he didn't want to pay.

"Remy?" a voice—Vivi's voice—said. He heard hustle around her—cars and movement and the swish of fabric.

"Hey, uh, Vivi," he said. He nearly asked her how she'd gotten his number, but that was stupid. Of course she had his number. He wondered if this was hers or just a lackey's phone.

"I'm so sorry. I had a meeting with the Grammy Museum people, and then had to meet with Noel's manager, and then there was some sort of storm that delayed my plane leaving Philly, so now I'm stuck in New York for another few hours or so."

"Oh, it's cool. We can do it another time," Remy said, while wondering what sort of *meeting* one had with one's significant other and his "team."

"No, no, let's do it now," she said. "I'm going back to my hotel room. I just sent you a new rough cut of the song—did you get it?" To answer her question, Remy's laptop beeped at him. The email had arrived. It was from Webmaster@ViviSwan.com—not her personal address. Did she have a personal address? Did people as famous as Vivi Swan check email?

"Okay, I'll listen and give you a call back," Remy said.

"No, just put me on speaker. I want to hear what you think when it plays," Vivi said. He heard the thud of something—bags? shoes?— hitting the floor of the hotel room, which he guessed was probably a thousand times more opulent than this bus, which was really saying something.

"Sure," Remy said. He set the phone down, feeling at least slightly more confident that she wasn't watching him on a camera—at least, not actively, since she was clearly not looming in front of a screen. He closed the contract, opened the song file, and hit play.

It was only marginally more done than it'd been on the bus from Portland—still mostly Vivi singing with a guitar track, though she'd added a layer of herself doing the lower side of the harmony. She also had a few more lyrics in place, now, and had changed the arrangement of others. It still sounded more like a template than an actual breakup song, but Remy heard one line—"whisper fights on anxious nights"—that made him think of her fighting with Noel in the hallway during rehearsals.

"What do you think?" Vivi asked as it ended. "I tried to replicate your drum stuff on my computer, but I'm pretty terrible at that. Could you do it, you think?"

"Yeah, definitely. And the piece still needs a really solid hook," Remy said, feeling oddly bold in this conversation. Perhaps it was because Vivi's hair and eyes and skin weren't there to distract him, or perhaps it was because this was a conversation he knew how to swim in, unlike that weird, murky casual-or-professional quagmire they'd wandered into for a time there.

Vivi said, "I agree. But I think it should be something that layers under what's there, so the vocals more or less stay the same—not the lyrics, necessarily, but the core of it." There was a lilt in her voice, like she expected him to contradict her.

"Mm, I don't know," he said. "I think if the vocals rise an octave there, it'll work better. It'll highlight it."

"Okay, maybe—hold on, let me play it that way," she said, and he heard the clicking sounds of her opening her guitar case. She strummed through the song again, singing along quietly, playing so softly that he suspected no one else in the hotel could hear.

"Yeah, there," he said as they came to the chorus. "Right there. And if we—I mean, you—had a solid beat under that, something heavy on strings? It feels like that sort of song, I think. Strings always break people's hearts."

They picked through the rest of the song, chord by chord, experimenting with different beats, different keys, different ways she could alter the chords to wrap the listener up in the sound rather than leave them simply bobbing their heads. It was different from writing with Val, and not only because Val Young had never written a breakup song in his life—different because this felt almost like an entirely different form of creation.

With Val, Remy was always seeking ways to prove Val's

words—chords and beats and hooks that would drive home what Val was trying to say in a way listeners could understand. Make an angry song angrier, a forlorn song more forlorn, and a sexy song hotter. With Vivi, it was like they were working toward the end feeling, rather than from it—like she was finding ways to make the breakup hurt more rather than singing about something that was already there. This wasn't an unpleasant realization—it felt more like he had a hand in creating the feeling the song generated rather than just a role in highlighting it. The sun was gone by the time they hit the final chords, and Vivi still hadn't left New York.

"I think I'll have to stay here tonight. Which means I'll have to reschedule tomorrow." She sighed into the phone.

"Yeah?" Remy asked. "You mean the show?"

"No, no, I wouldn't cancel the show. I'll walk back to—where are we? Phoenix. I'll walk to Phoenix if I need to. But I had an interview with Records and a radio thing."

"You could do them over the phone too," Remy suggested.

She laughed. Her voice was breathy and low, almost muffled—she was lying down, Remy suspected. "I hate talking on the phone," she said.

"We've been on the phone for…Jesus Christ, two hours," Remy said, glancing down at his phone screen.

"Yeah, but we've been working, so it doesn't count," she said. "Though, wow, it's one o'clock? What time is it there, again?"

"It's only eight. And I drank all your sparkling water, by the way," Remy said.

"Have you eaten? There's food in the fridge. You can have it," Vivi said.

"That's not food. That's hummus and vegetables and yogurt."

"That's organic hummus and fancy-cut carrots and…well, yogurt. It might be fancy yogurt."

"I'm not a yogurt guy," Remy said. "I think we've got Hot Pockets in the band bus. I should go back there and make one."

"No, you'll lose me," Vivi said suddenly.

Remy went still, unsure how he'd so suddenly found himself in the quagmire again. "What?" he asked.

"Your phone. I've got a microcell in my bus to get a better signal. If you leave the bus and it switches over to a tower, the line will go dead," she said.

"Oh."

This shouldn't have mattered, because they were done working on the song. They were talking about yogurt. And besides, he could call her back or she could call him back or they could just talk again when she got into town the following morning. But there was something about hanging up, about ending the call at two hours twenty-one minutes and seventeen seconds that felt wrong—wronger, even, than the fact Remy was about to continue a phone call with his boss that had swiftly turned into something personal rather than professional.

Wronger than the fact that he liked it.

"I guess I'll eat yogurt then," Remy said quietly. He paused. "Do you have cameras in here?"

"That's a creepy question, Remember Young," Vivi said, but he heard her smiling, unsure how, exactly, he'd learned what her smile sounded like.

"No creepier than having a secret camera on someone," Remy refuted.

"There's a camera," she said, "but it's on the front of the bus. To see people boarding. There's nothing in the lounge. Why do you ask?"

"So I can eat my yogurt in private, obviously," Remy said. "My brother would kick my ass if he saw me eating…what is this…Fruit on the Bottom Razzmatazz."

"That's the best one!" Vivi said. "What's your brother got against yogurt?"

Remy shrugged a little and, now that he knew a camera wouldn't catch him, sat on the couch that was more or less the most comfortable thing he'd ever sat on. He peeled open the yogurt as he answered, "My brother believes in a few basic food groups. All involve off-brand Fritos, much to his girlfriend's dismay."

"Val is older, right?" Vivi asked. Remy made a noise of concurrence, and she went on, "I have a younger brother."

"Oh, yeah?"

"Mm-hmm. Three years. He wants to be an actor. Maybe. He's studying drama, anyhow."

"You guys close?" Remy asked, staring at the spoon absently as he spoke.

Vivi hesitated for a few moments—long enough that Remy stopped staring at the spoon and became very certain he'd asked the wrong thing. Finally, she said, "Not really. He was only ten when my first album released, so he's kind of…I mean, he's been Vivi Swan's little brother ever since, you know? People online are so terrible to him. It's like, when they get tired of calling me overrated or fat or a heartbreaker, they set in on him," Vivi said.

"The internet is full of assholes, though. I'm sure he knows that."

"Yeah, but he also knows why those assholes came after him," Vivi said, voice a little sharper. It made Remy still, though not from discomfort—from familiarity. He knew this tone, this exhaustion, the weariness of being told something wasn't your fault when it so clearly was. It was always terrible to be lied to but even worse when you'd already accepted the truth.

"What about you and Val? You've always been so close?" Vivi asked, sounding both eager and hesitant to change the subject.

"Yeah—definitely. We were all we had. Crazy weird religious family thing," Remy answered.

"Makes sense," Vivi said thoughtfully. "What about your parents?"

Even Celeste only knew scant details of his and Val's life in Florida, their family, their past, and she'd had to earn that knowledge over the course of years. Yet here he was, wondering if he should grant Vivi rights to it in…days? Twelve *hours*, maybe, if you lined up every conversation they'd had end to end. Vivi had one of those voices, though, one of those faces and those eyes and that tone that made you want to tell her things.

Remy fought it back.

"It's complicated," Remy said, settling for an incomplete truth. "They never really believed in the music thing."

"Really? Even after Quiet Coyote?"

"Especially after Quiet Coyote. If it's not a praise song played on an organ, they're not interested," Remy said.

Vivi exhaled loudly into the receiver. "Can't please everyone, I guess," she said. A long pause went by, and Remy found himself smiling through it, though he wasn't sure why. "Anyway, I guess I shouldn't keep you on the phone just to entertain me, huh? I can go work on the song."

Remy nodded, even though she couldn't see him, and thought about how he'd agreed to attend the Bus Three group thing in the hotel tonight. The prospect sounded terrible, now, when there was… this.

Remy grimaced as he spoke. "Yeah, I should probably get back anyway. Besides, I already drank all your sparkling water. If I stay, I might eat all this yogurt."

"You can have all the yogurt," Vivi said immediately.

"Oh." He paused then spoke cautiously. "Want to work through the song again and I'll just hang out on the line and jump in if I hear anything? I have some work to do on my laptop anyway."

"Yes," she said, sounding almost relieved. She was smiling, though again Remy wasn't sure how he knew that. "I'll put you on speaker. I'm putting the phone down now."

"Got it," Remy said and listened to the rustle of movement. He passed the phone back and forth between hands to make it sound like he was doing the same. Instead, he lay back on the couch, toeing his shoes off as he did so. He didn't have anything to work on, not really—or at least, nothing more interesting to him than the idea of closing his eyes to screens for a little while.

He listened to the hushed scratch of Vivi playing the song, notes dancing off her fingertips so quietly that he could barely hear it. She must have been writing something down as she did it, as she'd pause every now and again and he'd hear the rustle of paper. Remy wondered how her fingers looked on the strings—he'd never seen her play so quietly, never seen her play without being on a stage surrounded by lights. He thought her fingers might arc over the strings like jointed rainbows.

He thought they were probably beautiful. How could they not be?

Chapter Eleven

Remy inhaled. The air smelled like coffee—the good kind of coffee, the sort he picked out after paydays. He turned over, reaching instinctively for the strap that would release him from his bunk. He felt groggy, like he'd been woken in the middle of a sleep cycle, but like hell was he missing out on good coffee.

There was no belt. Remy frowned then creaked open his eyes.

He wasn't in his bunk. In a flash, he remembered—he'd lain down on Vivi's couch, she was on the phone, it was after midnight, he was going to listen to her play while he worked, and then—

Well. Then it was seven o'clock in the morning, according to the clock on the sleek miniature microwave just visible if he craned his neck correctly. Also visible: Vivi herself.

"You're awake," she said, like he'd accomplished some great feat.

"Oh, god," he said, sitting up too fast. He fought dizziness by running a hand over his head. "I'm so sorry. I don't know what happened. I didn't even know you came in."

"Well, I'm wearing flats," Vivi said, motioning to her feet as if this fully explained how he'd managed to sleep through her security team sweeping the bus, her entrance, the shuffle of putting down bags, and the brewing of coffee.

"I'm so sorry," Remy said, a swell of guilt building in his stomach. He was a professional—and professionals didn't fall asleep in the talent's bus. He should have left, should have let the line disconnect if that's what it meant. His worry wasn't helped by the fact Vivi wasn't smiling or laughing or even teasing him; she was just somewhat stonily making coffee. She looked pleasant, the way she always did, but there was nothing forgiving in her face. She said, "It's done. You're here, and there's no way people will miss you getting off my bus, so we've just got to deal with it. But I'm not dealing with anything until I've made coffee. So just give me a minute, okay?"

Remy licked his lips, breathing through his mouth to quiet the sound of air, like he used to do when playing hide-and-seek with Val. Vivi moved intentionally, one scoop of sugar, a little half-and-half, her face expressionless, almost robotic. When the coffee was done, she turned and leaned on the counter, without looking at him, then took a few careful sips.

"Okay," she said, exhaling. "Okay. The band will have missed you on your bus, so even if you get out of here without a photo, someone will figure it out."

"I'll say I booked a hotel or something—"

"No, no, if you make too many excuses, someone will *really* know something's up," Vivi said. How was her voice so frightening when it was so calm? Perhaps it was the threat of that calm breaking, becoming a shouting match? Remy pressed his lips together. "People will think we were here together, and that'll just make everything happening with Noel right now worse..." Vivi said.

"Are you sure? Aren't there pictures of you in New York to prove—"

"Remy, I've done this before, okay?" Vivi said, voice commanding. "Let me fix this."

"Sorry. Right. Sorry," Remy said, hating himself harder than he thought possible. Who the fuck fell asleep on their boss's bus?

Vivi nodded to herself then pulled out her phone. She laid it on the table, on speaker.

"Hey, Vivi! What's up?" a cheery female voice asked—though there was a groggy undertone that made it pretty clear she'd been woken up.

"Hey, Aspen. I want to get ahead of something."

"On it, on it, on it," Aspen said, and there was a shuffling of papers and sheets. "Go."

"My drummer, Remy Young, has been working on some production stuff with me, but we haven't announced it. He fell asleep on my bus last night, while I was in New York."

"Oh, for fuck's sake. Who does that?" Aspen asked.

"Me," Remy muttered.

"Oh, he's still there?" Aspen said unapologetically.

"I'm waiting for a plan. I'm thinking we just announce that we're working together?"

"That's big. Is there time to do a check?"

"Not really. We did one before the tour that came up clean."

"Remy—Remember Young, right? Quiet Coyote…" Aspen muttered. Remy found Vivi's eyes for a scattered second but couldn't discern if Aspen was talking *to* him or through him. "Alright, Remy, listen—is there anything we want to know about you? Anything not on your record check? Crimes? Anything? Tell me now. Right now. This is your only chance to come clean before shit gets real."

"Um—" Remy said, voice strangled. "Nothing. I mean, nothing that I think is a big—"

"Let me be the judge of that. Tell me anything that the media might like."

"Uh, I guess—" Remy said, looking at Vivi, hoping the pain in his eyes wasn't too profound. "My brother was an addict. But he's clean now. My family is really religious…" He stumbled, unsure where to go next. What constituted a scandal in Vivi Swan's world? He swallowed, mentally thumbing through his secrets.

"Religious how? Cult religious?" Aspen asked.

"Aspen, you're sort of intense," Vivi broke in gently and laid her hand on top of Remy's for a fraction of a second. It was enough to make his heart race and breath slow at once, which made him feel even more unhinged, a car engine trying in vain to turn over.

"Vivi, I'm just trying to make sure we're not in the middle of a Scientology disaster. You remember what happened to Serena Evanson?" Aspen said politely.

"My family is Pentecostal," Remy said before Vivi could respond.

"Scary religious, not cult religious. Okay. Any DUIs? Drug arrests? Hookers?"

"No."

"I'm serious about the hookers—ever been to a massage parlor? That counts."

"No."

Aspen said, "Okay. I'll leak that you're working on a song together. Just loose, casual, because-he's-on-the-tour-anyway type stuff. Do you want me to call Noel's managers?"

"Call George, but don't call Noel. I'll handle him," Vivi said, pulling her hand back and sounding battered. "After yesterday's disaster with him, I need to be the one to head it all off."

"Okay. Remy, make sure you look clean and put-together when you leave. You need to be carrying your laptop where everyone can see it. Put together a notebook and write *Untitled Vivi Swan Song* at the top, carry it so if there's a photo, people can see it. Vivi, make sure you stand in the doorway for a second, have an instrument— you've got a guitar on the bus, right? Make sure you've got it in your hands."

"Got it. Thanks, Aspen," Vivi said, voice sounding a little gentler, a little more relaxed. Remy wondered if it was the caffeine taking effect or the fact there was now a plan for the whole Remy-slept-here thing.

"Literally what I'm here for," Aspen said. "I'll call back in three hours to let you know if anything leaked, okay?"

"Thanks," Vivi said and hung up before Aspen could respond— though Remy got the impression traditional phone etiquette wasn't really a thing with the two of them.

"I'm so sorry," Remy said again, slower this time, wishing he could crack himself open and show how really, truly, very sorry he was.

Vivi nodded and sort of half smiled. "I convinced you to stay."

"But still."

"But still," she agreed. "It might be nothing. Better safe than sorry, though."

"Hey, I understand," Remy said reassuringly, though given the fact there were still pillow lines on his face, he wasn't sure he was being particularly convincing.

They sat in silence for a long moment, Vivi sipping her coffee, the idea of a smile toying at her lips. Remy ran his fingers along the lip of his laptop. It was the sort of silence that wasn't easy or simple but was so warm and rose-scented, he didn't want to break it. He was content to let it stretch out, dissipate into nothingness, rather than cut into it directly. When Vivi finally sighed, they both had the look of people rising from sleep.

"What I said before, about the disaster—with Noel, I mean…" she said.

"Nondisclosure," Remy reminded her. "I won't say anything. And I don't know anything about it anyway."

Vivi looked some combination of wounded and relieved, an expression that made her eyes wider and lips more heart-shaped all at once. "No, it's not that. It's…things are sort of tense with me and Noel. It's hard, in this industry. You're not just dating a person, you're dating a brand. And, well…Noel's brand isn't always my thing. But the clean-cut boys were always breaking my heart, so when our managers introduced us, I figured I'd give a broody bad boy a shot, you know?" She forced a laugh at the end, like she was working hard to make the phrase into a joke if the conversation turned that way.

"I can see how that'd be a problem. Your brand is so…" Remy began with a nod but found himself afraid to finish. Glitter? Sparkles? Revenge? Romance? The words sounded both like an insult and woefully incomplete—like describing himself simply as *short* or Val as *angular*. "Your brand doesn't mesh with his," Remy said, trying to save the sentence.

Vivi gave him a sardonic look, all eyes and a half smile. "No," she said then inhaled. "My brand is Disney love. Kissing and grand gestures and getting ice cream with your girlfriends when he leaves you. It doesn't really line up great with dark-poetry eyes."

"Maybe he'll become less…dark?" Remy offered, unsure what else to say—it wasn't like he felt comfortable shit-talking her boyfriend to her, and he was hardly the guy to give sincere relationship advice.

"Ha," Vivi said with a humorless laugh.

"What about you, then? Maybe you can go dark? Like that last scene in *Grease*. He won't change, so you put on leather pants and go to the carnival. And then a car inexplicably flies," he said, and it made Vivi *actually* smile—which made Remy feel like he'd slain a Noel-Reid-shaped dragon.

"The flying car, I could work with. That feels on-brand. The leather pants…don't think I can go there," she said, still grinning, still making him feel lightweight. She exhaled. "Noel would be into that, though. And hey, we could share eyeliner."

Remy snorted despite his best efforts to hold it back, which made Vivi smile harder. They sat in comfortable, sunshiny silence for a moment. Remy finally tapped the table lightly and said, "Hey, can I say something without getting fired?" Vivi nodded, and Remy went on: "I don't think he's all that dark. He's like Fisher-Price dark. Dark Ken doll."

Vivi grinned. "He does work too hard at the whole emo kid thing, doesn't he? He's from Beverly Hills. His backstory isn't nearly as dark and broody as he wants it to be."

"Here's the real test: Does he eat kale?" Remy pressed.

"I do believe he's ordered a kale wrap before."

"Yep. No one who eats kale can authentically brood," Remy said.

Vivi laughed brightly then reached into one of the galley drawers. She slid him a crisp, fresh legal pad. "Alright. Better get your paper ready. *Untitled Vivi Swan Song*, aka: Kale Me Phony."

"That was a terrible pun," he said, shaking his head in faux shame.

"You laughed anyway. Besides, we'll work on it. We have to, now."

"Right," Remy said and pulled a pen from his bag then scrawled *Untitled Vivi Swan Song* at the top. Vivi rose and vanished to the back bedroom, returning a few moments later with her guitar.

"Ready?" Vivi asked.

"Sure."

Vivi nodded, grabbed her phone, and texted someone. A moment later, there was a thunderous knock on the door. "That's security. Go on out," she said. Remy rose, and she followed him a few steps to the door.

"Hey," she said, just as he reached for the handle. He turned, and she smiled again, and her voice changed a bit. "I'm excited to work with you, Remy Young."

"Likewise," Remy said through a somewhat unexpected breath then opened the door and walked toward his own bus—trying desperately to avoid looking for prying eyes. It truly wasn't until he was back on the band bus that he realized he'd just gotten the career boost he'd hoped for when signing on for this tour.

And rather than being ecstatic about *that*, he was hanging on her words—or rather, on the way she'd said them. The way her voice was a little soft, a little gentle, a little nervous, almost. The way she'd paused for a millisecond before the word *work*.

I'm excited to work with you, Remy Young.

Then

Val was getting better at guitar.

Remy was getting better at percussion.

But Mercy wasn't getting any better.

They spent every Sunday afternoon and evening praying—the boys, their father, their grandparents and neighbors and Pastor Ryan. It wasn't the quiet, contemplative sort of prayer. It was the shouting kind, the angry kind, where their father spoke in tongues and the lady who babysat them sometimes convulsed on the floor. They sweated and shook and felt delusional and feverish, and around sunset, when the frenzy tapered, the pastor would look proud.

"That was God's presence," he said. "That was God visiting us. God telling us about his great and mighty plans to heal baby Mercy."

After prayers were over, Val and Remy slipped outside in the bustle of people gathering hats and purses and toddlers. Even in Florida, the evening air was cool, and the humidity pressed against their skin like a damp cloth. This part of the state was ridiculously flat and grassy, and seemed quiet and still until you realized you weren't hearing silence—you were hearing the calls of a thousand crickets trilling. Remy had always been particularly intrigued by how crickets could be so loud and so quiet at once.

Val took his shirt off—he hated wearing button-up shirts— revealing the crudely drawn tattoos he'd put on his chest in marker. Remy looked nervously back at the house, far more afraid of his brother getting caught than Val himself was. The fake tattoos were supposed to look like the ones on a rock star whose CD cover they'd seen at their music teacher's house. They made the rock star look tough. They made Val look skinny.

"You know something?" Val said, slumping into the grass and stretching out like a star. "I don't think that was God."

"What was?"

"All of that. I don't think that was God."

Remy dug his toes into the grass. Val said things like this; Remy never did, even if he thought them. Thinking them was sinful enough but at least deniable. Saying them meant it was real.

"Who do you think it was, then? The Devil?" Remy asked.

"No," Val said and plucked a long blade of grass from the ground. He stuck it between his teeth. "I think it was Pastor Ryan."

Remy didn't say anything, but he sat down next to his brother. He watched members of the Lake City Assembly of God file out of the house, slip into cars, or start walking toward their own homes. He and

Val shrank back into the darkness to hide themselves a little better, and Remy caught Val reaching for his shirt, in case he needed to hide his pretend tattoos.

The crickets went quiet and then loud again as Pastor Ryan and their parents stood at the front door, speaking in hushed voices. Remy opened his mouth to ask Val what, exactly, he meant about it being Pastor Ryan, when suddenly a car pulled up. It was white, and even in the sunset, they could see the gold and blue stripes along the side. The last rays of sun licked at the reflective lights across the top.

"Why are the police here?" Remy asked, voice quivering. The police were no good. The police came when you were in trouble, when things were about to get dark, when someone was going to jail. "Put your shirt on, Val," he said to his brother. He knew it was illegal for a kid to get tattoos—did Val's pretend tattoos count? Were the police here for him?

"Are they here for me?" Val asked, not speaking to Remy in particular. He stood, tattooed chest still uncovered. Remy stared at his brother. Val's voice hadn't been fear-stricken, like Remy's. It had been curious. Perhaps even hopeful.

Their mother wailed. It was a keening, broken sound, not a scream, not a cry, but a sound like air being squeezed from her lungs. Their father was shouting. Pastor Ryan appeared, he yelled, the policeman returned to his car and spoke over a crackling radio. Remy finally convinced Val to slip his shirt back on, and together, they walked toward the house.

"Boys! Get in here!" their father yelled when he saw them emerging from the trees. The policeman's eyes darted toward them, and for a moment, Remy thought he was going to lunge for them. What then? Run toward their father or toward the tree line? If they got away, they'd be in the woods by themselves after dark. Being caught by the policeman would be worse, Remy guessed.

But the policeman didn't lunge, and the boys scurried into the house, where their mother paced in the kitchen, clutching the tiny bundle that was baby Mercy to her chest and weeping openly. Her long, pious skirt whipped around her legs like a tangle of sheets, and Pastor Ryan stood nearby, hand lifted to the sky like he was waiting for God to reach down and touch his fingertips.

Val brought three fingers to his mouth, kissed them, then waved goodbye to Mercy's tiny form.

"Pray with us, boys," Pastor Ryan said, creaking open an eye when he heard the brothers shuffle in.

"What's happening?" Val asked.

"It's the government. They want to take Mercy away. They'll take her to a hospital. They'll mock our faith by trusting man to heal what they think God cannot. But he can, boys, and you know that. We just need to pray."

Val and Remy fell silent beside Pastor Ryan, pretending to pray but stealing glances at each other. Pastor Ryan begged aloud for forgiveness. Their mother wept openly. Baby Mercy tried to cry but didn't seem to have the energy.

So Remy prayed, because it was the only thing he knew how to do when it felt like everything was breaking. He asked forgiveness for his sins and, in doing so, began to count them: He ate candy at the music teacher's house. He didn't avert his eyes from the magazines with ladies on them at the supermarket. He wrote songs with Val that weren't about God.

He *loved* writing songs with Val that weren't about God. He loved playing them. He loved slowing them down and speeding them up and recording them on the karaoke machine they had upstairs while their parents were manning the community kitchen. He loved the way music felt alive, vibrating the drumsticks in his hands and rattling his brain around in his head.

So perhaps this was why the government had come for Mercy. Because he loved music, and Val, and playing music with Val—because he loved all the wrong things and none of the right ones.

Chapter Twelve

Life on a massive arena tour was, alarmingly, similar to life on a small bar tour—boring and suitcase-laden in the morning, followed by a rush of adrenaline in the evenings. While Remy tended to the whiplash of those sensations, Vivi flew all over the country, constantly being rushed into and out of cars, appearing on morning shows filmed on the opposite coast, being photographed with Noel Reid in LA.

After all the frenzy, no one spotted Remy leaving Vivi's bus. Rather than being relieved, Vivi considered it a near miss and didn't ask Remy for any more late-night visits to her bus. There were days, in fact, where the only time they really saw one another was the tiny moment of eye contact they always made in the seconds before Remy's platform began ascending onto the stage. Vivi would take her place in her glittering pearl-colored dress and nod at the stage manager. Remy's platform would grind then start to climb. Vivi would look over and smile, and Remy would catch her eyes and smile back until her face vanished from his view.

It was such a small thing, but the look felt like an ember inside him—smoking, threatening a flame, but never quite catching. He hated it until the moment it happened again, at which point it felt like sunshine in his chest.

The morning they arrived in Dallas, Remy lay in his bed, staring at the ceiling as the sunshine feeling dissipated and the frustration returned. He rolled out of his bunk and climbed down the ladder. The rest of the musicians and singers were spilled around the lounge, watching an old *Behind the Music* tape that supposedly showed David shirtless, with a six-pack, having panties launched at him. David insisted it was just lighting, that there were no panties; Michael insisted that he'd been in the audience, and there weren't just panties but bras. The tape, which to Remy's amazement Walter's assistant had hunted down for them (and the VCR to play it), was supposedly going to prove who was correct once and for all.

"Here it comes," David said. "Here we go." He took a long swig of a lime-flavored beer then used it to motion to the screen.

"No, it's not here. It's later," Michael said. "It's when you start that shitty song."

"Man, these are *all* shitty songs," Laurel said, laughing.

"Wait, you played with 78 Devils?" Remy asked, when he realized just who the band young (and indeed, six-packed) David was playing with.

"My first tour. Talk about parties, man. Being on tour with them was the kind of thing you have to train for. Like, don't even board the bus if you can't down a case yourself and still play," David said, shaking his head. "And then we'd drive all night, hardly any sleep, with girls on the bus, and play another show the next day. No wonder Declan got on coke. How else would the guy have stayed awake?"

"My brother and I loved this band when we were kids!" Remy said, sitting in the center of the floor between the rest of them.

"Fuck, man, way to make us feel old," Michael said, shaking his head.

Remy laughed. "Seriously, though—we weren't allowed to listen to music like this, but we found out our parents secretly had cable, they just never plugged it in. So, when they left, we'd hook it up and watch MTV. What was this, 1996? I feel like I saw this video a thousand times."

"I think 1996. Maybe 1995?" David said. "A lifetime ago. I was so new. We were all so new. We had no idea what was ahead—"

"There! See! Panties!" Michael said, pointing at the television.

There was some debate, some rewinding, some slow motion. Shirtless Young David ducked *something*, though they were either very large panties or a wad of paper towels. Later on, however, the entire bus—driver included—agreed there was definitely a bra being thrown, which led them to suspect the first toss was, indeed, underwear.

"Fine, fine, maybe it was. My money's still on paper towels, though," David said grouchily, shaking his head. "I mean, no one throws panties at the keyboardist. That's for the guitarists."

"Got that right," Parish said, and he and Michael high-fived, grinning.

"Come on, assholes—these guys, not you, ladies. You're not assholes," David said, rising and running a hand over his hair. "Let's get moving." It was nearly three thirty, which meant the unload was almost finished and sound check was about to start. They all had to shower or shave or arrange their hair into the Vivi Swan Sweethearts Tour–approved styles.

The dressing rooms were elaborate and, as per usual, immaculate. Remy skipped showering—he got so sweaty drumming, there was hardly any point—but carefully pulled on one of the many short-sleeve, label-less (yet designer) T-shirts the tour had provided him.

Walter's assistant had handed him a new stack of ripped jeans back in Kansas City, saying the ones he'd been wearing had become "too ripped." He wondered if this was an observation straight from Vivi or from Walter.

Remy had just grabbed a bottle of water when he heard a quiet acoustic guitar being played, a tune he recognized—the one he and Vivi had been working on. He stood still and listened for a few moments. The music was coming from behind Vivi's dressing room door. He took a few steps closer, closed his eyes, and leaned into the sunshine feeling that washed over him.

She played it again, stopped. Again, stopped. He heard paper flutter—was she writing on it? He eased closer, and rather than the sound of a pen clicking or the *slink* of her returning to the strings, he heard a heavy sigh. Not a frustrated one—a sad one. A sigh that felt on the verge of tears or perhaps in the middle of tears. He frowned and, before he could second-guess himself, knocked softly on the door.

"Yes?" Vivi called out.

"It's Remy," he said. The words fought his lips, and he took a breath. Knocking on the talent's dressing room door—especially over something like this—was not professional. Listening to the talent songwriting was not professional. Inquiring about the talent's potential tears was not professional.

But he spoke again anyhow. "I was just walking by and heard you working and, uh…"

There was a noise, sort of a mix between a laugh and a sniff. "You can come in. The door code is four-two-three." Remy looked down and realized there was a keypad. The band dressing room didn't have one, but then, the band didn't include anyone who looked like Vivi Swan. He fingered in the numbers, and the door gave a mechanical click, a light on top of the knob glowing green. He pushed into the room.

To his surprise, Vivi Swan looked perfect—the kind of perfect she looked onstage, not the kind of perfect she looked when they were alone. Her face wasn't red, her mascara wasn't tear-streaked, and she wasn't curled in a ball on the pristine white sofa that sat opposite the door. She was smiling, lipstick perfect, eyes perhaps the tiniest bit glassy from the tears he'd heard before—but deniably so. He lifted an eyebrow as he stood in the doorway, intentionally not letting the door click shut behind him. Being on the bus alone was one thing—there was a driver, after all, so they were never truly isolated. Being in a closed, locked dressing room alone was quite another.

"What's up?" Vivi asked cheerfully.

"I thought I heard you crying. And playing," he said, motioning to her and the guitar and back again. Had he lost his mind entirely? This girl hadn't been crying, clearly.

Vivi shrugged, smiled a little, then nodded at the coffee table— her black Moleskine notebook was there, open, with a ballpoint pen splayed across the pages. "I was working on that song. Trying to put some lyrics to it. It's funny how this is one of those songs—the melody, not the lyrics—that just works. Like, it can be cheerful or sad or angry. There aren't many of these. Golden songs."

"Why *golden*?" Remy asked.

"Because they go with everything, obviously, like gold jewelry," Vivi said a little teasingly, like this was a piece of fashion advice he ought to have known.

"Right," Remy said. Without thinking, he stepped forward, and the door clicked shut behind him, automatic lock whirring as it sealed. To his surprise, with the door shut, the space did feel more like the bus—just the two of them, working on music together.

Vivi's dressing room was really a series of rooms; there was a treadmill in a back room, along with a few of those giant exercise balls. In the main room, there was a table of fancy deli meats, the makings for nachos, water, and Diet Coke. It was softly lit and draped in fabric an almost white shade of pink, and there were two humidifiers whirring in either corner. Everything was intentional, displayed like they were in a store, almost—which, of course, Remy guessed was on account of a detailed performance rider.

Remy watched Vivi's fingers running aimlessly back and forth across the guitar strings. "So…it's a sad song, now?"

She exhaled. "I don't know. Yes? Long story short, Noel was out with some girls at a club, and I tried to ask him about it, and we fought and just…" Vivi stopped, and when she spoke again, her voice was a little distant. "There's this joke the media likes to make about the songs I write—that maybe it's me. Maybe it's all my fault." She blinked. "They wouldn't say that to a man, you know."

"They wouldn't," Remy agreed then stopped. "Maybe that's the song."

"I've done two songs about the way the media treats women differently—you *play* them in the show, Remy," Vivi said, looking both amused and offended.

"No—that's it. Write a song about how *maybe it's you.*"

Vivi frowned, considering it, then played the first bit of their song, humming through the unwritten lyrics before singing it as the main line of the chorus: "*It's probably you, but maybe it's me.*"

"Golden," Remy said, smiling at her.

"Genius," she answered, nodding to him. "Although that makes it a breakup song, sort of. I'm trying to get away from those. I've got a million already, and honestly, they're getting harder."

"How's that?"

She put her guitar down and fiddled with the tuning keys absently. "Don't you feel like you get over your heart getting broken faster, now? I mean, compared to when you were, like, sixteen. It's just another thing you do once you're an adult."

Remy snorted at her words then held his hands up in apology—her eyes said that she thought he was mocking her. He said, "No, it's just, I don't know that I've ever had my heart broken. Not really."

She rolled her eyes. "Guys are always so afraid to call it that. You've been in love, right?"

"Uh—I don't...no, I don't think so."

Vivi looked surprised. "Seriously?"

Remy shrugged, suddenly embarrassed. "Not really. I mean, I've had girlfriends, but it wasn't love. Not really."

Vivi looked doubtful. "Just because you wouldn't call it love now doesn't mean it wasn't love then," she said, pulling a knee lightly to her chest. "You've at least had that moment when you didn't know what you'd do next, because everything that *was* suddenly *wasn't*. Right?"

He blinked at her, wondering if she was reading all this from the recesses of his mind. Thoughts of leaving Florida. Of Val using. Of the label killing their contract. Of realizing the life he'd thought stable was anything but. Even of Val secretly writing a new song without Remy's help.

She was right: he'd never thought to call it that, but it was definitely heartbreak.

Vivi must have known by his expression that she'd proven herself. She went on, "So my point is just that all those emotions are harder and louder and more painful when it's the first time. They're almost easy to write about when you really do think your world is over. But now...it's like I'm immune to the whole lost-love thing."

"You're in love with Noel?" Remy asked, voice foolishly doubtful. He immediately scolded himself. He shouldn't have said that. It was too personal. It was too serious.

Vivi stared for a second, a moment too long—then seemed to snap awake and said, "Of course." Her voice was clipped and cheerful.

She was lying.

Though, to be fair, Remy wasn't entirely sure she realized it. *He* only realized it because he'd seen the same look in Val's eyes when Val promised, swore, vowed that he really *wanted* to get clean. Val hadn't wanted to, not really. At that point, he truly believed the drugs fueled the music, and he'd have never traded one if it meant losing the other.

Vivi didn't love Noel; she was convincing herself she did so that she'd be able to tap into that pain when they split up. That she'd be able to drum up some hurt and pain and turn it into a song. The other boys were the same, according to Celeste—they'd all served the same purpose. How far back did it go with Vivi? When was the last time she *didn't* want to get her heart stomped on and turn it into a Grammy? No wonder she was always writing in that Moleskine—she was always in pain, always in the song.

Vivi exhaled. She looked at the clock.

"Probably about time," Remy said.

"Yep. We start makeup early," she said. Remy looked at her and noticed the smallest bit of her lipstick had smudged onto the lip of the teacup. If he studied her bottom lip, he could almost, sort of, kind of see the natural color of her lips through the stain.

Remy rose. "Alright. See you out there."

"Absolutely," Vivi answered.

Chapter Thirteen

"I bet Vivi is pissed," Michael said from the dressing room sink, where he was shaving disturbingly close to a fruit tray. "I think they're actually friends and all, not just show friends, but still."

It was hours before the Salt Lake show, and Tuesday Rivers, Vivi's longtime friend and fellow tabloid constant, had suddenly canceled her guest spot in the show. The band had learned the mash-up of Tuesday's new single and one of Vivi's staples, lighting had been adjusted, coordinating costumes had arrived, and Tuesday's dressing room was already set up—which, incidentally, was why the band had been offered a variety of spiked seltzers, seeing as how they'd otherwise go to waste.

"Wonder what the reason will be," Parish said, sipping one of the seltzers and making a face. "Laurel texted that there was some drama with Nick Maddon getting a DUI with Tuesday in the car. Hey, actually, maybe *Vivi* threw Tuesday out of the show over that. DUIs don't fit with her image."

"Possible," David said from the couch, where he was stretched out with a plate of chips balanced on his stomach. "Are *your* people still coming tonight, Remy?"

"They are—about ten minutes out," Remy said, keeping his voice level. He didn't feel level, though, even before the change of plans with Tuesday's cancellation. Two very different parts of his life were converging, tonight—Val and Vivi, old and new, bright and dark. He hadn't quite realized that the tour had laid claim to part of his life until Celeste confirmed that she and Val were going to be able to make it to the show. But now they were coming, which meant Celeste and Val and Remy's old life would be face-to-face with the arena and the lights and his new one.

He hardly expected those two lives to explode like volatile chemicals when they met, but he didn't expect them to stir together neatly either.

Celeste texted again, reporting that she and Val were just outside the loading docks. Remy hurried to retrieve them; Val wouldn't do so well if security hassled him, and there hadn't been time to mail them their backstage passes beforehand. Remy made his way through the concrete maze under the arena, running his hands through his hair, trying to remember how his expressions felt before he met Vivi so he could fake them. And then—

"Brother!"

Val's voice shot down the hall, echoing as it went. He was standing behind a very large but not particularly menacing arena security guy. The security guy looked back at Remy and scowled; Val gave him an obnoxious thumbs-up in return.

"You've literally been here one minute and already annoyed security?" Remy said, but he was grinning as Val hugged him tightly, wondering why he'd been worried. This was Val, this was him and Val, this was who he was deep down in his bones.

Val hadn't changed. Not that Remy expected him to be different—it'd only been four weeks—but Val was a wild card, someone who could very easily have changed in that period of time if he'd opted to. Celeste was wearing flawless LA makeup and smelled like honey and salt. She hugged Remy just as tightly as Val had, though her arms felt like the conclusion of a promise. *See, I told you he'd be fine. See, we've done it. See, it's okay.*

"This is legit, man," Val said as they passed racks of costumes, roadies with cables slung over their arms, harried dressers wearing rows of safety pins like medals on their shirts.

"Wait till you see the pyro," Remy said, experiencing a swell of pride and relief at Val's approval.

Remy took them back to meet the rest of the band, whom Val instantly charmed, talking music and equipment and obscure songs no one else on the planet would know about. Remy felt a rush of affection for his bandmates, who all mentioned not just Quiet Coyote but specific complex licks or clever song lyrics from their repertoire. Not just the fame but the heart.

"Aren't you going to introduce us to Vivi?" Celeste said, looking disappointed when Remy suggested they go across the street for dinner before his call time.

"She's doing a fan meet and greet—"

"We're fans," Celeste said, pouting.

"Aren't you hungry, though?" Remy said.

Val said, "You've literally got an entire room of food you could eat for free. And I want to know who you ditched me for."

"You *do* know. Her name's Vivi Swan. Didn't you see her name on the signs?" Remy said.

Val gave him a look, one that was a little too intense, a little too scrutinizing for Remy's comfort. The truth was he felt a desperate need for Val and Vivi to meet—and an equally powerful need for them to never, ever cross paths. If he kept making up excuses, though,

Val would realize something was up. Might realize Remy wasn't just playing in Vivi's band but was actually...writing songs with her? Talking to her? Liking her?

Remy forced a laugh. "Okay. Yeah," he said. "Come on."

He led them back through the underbelly of the arena, following signs to the meet and greet—it wasn't like he knew the venue any better than Celeste or Val did. He could hear Vivi's laughter from the conference room and saw a scattering of teenage girls in varying states of mental breakdown waiting just outside the door for their turn to behold her. One of them was hyperventilating to the point that Walter's assistant was watching her carefully from the doorway, clearly trying to decide where this was on the scale of emergencies.

"Hey, Wal—" Remy stopped, realizing he still didn't know the guy's name. He waved and started again. "Hey, man—I didn't put us on the schedule, but this is my brother, Val, and his girlfriend, Celeste. Can we jump in really quickly?"

Walter's assistant smiled in a way that made Remy certain the expression was for the benefit of those watching, not a result of anything actually smile-worthy. "For *you*, Remy. But only because it's you," he said in a way that was part sincere, part the words of a man with a fifty-seven-page-long to-do list on a clipboard.

Remy smiled and patted him on the shoulder; he heard Celeste say, "Thanks, doll!" behind him and could feel Val's indifference to fussy men with clipboards as they followed. Vivi was on the far side of the room in front of a large Sweethearts tour backdrop.

"They're always so much thinner in person," Celeste said under her breath.

"So that's your boss?" Val said at nearly the same time.

"That's her," Remy said.

Vivi looked up at the sound of his voice, and he felt himself soften as her eyes found his and, nearly instantly, processed who was standing nearby. She immediately returned her attention to the girl at her side—a tween who was gushing, voice rocky, about how Vivi helped her through a recent breakup with her boyfriend of three whole weeks. It was something Remy found himself wanting to mock, but Vivi didn't. She looked solemnly at the girl, nodded knowingly, and then hugged her close.

"It isn't easy, is it," Vivi said to the girl, so quietly that Remy had to strain to hear, "when the person we think is our soul mate just turns out to be a life lesson."

"Exactly. Exactly! I love you," the girl said, and now she was crying, grinning, shivering all at once. Vivi angled the girl a bit and tilted her head down so they could grab a picture.

"There are some cookies over there I made just for you guys," Vivi said, pointing the girl to a table that was layered with chocolate chip cookies. He made a mental note to ask her later if she actually *did* make them. Vivi turned her attention to the next in line—Remy, Val, Celeste.

"*You* must be the infamous Val Young," Vivi said, grinning, red, red lips on sparkling white teeth. Remy stood by, stomach twisting, as Vivi hugged Val then immediately turned to Celeste.

Celeste smiled at her. "I'm Celeste—Val's partner."

The use of the word *partner* threw Remy. Partner? She was his girlfriend. *Partner* was so much more...so much more everything. *Remy* was Val's partner. Remy was Val's only partner, and Val was his—

"Celeste," Vivi said. "Of course. I know! Remy told me all about you. Though, actually, have we met before? You look a little familiar," Vivi said, tilting her head at Celeste. They hadn't—of course they hadn't—but Remy saw what this was: another Vivi Swan move, another clever way to make Celeste feel special and important. Clever, clever as hell.

"No, I'd definitely remember that," Celeste said with a bright smile.

"Well, maybe you've just got one of those faces, yeah? Anyway— I'm so glad you guys could come to the show tonight," Vivi said. "And that you didn't mind us stealing Remy to save our butts."

"I wouldn't say we didn't *mind*—" Val began, but Celeste jumped in.

"Glad to be here. I love this album," Celeste said, expertly stopping whatever too-honest thing Val was about to say.

"Thanks! Speaking of—we listened to Quiet Coyote's album on the bus a few weeks ago. You are so crazy talented, Val. Seriously, the lyrics, just…wow. And Remy's such a great producer. I wish you'd release another album."

Celeste and Remy flinched in near unison—and even Vivi seemed to realize the carelessness of her words as soon as they left her mouth. Her eyes jumped to Remy's apologetically.

"We're not really recording these days," Val answered, rubbing the back of his neck. "It's really all about the live show, about music being *real* instead of sounds in a file."

Vivi didn't falter despite Val's Val-ness—in fact, she looked almost relieved, like he'd led her neatly out of the faux pas of suggesting a dropped band release a new album. She said, "I understand that. I like recording, and I like my music being available to people. But I like the live show. When I feel the song in my knees."

"Your knees?" Remy said, smiling, fighting to keep his voice a level of disinterested that wouldn't spike Val's curiosity.

Vivi gave him a little embarrassed sort of shrug. "That's where I feel the beat. Some songs, anyway—they start at my knees and pulse up. But some of them, like maybe…'Forget Her'? Those I feel in my elbows first. Sometimes this bone in my jaw." She put a perfectly manicured hand up against the edge of her cheek.

"That's cool," Val said, *almost* approvingly. "I get that. Music's bigger than just what you hear. It's a body thing, not a listening thing."

"Absolutely," Vivi said and smiled.

Remy fought the urge to grin, to shake his head. Somehow, Val had managed to meet both Vivi the girl *and* Vivi the product and seemed to like both. Well, to like them as well as could be expected, anyhow.

"Do you guys want to get a picture?" Vivi asked.

"I do!" Celeste said. Remy and Val glanced at each other and stifled laughs at the prospect. Celeste's enthusiasm, however, meant they edged around Vivi—Remy on her immediate right, and Val beside Celeste on her left. Vivi put her arms around Remy and Celeste, pulling them in close, letting her weight sink toward Remy in a way he didn't entirely comprehend until she pulled away and left a cool void by his side.

"See you out there, Remy," Vivi said cheerily, and then Walter's assistant and security were on to guiding other fans over to Vivi—twin teens in homemade VIVI FOR PRESIDENT shirts. Their little sister was wearing a matching one that said TUESDAY RIVERS FOR VICE PRESIDENT—Remy guessed they'd made them before Tuesday bailed.

Val gave the group a wary look then said, "Let's go. I want to see the stage, and this room smells like candy or something. Cherries."

"Vanilla. All her rooms have vanilla-scented things in them," Remy said. Val gave him a weird look then started for the door. Celeste shrugged and went after him, leaving Remy little choice but to follow.

The stage was a strange place between the sound check and the show. The lights were set, props were in place, instruments were on stands, but it was more or less a ghost town occupied by a few haunting crew members in black left to guard it all while the others grabbed dinner. They nodded politely at Remy then went back to their own conversations.

"This is it?" Val said as they approached the drum set. Remy nodded then turned back and saw Val wasn't looking at the drum set. He was walking in slow, almost dreamlike footsteps toward the middle of the stage, where Vivi would rise when the show began. His eyes were out at the thousands and thousands of empty seats in the arena, seats that were so far back, they were indistinguishable from the concrete steps and iron handrailings. Seats that still probably had a face value of a few hundred dollars.

Val was silhouetted in the light, a dark, almost genderless figure. It was a twisted version of a familiar view; when Remy couldn't see the Sweethearts backdrops or pink sparkly microphone stands, the scene looked *almost* like it always had in the hours before a Quiet Coyote performance—save the massive array of seats ahead of his brother. This was the way the hours before a Quiet Coyote performance might have looked if they'd found a second song, if they hadn't been dropped, if they'd grown into the sort of band that did arena tours.

Remy allowed himself to imagine that was the case for a moment. It's what they'd planned on, after all, and no matter how much Val talked about the *music* and the *feeling* and the need to let it *live*, Remy knew being dropped from their label still ate at him. Val had been so focused on music getting them *out* of Florida, he'd never really considered the possibility that it might do that but nothing more.

"How are you liking it? Being on the tour?" Celeste said quietly from just off Remy's shoulder.

He turned to her, ready to lie—to say *it's fine* with a shrug, the same answer he was trying to telegraph to Val. Noncommittal and uninterested. Celeste could see through lies, though, and so he still shrugged but said, "It's pretty good. It's great, actually. It's like this well-oiled machine. Stand here, play this, bow now."

"Val would *hate* this." She laughed a little.

"Yeah," Remy agreed.

"What about Vivi? Is she cool?" Celeste asked.

Remy almost answered but stopped himself. "Nondisclosure. No site talk."

Celeste rolled her eyes. "I'm just asking as a friend, not as a reporter. Look, Val is worried about you. I know this is a great gig, you know it's a great gig, but Val is worried that you're miserable and afraid to tell him. He thinks he's at home working on a song without you, which is absolutely freaking him the fuck out, and that you're here on a sad bus with strangers being sad."

Remy frowned. "What? No." No, he wasn't sad. No, Val didn't worry about *him*.

Celeste rolled her eyes. "Yes. I'm just saying, you now know that he's okay. Let him know you're okay."

Remy hadn't once, in his entire life, gotten advice on how to be Val's brother. The feeling in his chest wanted to rear up, wanted to remind Celeste that he'd been Val's brother longer than she'd been his girlfriend.

It wouldn't help, though. He nodded stiffly and looked back toward Val, who was walking back to them, shaking his head.

"This shit is nuts. Absolutely nuts," he said.

"Pop music is where it's at," Celeste replied, and her face went from concerned or hurt or annoyed to grinning. "Come on, Remy— show us where we're sitting?"

Their seats were close to the stage for the show—close enough that Remy could see Celeste singing along when the lights flashed over her. It was a good show—the same show it always was, the shared gaze before his platform ascended, the brilliant videos on the screens above. Vivi spoke to the audience during her acoustic sections, pausing as if thinking of what to say next, and the crowd screamed and cheered and called her name over and over and over until her name wasn't made of words or letters anymore but just a sound, like a war cry.

Afterward he, Celeste, and Val—along with Laurel, Ro, and Parish—walked to the soda shop across the street from the arena. It was one of the few things open in Salt Lake—it and a handful of ice cream parlors all within hopping distance of one another. The soda shop had a long menu of sodas mixed with fruits and juices and ice creams, a Mormon-friendly cocktail.

They sat on benches outside with a handful of other young people from the city's colleges. Remy blended with them well enough, but Celeste, with her ultralow top that would have been conservative in LA, and Val, with his Val-ness, looked like exotic flowers stuck into the salt flats. Celeste and Ro were talking marketing strategy for Laurel's singing videos she posted on social media—Celeste had a thousand ideas about how she could land bigger sponsors, none of which Remy understood. Remy and Val talked shop with Parish for a while, until he gradually sank into his phone, and it was just Remy and Val, Val and Remy, alone in a crowd like they always were.

"So, hey—Celeste said you're working on a song?" Remy asked, trying to sound casual.

Val nodded. "Yeah. It's coming. It's good."

There was a long pause where Remy debated asking Val if he could hear it. It wasn't that he was afraid to ask—it was that he was afraid of the fact that he felt like he had to, for the first time in his life. Val had never held music back from Remy. He'd played it for him, like it or not, over and over as he meddled with notes and ideas and curses. A performance artist figuring out what the performance was.

Val bathed in the silence then exhaled. "I'm still kind of…I don't know. I've never really done a song by myself, and it's like, since you're not home anyway—"

"It's fine," Remy said, unsure if he was lying. "I can hear it when it's done."

"Not done," Val said quickly. "It won't be done till you fuck it up, obviously. Don't worry."

Remy laughed, sort of. *Don't worry*, Val had said, which made sense—because Remy worried about Val, not the other way around. And yet the hitch in Val's voice, the way he'd so quickly tried to explain away the song… Val was worried about Remy, and Remy had been too worried about *Val* to notice.

Let him know you're okay.

Remy looked at the stars for a second then said, "So, actually, I'm working with Vivi on something. On a song."

Val went still. "Like, the Vivi we just saw perform?"

"Not a lot of other Vivis on the Vivi Swan tour," Remy answered.

"Right," Val said, as if that hadn't been a jab. "Is it—what kind of song? I mean, is it your song, or is it hers?"

"Hers," Remy said quickly. "I'm helping with hers. Just here and there."

"Nice," Val said.

And they sat quietly some more, unable to be mad at each other but unable to be *happy* for each other either. Unable to be much of anything, other than brothers.

"That's the look. That's the one." Celeste's voice cut across them. They lifted their eyes to her in unison, only to discover she was pointing them out to Ro, Laurel, and Parish. "See?"

"Holy shit, you're right," Laurel said.

"What's she right about?" Val asked.

"I said that you guys don't look anything alike, but she said you do when you do that eye thing, that, like…angry, frowny emo-kid eye thing. Suddenly you're twins," Ro said. "Remy just needs some eyeliner."

"Please. Everyone knows I'm the hot one," Val joked.

"Only when you're standing beside me, which isn't saying much," Remy added.

"It's true," Celeste said. "That's why we haven't been having sex. Without Remy around it's like…meh." She grinned, and Val rose to swing his arms around her waist and kiss her, and it was sweet and tender and a reminder that, when they were apart, Val was still part of a duo. He wasn't alone writing music—he was with Celeste. His partner, just like she'd said.

And Remy was writing music with his boss. Right?

Chapter Fourteen

Celeste and Val caught a late flight back to LA, and their leaving made Remy feel every bit as uneven as their arrival had. He waved as their ride service pulled off, then he poked around the buses for a while, trying to fill the moments until he became tired enough to justify going to sleep. David and Michael were visiting local friends, Parish and Laurel had vanished together, Ro was on the phone...everyone was busy with someone or something.

So Remy went to Vivi's bus.

He wasn't entirely sure when he made the decision to go—his feet seemed to take him there of their own accord. As he walked, he reminded himself that he couldn't just drop in on Vivi Swan without warning—but he didn't stop. Lights were on inside her bus, and he was surprised and pleased when the security team hovering around didn't stop him from knocking gently—

The door swung open, so fast and hard that it clacked against the back wall. Remy's eyes widened. Vivi was standing in front of him, and while her lipstick was flawless, her mascara was heavy around her eyes. Crying, Remy realized. She'd been crying, and not in that just-writing-a-song way this time. Upon seeing Remy, Vivi took three fast, shallow breaths then forced her lips into a smile.

"Let's just talk later, okay?" she said quickly, and Remy realized she was on the phone. She turned and dropped her voice, though it did little to keep Remy from hearing her say, "Tuesday, please. Later."

Then she lowered the phone and, as she turned around, hit a button that dimmed the lights, casting her face into enough shadow that it hid the tearstains.

"Uh, sorry," Remy said quickly. "I shouldn't have come unannounced. I should have texted or…I don't know. Something. We'll talk later." He was already backing away, holding his hands up as if she were a wild animal.

"No, no, it's okay!" Vivi said, voice a little high. She smoothed her hair. "It's fine, seriously. Anyway. What did you need?"

"Um," Remy said, cycling through his thoughts, his excuses, his justifications. What did he need, exactly? Vivi watched him from the near-darkness, waiting. He took a long breath, puffed his cheeks out as he answered, "I figured you'd be watching *House Hunters*. Thought I'd come watch with you. But if you're busy, I can…go."

Vivi didn't react for a second too long—long enough for Remy to hate himself and every word he'd ever uttered. But then she smiled, her teeth glinting in the pale light. "See? That show gets under your skin," she said. "Give me a minute to change?" she asked. Remy nodded, and she stepped away from the door, leaving it open for him. By the time he boarded the bus, she'd run into the back rooms. Without a laptop to busy his hands, he reorganized her sugar packets.

When Vivi reemerged, her makeup was tidied and polished, her hair neat, and she had changed into something that looked moderately comfortable but stylish enough to be in a magazine—burgundy fitted jeans and a striped shirt. She'd even put on a necklace that matched the entire thing, as if she were dressing for a day out rather than watching *House Hunters.*

"Did your brother like the show?" she asked, voice a bit clipped as she opened the fridge then ducked her head down to riffle through it.

"He did. It's very different than anything we ever did. Not just the size of the audience, just the show altogether."

"He's not a fan of pop music," Vivi said, rising with a bottle of water in her hand. She smiled, teasing the answer from him.

"He's not," Remy admitted.

"People are afraid of what they don't understand," Vivi said. "Especially when so many people *do* understand it."

Remy frowned, and Vivi's face faltered, concerned she'd offended him. "No, no—that was just...that was a great way of putting it," he assured her.

"Thanks. It's like that in country music too—people don't like me because I started in country, but now I'm more pop...but they still play me on country stations. There are whole websites devoted to me *not* being a country artist anymore, like it's something that needs to be proven," she said then sat by him on the couch. She was unbearably close, close enough that when she pulled her legs up and crossed them, her knees brushed his thigh. She took the remote and flicked through the television channels, stopping immediately when the show popped up.

"Have you seen this one?" Remy asked after grounding himself. He leaned back a little, forced his spine to relax, an action that drove her knee farther into him.

"I think so," Vivi said. "They pick the good house. It's not the nicest-looking one, but you can tell it's the one they'll be happiest in. Like, it's the sort of place you know they'll live in for ages and put kids' growth charts on the wall and...all that sort of stuff."

They sat quietly on the tour bus for a while, watching the house hunters prowling around mansions on exotic islands, but there was something heavy settling over them, a drowsiness or a loneliness or a sigh. The couple had nearly chosen a house when Remy felt the slow, gentle touch of her hand sliding over his. Her fingers were warm and light, and she closed the tips over the top of his hand delicately. He felt the corner of his mouth pulling into a smile he couldn't resist, then, carefully, turned his hand over so their palms were touching and wrapped his fingers around her hand. He waited, worried she'd pull away, but she didn't. She didn't move, save to exhale a breath that sounded like she'd been holding it for some time.

They sat there silently for so long that the sparking, electrical feeling between their palms faded into a steady buzz that wasn't shocking so much as comforting. Remy caught himself running his thumb over the ridge of her knuckles, counting the spaces between them, memorizing the geography of her hands. She settled her hand deeper into his.

"I just feel like I'm losing her," Vivi said quietly.

Remy didn't speak for a few long breaths—it felt like she'd perhaps said that by mistake, and his responding might startle her away. Finally, though, he asked, "Tuesday, you mean?"

She nodded. "She never would have bailed on me like this before. But the longer she's with Nick, the worse it's gotten, and it's like—it's like being with Nick is who she is, now. She's Nick Maddon's girlfriend. Professionally, personally, emotionally…but it's not like I can make her choices for her. Maybe we're just growing apart and we're driving each other crazy trying to hang on. I don't know. It's stupid. Forget I said anything, actually." She turned back to the TV and stared, eyes too focused on the screen.

Remy inhaled and spoke, voice low. "My brother is…he's writing a song. Without me."

Vivi unlocked her gaze, looked to him. "Oh?"

"And I'm working with you and not him. He and I talked about it tonight, and it's weird. I feel like I'm losing him but also like he's… better. Like it's good for him. And I hate that and then feel shitty that I hate it."

Vivi smiled the tiniest bit. "I think there's a pretty distinct possibility that you and I are just really worried about being left behind by the people we love."

"Well, to be fair, there's not many people I love, so losing one is a big deal."

"Same," Vivi said faintly, and Remy thought of the arena of people chanting her name, the thousands and millions of people who loved her but didn't know her. He thought about how she was sitting here with him, and somehow, they had more in common than they'd ever had before.

"You're not going to lose your brother. That's not how being a brother works," Vivi said after a long pause.

"I lost my sister," Remy said quietly.

Vivi started, her eyes jumping toward him. "Oh, god, I'm sorry—I didn't know she was—wow—"

"No, no," Remy said. "She's not dead. She's back in Florida. I guess we didn't lose her, exactly. Val and I left her behind. We had to."

They had to. Right?

"Why?" Vivi asked, and the question sounded so sincere, Remy knew he couldn't do anything but answer honestly.

"My family—the religious thing. You can't just leave halfway. It's all or nothing. If she'd been old enough to come with us, or *well* enough to come with us…but she was little and sick. *Medically fragile* was the term."

Vivi nodded a bit. "I do hospital visits sometimes for kids like that. Maybe…I mean, if I'm in Florida, I could…" She trailed off then flushed deep red. "Sorry."

"For what?"

"Just…" Vivi waved a hand. "Fame and pop music can't fix sick kids, I know that. I just thought I would offer, but then it sounded so dumb when I said it out loud."

Remy smiled. "I appreciate it. But trust me—if it's not praise music, my parents aren't letting it anywhere near my sister. Look what happened to Val and me, after all."

"You're absolute disasters," Vivi said, nodding solemnly.

Remy laughed under his breath, because his parents would have said the same thing with complete sincerity. "You're not going to lose Tuesday, though. Not if you care this much about keeping her."

Vivi made a face. "Please. Have you met me, Remy? I can lose anyone," she said, and while the phrase started as a joke, in the end a breath released from her body that seemed far too big for someone so small to contain. Tension released in her hands, her ankles, her shoulders; she closed her eyes for a long time. When she opened them, she was humming lightly—

"What's that?" Remy asked, brows knitting.

"*I can lose anyone*. It's a solid lyric for something. *I can lose anyone*. I need my notebook." She murmured the last bit to herself. She sniffed and wiped at her face a little then shook her head like she was apologizing for something. Vivi drew her hand away—

"Maybe it's me," Remy said at the last instant, when only Vivi's fingertips were against his skin. She stilled, and a smile played at her lips, something hopeful and sweet.

"What did you say?" she asked a little hazily.

Remy licked his lips. "'Maybe It's Me'—those lyrics line up with the start of the chorus you've already written for 'Maybe It's Me.'

Maybe it's me, it's my fault all along, I can lose anyone… It works great as the break in that blank section."

"Oh!" Vivi said and smiled broader but falser. "Yeah, it does. It works great there," she said a little rockily. She pulled her fingers away from Remy's palm, leaving it cold and clammy. Vivi walked briskly toward the kitchen counter, where her Moleskine was by her phone. "Still a breakup song, though, isn't it? Just about me and a friend instead of me and a guy," she said as she flipped the notebook open.

"No," Remy answered, shaking his head. "It's not a breakup song. Because you aren't breaking up with Tuesday any more than I'm breaking up with my brother. It's a…it's whatever the opposite of a breakup song is."

"A love letter," Vivi said thoughtfully.

Remy looked down at his hand, the place where her fingers had been a few moments ago. "Maybe they're all love letters."

Someone knocked hard on the bus door, the sound sharp as a foreign curse against the room's delicate melody.

"Come on in," Vivi shouted, trying to pretend she hadn't literally leapt into the air in surprise.

"Hey, doll." Walter's assistant poked his head in the open door, his voice loud and too bright. "Just checking—is Remy Young on here? David said he snuck off Bus Three, and we can't find him."

"I am," Remy said, jumping to stand, as if being on the couch was something incriminating.

Walter's assistant's head popped up, and there was a knowing look in his eyes. He wasn't surprised at all to find Remy on Vivi's bus, nor was he particularly happy about it. "You guys working?" he asked in a voice that said he knew they hadn't been working—even if he didn't know what, exactly, they'd been doing.

"Yep—playing around with a song," Vivi said swiftly, almost

sounding a bit panicked at his obvious suspicions. She tapped the notebook on the counter, like it would provide the proof she couldn't.

"Inspired by *House Hunters*?" Walter's assistant asked teasingly, nodding at the still-on television.

"The great love story of an upper-middle-class couple and a Grecian bungalow," Vivi said, flashing a kind smile at him—though her voice was firm and discussion-ending.

Walter's assistant chuckled under his breath warily then forced a smile. "Right. Well, Remy, we're pulling out in thirty—you riding here?"

"Oh, I—no," Remy said quickly. "No, I wasn't planning on..." He stopped when his eyes drifted to Vivi's and, to his frustration, he found he couldn't read her expression from this distance—not when he couldn't see the corners of her eyes, judge the way her breath rose and fell. From just a few feet away, she became Vivi Swan again, unreadable and famous and flawless. Everything he knew about Vivi Swan said she wouldn't want him to stay, but Vivi the girl might...

"No, I'm not," Remy said slowly, letting his eyes slide back to Walter's assistant, who nodded approvingly—if slightly—at Remy's words.

"Well, get back then, now. I want everyone where they're going to be in the next ten," Walter's assistant said then vanished, his walkie crackling as he moved on to the next bus.

Despite the fact the television was still muttering in the background, the bus was thrown into a heavy silence that sealed Remy's mouth shut. It seemed to have the same effect on Vivi; she flipped her notebook closed and ran her fingers along the edge of the granite countertop. Watching the action made Remy's hand hum, made him remember the way his breath felt small when those fingers were wrapped around his, how they felt tiny and delicate and not like fingers that had signed millions of autographs and massive record contracts.

"Thanks for coming over," Vivi said breezily.

Remy swallowed hard. His lips parted, and words seemed to bloom without much assistance from his brain. "Of course. Anytime."

Vivi looked like she didn't quite believe him but wanted to, and it was too much—something felt hooked in Remy's stomach, pulling him forward, one step, two steps, he reached out with one hand to take hers again—

Vivi stepped away, breathing in sharply, reaching for an upper cabinet. "I think I'll make some tea and go to bed. See you tomorrow?"

Remy froze in place, unable to think fast enough to act as though he'd just been rushing toward her for some other, less totally inappropriate reason. He rocked back then nodded, knees wobbling like the joints of an old toy. "Yeah," he said, alarmed to see he wasn't entirely unsuccessful at matching her false tone of voice. "Tomorrow, and I'll bring my laptop so we can work." Work, because this was Vivi Swan, and he was her drummer-slash-producer, and she was his boss, and so that meant they had a *working* relationship.

"Alright. See you then," she said, taking down one, two, three boxes of tea and arranging them on the counter. Remy paused, waited one more second, then dared to brush by her, sucking in on himself so their skin and clothes and fingers and breath didn't touch. He hurried down the steps and pulled the bus door shut behind him, taking a deep, heady breath of dry Salt Lake air.

Vivi's New Man
Nighttime tour bus rendezvous!

Vivi's got a secret weapon on her tour—producer-slash-drummer Remy Young, formerly of indie band Quiet Coyote. Rumor is that the two have been spending a lot of time on Vivi's tour bus lately, but there's no need to worry, Noel Reid—they're songwriting together. Vivi has reportedly been in search of a new sound, and while Remy doesn't have any major credits to his name, he's respected in the industry as a musician and producer. Despite her sold-out Sweethearts tour, media outlets have been reporting that fans are getting a little tired of Vivi's unlucky-in-love routine. Will Remy Young be the one to break the mold she's cast herself in?

One thing's for sure—with Noel Reid in the picture less and less, these days, Remy's got his work cut out for him if he wants to produce a new breakup song.

Comments: 79

Author: Bianca Treble

Chapter Fifteen

Despite what they'd said as they parted ways, Remy didn't see Vivi much the following day—she was busy with promo stuff before the show, and afterward she flew out to the next tour stop so she could do a magazine shoot in the morning. Remy found himself following Vivi's movements the same way so many fans did—via cell phone and paparazzi photos on sites like Celeste's and Vivi's own Instagram account.

The show was done, and Remy was back on the bus, falling asleep to the hum of the road beneath them, when his phone chimed.

Vivi Swan: Good news and bad news

Remy Young: Good first

Vivi Swan: I have workable lyrics for basically the whole Maybe It's Me song now.

Remy Young: Bad news

Vivi Swan: It just came out we're working together

Remy Young: Ok

Vivi Swan: Is that ok

Remy Young: Why wouldn't it be

He rose and slid out of the bunk, avoiding David's hand slung through the ladder rungs. He tiptoed to the galley and pulled the door shut, closing off the sleeping area, and called her. Actually *called* her, which felt weird and wrong but still rather like a trophy marking just how familiar they were now.

"Hey," he said, rubbing the back of his neck both from the exhaustion and the warm, rushed feeling he got whenever he started a conversation with her.

"Hi." Vivi's voice was small and precious, and it slayed him.

He inhaled the sound. "So. We're caught?"

"Apparently. I'm not sure who leaked it—maybe Eddie?"

"Who?"

"Walter's assistant?" Vivi said, sounding alarmed that Remy didn't know. "It could be anyone on the tour, though. I'm thinking I'll put a few plant stories out there and see what shows up so I can pinpoint who it was. But Eddie came by last night, I said we were working on music, and then the story leaks today…I don't know. It's fine, I'm just…ugh. I'm sorry."

"I'm not mad. I'm not sure why I'd be mad to begin with," Remy said as he slung onto the couch. There was warmth on the phone line, flickering between them and conquering the chilly, vacant feeling the bus always had this time of night. Every so often the moon broke through the rain clouds to make the gently sloping mountains look blue and storied. Remy watched the highway zip by, trying to shake the remaining sleepiness from his bones.

"I guess I just… It was ours, you know? It's this celeb blogger named Bianca Treble—she's been a pain in my ass for years. It's like the minute I plug one leak with her, another one pops up. You and I should have done everything by phone…"

"I—" Remy found himself unsure what, exactly, to say. He inhaled. "I don't think it would have worked as well that way."

There was a long stillness, then, "Yeah. You're right. Yeah. Anyway, I just wanted to tell you before someone else did."

"Well, it's two o'clock in the morning, and I don't start accepting social calls from the general public till three o'clock, so good move," he said, smiling into the phone.

"Damn it, did I wake you up?"

"Of course you woke me up. It's two o'clock," Remy joked. Vivi made an apologetic sound, but Remy cut her off. "It's fine—it's not like I don't have all morning to nap. What about you?"

"I have a Make-A-Wish thing tomorrow afternoon, but that's it. So I can nap too, can't I?" Vivi said in a way that told Remy she hadn't thought about sleep all that much. They sat in silence for a moment, listening to the sound of each other's breath.

"Play the song for me," Remy said, dropping his voice a bit—he thought he heard someone stirring.

"Right now?"

"Yeah. Please? I want to hear it with the new lyrics in, especially if the Vivi Swan fandom is about to know all about it."

Vivi laughed a little, more a breath than anything else. "Alright. Hold on—I'm putting you on speaker. Don't hang up." He heard her rustling around then the hollow zip and twang of a guitar being lifted. She tuned it swiftly then called, "Ready?"

"Ready," he said. He found himself picturing her on her bus, all the lights on, *House Hunters* muted in the background. She was sitting on the edge of her couch, he wagered, and he wondered what she was wearing—designer jeans, or something else that looked like casual clothing but cost ten times as much? It was impossible to picture her in something like the ancient pajama pants he was wearing— impossible to picture her messy, her hair unbrushed, her face free of makeup.

"Hey," he asked, curious, daring, "where are you?"

"On my bus," Vivi said as her fingers danced across a chord—she'd been just about to start.

"I mean, where on the bus? I'm trying to get the whole picture," Remy said, grabbing someone's—Parish's?—jacket from a chair to sling over his torso and fight the chill.

"I'm in my bedroom," she said cautiously.

"Oh. Well," Remy said, acutely aware of how creepy his question had just become and simultaneously disappointed he couldn't truly picture this—he'd never been into the back of her bus. Any lingering sleep was pushed aside to make way for feeling fumbling and awkward.

Vivi paused then said, "White quilt. Peach walls. Too many pillows on the bed. And the phone is on the dresser opposite the treadmill."

Remy grinned, the room coming into view in his head. "You have a treadmill on the bus?"

"Britney Spears had a tanning bed," she said defensively.

"I wasn't questioning it, just…I wouldn't have thought to put a treadmill on a bus," Remy prodded back.

"They notice if I put on three pounds. That's the magic number—three. If I stay under three, I'm good. If I go over three, they say I look *well-fed* or something like that. If I go over five, it gets mean." She said this practically, without any emotional attachment—*just the facts, ma'am.*

"Hence the Razzmatazz yogurt?" Remy asked.

"Hence the Razzmatazz yogurt," she said. "Ready now? For real?"

Remy took a breath, locking the imagined picture of her room in his head. He managed to picture her in pajamas—the type with a matching top and bottom, yet not the sexy sort—but couldn't imagine her without the lipstick. "Go ahead," he said.

Vivi played through "Maybe It's Me," playing confidently and singing loudly, no longer working her way through a draft of it. It was lovely—melancholy and pleading and touching. When she sang the chorus, Remy noticed that her voice went huskier, like she was singing in Tuesday's voice. Better yet, it was the type of song that could take on multiple meanings. It was about Tuesday, but when Remy let the song sweep through him, it became about Val. It could be a love letter to anyone.

"That's how pop songs work," she told him when he commented on this. "That's why they work. They're about everyone."

"Val would say they're about no one," Remy said with a slight laugh.

"That's because Val doesn't want to be connected to anyone but you. And Celeste," Vivi answered knowingly. She paused. He heard the click of her guitar case closing, and then her voice got closer and clearer. "Thanks for working with me on it, Remy. I kind of don't want to ever be finished with it, you know?"

"It's been my pleasure," he said. He leaned as close to the window as he could without pressing against the cold glass, trying to see her bus— it was, in theory, the next one up in the caravan, but the most he could get was glimpses of the red brake lights now and again. They bounced off the water that slicked the sheared rocks bordering the road.

"We're here," Remy said a little suddenly, when his eyes rose to the horizon.

"Huh?"

"Nashville. I can see the AT&T Building," he said. "When Val and I first left Florida, we drove straight here—something like twelve hours, and we just traded off. We didn't want to go to our first meeting looking unprofessional, so we pulled over and painted the band name on the side of the van and changed shirts."

"And that made you look professional?" Vivi asked.

"No, apparently it made us look *homegrown*. That's the word the label execs kept using. Nouveau garage band! Homegrown rock! The band next door!"

"When I moved here, I thought I'd hit it big," Vivi said.

"She said from her exquisite tour bus."

"I know, I know, but that's not what I mean—I thought I'd get here and more or less be famous. That was sort of what my parents let me think. But I ended up playing festivals and bars and this little twenty-four-hour cafe near Vandy about three dozen times. It was amazing." Remy was about to ask what, exactly, was so amazing about Cafe Coco—he knew that had to be it—when she went on, "It was amazing, looking back, I mean. I had all that time to figure out who I was and what sort of music I wanted to play. I wrote my own songs and played them and changed them depending on how people reacted. It's so different than someone like Tuesday—she came off the Disney show, and people sort of told her sing this, wear this, be this. But I got to find my own way. With a bunch of high Vandy kids cheering over mochaccinos."

Remy laughed. "I played there a few times."

"Oh, yeah? Did you like it?"

"Loved it. Val is good with that sort of crowd—college kids, hungry people, caffeine addicts. He sort of appears and hypnotizes them. You really should come see him at a show," Remy said then stifled a sound of alarm when he pictured Vivi Swan at a Quiet Coyote show. Even in LA, where the shows usually had twice the sparkle and three times the deodorant, she would look ridiculous, a real diamond in a shaken box of cut glass.

"I'd like that," she said, a bit quieter. "Oh, I can see the AT&T Building again! I can't believe I didn't notice the airport."

They sat on the phone in silence for a few moments, staring

at the same thing—the small but shining Nashville skyline. The AT&T Building dominated the view, but a handful of other buildings stretched into the sky. Nashville's beauty wasn't in the sky, though—it was on the ground, in the little ancient brick buildings with house bourbon and original hardwood stages. It wasn't a thing like LA, where everything was clean and citrus and salt. Nashville was old in a way that made you want to settle into its woodwork just like the grit that never could be scrubbed away.

"Do you want to get breakfast?" Vivi asked. They were getting off the interstate now, drivers gently weaving down ramps so as not to jostle those sleeping in bunks.

"When?"

"Now."

"Seriously?" Remy asked, stunned.

Vivi sighed and sounded like she could very easily be convinced this was a terrible idea. "If I want to go later, the whole security team will have to come, and there'll be pictures and paps and...I don't know. I just want to go to breakfast like a normal person, right now."

Remy nodded. "Yeah. Okay. Let's go be normal, then."

The buses turned left, and the arena—spaceship shaped and gray—loomed ahead of them in the dark. Police motorcycles were blocking the cross streets to allow them through; there wasn't much point—there wasn't a car in sight. Vivi's bus pulled straight into the loading area; Remy's pulled up directly beside it.

"Meet me here in five?" Vivi asked, sounding excited. Remy rose and looked out his window, trying to see into hers. It was all darkness and reflections until she suddenly flipped on the lights and came into view, standing, looking back at him. She was, as he'd guessed, wearing designer jeans and an artfully torn T-shirt. Her face was darkened a bit by the tint on the windows, but he squinted—she wasn't wearing eyeliner or mascara, and it made her eyes look smaller but more like pinprick stars.

"Remy? Five minutes?" Vivi asked when he didn't answer. Remy reached over and, without looking, flicked on his own light. Vivi smiled when he came into view.

He smiled back. "I'll be there."

***

"Here we go," Vivi said warmly as a black SUV rolled up to her and Remy. They were standing on the curb outside the arena. The sky was still pitch-black, the world around them still, save the beeping of delivery trucks and the occasional whine of a police siren.

One of Vivi's security guys was driving; he got out to hold the door open for Vivi, while Remy hurried around to the other side and got in on his own. Vivi had refreshed her makeup, and though she was wearing flat shoes, they were sparkly and had cherry-red soles that matched her lipstick. Remy, meanwhile, had hurriedly tried to flatten wrinkles out of a dress shirt and failed entirely, the finer points of wrinkle-free folding still a mystery to him.

"Loveless Cafe," Vivi told him. "It'll show up in the GPS. Thanks for driving us, Steve."

"No problem, Miss Vivi," Steve said. "They expecting you?"

"Yeah—Eddie should have called ahead. They won't even be open, so it shouldn't be a security problem."

Steve nodded, pecked the name into his GPS, and they eased off. He turned the music up a bit, just enough that the car wasn't awkwardly silent.

"They're not open?" Remy asked.

"The cooks get there at two or three, though, since they make stuff that has to rise," Vivi said reassuringly. Remy glanced at the clock—it was a quarter till four.

"They're opening the restaurant for you," Remy said, realizing.

"I'm Vivi Swan, remember? I'm the worst," Vivi said, elbowing him playfully, and Remy snorted, shaking his head.

They wove back outside of Nashville, slicing through trees and squat buildings and massive houses on stately hills. The Loveless Cafe finally appeared, a restaurant built on the bones of an old, single-story hotel. The neon sign wasn't on, but the lights inside were pouring out into the darkness like a beacon. Steve got the door for Vivi, leaving Remy to his own devices again. No sooner had his door slammed shut than a man in a nice shirt with a too-clean apron on appeared at the café door.

"Miss Swan," he said warmly. "What a pleasure to have you again."

Vivi walked forward in big, long steps. "Thanks so much for having us! I was afraid I wouldn't get a chance to come by this trip."

"Our pleasure. We're here early anyhow," he said, shaking her hand. He extended the same hand to Remy, smiling, face certain that this boy in the wrinkled shirt was every bit as important as Vivi.

"Remy Young," he said.

"Michael Owens," he—the manager, Remy reasoned—said.

"He's a producer on my next single," Vivi said swiftly.

"I can't wait for it!" the manager said and ushered them both inside. Vivi met Remy's eyes briefly and gave him a small, conspiratorial sort of smile. Remy was both delighted and annoyed by it, he found—delighted that they were getting in somewhere off-hours and annoyed that Vivi thought this was something conspiratorial. It was fame, simple fame, not something cunning on her part.

But then he decided he was being an asshole, so he shook it off.

The café was warm and inviting, even without any other patrons. Brick walls and checkered red-and-white tablecloths, rows of jellies and jams for sale at the counter. A fireplace was blazing despite the fact they were scarcely through summer, its light flickering off the frames of hundreds of celebrity patrons' photos through the years. Remy reasoned Vivi's photo must be up there somewhere but couldn't begin to know where to look.

They were seated at a table for four—two seats had already been removed, giving them plenty of room. There were already waters at the table and a carafe of coffee. The manager pulled out Vivi's chair for her, once again leaving Remy to help himself.

"I used to come here with my dad after gigs," Vivi said, smiling as she looked around.

"They're in Nashville, right? Are you going to visit them while you're here?" Remy asked.

"They're actually not in town. My brother has a play at his college, and I told them they should go to that instead," Vivi said. She paused then said, "It's weird now, with them."

"Weird?"

"It's hard to not…it's like, when I'm in Vivi Swan mode, it's hard to suddenly just be their kid. Even though obviously I'm still their kid. I don't know."

"You can't go home again," Remy said, nodding. "I get it. My parents are always my parents, but…I'm not sure we know one another very well anymore. I don't know that they'd even recognize me if they saw me, to be honest."

"Yeah, I think that's it," Vivi said, looking disheartened. "They'd recognize my face but not *me*."

Their conversation paused when a heaping plate of biscuits arrived at their table, along with a dish of red gravy. The biscuits had a myriad of fillings—ham, eggs, fried green tomatoes, sausage, honey, sorghum. Vivi carved several into pieces to sample everything.

"You can order a meal too, if you want. But the biscuits are where it's at," she said, grinning. He followed suit, taking a whole sausage biscuit and a sampling of the others.

Once they were on his plate, he looked back up at Vivi. Remy watched the way she ate delicately to avoid smudging her lipstick. "Can I ask you something?" he said.

"Of course," Vivi said without lifting her eyes.

"Has Noel ever seen you without lipstick on?"

Vivi looked alarmed by the question. She set her fork down thoughtfully. "I guess no. Not really. That's a weird question. Why do you ask?"

"Just wondering," Remy said. "It's nothing."

Vivi looked bemused, licking strawberry syrup off her index finger. "So I was thinking—maybe we could try to do a rough recording of the song soonish?"

"Sure," Remy said. "When were you thinking?"

She lifted the carafe to pour herself another mug of coffee. "Maybe in New York when we stop in East Rutherford? But it'd probably be easier to just do it at a studio in London."

Remy blinked at her; when she stared back, he said, "Uh, it'll have to be East Rutherford."

"Why—oh!" Vivi said, eyes suddenly widening. She lowered the coffee, focused on wiping away the drip running down the glass for a beat too long. "You're not going to Europe." It was a statement but sounded like a question at best and a confession at worst.

"I'm not going to Europe," Remy confirmed.

Vivi stared into her fresh coffee for a moment, brows drawn together in a way that created a wrinkle between them, the one girls in LA usually Botoxed away before it got too deep. "Huh."

"Yeah," Remy said and couldn't help but realize that, for all their newfound similarities, *this* was the symbol of just how different he and Vivi were. She'd forgotten she hadn't hired him for an entire world tour; he'd always known the day the paychecks would stop being direct-deposited into his account. He'd put it out of his mind, sure, but never forgotten.

"Maybe you should just come," Vivi said. "You can, you know. If you want to."

Remy inhaled at how the hope in her voice made him feel lifted. Yes. Yes, he wanted to do the Europe leg. Because Europe, because paychecks, but because it meant more strange and quiet and pretty moments like this. He'd never be able to get this weird arrangement with Vivi back, not once he went home. He'd be in LA, and she'd be wherever it is celebrities go, and they'd text, but then, eventually, she'd stop answering. Tour was its own little world where they could ignore their differences, but real life would only highlight them.

But the real world was inevitable, wasn't it? It was better to get out now, to stop before the pull to be with her became a need rather than a want.

"It's just—I can't do that to the other guy," Remy said. "I can't take a guy's job the week he's supposed to fly to Europe. It's hard enough to find work as a musician as it is." It was the tiniest part of the truth but the truth all the same.

Vivi nodded, but a flicker of guilt crossed her face—she hadn't considered this. "Well. If I'd remembered, we could have handled it all before now. I just can't believe I forgot," Vivi said, shaking her head like she'd let herself down. She began to cream and sugar her coffee, doing so with such intention that she looked like a scientist.

"When?" Remy asked.

"What?"

"When would you have asked me to stay for the whole tour?"

Remy asked, voice dropping a bit. This felt important. When did she...want him there?

Vivi started to speak then paused, thinking through her answer. She lifted her coffee mug and sat back, rolling it back and forth on her palms. "I don't know," she said, which was a lie, Remy could tell—and it must have been obvious, because she took a breath and said, "After that phone call. The one when we were working on the song and you fell asleep."

"Really?" Remy asked, a smile playing at his lips.

"Yeah," Vivi answered, voice smaller than normal. "Do you know the last time I've had one of those phone calls? Where they last for hours? Probably...god, probably sixth grade."

"So I get the nostalgia vote," he said.

"I didn't know there was anyone I wanted to talk to for that long," she said, and it was so sincere that the clever smile on Remy's face over his nostalgia-vote comment instantly faded. Vivi lifted her eyes to his. "Did *you* remember you were leaving?"

"Of course."

Vivi's brows knitted again, that wrinkle reappearing. "Do you *not* want to go to Europe? Is that it?"

"Of course I want to go to Europe with you," Remy said, instantly regretting the fact that those last two words—*with you*—had made it from his brain to his mouth.

Vivi noticed them and shook her head, eyes hurt but voice tense—angry, almost. "I can't believe you didn't say anything. We could've set it all up!"

Remy felt a jerk in his stomach at the prospect. Vivi didn't see why he would remember something like this and she wouldn't, and she didn't see why he could never have just asked. It seemed unbelievable to him that he had to explain—that despite how real Vivi was, she still had these starlet tendencies underneath. The realization was somewhat disappointing.

Remy half laughed. "Vivi, I can't just tell my boss I want her to fire her drummer so she and I can hang out more."

Vivi looked like he'd slapped her—her face long, mouth open, eyes wide. "Your boss," she said.

"Yes, Vivi, my boss," Remy repeated, lifting his hands in surrender. It didn't remedy her expression, so he spoke quickly. "I don't mean—it's not a bad thing. But I can't just ask for a favor because we watch *House Hunters* and go out for breakfast and work on a song in between all that."

"Of course you can! This whole damn industry runs on favors," Vivi said, almost yelling but not quite.

"But I wouldn't be with you as someone from the industry. I'd be with you as…"

And then he stopped, because he wasn't even sure what the word was. *Be with you as…* The end of the sentence hung in the air around them, pushing their hearts deeper and deeper into their bodies.

"I wanted to keep it professional," Remy said, slowly, carefully. "Or at least I wanted to try. I didn't want to assume anything or for you to think I was just using you for a trip or a gig or…you have Noel and…I just wanted to be professional." He wasn't entirely sure if he was saying this to convince Vivi or to convince himself.

"Fine," Vivi said. "It's fine."

Chapter Sixteen

Nashville to New Jersey was a longer hop than Remy expected—a little over thirteen hours. He was grateful that everyone had reached a certain point of tour exhaustion and more or less went straight to bed after the show. He was even more grateful that he didn't see Vivi again that evening. The buses pulled into the MetLife Stadium parking lot just as the sky was starting to lighten, but Remy was barely aware of it. It felt like all those late nights and early mornings with Vivi were finally catching up with him; he slept until almost noon.

"Remy? Are you dead?" Parish's voice floated through Remy's sleeping mind. Remy blinked—his phone alarm had gone off, but he'd been hitting sleep for…from the looks of it, three hours.

"I'm alive," Remy said, voice gravelly. He slid back the privacy curtain in front of his bunk to see Parish standing in the bedroom doorway.

"Good, because your presence is requested on Bus Three," Parish said.

Truthfully, Remy wanted to stay on the bus and wait for a text or call from Vivi, because surely they'd hang out before the show, right? But he was keenly aware of the fact this was his final show, and that whatever happened with Vivi, the musicians had been incredibly welcoming to him from the start. So he heaved himself from his bunk, found a fresh T-shirt, and stepped out into the bright daylight.

It was beautiful outside—one of those perfect days where the sky was epically blue and you wondered how anyone might think New Jersey was a dirty sort of state. Several buses had their panels pushed out and sunshades pulled up—the dancers drinking Bloody Marys on folding chairs waved to him as he walked by. Bus Three had their panels extended as well; when he arrived, Laurel was coming down the steps with a carafe of water. She placed it on the ground between the band, Ro, and the other two backup singers, all of whom were eating takeout from the burger place across the street.

"The guest of honor arrives!" Michael said. Remy grinned.

"We got you a goodbye hamburger," Laurel said, thrusting a paper bag his way. "Know I had big plans to make a cake, and then those changed to plans to buy a cake, and now it's just burgers. Though we did upsize your fries."

"I like burgers more than cake anyway," Remy said. "This is great. Thanks, guys."

"Thanks for not being all that interested in skateboards," David said, raising his fast-food cup to toast Remy. The others followed, one at a time; Laurel leaned over and kissed his cheek quickly.

"So what's the plan when you get back?" David asked. "Keep on Quiet Coyote-ing?"

"Probably," Remy said, which was the truth. The lie, however, was in the way he smiled and nodded, the way he implied this was exactly what he wanted to do for the next five months. "But I'd like to keep doing some songwriting and producing, like I was doing with Vivi," he added quickly, like he was trying to sneak in the confession of how he really wanted to spend his days.

"Smart," David said, pointing a fat finger at him. "Be the one making the music, not just the one playing it."

"That's the goal," Remy said and smiled at him.

"You got a contract for that song you worked on with her, right?" Parish asked.

"I—no, actually. We never got around to it," Remy said, embarrassed.

Eyebrows raised—all eyebrows other than his, in fact. "Well," Parish said, giving a forced shrug, "we can vouch for you if she tries to cheat you. We could hear you guys working on it in Dallas in her dressing room. Plus, you hum it all the damn time."

Remy frowned, unaware that he hummed, period, much less that he'd been humming the song. "I don't think she'll try to cheat me. But thanks. Seriously," Remy said. The fact they were offering to go to bat for him—against their boss, no less—was genuinely touching.

When Remy left Bus Three, he intended to finish packing up his things but found himself wandering toward Vivi's bus. He wanted to apologize—maybe. Or perhaps he wanted her to apologize to him. Or was it that he wanted to tell her never mind, he'd go to Europe? Or to call him? Or that he'd call her?

He just needed to see her. It wasn't a crushing, desperate need—it was more a dull ache, a want that could be ignored but only if you were willing to make yourself miserable. He needed to see Vivi, and even though he could have come up with a thousand excuses as to why, the truth was that he simply *needed* it before he left the tour and perhaps never saw her in person again.

She didn't answer when he rapped on her door, nor did his text to her show that it'd been read. Remy scouted around until he saw

Walter's assistant flitting between buses, his clipboard thick with papers, talking into his headset.

"Hey! Any idea where Vivi is?" Remy asked, jogging up to him.

"It's three o'clock," Walter's assistant said, looking at the digital clock on his clipboard. "So I believe she's in her fitting for her CMA dress. Probably in her costuming trailer."

"Where's her costuming trailer?"

Walter's assistant lifted an eyebrow, and Remy fought off flushing. "I just—we needed to talk about some stuff with the song," Remy tried, but it sounded as stupid out loud as it had in his head. He hoped this guy wasn't the one who'd leaked their working together. If he was, Remy's face was probably giving him plenty more stories to sell.

Walter's assistant rolled his eyes unapologetically then pointed in the direction of the trailer.

The trailer's door was shut, but he could hear voices inside, Vivi's included. He lingered, waiting for a break in the conversation to knock, enjoying the soft melody of her words—even when she wasn't singing, her voice had a cadence, almost like a love song. Her words were punctuated by a loud, meaty laugh—one of the dressers—and then the same voice asked, "So what is Noel wearing?"

"I'm not really sure. That's sort of why I'm wearing white—he'll have to work hard not to match it," Vivi's bright, shiny voice responded, and a few others laughed.

Right. Noel. Her boyfriend.

It didn't matter that she and Remy had shared more than a few quiet, soft moments, that they'd clasped hands and run their fingers over each other's palms. She was still with Noel. She'd still be with Noel if Remy went to Europe. She'd be with Noel if he apologized to her, if she apologized to him. She was with Noel, even if she never saw him, even if she rarely mentioned him. Remy was just someone she spent time with, someone she had plausible deniability about, someone who was contractually obligated to never tell a soul how her eyes softened when she looked at him.

Remy took a step back from the trailer.

It was done. Whatever *it* was, it had to be. The job, Vivi, the tour, his role in it, and her and the music. It was over almost as suddenly as it had started—the rest of the tour would belong to the original drummer, which was appropriate. It belonged to him, after all—this entire experience was just something Remy had borrowed for a time. Like being a one-hit wonder. Like living in Florida. It was a slice of a life, not a life.

After the show, when the crowd had filed out and the custodians were winding their way through the seats, Remy returned to the stage. He'd changed from his show clothes to his own, washed off the bits of glitter and confetti fired from the cannons during the finale. He walked to the front of the stage, looked back at the crew breaking down sets, coiling cables, talking into walkies. Things had to get packed quickly so they could leave.

Remy looked out at the empty seats, took a deep breath. He kissed the pads of his middle three fingers and waved in a small way, keeping his hand close to his chest. It was Quiet Coyote's goodbye. That was the only thing that was truly *his*—his past, the band, his brother.

He lowered his hand, shoved it into his pocket, and walked away from the tour as he'd walked into it—alone.

Then

The music lessons stopped.

At least, the ones with the music teacher they liked stopped. Now, every Wednesday night, they met with a very old woman who taught

Val to pick apart praise songs delicately. She knew nothing of drums, really, so she more or less just drilled Remy on reading sheet music, trying in vain to get him excited about playing the piano instead. He obliged but hit the keys too hard on purpose.

Remy thought they were lucky, frankly. Their father made it no secret that he blamed their music—the secular songs, the outside-of-the-church teacher, their supposed neglect of Bible study at the hands of music study—for everything with Mercy. Remy was surprised they weren't forced to drop music lessons entirely.

Val did not feel they were lucky. His eyes would go dead as he sat through music lessons; whenever their parents were out of the house, he snuck onto the computer and watched videos that taught him how to play the songs he liked or sometimes worked on his own songs, shouting draft lyrics over and over until the right series of words snapped into place. Without a drum set at home, Remy aided in the songwriting by playing on jugs or tables. He learned the key in which the cabinet glass rattled when shut just hard enough, how to flip and turn plastic cups to create beats, a thousand sounds he could make clapping his hands in different ways.

And still, he felt guilty. It was a deep, gut-twisting sort of guilt—that he'd not only caused Mercy to become ill, but he'd kept her that way. What if she fell sick again because he couldn't help but layer rhythms underneath Val's voice? What if this time it was their mother? Or Val? If left to his own thoughts for too long, he felt dirty for his disobedience. When he heard his parents leave, he'd count down how long he made it before joining Val in the kitchen or bathroom, where the tile made his guitar sound haunted.

"I was going to read a book today instead," Remy said one day when he met Val by the computer.

"You don't want to read a book," Val said without looking at him.

"Val—" Remy began.

"You have to help me," Val said firmly. "Everything I write is better when you help."

"I don't want us to get in trouble."

Now Val sighed and turned to look at him, eyes soft and older-brotherly and surprisingly lifelike. "We won't get in trouble. We're doing this together. Who's going to tell?"

"Even if no one tells…" Remy said then darted his eyes upward, toward heaven.

Val scowled. "Why would we love music at all, if we weren't supposed to?"

"But Pastor Ryan thinks—"

"I don't believe Pastor Ryan," Val said flatly. "Or Mom, or Dad. I think we love music because we're *supposed* to love music. I think we love music because God wanted us to have a way out."

"Are you sure?" Remy asked, looking a little longingly at the video that was cueing up—an artsy, black-and-white video of someone playing a slow and soulful song.

Val shook his head. "I'm never sure of anything. Except us, brother." He paused then cocked his head to the side. "Write that down. Those words."

Remy grabbed a piece of paper and did so. The video was paused then forgotten, as together they picked their way through a song about that: the feeling of floating, of being certain of nothing whatsoever. Nothing except the person who was standing next to you.

Chapter Seventeen

It took two flights and one unfortunate layover in O'Hare for Remy to get back to LA. He arrived at five o'clock but, to save Val and Celeste's sanity, waited for rush hour to end before calling them to get picked up. They arrived at LAX in Celeste's car; Val leapt out of the passenger seat and hugged Remy tightly.

"How does it feel to be done?" Val asked, helping Remy chuck his bag into the trunk (which was full of off-season clothing Celeste couldn't fit in the house).

"Great," Remy replied. "Plus, LA weather trumps everything." He slid into the car, marveling at how it smelled like their house: sunscreen and lavender and oranges and figs and the tang of cigarette smoke underneath it all.

"No kidding," Celeste said, glancing at him in the rearview mirror. "You look rough, man."

"He looks like shit," Val corrected. He'd joined Remy in the back seat, making Celeste look like something of a chauffeur.

"Yeah, yeah. I'm just tired. I'm exhausted," Remy said, and the reality of this statement didn't hit him till he said it aloud. He was beaten and worn, and his mind felt rubbed in places where there were no calluses. "How did we survive touring?" he asked Val.

His brother laughed. "We were young and dumb and were still excited about eating fast food instead of disgusted by it. Celeste made fig-and-pepper bread for your coming-home party, which isn't actually a party, because we knew you'd hate that."

"The bread was supposed to be a surprise." Celeste scowled back at them then shouted a few obscenities at a limo for cutting her off. The car felt alive and wicked, not at all like the slow, lumbering buses.

"Thanks. For the bread, and for not throwing a party," Remy said then yawned and leaned his head back.

Walking around the house felt like wandering around a dream, where it seemed familiar and foreign all at once, with things he'd never even noticed—dents in the doorframes, the way bloomless climbing roses conquered the drainpipes, the triangular shadows on the dining room walls cast by 1980s light fixtures. Celeste's office looked even more like a war room now; since he'd been gone, she'd hung up a corkboard with dozens of articles, snippets, numbers, business cards, and lanyards tacked to it. The living room looked massive because the couch bed was folded up and the pillows neatly propped in the corners of the couch.

"We'll move back out here," Val said immediately when he saw Remy noticing the couch. "We meant to do it before we picked you up so you could crash immediately, but Celeste had to chase down some girl or something."

"I had to *interview* a source about one of the Sebastian girls," Celeste said.

"Teasing," Val said affectionately, and Remy could tell that, unlike many times before when he'd been teasing, it was in good fun rather than as a means of personal commentary.

When dusk fell, and Remy grew tired earlier than normal on account of his addled mind having no idea what coast it was currently residing on, he quietly unfolded the sofa bed and, before Celeste or Val could really see what he was doing, climbed into it, feigning sleep when they poked their heads around the corner to see what was happening.

It wasn't that he wanted to give up his bedroom. It definitely wasn't that he wanted to sleep on a sofa bed, which was inexplicably even less comfortable than the tour bus bunks. It was that he'd looked at his old bedroom and seen what Celeste and Val had done with it in the six weeks he'd been gone. The mattress was actually on a bed frame, and there were nightstands on either side (one made of a fruit crate, but still). The bed was made. Celeste had decorated with bits and pieces she'd crafted into the sorts of things they sold at interior design stores to the stupidly wealthy.

They'd turned his bedroom into *their* bedroom, and Remy knew they'd done it by accident, which made it all the more…untouchable. It'd have been one thing if they were playing house, dressing up the room the way you put your stuff in the drawers at a hotel. But Val and Celeste had simply moved in and let their lives fill in all the cracks.

When the two of them finally went to bed, Remy sat up and stared at the darkened house. He scooted back till his shoulders were against the couch then turned the television on, immediately turning the volume down to nothing so as not to wake the others. It was on E!, which was no surprise, given that Celeste lived here. Remy hurriedly changed the channel, suddenly worried Vivi would appear and afraid of what his mind or heart or throat would do if he saw her.

"I knew you were faking," Val's voice called from the doorway. Remy's eyes shot up to find his brother looming like some sort of wraith, the television—now tuned to a late-night prayer channel—light bouncing off his marble-white chest. Val walked over and slumped down onto the couch bed beside Remy, stretching his legs comfortably.

"Join me, won't you?" Remy said, smiling.

"Watching the Jesus network? See, this is why I don't like you writing to our parents," Val said, but he was smiling too—the prospect of Remy watching a prayer channel was too outlandish even for Val's fears.

"What was it like when I was gone?" Remy asked a few moments later, as he scanned through the channels in order to have something, anything, to do with his hands.

"It sucked. The drummer we hired was basically a high school marching band kid with decent hair."

"I mean here. Like, with you," Remy asked, staring at the television.

Val made a bored noise. "I don't know. It was fine. It was weird."

"Yeah."

"Was it weird being away for so long?" Val asked, and the bored noise was gone.

"It was weird. But it wasn't bad."

"Yeah. Same."

They stared at a Super Shammy commercial mindlessly—it could hold up to five gallons of water, you know. Val groaned then chucked the remote across the room, seemingly pissed that there wasn't anything decent to watch at one o'clock in the morning. He turned to Remy. "Also, we had sex in your bed."

"You motherfucker."

"More than once."

"The hell is wrong with you?" Remy asked, punching Val on the arm.

Val cackled and swung his legs off the bed, rising to get out of Remy's reach. He stretched his arms to the ceiling and yawned. "I have that new song almost done. Want to hear it?"

This was said so casually, so effortlessly, that Remy did a sort of mental double take, where his mind processed the words then had to immediately do so again. He met Val's eyes and saw recognition there—that despite the yawn, despite the effortless words, Val knew how big a deal this was—yet also wanted, desperately, for Remy not to recognize it as such.

"Sure," Remy said and shrugged, while his internal organs rearranged themselves. Val was writing again. Val was writing again. Val was writing again—no, wait: Val was *finishing* again and doing it without drugs. It was the inverse of hearing that Val was using again—a level of joy that would have perfectly mirrored Remy's devastation.

Val retrieved his guitar, and they went out to the patio, where the air smelled like salt and sugar from the ocean and fallen figs. The patio light was covered in abandoned spiderwebs and attracted purple and yellow moths; Remy swatted them away from his face, while Val walked through them, untouched by feathery wings.

Val took a seat on the table and, without any regard to the hour or the neighbors, launched into a song. Val's guitar work was the opposite of Vivi's—loud where hers was soft, demanding where hers was questioning. Still, though, Val's new song felt delicate to Remy's ears, something poking its head out of a burrow to see if it was spring yet. All the words were in place, all the melodies, but it still felt fresh. Val's lyrics were always a sea of metaphors, harder to follow than Vivi's straightforward, diary-esque songs, but Remy knew it was about saying goodbye. It was a song about saying goodbye to Florida and drugs and even Remy, to a degree.

It was a love letter, from someone to their past.

"It's great," Remy said huskily when Val finished. Val looked almost startled; Remy knew his brother had more or less forgotten he was here.

"It's still getting there," Val said but grinned. "I've got a few others I'm working on. Nothing done. Anyway." He picked at the guitar for a moment. "What about the songs you were working on with Vivi Swan? Those get done?"

"It was just one song," Remy said. "And it wasn't done, really, so I guess it won't be. I'm not sure."

"Was it any good?"

Remy felt his lips betray him by curling into a smile. He exhaled. "Honestly, yeah. It was one of those songs that works a thousand different ways—we'd speed it up, or slow it down, change the words. It worked no matter what we made it about."

"Golden," Val said.

Remy lifted his eyebrows. "That's exactly what she called it."

"We're twins," Val mocked, but he seemed good-natured enough about it. He leaned back on his palms, looked at the sky for a moment. It was velvety black, not a star visible, given the light pollution. "Maybe we are twins. Me and the pop princess both keep playing the same old shit. Breakup songs and Quiet Coyote."

"You've both got more to you than that," Remy said.

"I know. I just wrote new stuff. I contain multitudes, little brother. Does your girl?"

Remy laughed again, the same barking one—it was a laugh for liars. "Hardly my girl."

"Maybe she's got multitudes you're too thick to see," Val answered, giving him a mysterious look.

"Are you writing lyrics or just being a pain in the dick?"

"Same thing," Val said. Then, he strummed the guitar and sang, loudly, into the night, "Pain in the dick! I'll make you fucking sick! I'll be a pain in your *dick*! Hey, one plus one, the arithmetic says I'm gonna be a big pain in your—"

Celeste's voice screeched through the house, out the door. "My hand to fucking God, I will cut *both* your dicks off if you don't stop."

"Sorry, lover!" Val called back then devolved into snickering, whispering laughter that Remy couldn't help but match.

Vivi Stuns (and not just in her dress)
Singer is apparently still on again with Noel Reid

Vivi Swan appeared at the CMAs with the most surprising accessory of all—boyfriend Noel Reid. For weeks now, they've rarely been spotted together, and Noel hasn't been shy about hitting on other girls. Vivi has a reputation for dating the wrong guy, but come on, girl—even *we* can see you need to end things with him, no matter how sweetly he can play the acoustic guitar.

The two looked gorgeous though, as per usual, and were arm in arm for most of the night. They even kissed quickly when Noel picked up an award for Single of the Year (shared with country star Waylon Focus, who provided the C to the win's MA). Interesting, though, that other than that, our cameras never caught them looking at each other. Anyone else sense a new breakup song on the horizon?

Comments: 143

Author: Bianca Treble

Chapter Eighteen

"I like Vivi's dress," Celeste said, studying the photo the next morning moments after sunrise. "It's one of the better ones from the CMAs. She's sort of becoming a thing in the fashion world, you know?"

"Sure," Remy said, turning away from the photo. He had to turn away—if he looked too long, he knew it would paralyze him, like one of those heroes turned to stone by mythical lady creatures. Even after he was focused on going through the variety of junk mail that'd arrived for him, the image was burned in his mind. Vivi, in a long white dress. Backless. It'd been backless, and the photo was posed such that he could see the curve of her spine and the peaks of her shoulder blades. He hadn't realized he wondered what they looked like until that moment, and now, he couldn't help but want to see them again.

He focused on tearing up a variety of credit card offers instead. Celeste didn't seem to notice anything amiss, continuing to rapidly click through photos on Getty Images. Val was still asleep—having the bedroom meant he didn't have to force himself awake when Remy (or Celeste) rose.

Remy took a long drink of his coffee and looked out at the

orange-and-purple sky. "My sleep schedule is so jacked from that tour. If I'd gone to Europe, I'd be a wreck right now."

"Probably. Sucks that you didn't get to go," Celeste said without looking up.

Remy paused then said offhandedly, "She asked me to go, sort of."

Celeste's eyes shot to him. "Wait, are you serious? Why the fuck are you here, then?"

Remy stepped back from her intensity. "I just…I didn't want to take the other guy's job by begging to join up last minute," he said, settling on the simplest explanation. Saying, *She sort of forgot I was her employee* or *I don't know who I am when I'm around her, and it's insane,* to a woman literally working on her gossip website was probably unwise, near-family or not.

"Remy, that was an amazing gig you passed up," Celeste said, shaking her head. "Is it because of Val? Because he's fine. You know he's fine. You both are, frankly, better than I'd thought you'd be after so long apart."

"It's not Val," Remy said, surprised this was the truth. He followed it up with a lie. "It's just the other drummer—"

"There's always going to be another drummer. If she chose you, she wanted you," Celeste said.

Remy considered this longer than he meant to; his eyes flicked to Celeste's computer screen again. It was another image of Vivi, this time from the front. White dress, sharp shoulders, sparkling designs running up and down the bodice. And a man on her arm. *Noel* on her arm, her fingers delicately splayed across the fabric of his suit jacket sleeve.

"Well, next time," Remy said.

"There probably won't *be* a next time," Celeste argued.

Remy shrugged and didn't say what he was thinking—even as

the thought made him nauseous. *I'm counting on there not being a next time.*

Val had arranged a homecoming show that evening at SALT, where Remy would make his triumphant return to the drum set. They arrived at six o'clock, which in some ways felt as much like coming home as going to their actual house had, for Remy. The place still smelled like beer and sweat and wood and ocean, and bartenders and regulars who were more or less just other-side-of-the-bar bartenders clapped him on the back and celebrated his return. Remy fell into work alongside Val, checking mics and lights and finding his brother's obsession with both charming, for once, rather than exhausting. It wasn't until they were in the green room that Remy realized he hadn't felt compelled to double-check it for alcohol before Val got his hands on it.

"You still know the music, right? Don't start playing that one and three pop shit," Val said, bumping him on the shoulder.

"You know, Val, it's worth mentioning it was the pop stations that played 'Everything but the World,'" Celeste said, grinning, glowing. She looked new, refreshed to see Remy and Val back together—or maybe just to see Val like this.

Val laughed and kissed her quickly. "Are you trying to make me quit music entirely?"

"Obviously. Your true calling is so clearly being an elementary school teacher. Third grade," Celeste answered. The lights flashed at eight o'clock, signaling their start time, and they made their way out onto the stage. Somehow, the crowd was louder than Vivi's had ever been—perhaps because they were closer, perhaps because he could see faces, perhaps because they were chanting for them rather than a girl in gold. Val writhed in the sound, sang through their songs like an animal moves through trees, and it felt so different from what Remy had done for the past six weeks that it was almost impossible he'd been playing the drums on both occasions. Vivi's music was a production, a play, polished and flawless. Val's was moody and had to be tamed every few moments, lest Val run away with the song in his jaws.

But both pop songs. Both music. Both amazing, in very different ways, ways Remy didn't fully appreciate until they rounded the final song before their intermission. Val didn't like to talk during breaks—he felt it broke his focus—so Remy made himself scarce, lingering at the end of the SALT loading docks by himself. This place was so desolate during the in-between moments—not at all like the Sweethearts show, where the backstage flurry never stopped. He exhaled and leaned against the wall then slid to the floor and pulled out his phone.

Where was Vivi now? He pulled up her number to see their most recent text chain. Could he send her a message? What would he even say? *I liked your dress but not your boyfriend?* Or *I'm mad you didn't demand I stay for the Europe leg?* Or *Hey, sup?*

Remy decided that, as wonderful as tonight was going, he hated everything.

"There you are!" someone said—one of the bartenders, a burly guy that straddled the thin line between hipster and lumberjack.

"Everything okay?" Remy asked, alarmed by the guy's wide eyes.

"Yeah, dude, but my boss said they need you in the office. Like, now."

"Is it Val—"

"No, no, I don't know what it is. But they took me off the bar to find you, so it's gotta be serious. I hope everything's okay," he said, looking almost frightened for Remy.

Remy leapt to his feet, mind running through scenarios. Did the house burn down? Was it Mercy? How would their parents even find them at SALT, though? If it couldn't wait till after the show, it had to be intense—Mercy had to be dying. Or was it a collector? Some repo guy? They owned everything outright, but still, shit happened.

Remy nearly ran down the halls after the bartender; he called out for Val as he passed the green room, but his brother had headphones on and didn't hear. Celeste lifted an eyebrow, but Remy was gone before he could explain. Down the hall, up the fire stairs, to a tiny, tiny office door covered in ancient band stickers and the occasional piece of gum. The lumberjack bartender had abandoned him at the turn, eager to get back to his bar and his tips; Remy lifted a hand and knocked hurriedly on the door.

It swung open almost immediately to the grinning, nearly chaotic-looking face of the SALT general manager.

"What's going on?" Remy asked.

"Come in," the manager said, stepping aside—

And revealing the reason Remy had been sent for.

"Vivi," Remy said, the word louder than he intended, panic still on the syllables.

"Thanks so much for getting him," Vivi said to the manager, who was still grinning almost clownishly over the fact that *the* Vivi Swan was in his club. "Can we borrow your office for a second?"

"Of course, Miss Swan. Make yourself at home. Sorry it's such a wreck," the GM said, flushing a little as he noticed a stack of pizza boxes, the top one open to reveal a handful of uneaten crusts. The room made Vivi glow like a beacon in the night. Or maybe a beacon in a dumpster.

"Thanks—Steven, right? I appreciate it so much," Vivi said brightly. "And trust me, it's fine. I've been on a tour bus for weeks. Anything not on wheels feels like a five-star hotel."

This was unconvincing to Remy and, based on the GM's expression, equally unconvincing to him. Still, he backed out of the room, almost jittery, and let the door latch shut behind him.

Remy turned back to Vivi, heart beating to the sound of her breath, which appeared to be moving to the house bass blaring downstairs.

"Hey," Remy said, though he wasn't quite sure how he'd decided on saying that. There was some sort of disconnect between his body parts—head to mouth, mouth to heart, heart to hands.

"Hi," Vivi answered, lips curved a little, and the action reunited his organs. She was wearing a short skirt and tall boots, with a light-pink sweater which made her lipstick look particularly cherry-red. Remy fought the urge to run his eyes up and down her form.

"You're here," Remy said. "I thought you went to Europe today."

"Later," Vivi said, nodding, rapping the desk with her nails. "I was back in Nashville for the CMAs—"

"I saw," Remy said.

"Yeah. And I just thought I'd stop by and see your show before I left the country," she said cheerily, voice becoming a little false.

"Nashville isn't exactly a stone's throw from LA," Remy said, furrowing his brow.

"Yeah," Vivi answered, and she looked so unrehearsed, so unpracticed, that it felt as if Remy was seeing an entirely new model of Vivi Swan. "I guess," she said then stopped for a long time. She studied some papers on the desk, an order for bulk maraschino cherries. "I guess I didn't really get an actual chance to say goodbye to you. And that felt weird."

Remy nodded, mentally calculating the distance between them. Six feet? Six miles? Six inches?

"And I was also thinking about what you said. About how you couldn't ask me to come on the European leg because I'm your boss—"

"Vivi—"

"Wait, wait, let me finish," she said, swallowing and lifting her eyes to his. "I should have asked you. Not because I'm your boss or whatever, but because I knew I wanted you with me basically from the night I got stuck on your bus. So I should have just said it aloud instead of waiting for you to say it."

"Thanks," Remy said, which sounded stupid as hell. He licked his lips and looked down, unable to keep his eyes on her, feeling crushed by the weight of her irises.

"And…I guess…that's what I'm asking now. Will you come to Europe with me? Please? I'll pay the other guy's salary. All of it. He'll be fine. But will you come?" Vivi said, voice softening.

Remy dared to look up and nodded.

"Okay. Well. Good," Vivi said, taking a breath and smiling. "Great. I'll call Walter and have him book your tickets. We can fly over together."

The house music faded—Quiet Coyote was about to come back onstage. Remy glanced at the door, wondering where Val would assume he'd gone off to. Not here. Certainly not here, certainly not with Vivi Swan, certainly not with his hands sweating.

"Why didn't you just call me?" he asked.

Vivi shrugged, a tiny movement that barely moved her shoulders. "I don't know."

"Really?"

"I was afraid you wouldn't answer," she admitted.

"I would have answered," he said, and Vivi smiled.

"I guess you should get back. I'm going to watch the rest of your show from backstage, okay?" Vivi said, looking winded—like the entire conversation had taken something out of her.

"Yeah. That'd be great, yeah," Remy said, nodding. Vivi pressed her lips together then turned around and grabbed for the doorknob. It felt like the room was shrinking around them, forcing them closer together—especially when the doorknob stuck.

"Oh, there's a trick to it. The place is all settled, and it doesn't turn—pull—here, let me do it," Remy said hurriedly and walked to the door. Vivi dropped her hand from the knob just as Remy slid his over it, but instead of pulling and turning and performing the alchemy required to get the door open, he froze. The room had shrunk again, and now his and Vivi's arms were pressed together.

He kept his eyes on the doorknob, unblinkingly afraid to look anywhere else but likewise afraid to move, afraid to breathe, afraid the room would get smaller and kill them both. Vivi lifted a hand—she was staring down at the doorknob too—and let her fingers dance along the sleeve of Remy's shirt before she took hold of a scrap of fabric.

It happened fluidly, like the entire movement was choreographed. Remy turned toward her, and Vivi sank against him, tucking her head underneath his chin, wrapping her hands under his arms to rest on his shoulder blades. Remy's arms encircled her, and suddenly the feeling of the room shrinking wasn't dangerous but welcome as it pressed them closer.

Vivi breathed a laugh that sounded disbelieving, which tempered Remy's matching feeling. "I'm really glad you're coming to Europe, Remy," she said. He could feel her breath through the fabric of his shirt.

"So am I," he said and didn't even try to stop himself from inhaling the scent of her hair as he spoke. He didn't stop himself from liking the way she felt small against him or the way he could feel the back of her bra underneath his thumb.

It felt like he was stumbling forward, forced to place each foot in front of the other—all the things he'd refused to dwell on too long, that he'd tried to talk himself out of: thinking of Vivi as a woman, not a boss, not a neon star, not even a colleague. Wanting to be close to her. Wanting her to want him back.

She tilted her head upward, and Remy leaned back so he could meet her eyes. Her hair rained away from her shoulders, brushing the side of his hand. This close, he could see the way her eyes were a kaleidoscope of blues, the inside edge of her lips where the lipstick didn't quite reach, the piercing marks on her earlobes where she wasn't wearing earrings. That, of all things, was what he was looking at when she rose onto her toes, slid one hand off Remy's back and around to the side of his chin. She brought his head down, tilted her own back, and kissed him.

It wasn't deep, or passionate, or hard; it was light, and nervous, and gentle. Tentative, and Remy returned it in kind. He was struck by a sense of disbelief, at how naturally her lips curved against his, but also a steady calm.

She pulled back the smallest amount; he could still feel the heat of her mouth, the sweep of her breath. Her hand slid farther up his cheek; there was a tremble there, one she was trying to hide. Or perhaps he was the one trembling? He couldn't tell—he couldn't truly focus on anything but the nearness of her.

"Sorry," Vivi said quietly, perhaps even sincerely.

"It's fine," Remy answered just as softly then pulled her slightly closer and dared—because it felt like a dare, the gleaming, shouting, childhood playground kind of dare—to kiss her again.

The door flew open, banged against the back wall.

"Holy motherfucker," a voice said. No, not *a* voice—Val's voice. Remy and Vivi sprang away from each other, frantically putting space between them as Val's mouth hung open.

"Um," Val said.

"Hey," Remy said, because this was apparently how he opened awkward conversations now. He hated everything once again.

"So we're doing a show. If you're done up here," Val said, though not unkindly—not exactly kindly either. It was an actual question.

"We're, um—"

"We're all done," Vivi said in a panicky voice. "I mean we're not—I just—"

"Val, look, you can't say anything—" Remy cut in.

Val held his hands up. "Trust me. This is too messed up even for me. I just need my drummer back."

"Yeah," Vivi said, swallowing. "Okay."

Remy adjusted his shirt at his waist to hide the consequences of that kiss, and Vivi wiped at her mouth, trying—and failing—to tidy her lipstick. She stayed behind as Remy went to the door, shouldered past Val, fought to regain his breath. He was halfway down the stairs when he heard Val's voice.

"Well?" Remy turned to see Val was talking not to him but to Vivi, now hidden from view in the office.

"Hm?" she asked, voice fractured.

"Are you going to sit up here, or are you going to come down and see a fucking amazing show?" Val asked.

Vivi laughed nervously. "I'm coming to see the show."

Val nodded then turned, feet slapping down the steps as he spoke. "Good. If you'd said no, I would've had to ban you from kissing my brother."

Then

Val and Remy were lost causes.

This was something their parents never said, not outright, but it was obvious with the way they let little things slide—Remy's untucked shirts, the fact they were always an hour or so late coming home, the shadow of eyeliner that was still obvious despite Val's attempts to rub it all off. Once upon a time, they would have been placed front and center at the church so the entire congregation could scream prayers at them. Now? Their father just tensed his jaw and averted his gaze, and their mother occupied Mercy's time—keeping the girl busy would get her away from her brothers' influence.

They'd long outpaced the little old lady from the church and her 4/4-time, gentle music lessons. When Val got a job mowing lawns in the neighborhood, he put the money toward music lessons in town for both himself and Remy—and did so without asking, with his newly acquired Val Young swagger that even his parents didn't seem able to contest. Perhaps they kept silent on it because he donated a quarter of his earnings back to the church—more than the fifteen percent the pastor asked for—or perhaps it was just because Val and their parents never spoke, not even to argue anymore.

Val wrote songs and Remy polished them. They burned CDs and sent them to labels and agents and famous musicians. Val began to chant a low, blood-level refrain: Music will let us leave. Music freed us the first time, and it will free us again. Remy offered no opinion on the matter but maneuvered the melodies of Val's songs so the longing became clear in the chorus. Crowds at bars, where they lied about their ages to be allowed to play, sang along, fists pumping, eyes shining.

And then, on a Sunday, one that wasn't unlike most other Sundays, things changed.

"Today we have a special prayer," Pastor Ryan said, his eyes wandering out over the congregation of the Lake City Assembly of God. "A special prayer of healing for one of our most vulnerable parishioners. Valor Young, son—will you come pray with me?"

Val frowned, while Remy startled—unlike Val, he hadn't been paying particularly close attention until that moment. It wasn't unusual for someone to go pray with Pastor Ryan, but it was unusual for that someone to be Val or Remy—besides the fact they were considered lost causes, it was usually Mercy who needed prayers, especially as she continued to go in and out of the hospital. Val rose, adjusted his collar, and walked to the front of the room.

"Our young brother Valor is a man now—nineteen years old, a real adult. But man is fallible," the pastor said, pausing so people could shout *amen!* between each sentence. "And our young men, they are so at risk in this world. In these times, it's so easy for them to get confused, mixed up in the head. Valor's parents have made the very difficult decision to get him help."

A murmur went through the crowd, and Val's jaw clenched. Remy, however, looked at his parents, shocked. A therapist? Maybe a psychiatrist? That was so flatly against everything the church believed in.

"Valor," the pastor said, wrapping an arm around Val's shoulders and pulling him close. Val didn't resist. "I know you struggle. I see the pain in your eyes. I know the doubt in your heart. We've all gathered together our pennies—even your pennies, from your tithings—to pay for you to go away for a spell, to a special camp that will help you become a stronger, happier man of God."

Val never resisted, never shouted, never faltered; he stood still for the rest of the service while the pastor regaled him and the rest of the congregation with stories of the camp, how it made young men turn away from drugs or alcohol or sodomy. It was Remy who glowered at his parents, at his mother's quivering chin. It was Remy who, for the first time in his life, screamed at his parents when he arrived home, the threat of Val going away to a conversion therapy camp finally shattering his stoic, quiet nature.

But it was Val who acted.

He packed his bags of clothes, took the pamphlets from his parents that featured happy young men with their arms slung around one another's shoulders and proudly discussed the benefits of electroconvulsive therapy and exorcism. Remy finally shouted at Val—what was he doing, going along with this? Why wasn't he fighting?

How could Val willingly leave Remy here alone?

Remy wondered this all the way up till three o'clock in the morning, when Val shook him awake and motioned to the window. Without a single word, they unloaded Val's lawn equipment from the van, replacing it with Val's personal belongings. With nothing but a long, shared look, they then loaded Remy's. It was almost four when Val slipped into the driver's seat. The van would squeal when the engine turned over—it would surely wake everyone up.

"Ready?" Val asked.

Remy wasn't entirely sure if Val was talking to him or to himself, but he nodded all the same. "Where are we going?" he asked.

Val shook his head. "To the real world," he said.

He turned the engine over.

Sure enough, the van squealed to life. Val kept his eyes on the road, but Remy watched in the side mirror as the lights in the house flicked on. Their father ran out first, clad in boxers and a stretched-out undershirt. He was shouting; when their mother ran up behind him, she was wailing. Mercy appeared at her bedroom window. She was watching, motionless, the smallest of curious expressions gracing her face.

Val pressed the gas, and in a rumble of smoke and backfires and clatters, they sped out of Lake City for the first and last time.

Chapter Nineteen

Remy was going to Europe.

Val was sworn to secrecy—even from Celeste.

Vivi was seen at a Quiet Coyote show "to support her new producer," and their sales spiked for forty-eight hours, which meant the van was getting new tires.

Even Vivi's superstar powers couldn't get Remy a seat on the flight to Europe with her. They didn't kiss again before she took off for London, both because they didn't have another moment alone *and* because neither could remember just how to act in the other's presence—they were both fidgety hands, sideways glances, and too-loud conversation all the way till the moment Vivi's driver picked her up from SALT. The following day, Remy spent the entire flight to London watching HBO shows but accidentally picturing him and Vivi instead of the characters in each and every steamy scene.

It was a very long flight.

The band hotel was adjacent to the venue—Hyde Park. Remy had heard of the place plenty of times but was still surprised to see it was an actual park—with rolling green meadows and big, ancient trees.

It wasn't an arena, like the other shows—it was an outdoor concert. The stage was framed by massive fake trees on either side that held up one side of the video screens and hid some of the lighting rigs. The whole area was fenced off, making it feel as if they weren't in a city but rather some sort of private, fairy-tale forest. That happened to have two dozen speakers hanging from tree limbs.

"What the hell are you doing here, kid?" a voice asked cheerfully as Remy walked up. It was David, and he was grinning. He strode across the stage, guitar patting against his chest as he moved. Remy smiled through his surprise at learning the band hadn't been told he was returning then rose and hugged David lightly.

"Looks like I'm not leaving after all," Remy said.

"Where's Jason, then?"

Remy shrugged. "Don't know." It wasn't exactly a lie, right?

The rest of the band filtered on, all equally surprised to see Remy but seemingly pleased. Laurel shrieked and hugged him, which made Parish roll his eyes a little. Even a handful of the dancers gave him welcome-back nods. It was like he'd never left.

At least, to *them* it was like he never left. Remy himself had a blurry, almost out-of-body feeling about it all. He'd already mourned leaving the tour, returning home. He'd mourned whatever he had with Vivi. Getting it all back and then some was an unbalancing sensation, despite the fact it was also a pleasant one.

Vivi returned from her interviews just in time for sound check, but both she and Remy were too occupied with their professional responsibilities to do anything more than glance at each other and smile in small, secret ways. They played through four sound check songs, managing some acoustic gymnastics that were necessary for the outdoor venue. By the time Vivi went back for hair and makeup, the sun was setting, and the gray sky had been split into bright oranges and purples that silhouetted the handful of buildings stretching over the tree line. Venue employees had arrived with flashlights and were manning the faraway gates already packed with eager concertgoers.

It had been ages since Remy played a concert outdoors, and he'd never played one of this magnitude in the open air. Instead of feeling like the sound was sucked up by the audience, it seemed to spread out everywhere, absorbed by the people and the trees and the grass and the stars. The lights filled the night sky, and Vivi's amplified voice could surely be heard across the city, her between-song inspirational speeches landing in the hearts and ears of London.

When the lights flared then extinguished at the end of the show, the world felt suddenly dark and cold—not at all like the muggy, summer black that he'd felt in the closing moments of the arena shows. He panted from exertion, and his hands vibrated—he wanted to play more. He wanted to keep going, for her to sing again and the crowd to roar and for him to inhale the power that was being a part of something he thought he'd lost.

But he couldn't, of course. The curtains suspended from the tree limbs closed, sealing the stage off from the still-screaming crowd. Vivi was already gone, and the dancers were dropping their comically large, cheerful smiles as they hustled backstage. Parish unplugged and handed his guitar to a roadie; Remy finally rose, set his sticks on the snare, and backed away.

"Like you never left," David called over from the keyboards then grinned.

"Yep," Remy said, though this couldn't feel further from the truth for him.

After the crowd was hustled out and they'd changed out of concert clothes, the Bus Three crew made their way to a late-night curry restaurant by the hotel. The place was little more than a hole in the wall, with a flickering sign and room for about ten people inside. They nearly filled the place—there were six of them all together—but they crowded around a tiny table and made it work. After they ordered all the menu items with five peppers pictured beside the name, they fell into standard shoptalk—complaining about the show, discussing past tours, about the costuming, about whether they should insure their voices and—

"Here's what I want to know, Remy—what's it like? Working with her? I mean, *actually* working with her, not just singing behind her. Does she *ever* loosen up?" Ro asked. It wasn't an unkind question, but it was one asked with a certain expectation—like she couldn't so much as anticipate anything but a *no*.

"She's professional. We both are, so it works well," Remy said. He had no idea if he was lying or not. Surely he was, right? But no, he and Vivi *were* professional...they were just also being hyper-unprofessional. Conversation paused while the waiter delivered steaming-hot bowls of curry—a few bright lemongrass-green, the other two red-brown and creamy—before them, along with an enormous bowl of sticky white rice.

"That's true, you are professional," David said, spooning rice onto his plate before slathering it with the green curry. "Which I mean as the highest compliment. It's why I like you better than Parish."

"Dude," Parish said, offended.

David grinned. "*Remy* follows the rule about disposing of condoms *outside the bus trash can*."

"To be fair, I haven't had any condoms to dispose of," Remy said.

"That's probably not something to brag about," Ro answered, looking sincere.

"Well, I'd like to point out that you're both professional, but you're the only one who'd dare to eat curry with us. She's such a fucking ice princess," Parish said, shaking his head then frantically fanning his mouth as the green curry spice kicked in—apparently in levels he hadn't expected.

Michael rolled his eyes. "You're like one of those little girls who gets bitter when people don't come to her birthday party, Parish. Also, your eyes are watering."

Parish snorted and took a long drink of his mango lassi then coughed. "Uh, yeah. Because my birthday parties are awesome. And also, who the hell doesn't want to come to a birthday party? It's a *party*."

"Did…Vivi not come to your birthday party?" Remy asked.

Everyone else cracked up, loud enough that one of the tables near them muttered something about "loud Americans."

"No, no—Parish has a point though," Ro said. "I've done plenty of tours, and Vivi is the only one who is like some sort of…I dunno. Precious art installation. We never see her, she never talks to us, she never hangs out with us. When I was touring with Mimi Martinez, it was totally different. Mimi would be here eating curry with us, if we were on her tour, because she understood we were part of her machine. If we stopped working, she'd stop working. But with Vivi, it's like we're not even her machine. We're just set dressing."

The conversation steered away from Vivi—which Remy was grateful for, as he didn't like hearing her insulted and also didn't trust himself not to slip up, saying something about the way she kissed or how her hair smelled bright. It was after midnight when they finished up and headed back to the hotel. Remy said goodbye to Michael and David, who were headed to their rooms, then Parish, Ro, and Laurel, who were setting up at the hotel bar. He stood at the door to his room, key card in hand, when his phone chimed with a text.

Vivi Swan: Do you want to go somewhere tonight with me?

Remy Young: Where?

Vivi Swan: I know a place where we won't get mobbed

Remy Young: What time?

Vivi Swan: It has to be late, maybe 1?

Remy Young: Your place or mine

Vivi Swan: There should be an eye rolling emoji. I'm at the Dorchester. Meet me here.

Chapter Twenty

From the far side of Hyde Park, the Dorchester wasn't anything to write home about. It looked, truth be told, like a cream-colored apartment building with extremely well-manicured gardens out front. As Remy walked closer, though, the evidence that it was Vivi Swan worthy began to appear. Alert doormen in crisp suits and top hats. Valets taking the keys to cars Remy couldn't so much as name, much less imagine driving. The warm glow of a gold-plated lobby. Remy shoved his hands into his jacket pockets, fighting both the chill of the hour and the city, and approached.

The doormen didn't stop him, though he saw their appraising looks. The attendant just through the doors, however, gave him a smile that clearly said, *Just a moment*.

"I'm meeting a friend here," Remy said, smiling politely.

"Of course! I'll give them a call. Which room?" he asked in a chipper British accent. His teeth were flawless; Remy wondered if bad British teeth were a stereotype or if this was just the sort of hotel where bad British anything was unacceptable.

"I'm not sure, I'm afraid. I'm producing with Vivi Swan, and she asked me to meet her," he said smoothly. He'd prepared to be stopped—he looked perfectly fine but not like someone who had a room at the Dorchester—and had prepared for the look of surprise that the attendant was now giving him.

"I can wait for her. She's meeting me here," Remy said then brushed past the attendant to sit on one of the camel-colored benches in the lobby.

The attendant looked torn between his responsibility to maintain a high-profile guest's privacy and Remy's calm. It was ultimately decided when the elevator arrived and Vivi stepped out, precisely at one o'clock.

"Remy," she said, smiling at him. She was done up as ever—lipstick, eyeliner, heels—but she was wearing a long tan coat with fluffy lining and a knit cap that made her hair frame her face prettily. She was holding an acoustic guitar case. Remy wanted to kiss her, but this wasn't SALT, and he wasn't sure where his feet were.

He swallowed.

"Miss Swan," the attendant said kindly, bowing a bit as she breezed past.

"Have a lovely evening," she said then tilted her head at Remy, indicating he should follow her. They went not out the front door but rather through the kitchen and through an employee exit that put them out in a parking deck.

"I know all the ways out of hotels," she said when Remy gave her an impressed look. "The hotel in Berlin has a secret cellar exit that lets you out on the other side of the street."

"How spy-like," Remy said, following her through the deck, which dumped them into what was, essentially, an alley.

She laughed lightly. "Europe has better secret exits than the States. I think because the buildings are all old and elaborate? But it's great for escaping without being followed. It almost makes me feel like I'm just…you know. Some girl, exploring a city. Like in a movie," she said, sounding almost wistful. The tone of voice, what it did to her eyes and her lips, made her particularly beautiful.

"Alright. So where are we escaping to, exactly?" Remy asked softly.

"To London," she answered, smiling up at him. Remy badly wanted to reach for her hand, but he could tell from the way her eyes kept scanning the darkened windows that this was probably a risk she wouldn't appreciate, no matter how clever her escape route. Instead, he offered to take the guitar from her, and when she allowed it, gripped the handle hard to squeeze the prancing energy from his body.

London's streets were dark and almost, but not quite, eerie. It wasn't that they felt dangerous or malicious—it was that they felt so *old*. At night, without the distraction of cars and phones and people, it was as if the ghosts came out. Remy didn't spook easily, but he was surprised Vivi was so calm about walking through a city in the middle of the night, not because she was Vivi Swan but because she was a hundred-fifteen-pound girl in heels. He hoped very badly that he wasn't going to be expected to fight a British punk to defend anyone's honor.

They walked past Buckingham Palace, which Remy recognized from movies, then past gardens and another massive park of rolling hills and trees stretched up into the cold stars. They approached the river, still and black and hemmed in by stone walls. Westminster Abbey—Vivi told him what it was—appeared before them, its two towers glowing gold in the navy sky. She was clearly familiar with London and clearly eager to share that familiarity with him.

"The royals get married there. I was so obsessed with Harry and Meghan's wedding."

"So was Celeste. Why?" Remy asked.

Vivi shrugged. "The spectacle of it, I guess? I mean, that was a hell of a thing for Meghan to do, marry into royalty. And then, to watch her take her life back after they hurt her, to just leave with Harry and their family and...I don't know. I admire it," Vivi said and took a step that brought her closer to Remy, close enough that their elbows knocked against each other, soft through layers of coat material, sending the guitar case wobbling on its handle for a moment.

"Can't have been easy," Remy mused. "When Val and I left Florida—not that it's the same, but you know what I mean—it was like cutting off a limb. It had to be done, but..." He took a deep breath.

"Would you have done it without Val?" Vivi asked.

Remy immediately shook his head. "Not a chance. He and I are a packaged set."

"Where does Celeste fit in, then?" Vivi's voice was caught between amused and sincere.

Remy sucked air through his teeth. "That's...something I'm figuring out."

"Three's a crowd?"

"Something like that," Remy said.

"You sound jealous, but I'm not sure if it's of Val or Celeste," she teased and then linked her arm through his playfully, like an apology—but one that came with a leap in his heart. It was the first real touch, the first significant one, since the SALT office, and it felt dangerous and glorious and perfect. Vivi left her arm linked with his as they approached the river, but Remy saw her scan the area, looking for prying eyes or phones, fighting an internal battle over the desire to be close to him and the desire to stay off the tabloid pages.

"You don't have to," Remy said to her quietly, looking down and nodding toward their arms.

"Thanks. Maybe just…just not yet," she said and withdrew her arm with a sad look his way. Remy had hoped she'd argue, remind him that she was *the* Vivi Swan, remind him that it was nearing one thirty and there was no one around to see, so who cared? But he knew better: Like she'd once said, camera phones were everywhere. One picture and there'd be nothing quiet or secret or precious about whatever was happening between them.

They walked along the edge of the river, so still and black and massive that it looked like a floe of obsidian ice reflecting brake lights and streetlights and even the dim glow of cigarette tips from smokers who leaned over the railing, gazing into it. It was so unlike anything Remy had seen before that it felt like a movie set or an alternate universe. Not a different world—the same one, poured into a totally different mold.

"Here. This is it. It's my favorite place here," she said, motioning to the left. It was hard to tell exactly what she meant, at first, as she more or less seemed to be pointing to a void in between an office building and a tall apartment building. As they neared, however, the space took shape. A tower, not entirely unlike the ones at Westminster, only smaller and cream gray rather than gold. Walls, the same type of stone, covered in ivy and trumpet flowers, not in a decorative way but in an aged, ruinous way.

"It was a church. It got bombed in World War Two," Vivi said as they crossed back over the street, away from the Thames. "It's great—no one's ever here."

"Likely because it closes at seven," Remy said as they passed a placard posted on the exterior wall.

Vivi grinned at him mischievously and plucked the guitar case from his hands then brushed past the CLOSED AFTER 7 P.M. OR DUSK sign and into a courtyard. There was no ceiling left on the church, no glass in the windows—just mossy walls and crumbly arches and little altars with fountains or statues in the center. The space took up perhaps half a city block, but standing in the middle, it was difficult to measure it in terms of the city, or in years, or in people. It was the sort of space that seemed to exist outside of time, like it had been paused while the rest of the world played on.

"This is amazing," Remy said, jumping a little at how loud his voice sounded in the secret garden. He turned around, taking it in. There was nothing in the States like this, nothing this old or wise. He walked to the nearest wall and brushed his fingers along the stone, letting it scratch his nails and not caring one bit. He turned back and saw Vivi had taken a seat at one of the benches in the middle, illuminated by the moonlight that bounced off the tiny, water lily–filled pool at her feet.

She lifted her eyes to his, pulling him toward her with her gaze until he sat on the bench, six safe and terrifying inches between their legs.

"I've worked on 'Maybe It's Me' again. I changed some of the lyrics. Almost all of them, honestly," she said. Her nose was pink from cold.

"Oh, yeah?"

"Yeah. And I took a few of the minor keys out. Hence why I brought the guitar. I want to play it for you." She leaned down and gently set the guitar case on its back then opened it and pulled out the instrument. It was already a beautiful guitar, made more so by the pale of her fingers and the blue of the moonlight bouncing off it. Vivi took a deep breath then played through "Maybe It's Me" at barely more than a whisper.

The words had changed—the words had changed entirely. It was a different kind of love letter now, one about kissing. About kissing him—about finding him in a place of salt and smoke, about all the moments before when they'd wanted to kiss but hadn't, about holding hands on buses carving through long nights.

"Maybe It's Me" was about hoping you were the one. The song bounced off the stone walls and path and spun into the sky. Vivi smiled at her echo then looked at Remy.

"I like it," Remy said, voice low and quiet and unsure.

"Yeah?"

"Yeah."

"I wrote it so it sounds like you," Vivi said, glancing down, blushing a little.

Remy stopped then smiled. "What do you mean?"

"When you talk to me, there's a way your voice goes. It sort of sounds like everything is a question, but in a good way, and it feels…" She paused and looked particularly embarrassed; when she met Remy's eye, she finally went on, "It makes me want to answer them."

Remy swallowed, unsure how he hadn't touched her yet, unsure how he hadn't kissed her again. He worked hard not to stare at her mouth as he said, "I think we should change the lyrics to the chorus, then."

"You think? I like them," Vivi said, pouting a little, which made it even harder not to stare at her mouth.

"Yeah, but it's not quite the same feeling. We should make the lyrics the question and the chorus the answer. *Maybe it's me*, then *yes, it is*."

Yes, it is.

"That's a great idea. I love that," Vivi replied softly. Remy felt his cheeks heat and was relieved when Vivi took her eyes off him in order to duck and put the guitar back in her case. While she was leaning over it, Remy cracked. He placed his hand on her back, between her shoulder blades, fingers teasing at the end of her hair. It was almost an involuntary act—his hand was there before he'd even truly known he was going to move it. Vivi felt the touch through her coat and jumped.

"Sorry," he said immediately, yanking his hand away.

"Don't be sorry," she said, pressing her lips together. She moved shakily closer to him, tilting her body toward his chest; Remy immediately pulled an arm around her then reached across his lap to take her hand, like her motion had unlocked a matching one in him. Vivi drew her knees in slightly against the chilled air then twisted and ran her still guitar-string-lined fingers along the side of his jaw.

He closed his eyes without meaning to, which made Vivi breathe the sound of a smile. She lifted her chin and lightly, very lightly, brushed her lips across his cheek, asking him without words to turn his head, to kiss her for real. He tilted toward her, found her lips, found they were exactly as delicate and lovely as he remembered. This time, though, there was far less fear, far less disbelief, just the chill in the air, her small and warm body, the vanilla scent of her skin.

"Vivi Swan," he murmured when she pulled away, bringing up a hand to smooth her hair. "Did you bring me to a bombed-out church in the middle of London to get lucky?"

Vivi laughed, loud and barking and so unexpected that it slayed Remy as well. She play-shoved him, her face red and eyes sparkling and everything about her a thousand times more beautiful than she looked in any magazine photograph.

"I just wanted to prove that gentle acoustic guitar music works as well for women as it does for frat boys," she teased back, and when she went to shove him again, Remy caught her arm lightly and, without reservation, pulled her closer and kissed her again. She swayed against him, locked her arms around his neck.

Everyone in the world seemed to know the words to her songs, and her array of exes, and her favorite brand of lipstick, and they thought that meant they knew her; like her being was the sum of her products and dating history. They didn't know about her fears, or how she liked ugly baby songs, or how she worried about Tuesday, or how she kissed like she was searching for someone who kissed her back the way she wanted to be—needed to be—kissed.

So Remy kept kissing her, hoping to be that person. Hoping to be *the one* the song was about.

Chapter Twenty-One

The band flew from London to Barcelona the following morning, while Vivi took a private plane so she could swing by Portugal for some sort of birthday party for another famous person or an agent or executive or something. Barcelona was a strange combination of touristy old-world Spain and bustling city—yellows and golds and creams against sleek steel and tinted car windows. Remy knew a fair amount of Spanish—he was from Florida, after all, even if it was just the panhandle—but found it was utterly useless given the speed and accent of the Spaniards who warmly smiled but bustled about their lives around him and David as they ducked out of their hotel to find something to eat.

"Never been here, right?" David said.

"Never left the United States before London."

"You picked a hell of a way to do it," David answered, grinning. "Street food in Barcelona is amazing, man."

David was right. The churros they bought from a vendor were so good that Remy didn't hold back when they passed a butcher shop selling bocadillos—strange little crusty bread sandwiches full of meats or cheese or fish—at a table by the street. They were in line to buy horchata to drink when Remy's phone rang. Vivi's name popped up and, likely without meaning to, David saw it.

"Boss is calling," he said, lifting his eyebrows.

"Yeah, um—"

"Go on, I'll get you one," David said, waving him out of the line. Remy gave him a quick smile and answered, holding the phone tight to his ear.

"Hey," he said.

"Hey," she answered, and she sounded relieved. "I'm on a plane from Portugal right now. It's the first free moment I've had basically all day. I'm sorry I missed you last night."

"It's okay," Remy said. "I was just—I thought—"

"I missed you," she said plainly, and Remy found his eyes wandering skyward, like she might be able to meet his from a plane window. "Sorry," she said quickly. "Is that weird? I made it weird."

"It's not weird," Remy said.

"Anyway—I found some studio space in Madrid, if you want to go put down rough cuts of that track there. Do you have time?" she asked.

"I can pencil you in," Remy joked, wondering what else she thought he might be doing—and wondering if she even remembered that she'd told the radio station, not him, that they'd be recording the song soon.

"'K—tomorrow morning? We're supposed to be there by ten o'clock, if the buses leave on time tonight."

"Sounds good," Remy said. "See you then."

Vivi paused. "Are you with someone else? Someone that you're trying to be all…what the hell was it—buttoned up. Yes—all buttoned-up Remy with?"

"I am," Remy said curtly, simultaneously relieved that she didn't think he was being cold to her and humored that she'd caught him.

Vivi made a sound that Remy knew came with a particularly sneaky sort of smile she wore sometimes, something between a sigh and a laugh. "Does this mean it's a terrible time to say that I'm thinking about kissing you?"

"It's not the best," Remy said tightly.

"Because," Vivi said, voice dropping to a low whisper, "I have to be totally honest, I've been thinking about kissing you all day. If we're being *totally* honest, I've been thinking about kissing you more and more until it can hardly be described as *kissing* anymore—"

"Okay, Vivi, sounds good," Remy said in a choked voice.

She laughed. "I'll see you at sound check, if nothing else?"

"Of course," he said, swallowing hard and trying to think of particularly unsexy things—naked grandmothers and cold swimming pools and the smell of eggs cooking.

They were no match for the memory of kissing her.

***

He met Vivi in her Madrid hotel lobby—which was grandiose to the point of tackiness—the following morning. He'd raced back to the bus to get some sleep right after the show the night prior but hadn't slept particularly well; he felt foggy and slow. Vivi, however, was bright and shiny, with a large cup of coffee in hand and a loose sweater draped around her shoulders, falling to the top of high-waisted jeans that just barely hit her belly button.

"That's what you're wearing to record in?" Remy asked, looking at her banana-yellow heels. They made her a few inches taller than him.

"What?" Vivi said, concern flickering across her face.

"Nothing, I just—most people go for comfort when they're recording."

"Have you seen the stuff I wear? This *is* comfort," she said, teeth flashing as she smiled at him. She had a point.

The security guys led Remy and Vivi to an SUV via yet another secret staff-slash-famous-person hotel door then got in one of their own so they could travel to the studio separately. There was only one decent recording studio in town, Vivi explained, and it was on the other side of the city. They rode along in pleasant silence for a while, but it became awkward and strange with the driver right there within earshot—at least on the buses, they'd been able to shut the driver out of the main cabin.

"We're nearly there, Miss Vivi," the driver finally called back after twenty minutes of weirdness.

"You've been to this studio before?" Remy asked, gathering his bag.

"Nope. I just asked around last night in Portugal, and someone recommended this one," Vivi answered, slipping her sunglasses back down and lifting her purse.

"Hm—Miss Vivi, we have a problem," the driver said as the car turned onto a drive.

"What?" Vivi asked, frowning. She leaned forward to look through the seats then groaned. Remy pitched forward to look too.

"How'd they know?" Remy asked when he understood the nature of the "problem." Paparazzi—it looked like the entire country's paparazzi—were stationed outside the studio's slim brick steps. They saw the cars coming and were already taking photos hurriedly. The sound of shutters snapping was audible even from within their car at a distance of a few yards.

The security guys cleared out of their car in one fluid movement then surrounded Remy and Vivi's SUV. The driver slowed the car to a crawl, and the security guys walked it through the crowd, each keeping a hand on the car's exterior as if calming a mechanical animal.

"This is a mess," Vivi muttered.

"Should we just…not go?" Remy asked, because he felt he had to, not because that was a desirable solution.

"No, it'll be fine. I just…I sort of didn't want them to have a picture of us together this early. I mean, I have a boyfriend." She said this quickly, thoughtlessly, without so much as a glance toward Remy.

Remy stiffened. Yes, she had a boyfriend. Which he knew, of course, but which he didn't want to hear her say aloud. He finally took a breath—she was *with* him, not Noel, and that was more important, surely. "I'm just your producer," he reminded her and simultaneously grabbed her hand where it dangled between the seats and squeezed it discreetly. It was the first time they'd touched all day—the first time they'd touched since they'd kissed in the London garden—and Remy felt like if he looked down, he'd see his skin sparkling. A smile played with the corners of Vivi's mouth; she pressed her lips together and turned to Remy, exhaling in a soft, warm way that made him certain he knew how the breath would have felt against his neck.

"Right," Vivi said softly, raking her thumbnail delicately across his knuckles. "Of course."

They released hands as the SUV pulled right up to the studio's steps, the driver rearranging it so the door they'd exit through was directly in line with the studio's bright-blue front door. Security lined the sides; then, like ripping off a Band-Aid, they pulled the SUV door open. Shouts slammed into Remy, somehow louder even than the roar of the arenas. He was immensely grateful that, in the bright morning

light, there were few flashes popping—just the noise of shutters clicking rapidly, harmonizing till they sounded like a horde of insects.

Vivi moved swiftly, accustomed to this particular dance, and
Remy followed as close as he could behind her to avoid being
swallowed alive. The two of them were halfway up the steps when
Remy realized someone was holding the door to the studio open for
them—a swarthy-looking Spanish man with gelled hair and a skinny
tie. He kept his head up, and when Vivi made it to the door, he made
eye contact with a few of the photographers, making certain they had
a great shot of him with Vivi Swan.

"Mr. Young! Welcome!" he yelled over the photographers when
Remy reached the door. He clasped Remy's hand firmly and held it a
moment longer than necessary while the photo-taking continued. Remy
smiled tersely then shoved past him. One security guy ducked into the
building, quickly shutting the door. Outside, the paparazzi showed no
signs of dissipating, crowding the windows and shouting Vivi's name.

"Forgive them," Skinny Tie said with a thick accent. "You've never
come to Madrid before. They've never had a chance to get your picture!"

"I'm surprised they had a chance this time, since this wasn't an
announced session," Vivi said coolly, giving the studio owner a stern
look.

"News travels here, I'm afraid—no telling how they found out!" he
said, smiling too wide. "Come along, let me show you to the studio!"

It was a no-frills sort of studio, one with an assortment of instruments in one room and a separate booth for vocalists. The control
room was small, made for perhaps two people rather than entire
entourages of hangers-on like the ones in LA. Remy pulled his laptop
from his bag and set it on the control room desk, digging through a
pile of jumbled wires to plug it up to the mixer, while Vivi walked into
the studio, Skinny Tie on her heels.

"Is there anything you need? We have coffee and tea and an espresso machine—"

"We'll call down if we need anything. Thank you so much," Vivi said warmly. It was delivered in a voice tinged with kindness and finality—a declaration that he should leave now. Skinny Tie hedged, stalling by offering to show her how to use the mics, how she could light the candles if desired, by offering to untangle all the wires so Remy didn't have to look at them in knots. When there was nothing else he could possibly fiddle with, he finally left, reminding them he'd be just down the hall, but they'd have to crack the door to call for him or else he wouldn't hear.

The door shut behind Skinny Tie, and the room fell into the syrupy, sweet silence of a still recording studio. Remy was in the control room, separated from Vivi by a pane of glass, but still—they were alone together, finally finally finally. Vivi turned to him and smiled a bit then knelt to get her guitar out of its case. Her Moleskine was set on top of it, slid beneath the strings.

"Anything I should know about how you like doing this?" Remy asked over the intercom, sliding the headphones onto his ears.

"Literally the only guy to ever say that to me," Vivi replied with a snicker at her own innuendo. Her voice sounded lovely and solid over the studio mics, like something that could be tasted as well as heard. Remy's computer screen lit his face as he opened programs and checked peripherals.

Vivi rose from her case, the guitar strapped over her shoulder; she released the instrument to pull her hair back into a ponytail then tuned it slowly, carefully. Strands of hair worked their way free from the ponytail and slipped in front of her eyes, drawing attention to the fact she bit her lip when she tuned. Remy hadn't noticed before.

"Let's just get the base down so we have something to work off,

okay? And can you play the drum parts?" Vivi asked without looking up.

"Sure," Remy said. "And I want to add a snap to the hook—I'll
show you when we're there."

Vivi nodded. "Alright, let's do this. Ready?"

"Ready," Remy said, eyes on hers. He pressed a button. "We're
recording."

Vivi began to play the guitar section, mouthing the words. She
didn't ask for a metronome track, and she didn't need one—she kept
in perfect time as she played, closing her eyes and rocking slightly
when her pick hit the strings hard, dredging up the emotion the song
wanted. Remy didn't touch the track just yet; he looped the music back
through to Vivi's headphones so she could record the vocal track next.

"That wasn't great," she said when she'd finished. "Let me do it
again. I want it to be…bigger. More meaningful."

So she did—and again, and again, and then bits and pieces of the
chorus. Remy listened carefully, trying to think of the music rather
than the girl singing it. Truthfully, he rarely got to actually watch Vivi
while she sang. He always saw her back, or the lights, or the production. She smiled when she sang, batted her eyes, acted out the lyrics a
little—though the moment the song or lick stopped, she would shake
her head and fiddle with the guitar, nag at herself for some imperfec-
tion or another.

"That wasn't it either. Why I can't get it right?" she snapped at
herself—a tone Remy recognized, as he knew exactly what it was to
fight for perfection in the studio.

"How about I record the percussion and play with the file a little,
and we can come back to vocals later?" he suggested over the intercom. "Or we can lay down another song, if you need a break from this
one?"

"What other song?" she asked, frowning.

"You brought your notebook—I meant, if you want to get a good guitar recording of anything you're playing off, it might shake this one loose in your head. I can just run the board for you," Remy said, waving to the control room.

"Oh," Vivi said, looking a little astounded. "No—nothing in there is ready to be...no, I don't think so."

"Okay..." Remy said, hesitantly. "Really? I'm not saying you have to work on them with *me*, I was just offering—"

Vivi cut him off apologetically. "No, that's not it—I just don't think they're ready. They're not songs I'm ready to share with anyone, just yet."

Remy did his best not to feel hurt by this—after all, it was her music, and he didn't have a right to it just because he'd kissed her. He couldn't help but wonder what the songs were about that was more of a secret than the things she'd already told him about Tuesday, about her family, about what it was to be Vivi Swan. What the songs were about that was more sacred than "Maybe It's Me" in its current incarnation.

Remy shrugged off the curiosity as best he could and left the sound booth. He came around the corner into the studio, just as Vivi went to lift her guitar over her head. The action caused her sweater to lift the smallest bit, revealing a stomach smoothed by no doubt hours upon hours of private Pilates instruction. Remy noticed, however, not the arc of muscles beneath her skin but a tiny hint of ink at her hip.

"You have a tattoo," Remy said automatically. Vivi jumped then tugged at her sweater, turning away from Remy as if doing so would erase the memory of what he'd just seen. "Too late for that," Remy said, lifting his eyebrows. "What is it?"

"You weren't supposed to see that," she said with nervous laughter.

"Clearly," Remy said, stifling a laugh as he crossed the room. He was struck by the need to approach her cautiously, like she might sprint away—perhaps because they were in a studio rather than a garden shrouded in moonlight. It made every action he took feel intentional rather than dreamlike. Still, he drew closer, closer, till they were a foot or so away from each other.

"Ugh," she said and sighed as she dropped her hands to her sides. It was such a broken gesture that it softened Remy; he reached out a hand for her waist, sliding it over her hip, an inch or so above where the tattoo was hidden under fabric. Vivi closed her eyes a little and smiled then stepped closer to him.

"It's not even a good tattoo," she continued to argue, but her voice was melted.

The room was so quiet that Remy was almost certain he could hear her heart beating, or perhaps his—either way, it was picking up speed. Vivi shook her head, like she was surrendering, then lifted her arms up and looped them around Remy's neck, her weight pulling his mouth to hers.

Remy didn't care about the tattoo anymore, or the songs, or whatever other secrets she was keeping.

By now, the third time, Remy knew how to kiss her, knew how to lean in so she'd arch her back and smile against his skin. He knew where to find the wisps of hair at her neck and how chill bumps rose on her neck if he ran his lips along the place where her jaw met her ear. Vivi licked at his lower lip, so quick Remy almost doubted it'd happened, but then it happened a second time, and then again, until he dared to press his tongue against hers. She made a contented noise that swam down his throat and wrapped around his lungs.

"I wanted to do this right away, you know. But you went and locked yourself in the control room," Vivi whispered.

"Studio time is expensive," Remy said, and Vivi rolled her eyes then kissed him again, pressing against him hard enough that, were he braver, he'd lift her from the ground entirely. It was by accident that he saw the tattoo again—clearly this time. It was a treble clef, a simple design that had blurred a bit around the edges. He'd seen enough tattoos to know this one had been there for a while. Not ages and ages, but certainly five or six years.

"You saw it!" Vivi said accusingly, pulling away. She'd opened her eyes and seen where he was looking.

"I didn't mean to!" Remy said. "It's not a big deal."

Vivi sighed, but she was smiling a little, an embarrassed sort of expression. "It's stupid. Every girl in Nashville has one."

"That's not true. Some of them have eighth notes," Remy said and danced his fingers across her hand. Vivi scowled at him then pulled her top and pants away from each other so Remy could see the tattoo again. She tucked her chin so she could see it too, shaking her head at herself.

"I got it with a friend," she said. "Right after I signed my first deal. It was to celebrate—her brother did them. On his dining room table. It was super hygienic, I'm sure."

Remy extended his fingers to the design, running them across the clef. It was raised a tiny bit; he traced the shape until Vivi shied away.

"That tickles," she said then tugged her shirt back down. "Do you have any?"

"I don't. My brother does, though. He gets them for every musical milestone. Does anyone even know you have it?"

"Sort of? I think some old photos might have it showing," Vivi said. "I don't, like…*show it* to anyone. No one's seen it on purpose, exactly."

"Not even Noel?" Remy asked. Vivi shook her head then seemed to understand what Remy was really getting at. If Noel had never seen the tattoo, it meant he'd never seen Vivi naked. If *no one* had seen the tattoo, it meant—

"I guess you could say I showed it to Jonas on purpose," Vivi said slowly. "A long time ago."

Remy scoured his brain, thinking back through Vivi's boyfriends. Jonas was the one he'd read about ages ago—the one before Noel, the one she'd supposedly lost her virginity to. The fact that Remy knew that before Vivi told him suddenly felt embarrassing and toxic.

"Anyway," Remy said, shaking off the burn of tabloid news as best he could. He stepped forward and kissed her on the forehead, taking as quiet a breath as possible so he could capture the scent of her hair. "Get out of here. I'm recording percussion. You know how to use the program on my laptop?"

Vivi narrowed her eyes. "Please, Young. I used the old version of that program to record my first demo." She started toward the control room then glanced back at him. "I've got another tattoo, you know."

"Really? What of? Where?" Remy asked as he slid onto the stool behind the drum set. It was an overly complicated set, with shiny bells and whistles that no one really needed but rich people liked to buy.

Vivi gave him a mysterious sort of smile. "I'll never tell."

Vivi Swan and Producer in the House
America's Sweetheart takes a break from her world tour to record new music

Vivi Swan and new producer-slash-tour-drummer Remy Young (of Quiet Coyote fame) stopped by Casa Oro studios in Madrid yesterday morning. Sources say they were inside for approximately four hours and recorded a single. Paps swarmed the two as they arrived and left the facility, but they were all business—leaping into separate cars to jet back to the concert venue before their four o'clock sound check.

Who is the song about? The studio manager claims to know but wouldn't tell. Given that Vivi and boyfriend Noel Reid arrived together to publicist Anne Richard's birthday party in Portugal, we think Noel is safe from being the subject of the song—but then again, maybe Vivi just wanted a fresh dose of breakup emotion before the big recording session.

Comments: 511
Author: Bianca Treble

Then

Getting to Nashville wasn't particularly difficult, especially since they hadn't really intended to go there.

Staying in Nashville, however, was tricky. Val mowed the lawns of the rich and famous in Brentwood, and Remy waited tables and made coffee at a place downtown during the day. This left them free to play music at night, which they did to the point of exhaustion. Between the two of them, they managed to rent a studio apartment, which was comically small but still larger than their bedroom at home.

"We can do two shows tonight if we don't stop and try to sell merch afterward," Val said, peeling the bandage off a new tattoo—the word FREEDOM in massive script down his arm, a celebration of arriving in Nashville and pursuing music. He winced when the tape stuck fast but went on, "Besides, I won't have time to tune again unless you drive."

"I can't drive. I don't have a license," Remy said.

Val gave him a withering look. "You know *how* to drive. Just don't do anything to get pulled over, and we'll be fine. The venues aren't that far apart."

So they played both shows—Remy driving between them, sticking to the slow lane and using his turn signal to the point that Val said the clicking was driving him crazy. When they took the stage at the second venue moments after the headlining band finished, the crowd cheered with boozy abandon. Val grinned at them in such a way that they understood: he was one of them, so drink up, boys.

"We're the Lake City Millionaires," Val said. "And this first song is called 'Feverish.'"

Val kicked off the song with a quick, sharp guitar solo; the bassist, a friend of theirs they'd met at another gig, joined in, then Remy on the drums. The keyboard effects were run entirely off a keyboard Val and Remy pooled their money to buy used. It froze, occasionally, which meant they'd gotten used to improvising should it suddenly go off-tempo or become nonexistent. They played through their set to an increasingly wild crowd; Val whirled them up with microphone tricks and dance moves that weren't so much choreographed as convulsed. He'd done more and more of this lately, breaking into spontaneous movement, like his body was cracking and breaking now that it was free from Florida.

When their set ended, a group of girls gathered up around them; the bartender slid the brothers their comped PBRs, which neither particularly liked at that point but both had learned how to confidently swig.

"Where's Lake City?" one of the girls asked, shouting over the thumping house music.

"Florida," Remy said back, though the volume made his head hurt. "There are approximately zero millionaires there."

"Oh, yeah?" the girl asked. "How many bands?"

"As far as I know, there's us, and then the church group that plays praise songs," Val said.

The group laughed and ordered another round of drinks. The taste of beer was still strange and new to Remy, the sort of thing he was trying desperately to train his taste buds to appreciate but largely failing. Val claimed to like it instantly, but Remy knew his brother well enough to know he was lying. They'd never had it before Nashville—too afraid that if they snuck it while playing gigs, their parents would smell it on them. It was a reasonable fear—in a house totally void of alcohol or caffeine, the scent of booze would have stood out like high beams in the dark.

Val didn't get sloppy when he drank—not yet—he just got darker.

His eyes, his hair, his expression. It all became brooding and angrier and, if the people who draped themselves over him were any indication, sexier. Those who couldn't hold court on Val's lap reluctantly sat beside Remy, largely having conversations with one another over him. During a particularly loud conversation that involved squealing and shoving and delighted giggles, one of the guys that had joined them interrupted the girl on Remy's right. She responded by holding up a hand to him with her middle two fingers pressed to her thumb, pinky and pointer fingers extended into the air, like she was making shadow dogs on the club walls.

"What the hell is that?" the guy asked as she shoved her dog-hand in his face.

"Gang sign," Val said, and even though it wasn't a great joke, everyone laughed.

"It's a thing from elementary school," the girl explained as the laughing subsided. "You don't know the quiet coyote?"

"We didn't go to elementary school," Remy said, but Val kicked him sharply under the table, silencing him.

"It's a thing our teachers did to get us quiet. So, when everyone's talking, you just do this sign." She held up the signal again. "And it's the quiet coyote. Mouths closed, ears open."

"Mouths closed, ears open?" Val asked. The girl nodded. A slow, gentle smile crept across Val's face, and his eyes took on a faraway look.

"What is it?" the girl said cheerfully.

"Mouths closed, ears open," Val said. "That's everything. That's how it should be. That's how we should live."

Chapter Twenty-Two

"Maybe It's Me" wasn't really finished—not even close—but it was loosely recorded, which was something. Remy played around with the files, adding effects, increasing echoes, adding beats and breaks and the sound of camera shutters clicking wildly. Vivi had been right—there was something that didn't work in the vocals, but he hadn't figured out yet if it was the lyrics or something more. He was working on it in a Cologne hotel lobby when Celeste called.

"Hey," Remy said, smashing the phone between his ear and shoulder.

"You recorded the song?" Celeste asked excitedly.

"Yes. It's not done, but we have a scratch demo," Remy said. He tried to sound nonchalant, but there was a part of him buzzing over the entire thing. It was exciting to be recording again and exciting to be recording something that had a part of him in it.

"What is it about? It's the Noel breakup song, right?" Celeste asked eagerly.

"Nondisclosure," Remy reminded her.

"This totally doesn't count. I mean, the songs are half yours, right? She can't sue you for talking about something you own," Celeste said matter-of-factly.

Remy sat back from his laptop. "Look, it's not about if she can sue me or not. It's about…trust. We're working on that song *together*." *We're together. Or something.* I mean, obviously they were at least *something*, given what "Maybe It's Me" was about.

"Give me a hint. Is it an angry song? Sad song? Revenge song? Fuck Noel Reid song? Come on, Remy," Celeste whined.

"I'll try to come up with something you can use," Remy said, with no intention of actually doing that—since telling her that it was a love letter, that *all* Vivi's songs were love letters at heart, would definitely blow up on him. "I need to keep working. Tell Val to call me, okay?"

"Fine, fine. He's being weird about you. Or, actually, weird about Vivi Swan. He wants to see everything I write about her tour."

"Maybe he's a secret Vivi Swan fan," Remy suggested, forcing a fairly convincing laugh from his throat.

"Yeah, maybe Burrito Armageddon is a great band name," Celeste said, no doubt with an eye roll so hard, Remy could basically hear it over the phone. "I'll tell him to call you. Now go. Find something I can use on the site."

"On it," Remy lied.

***

Vivi Swan: ok Im done

It was the message Remy had been waiting about thirty minutes for—a heads-up that it was fine for him to dart to Vivi's hotel across the street. She'd had interviews with Italian *Vogue* and then a meeting with some sort of shoe person for some sort of shoe reason, but now they had a whole hour to themselves before sound check. Remy packed up his laptop and started across the street. There were a half dozen photographers at the entrance to Vivi's hotel. They looked bored, lolling against walls, talking to one another, talking on cell phones with their backs turned.

Remy walked to the front doors casually, pocketing his cell phone and glancing down Cologne's brown-and-green-tinted streets as he neared the hotel—

"Remy! Remy, hey, man!" someone shouted. Remy whirled around, certain he'd see someone he knew from the tour. No—it was one of the paps. That man's voice was like a signal cry to the others; they leapt off walls, shoved phones in pockets, jumped around him with their cameras clicking wildly.

Remy laughed aloud—seriously? He blinked at the handful of flashbulbs that popped then lowered his head when blinking didn't disperse the stars in his eyes.

"Remy, what's the new song like?" one of them asked.

"It's…it's great," Remy said. "Great." The paps danced around him, not exactly blocking his path, rather circling him like some sort of force field that moved when he did.

"You going upstairs to work on some new pieces with Vivi?" a pap said in a thick Italian accent.

"This for a new record or just playing around right now?" another asked.

"Just working on a song, keeping it simple," Remy said. The paps split as he reached the door, allowing him through. They all told him to have a great day, that they'd see him later, wished him luck on the music—the more stars liked you, the more likely you were to get exclusives on photos or scoops.

Stars, Remy thought, almost snorting in the hotel lobby. He was *not* a star. This was ridiculous.

Vivi had to buzz him access to the penthouse floor before the elevator would budge. She did, and a few moments later, the elevator doors opened to a room with a view of downtown Cologne—notably, a massive church with two spires and something that vaguely resembled the Seattle Space Needle. Between those were dozens of gray and green and brown and mustard buildings with dozens and dozens of windows stretched across their sides.

"Hey," Vivi said. Remy's eyes jumped from the view to her—she was coming around the corner, wearing a blouse and fitted jeans, the stretchy sort that seemed to be dance wear and denim all in one.

"Hi," Remy said. Vivi slowed as she neared him, a smile spread across her face. Her shoulders relaxed, her posture slouched the smallest amount, and her eyes brightened. The tension melted from him; it felt like he might become water and flow toward her, and the sensation locked a stupid, wide smile on his face.

"Hey," she said again, and Remy reached forward for her hand. He guided her toward him till their chests were pressed together, and then she tilted her head back and lifted her mouth to his to kiss him lightly. He leaned deeper in to her, but she put her hands against his chest, stopping him. "Lipstick," she said. "It's all glossy. I put it on for selfies with the *Vogue* lady. It'll get all over you."

"Might be worth it," he said without giving her any slack in his arms.

"You say that now," she teased. "Give me a second, I'll take it off."

Remy nodded as she disappeared into the bedroom. He busied himself setting his laptop up. When she emerged, Remy noticed she had indeed removed the glossy red lipstick, though she'd replaced it with her trademark cherry-red.

"You traded lipstick for more lipstick?"

"This one won't rub off," she said, swinging her arms around his neck and kissing him hard, as if to prove it. There was a moment where she released her weight against him, and he swung her legs around for a beat until their lips parted.

"Yeah, but you didn't have to dress up just to see me," he said, setting her down. She made a face, like she'd caught him in a lie, then kissed him again, whispering sounds of contentment that made his knees feel both tense and wobbly at once.

"Alright, alright," Vivi said, smiling and pulling away. "We need to work on the mix for 'Maybe It's Me.'"

"The photographers asked about it on the way in," Remy said.

"The paps stopped you?" Vivi asked, cringing. Remy nodded. Vivi went on, "Sorry, I—"

"It's not your fault," Remy said quickly.

"Of course it is. They stopped you because we were together at the studio in Madrid. What did they ask? What did you tell them?"

"It's fine. Seriously, it was fine. It was ridiculous, to be honest."

Vivi smiled, but it was uncomfortable. She spoke cautiously, her eyes drifting to the floor. "Look, Remy, I know you didn't say anything wrong, but this isn't ridiculous—it's my life. It's been my life for years. I just need to know what you said so I know what to expect online, okay?"

Remy inhaled, feeling guilty—she was right. It was her life; it was a huge part of her life, dictating where and when and how she went everywhere and did everything. He answered, "It was largely uneventful, I promise. I said the new song was great. That's it."

"Did you say what the song is about—"

"That's it, Vivi. I promise," Remy said, firmly this time.

Vivi startled, like Remy's words knocked her back to the real world. She stilled, leaning against one of the dining room chairs like a bird perched on a wire. "I didn't mean it like that. I just don't like the press to get anything I didn't give them."

"They caught me off guard. I shouldn't have said anything at all," Remy said after a too-long pause. He sat on the white leather couch, elbows on his knees.

Vivi nodded a little sadly and fiddled with the edge of her jeans, the spot where Remy knew the treble clef tattoo was. "Also, it feels like they're taking every little bit of what was just ours, for a while there. They get everything, in the end."

"Hey. I'm just a producer, as far as they know," Remy reminded her.

"But they still know," Vivi said, shrugging a little. She walked to the couch and sat down hard beside Remy, folding herself against him so easily, it was as if she'd done it a thousand times before. "Did they ask anything about Noel?"

Remy swallowed. "They didn't."

"That's good, at least," Vivi said, turning her chin so it was on his shoulder.

"Yeah," Remy said. "That's good."

He meant it—to a degree. He *was* glad that no one had caught on to the fact that he and Vivi were far more than colleagues. It meant there were no accusations, there was no infamy, there was no scandal. But he'd never been a secret before, and he was surprised to find that what had once been exciting was now sharp and pointed.

"Though if you're always walking over to my hotel, someone's going to start a rumor about us eventually," Vivi said glumly.

Remy nodded, ruffling her hair by his cheek. "Would it be insane for you to put the band and singers in the hotel with you?"

Vivi turned so she was looking at him, brows knitted. "I guess not. I don't really do that…"

"Is there a reason you don't?"

"I…well. Not really, I guess. No, that's not true—I sort of keep a distance between myself and the band and dancers and everything, usually. Obviously, not so much with you."

"Why, though?" Remy asked.

"I don't know. It's easier, for me, if everyone knows where they fall. If someone works for me but is also my friend, it complicates things. I know, I know, I'm the biggest hypocrite right now saying this to you, but…" She looked away. "Fame complicates everything. Absolutely everything. It's not that I can't trust people, it's just that I have to always remember where my relationship with them ranks. Like, is being my friend worth more to them than the hundred thousand dollars *Us Weekly* would pay for private photos of me? Is it worth more than the Instagram followers I could get them? Is it worth more than the record contract?"

Remy was struck by this and considered asking what she wondered about him—what she suspected his price tag was. One thing at a time, though. He said, "Okay, but I'm just saying—if the band stayed at your hotel, I wouldn't need to go past anyone to come see you. No photos."

"That's true."

"And, honestly, I think it might be good for you to do a nice thing from time to time for the band," Remy went on carefully.

Vivi gave him a startled look that quickly morphed to offended. "I do! I stock the buses with whatever you guys want. The hotels you're in are nice. I even fought to get you guys benefits for the tour. I—"

"I know, I know. I'm just saying that a more personal touch with the band might not be a bad thing. I know—they know—that you can't be their best friend, but I know as a musician it sucks to feel like you're canned music instead of a person."

"No one is canned music, but I'm not a band. I'm a solo artist who tours with a live band," Vivi said.

Remy blinked at the response. "So…doesn't that mean we basically are canned music?"

"No, I said you're not, of course you're not, I said that. I'm just saying that a band is a family, and so it makes sense for a personal touch. But I'm not a band, so when I try to treat people like family, it just leads to problems—where does the family line stop? The musicians? The dancers? The tech guys? Who do I have to treat like blood?" Vivi said, voice calm but stern. She'd gone hard against Remy, and he was suddenly aware of every place her weight was against him.

"Okay," Remy said, exhaling, avoiding her eyes. "You're not wrong, okay? But it doesn't have to be all or nothing. You can do the band a favor without owing them a life debt."

"I should be able to. But it doesn't always work that way. I do someone a favor, and if someone else comes asking and I say no—it'll be the second time that makes the news and makes me sound like a horrible person," Vivi said, pressing her lips together then forcing herself to relax against him. "I paid a fan's medical bills once. The next thing I know, dozens of little girls' families are asking me to pay their medical bills too. And it's just…it's awful, and I end up not knowing where to stop or where to not stop." Her voice came close to quavering, but she held herself back. She wound her fingers up with Remy's and added, "I know it's complicated. Everything is complicated with me."

"But I knew that going in," Remy said, running his thumb along her knuckles.

"I know. I didn't mean to snap at you. It just seems like I can never do quite what people need from me," she said. "I always get it wrong."

"That's not true, Viv," Remy said.

She laughed. "Did you just give me a nickname?"

"Hardly. I took off one letter."

"That's a nickname!"

"I was just trying it out," Remy said, smiling.

"It works," Vivi said then leaned forward to kiss him like this was something they'd done for years. "But only for you."

"I think I like *Vivi* better," he said then pressed his mouth to hers. He wanted to tell her exactly what he meant—that he liked *Vivi* far more than Vivi Swan. That it was impossible not to like her, once you pushed past all the people who loved her. And, ah, there was the conundrum, he knew: letting so many people in to see the real Vivi meant letting that many people in to moments like this.

They're taking every little bit of what was just ours, for a while there, she'd said. How much of Vivi herself had they already taken? Who was she, before the media got her, before they made her sleek and put-together and secretive and hyperaware of each and every action? Remy doubted even Vivi knew; she'd been famous since fifteen.

They get everything, in the end.

Chapter Twenty-Three

"Did you say something to her?" Laurel asked, bounding toward him in the hotel hallway. Her words were fierce, but her face was split into a wide, bright grin.

"Huh?" Remy asked, leaning in his hotel room doorway.

"I complain to you that she never puts us in a hotel alongside her, suddenly we're in a five-star Paris hotel? You said something, didn't you?"

"I might have said something," Remy admitted, and now he was grinning too. Vivi hadn't told him about the hotel, and so it felt like a surprise gift—one that meant something more than a room. It meant she wanted him nearby, she wanted him to be able to visit her more easily, she wanted him more than she feared what might happen if she did the band this favor.

Laurel flung her arms around Remy's shoulders. "You are seriously my hero right now. My actual hero. My room has a television in the bathtub mirror. Like, hidden in the mirror. It's crazy."

Remy laughed a little, letting his arms loop lightly around Laurel. She peeled away from him and bounced on her leopard-print heels. "We're going out for crepes after the show. Want to come?"

"Who is we?"

"Me, Ro, and Parish."

"I'll see—I might not be able to tonight," Remy said. He could tell from the falter in Laurel's eyes that she knew this was a no. He'd essentially only seen the rest of Bus Three in the dressing rooms and onstage since they left the States. It wasn't that he didn't *want* to spend time with them, just that he knew he'd regret not spending that time with Vivi. They'd given up on him, Remy suspected— they weren't angry or bitter or the like, but the camaraderie he'd had with the rest of them for the first few weeks of the tour was wilted at best.

"Boo," Laurel said. "Well, text me if you're able to come."

Remy wasn't sure he had Laurel's number but didn't say anything.

After the show, just before midnight, Vivi texted Remy to meet her in the back of the lobby. She was waiting for him there, a jacket pulled over her shoulders and her hair in a ponytail. It was almost casual, but when she turned to face him, he saw she was wearing her trademark red lipstick.

"For a minute, I thought you were dressed down," he said, smiling, fighting the urge to reach for her. It *seemed* like they were alone back here, but given how she kept a few feet between them, he suspected there were security cameras he just hadn't seen.

"Plausible deniability," Vivi said and grinned. "I don't look done-up enough that everyone will easily spot me, but if they do, I won't be embarrassed by the pictures. Paris is harder to sneak around in than London, so I have to play it safe if I want to act like a normal girl." Remy nodded, remembering how Celeste had once told him there were no bad pictures of Vivi. This was why.

"And where are we going?" Remy asked as they walked outside, keeping the space between them formal. There was a car at the curb, but other than that, no one in sight—which made sense, given that they were more or less in an alley lined with trash bins.

"It's a surprise. A lame surprise, maybe, but a surprise," Vivi said, grinning as she climbed into the car without acknowledging the driver holding the door open. Remy nodded at him as he got in behind her; the driver looked appreciative enough but didn't speak.

The driver shut the door, and in the few moments between him doing so and his reappearance at the driver's side door, she grabbed Remy's hand and squeezed it. There was something to it, something stronger than just a handhold, like a plea that things would go back to the gentle, sweet way they were before yesterday, when there was no discussion of the paparazzi or worry over how the band viewed her. Remy wanted to return there just as badly, and he squeezed her hand back.

They rolled through Paris, the road tiny and apparently lane-less. The streets looked far more desolate than Remy would have expected—somehow, he thought it would be more like New York, always buzzing and bright and tireless. Shops were covered with rolling security doors, many of which had been graffitied, a sharp contrast to the well-designed, elegant signs above the shop doors.

They wound up alongside a river, its water black in the night, save for the brightly lit tourist boats that shepherded drunk foreigners back and forth apparently at all hours. Vivi stared out the window like she was mesmerized.

"I've always wanted to do that," she said, pointing. The river was a level below their car, a canyon hemmed in by a wide footpath at its concrete banks. People were walking along the banks—so *this* was where the city was bright and buzzing and tireless. Couples holding hands, the orange glow of cigarette tips, the carousing of young people shoving one another playfully. It was easy for Remy to picture himself among them—their faces were silhouettes in the dark, so it could easily be him or Val or Vivi jumping up on the river's wall edge and balancing there.

"Is that what we're doing tonight?" Remy asked, trying to keep his voice low so the driver couldn't hear.

"No," Vivi said, sighing. She looked at him and smiled. "Too risky. Maybe one day?" The word *maybe* was loaded with hope, but the sort of hope that already felt defeated.

"One day," Remy said with a careful smile. "Because tonight, we're already busy going to…"

Vivi sighed happily then nodded ahead. Directly in front of them was the Eiffel Tower—orange and glowing and somehow both bigger and smaller than Remy had pictured.

"A lame surprise, but a surprise," Vivi said.

"What's lame about the Eiffel Tower?" Remy snorted in disbelief.

"Nothing! I mean, just—it's super touristy. But I never get to do super touristy things, and I've always wanted to see the Eiffel Tower, so…here we are," she said, sounding sweetly embarrassed.

"Isn't this just as risky as the river?" Remy asked. Surely the Eiffel Tower was crowded at night.

"It closed at midnight. They're opening it after hours for me."

"Celebrities," Remy said and rolled his eyes dramatically. Vivi scowled and smacked him on the arm then leaned toward him, like she wanted to kiss him, before remembering the driver might see. Instead, they watched each other for a moment, eyes wide and happy and wanting. Remy felt his stomach twist in a terribly pleasant way and took a deep breath.

"Here we are, Miss Swan," the driver said in a thick French accent. He got out of the car without ever looking in the rearview mirror— come to think of it, Remy had never seen any of her drivers' eyes flick toward him. He suspected this was contractual. Vivi gathered her purse and waited for him to open the door. Remy, for the first time, waited for the driver to round the car and open the door for him too. It made him feel simultaneously like an asshole and like royalty.

One of Vivi's security guys approached her, and they spoke quickly, their eyes always darting along the horizon, waiting for a telltale camera flash or the oddly still, catlike freeze of someone steadying their cell phone camera hand. They saw neither, and within a few moments, Remy and Vivi were standing at the base of the Eiffel Tower, at a cherry-red elevator. An older-looking French woman with an Eiffel Tower–embroidered shirt waved them on then climbed on behind them, holding down a series of buttons with a bored expression on her face. They arrived at the tower's first landing, disembarked, and all three of them moved to another elevator—this one bright yellow.

This was repeated once more—disembarking, walking to another elevator, the woman climbing on behind them and pressing a series of buttons. If the woman knew who Vivi was, she didn't show it—in fact, she barely looked at them. They couldn't see the city from here, despite the fact they were going ever higher; the iron structure's many bars and landings and supports meant it felt more like they were being lifted inside an enormous robot than a national landmark.

"Excuse me," Vivi said politely, as they reached what Remy knew was the final elevator—both because of a sign reading SOMMET/TOP and because unlike the others, this one went straight up, rather than at an incline. The woman didn't turn; Vivi repeated herself.

"*Oui*?" the woman said, smiling politely but with a fair degree of disinterest. Remy decided she clearly didn't know who Vivi was— which, he suspected, was why someone had elected her to be their guide to the Eiffel Tower after dark.

"Could we take the last one alone?" Vivi asked, flashing a bright smile.

"Oh, I'm sorry, *mais no*," the woman said. "I am not allowed."

"Are you sure? We wouldn't tell, obviously. We can be back down in a few minutes."

"I will be removed from my job," the woman said, shaking her head.

Vivi nodded, still smiling. "I understand. Are you sure, though? I'm happy to pay you for the trouble." Before the woman could react, Vivi was swimming through her purse. She emerged with a purple bill she barely looked at. The older woman was still protesting but nonetheless took the bill from Vivi's fingers. Remy didn't know his euros from one another, but as the woman folded it into her shirt pocket, he saw *500* in big indigo letters.

"Celebrities," he muttered playfully in Vivi's ear, and her eyes sparkled. The woman reached onto the elevator and provided quick operating instructions that were essentially identical to those of any elevator anywhere.

"Twenty minutes," she said. "No longer."

"Of course. Thank you again," Vivi said sincerely and stepped onto the elevator. Remy followed, and they stood a foot or so from each other after Vivi hit the Up button, as if they wanted to prove to the woman that their request for privacy had no illicit undertones. She smiled at them politely as the doors rumbled shut.

Vivi was in his arms immediately.

Not just in his arms—in his skin, in his lungs, in his eyes. He wasn't sure if he'd reached for her or she'd reached for him, but suddenly they were pressed together as the elevator took them into the sky, mouths together, tongues flickering across lips. They'd kissed so many times before, but this kiss had a current of hunger rather than experimentation. Vivi's hands ran up Remy's back then looped around his shoulders. She pulled herself higher against him, and the shift in her weight caused him to stumble backward till his back hit the elevator wall. She laughed, a single sound, before she kissed him again and then pulled herself farther up—

Remy had fought the urge the first time, but with the wall supporting his weight, he couldn't fight it now—he wrapped his hands under her legs and lifted her against him. Her legs clasped around his waist, locking her there, and he could feel her hip bones pressed to his.

The elevator slowed then rolled to a stop. Vivi pulled away from his face, and they smiled at each other, neither moving to set Vivi's feet back on the ground. When the doors opened, they relented; Vivi released her legs and slid away from him then turned to face the city.

"Wow," Vivi said. Despite the elevator's glass walls, they'd been too preoccupied to watch the city growing small beneath them as they ascended. Now, it splayed out, and the nickname *City of Lights* felt particularly apt. Paris looked like it'd been coated in glitter, or stars, or fairy dust. So far from everyone else, the world was silent, save for the chilly fall wind whipping around them, whirling Vivi's hair into a cyclone around her head. She brushed it away and stepped up to the rail, resting her hands through the large diamond shapes made by the wire that kept anyone from leaping into the sparkles below.

"It's so much prettier up here," Vivi said in a near whisper. "This is amazing."

"Why didn't you come before now?" Remy asked, stepping up behind her. He ran his hands down her arms then rested his chin on the top of her head as they both studied the world below.

Vivi shrugged, her shoulder blades carving up and down Remy's chest as she did so. "I didn't have anybody to come with."

"You could've brought a friend," Remy suggested.

Vivi made a breathy, laughing sound. "This isn't the sort of thing I want to see with a friend." She paused for a long time then said, quietly, almost like she was worried he *would* hear, "I think I was waiting to see this with you."

Remy closed his eyes, because the smell of her hair was more magnificent than anything he was seeing just then. He cleared his throat, because if Vivi was brave enough to say that aloud, then he was brave enough to say his immediate response aloud. "I think I was just waiting on you."

Maybe it's me.

Yes, it's me. It's you. It's us.

Vivi turned away from the city and stood on her toes to kiss him; he put a hand to the back of her head, raking his nails gently through her hair.

"I think..." Vivi began huskily, keeping her lips so near his that they brushed against each other as she spoke. "I think we need to go back to the hotel after this. Or maybe right now."

Remy nodded, his stomach and lungs and heart and ribs crumbling in his chest. He felt alive and electric and animal, and his toes kept curling and uncurling in his shoes. He spoke gruffly into her ear. "Let's go now."

Chapter Twenty-Four

Remy woke to a blur of sunlit whites and the scent of vanilla and lemongrass. There was no pause, no moment where he didn't remember where he was—he knew exactly, just as well as he knew who the warm person pressed against his back was. He opened his eyes, careful not to let the movement trickle down to any other part of his body. If he moved, she might wake up, and then *she'd* move, and then the beauty that was this particular moment would be over. You only got to wake up after the first time once.

He blinked, waiting for the room to come into focus. It was the penthouse, and through the still-open curtains, he could see the Eiffel Tower on the opposite end of Paris, rising high above the low-rise buildings that made up the classic part of the city. The room was decorated in creams and lavenders and wasn't nearly as large as he'd have expected for a penthouse in Paris—unlike the one in Cologne, there weren't a myriad of different rooms but rather one large, high-ceilinged one with a sitting area and no kitchen, just a fancy espresso machine. The space had a warm, homey feel, between the oversoft bed and the worn brass doorknobs.

He felt Vivi shift behind him, the smooth skin of her bare shoulder moving up and down his spine. Remy froze. *Don't wake up don't wake up don't wake up.*

"Are you awake?" Vivi whispered.

"I am."

She turned over, making certain the blankets were still pulled up around her chest. He looked over to see that while her eyes were still sleepy and her hair tangled, she had a pen in her hand, and her Moleskine notebook splayed out on the sheets.

"If you're writing a song about sleeping with me, I think you ought to let me see it," Remy joked. Or mostly joked. The truth was, seeing the Moleskine out the night after they slept together made him wonder what sort of song she was writing.

Vivi laughed. "No way. But I'll tell you this much: Of everyone I've written a song about in this notebook, you'd be the one most deserving to take a look."

"Does that mean you *have* written one about me?" Remy asked, now genuinely curious. The notebook had continued to be a point of mystery, to him—she never played anything for him from it, save "Maybe It's Me," but she had to have written at least a dozen other songs or verses or at least lyrics in there in the time they'd spent together alone.

"I'll never tell," she said and stuck her tongue out at him before flipping the Moleskine closed. He growled then reached to pull her to him. Vivi moved fluidly, rolling into his arms and resting her head at the spot where his shoulder met his torso, and it made him go still and forgiving and blissful.

"I can hear your heart," she said quietly, her ear pressed to his bare chest.

"What's it sound like?" he asked.

She was silent for a moment, apparently listening, then tilted her head toward him. "I'm trying to think of something poetic to say, but it more or less just sounds like a heart."

He smiled and kissed the top of her head. "Let me listen to yours."

"You're just trying to get to second base," she said.

"Please. I would never. This is purely scientific," Remy said and sat up a little. He leaned over her, pressing his ear to the spot just below her clavicle. Her heart beat beneath him; she wound her fingers in his hair gently as he listened. He slid his hands up her skin, smiling when he felt her heart jump beneath his ear.

"Anything special?" she asked after a moment, as her heart slowed back down.

"No," he said but didn't move away. He marveled over how her heart was every bit as unremarkable as his, and yet he didn't want to stop listening to it. She didn't seem eager to move him away; she settled her arms around his shoulders and head, breathing slowly. He finally lifted his head, looking down at Vivi's face. She'd washed her makeup off last night—she'd insisted on the importance of doing so, actually, despite the fact he felt too exhausted to even stand after two hours of tangled sheets and limbs and bodies.

"What?" she asked, raising a hand to her face, smoothing the hair around it.

"You're beautiful," he said.

"He told his boss," she joked but flushed a little all the same.

"Well, I'm trying to get a raise. Maybe dental benefits," he answered.

Vivi laughed then smacked him with a pillow, and he fell backward dramatically. She shoved her way on top of him, he fought back, they tossed and moved and fell over each other until they were both breathless and laughing and stupid. Vivi was wearing underwear with navy stripes and gave up on covering her chest after she realized it made it too easy for Remy to tackle her. They wrestled back and forth until Vivi gave in and collapsed backward, while Remy rained kisses across her shoulder blades, wandered his lips up her neck, and relished the way it made her shiver and sigh.

"Hey, wait a minute," Remy murmured against her skin. "You said you had another tattoo. But I feel like I've more or less seen you from every angle at this point but still haven't seen anything other than that music note."

"I lied to you," Vivi confessed, biting her lips.

"Really? Why?" Remy asked. He pulled away from her neck, knitted his brows together.

"It was back in Spain, when I thought...when I wanted to...do this. All of this. When I thought we might. So it was a last check. I told you I had a second one then watched the gossip sites, to see if anything about 'Vivi Swan's secret second tattoo' came up."

"You baited me?" Remy said, unsure if he was amused or hurt. Vivi had to know him better than that, right? Surely.

"Well! I just wanted to know before..." Vivi argued, though she was clearly embarrassed.

Remy forced himself into being more amused than offended—he didn't like making her feel embarrassed, after all. "Wait, wait, wait— you *planned* on sleeping with me? As long ago as Spain?" he asked, the corners of his lips curving up.

"I didn't *plan* on it like that. I just knew that I liked you and that I wanted..."

"Vivi Swan, *the* Vivi Swan, was fantasizing about me. That's what you're saying," Remy teased.

"That's not what I'm saying!" Vivi laughed, looking relieved that Remy wasn't angry with her. She shoved him and hit him with a pillow, which he caught and tossed away easily.

"Forget the tattoo story. This is what I'll sell to the press: how a lowly drummer managed to become an object of Vivi Swan's sexual desires."

"You are the worst," Vivi said, shaking her head, but she melted close to him and kissed him, her lips tight from the smile she was trying to hold down. When they pulled away, he looked at her, eyes serious.

"Did you really think I'd tell?" he asked, more intensely this time. They'd written a song together, one about being together, one about being each other's person—and yet, she'd still tested him? How could she both feel so strongly and doubt so strongly at once?

"I know now you wouldn't," she said. "Are you mad at me?"

"No, I'm just…I'm surprised," Remy said, narrowly avoiding saying that he was *just disappointed*. He went on, "I don't know. It's not exactly normal dating protocol, to write music together and spend so much time together and sleep together and then…bait me with a lie."

"Well, I'm not exactly normal," Vivi offered.

"No, you aren't," Remy answered with a deep exhale then kissed her again. "And I have to go."

"Why?" Vivi pouted.

"Sound check. Which means you have to go too—but unless you want us to walk into the arena together, I need a head start."

Vivi squeezed his hand. "Thanks for thinking of that."

"Of course," he said then pulled away from her. "See you out there."

They had a second night in Paris, but somehow, the entire show felt new to Remy. It wasn't just that he knew what she looked like under her glittery costumes or even that, lately, she made a point to wink at him during the finale, when she was encouraging the audience to roar for each member of the band. It was—pride. Yes, that was it. Remy was proud of Vivi, and as pride was something he thought adults only felt for children or perhaps puppies, it took him a long while to pin down the emotion.

But he was proud. Of how hard she worked on the show, of how hard she worked on the songs, on her image, on her interviews, on being Vivi Swan. It no longer seemed insane to him that a crowd of forty thousand would come out to scream for her—it seemed deserved.

"Where are we next?" David asked absently as the whole of Bus Three gathered in the band dressing room during Vivi's acoustic set. They'd leave for the next city immediately after the show, without so much as a stop by the hotel.

"Amsterdam," Parish said. "Which means legal drugs, friends."

"That's for a younger man. And I think there's a line in the show contract about it, so be careful," David said.

"Pshh," Ro said. "Who's going to tell?"

"The spy," David suggested. "Whoever it is."

"You still think there's a spy?" Remy asked, half laughing. He was surprised to see so many of them shrug in response—not a yes, but not the resounding *of course not!* he was expecting.

"I still think it's one of the dancers," Laurel said, avoiding Remy's eyes completely, almost as if he weren't in the room at all.

"Fine. I don't want to get high with them anyway," Parish said, ransacking the craft services table to make himself a turkey sandwich.

Remy stepped outside for the remainder of the intermission, propping the stage door open with his left shoe. It was straight-up cold out here, but the time change meant this would likely be his only chance to call his brother, and the venue size meant this would be the only place with a semblance of privacy. "Motherfucker!" Val answered the phone sleepily but far more cheerfully than the word merited.

"Hey. Did I wake you up? What time is it there? I seriously have no idea," Remy said, grinning at his brother's voice.

"It's two o'clock in the afternoon."

"Then why the hell are you asleep?" Remy asked, listening to the shuffle of Val climbing out of bed. It was easy to picture him making his way out of the bedroom and onto the patio—after all, the room had once been Remy's.

"I was up late. What are you, our mother? I have a few more new pieces I'm dicking around with. It's like a floodgate, man. It opened up, and now I can't stop it." It was the most joyful complaint Remy had heard from Val, perhaps ever. Val went on, "So how are things with...you know. I mean, is it still going...or?" Val said, pausing, navigating.

"Things are great," Remy said, working very hard not to think of the way Vivi had looked that morning amid the linen sheets or about the sight of her writing in the notebook when he woke up.

"Really?"

"You sound surprised," Remy joked. "No faith in your little brother's romantic prowess?"

"I'm not surprised, just...I mean, fuck, I don't know what it's like to date a Vivi Swan. Wait, are you dating? Can you date someone if you don't actually go on dates with them? Holy shit, Remy, you're *hooking up* with Vivi Swan."

"It's not like that," Remy said, but he laughed and turned around, checking to make sure no one was headed back to the stage yet.

"It is too! She's got that other guy for the streets and you for the sheets. Nice."

Remy's laughter stopped short at the mention of Noel, however playful Val had meant it to be. He spoke quickly. "Well, they don't really see each other. And it's complicated."

"I mean, they see each other. They were together in Portugal for something. I saw the pictures on Celeste's computer."

"Yeah. Well, still. Not often," Remy said, except really, his mind was racing. They were together in Portugal? That wasn't long ago at all. She'd called him from Portugal. She'd never mentioned Noel was there with her. Never mentioned the first tattoo, baited him with the story about the second...

Val was quiet for a moment—he knew Remy well enough to know his brother's voice had gone dark. "Things are going well?" he asked again, and this time, he sounded particularly sincere.

"Things are complicated with her," Remy said slowly. "But I really...she's great, Val."

Val made a sound that Remy knew meant he was nodding. "She thinks you're great?"

"Yes. I think so."

"Then it shouldn't be complicated," Val said wisely. "If you're both all in, it isn't complicated. Messy, maybe, but not complicated."

Remy considered the difference between the words. Messy was, perhaps, Noel. Messy was their time together being stolen. Complicated...

Complicated was Remy's lingering wonder if Vivi *wasn't* all in. If they were together only because it meant Vivi was able to scribble down songs about him in the early morning. *Messy*, after all, was easy to fix—so why hadn't she left Noel and gone public with Remy, if there wasn't something more complicated at work deep down?

They hung up a few minutes later, and Remy rushed back to the stage, trying not to let his brother's words gain weight in his mind—trying not to let them press out the memory of the way Vivi felt against him that morning.

Remy sat at his drum set, waiting for the safety checks. While stagehands flittered around the set, he lifted his phone and, with a sigh, pulled up the article Val was talking about—searching for *Vivi Swan* and *Portugal* brought it up nearly immediately. He tapped to open it.

Pictures pulled up. Vivi, in a short red romper with tall heels, standing beside Noel.

She'd been there with him, just like Val said. Which, of course, of course she was—she hadn't lied to him. But she hadn't told him either. Vivi had acted like Portugal was any other business trip, not one that involved another series of pictures proving that, so far as the world knew, she and Noel Reid were a couple. She and Noel were messy, perhaps, but not complicated.

Chapter Twenty-Five

Amsterdam came after Paris; Laurel, Parish, Michael, and Remy hit the streets of the city after the show there. This was largely because knowing Vivi had been with Noel in Portugal made him want to take a long, deep breath in both the literal and symbolic sense—and getting out with Bus Three while Vivi was at a photo shoot, mending that bridge even the tiniest amount, seemed like a good way to take that breath.

People described New York as a city that didn't sleep, but as far as Remy could tell, Amsterdam was the only one in the world that truly didn't. Between red-wallpapered nightclubs and tourists gawking at elderly sex workers in shop windows, there was, in some ways, more to do after sunset than there was to do during the day. Or, at least, he guessed there was—he'd spent all his daylight hours in Amsterdam with Vivi.

"Wait, seriously?" Laurel asked, pointing at a giant sign on the side of a building. "Are you fucking serious, Dutch people?" It was an advertisement for two contortionist sister sex workers.

"Wow. That's rough," Parish said, making a horrified face. Both sisters had the look of heavy smokers, and the bikinis they were

wearing were slightly too big and droopy for their frames. No wonder
Vivi refused to come out with him—a photo of her beside an ad for
aged sex workers wouldn't be great PR.

"I wonder how much they make though," Laurel said, tilting her
head at the advertisement. "Probably as much as we do."

"Are you looking for a backup career?" Remy teased.

Laurel snorted. "Would it even matter if I went from backup
singer to old lady hooker? It's all the same shit. People buy a piece of
you for entertainment."

"That's an awful biblical outlook on the music industry," Parish
said as they continued walking down the street. Calling it the *red-light
district* was apt—every single shop had glowing crimson neon lights
in the windows. It made the world look fiery; the canal that ran down
the street became inky black save for the reflections of words like PEEP
SHOW and SEX PALACE. It was, perhaps, the least sexy place Remy had
ever been, though that made it strangely exciting.

Laurel went on as they paused in front of a window where a
number of sex workers hung on or around or from circus equipment.
"Well, it's not the exact same as the music industry, I guess. But hell,
Tuesday Rivers just did a nude series for *Vogue* with that molester
photographer dude. A lot more people will see that than...what's her
name? Harmonie."

"What do you think her real name is?" Remy wondered as they
watched "Harmonie" text from her perch on a trapeze, like a particularly interesting zoo exhibit. She smiled at them lightly, aware she was
being watched but clearly used to it. *Harmonie. Remember. Valor.
Vivian.*

"I bet for the right price, she'll tell you. Or at least she'll tell you a
convincing lie," Parish said. "One of my exes was a stripper, and that
was her game—take a guy back, let him think he's saving you, give

him a real name, watch him offer you money to take you away from your life of sin."

"Did it work?" Michael asked. He hadn't spoken much since they arrived in the red-light area, though Remy couldn't tell if it was because he was over- or underwhelmed.

"Every time," Parish said, grinning. "She's a cam girl now, I think. Doesn't even have to leave the house to make stupid amounts of money."

"Gross," Laurel said then moved along. The others followed her down the street, past a series of coffee shops that weren't coffee shops at all, as far as Remy could tell, but rather weed dispensaries. He wondered if you could actually buy coffee in Amsterdam or if it was just magic mushrooms as far as the eye could see. A brightly lit sign at the end of the street flashed between EXTREMELY DANGEROUS COCAINE SOLD TO TOURISTS and IGNORE STREET DEALERS, like this entire place was a twisted version of Disneyland, complete with constant cameras flashing as people documented their eager sinning, like dangerous cocaine was something worth remembering.

"How about it, Parish? You going to magic mushroom up? Or shall we continue on to the Museum of Prostitution?" Laurel asked, slowing when they came to a particularly bright storefront that was indeed adjacent to a museum of prostitution. There were menus hanging in the coffee shop windows—hash menus, weed menus, mushroom menus. The type of high you'd supposedly get from each was beside the item: Happy! Spacey! Energetic! Inspiring!

"I've never had mushrooms before, so, yeah, obviously I'm sampling the goods," Parish said, studying the menu. One of the guys from behind the counter came over, and they fell into a deep discussion of the merits of Spacey versus Energetic. Laurel, meanwhile, decided on Happy without much debate.

"What about you?" Michael asked Remy.

"Eh. I'm not much the smoker. Or…mushroom-er," Remy said, watching Laurel and Parish get their purchases boxed up.

"Oh—yeah. I see," Michael said, in a way that told Remy he actually *did* see what Remy was trying to say: that he'd seen drug use a little too up-close to be interested in even the most banal of versions. "How's the producing thing going?" Michael asked, leaning against a stone wall that was probably ten times older than anyone they knew—yet still had penises graffitied all over it.

"With Vivi? It's going great. Really great," Remy said and heard his voice soften a little too late to stop it.

"Good. I'm glad. She sign a contract with you yet?"

"Not yet," Remy said.

Michael laughed a little. "Hey, I'm not your dad, kid. You do you. I think we're all just still a little shocked that she seems to actually *like* one of us peons."

Any answer Remy might have given was delayed by Laurel literally hopping out of the coffee shop. Remy had doubts as to whether the mushrooms had really taken effect *that* quickly but didn't say anything, even when Laurel grinned and grabbed his arm, swinging around his side.

"That was fast," Michael said, helping balance Laurel.

"I didn't get many. Also, mushrooms taste gross, magic or not," Laurel said. "And *yes*, I am totally shocked that Vivi likes a peon. I didn't think it was possible. Unless…you're lying, and she's a nightmare."

"She's not a nightmare," Remy said as Parish appeared, rustling through his box of dried, woody-looking mushrooms.

"Dude, we all signed the same nondisclosure. Be honest. We can tell each other the truth," Parish said with a snicker.

"She's not a nightmare. Seriously." There was no small urge to tell them more—about the way she looked in the morning, and the way she fit into the space at his side, and the way every now and then, she exhaled long and loud, and it sounded like she was remembering to breathe for the first time in years. He couldn't, of course. But god, how he wanted to.

"Okay, but, like, what are you even *doing* with her?" Laurel asked, picking up another mushroom from her box and popping it into her mouth. "Are you writing stuff, or just doing backing tracks, or shaping stuff, or just telling her she's a fucking genius? What realm of producer-dom are you living in?"

"Shaping, mostly."

"I want to hear the songs," Laurel said.

"Song. Single song."

"Whatever. Then I want to hear the *song*," she whined again. "It's the breakup song about Noel, right? I mean, obviously it is, everyone knows it. Ro read that the only reason she went to that party with him in Portugal was to get some fresh emotion right before you recorded it."

"That's insane," Remy said.

"You don't sound like you really think that," Laurel said, waggling her eyebrows. Remy rolled his eyes. She wasn't *right*, exactly—he didn't truly think fresh Noel pain was why Vivi had gone to Portugal. But the idea wasn't totally outlandish either, and it wouldn't stop circling his brain like a buzzard.

Parish snickered in the space between Laurel's delight and Remy's exhale then took another mushroom out of his box—one that was considerably larger than Laurel's.

"What'd you get?" Laurel asked, peering at his stash.

"A medley," Parish answered with a wicked kind of grin. "Come on, losers. I've got an entire box of mushrooms to go through and only eight hours to do it."

***

It was well after midnight by the time Remy made his way to Vivi's penthouse room, primarily because Parish's mushroom medley had resulted in him taking his shirt off, making out with a sex worker (who then yelled at him for not paying), and joyfully singing Nick Maddon songs at the top of his lungs. Remy and Michael finally managed to shove Parish into his own room; Laurel went to hers more easily, albeit giggling so loudly that angry hotel guests flung their doors open and glared. The smoky, flowery scent of Amsterdam clung to his clothing, overpowering the scent of carpet cleaner that he was beginning to think was as internationally consistent as the smell of Subway restaurants.

He knocked lightly on the enormous gilt door; Vivi opened the door in a bathrobe, smiling. She was wearing enough makeup that Remy was confident she hadn't gone to sleep yet, despite the hour.

"You were awake?" he asked as he stepped inside.

"Yes."

"This late?"

"I was making cookies for the next batch of meet and greets," she said at nearly the same moment the scent of chocolate chips and vanilla struck him. He looked to the hotel room's expansive kitchen and saw several trays of already-cooled cookies on the counter. The place looked like a luxe New York apartment, all minimalist and marbleized and, frankly, cold—which made the steaming plate of cookies feel particularly out of place.

"You really *do* make those yourself?" he asked, surprised. "Have to admit, I thought that was a line."

Vivi grinned, looking proud, and they wandered toward the kitchen together, drawn in by the scent of vanilla and brown sugar. "I make all the dough before the tour then freeze it and have it delivered. Sometimes someone else has to do the actual baking though, if I don't have time."

"That's…well, that's sort of adorable and ridiculous," Remy said, shaking his head.

Vivi blushed. "I know. But I always did it before things took off for me. I'd bring cookies and lemonade to my shows and recording sessions. It was a way to make me stand out, you know? A way for me to be special, make people stick around to listen to another song or whatever. Nashville is full of white girls with guitars, but damn if I couldn't be the only one who brought you chocolate chip cookies."

"Though to be fair, you also stood out because you were the only white girl with cornrows," Remy said.

"Exactly. I had to make people like me despite those," Vivi answered and reached for a cookie. She broke it in half, handed the free half to Remy, and nibbled on the one she kept for herself. "How was Amsterdam?" she asked, leaning against the counter as the timer ticked down on the batch in the oven.

"It was beautiful and vulgar in the best way," Remy said then told her about the old sex workers and the DANGEROUS COCAINE SOLD TO TOURISTS sign that people who hadn't watched their brother overdose thought was a riot. Vivi listened, pulling the tray of cookies out and replacing it with a final batch.

"And the places you get drugs—like the places for pot and mushrooms—are all called coffee shops. They have actual menus, like real coffee-serving coffee shops. Like, what to order to make you excited, or happy, or mellow, or whatever you want to be."

"I think I'd heard about that before. Tuesday does that sort of thing when she comes here," Vivi said thoughtfully. "She says it's

Amsterdam, that you're basically required as an American to do mushrooms. She and Noel both, actually…" She drifted off, too skilled at subject changes to stop short—but there it was in the air anyhow. Noel's name. There it always was.

"People think the song we're working on is about him. That it's your Noel breakup song," Remy said as casually as possible, turning one of the cookies a bit with the edge of his finger.

"Yeah. My publicist told me," Vivi said. "Ridiculous."

"Is there—is that what you're working on though, that you aren't showing me? A Noel breakup song in that notebook?" Remy asked.

"I don't…I mean…yes," Vivi said.

"I'd like to work on that one with you, Vivi," Remy said carefully, meeting her eyes.

Vivi pressed her lips together. "We will. It's not for lack of material, where Noel is concerned. I could record a whole album of breakup songs about him."

"Then break up with him, Vivi," Remy said. The words spilled from him, not desperate, exactly, but almost demanding—the way you speak to a character on a movie screen. He wanted to bring up Portugal, or the paparazzi, or the stupid haircut Noel had, but really all those points led to the same place: *Leave him. Please, leave him. Be with me, in public and private and everywhere in between. Leave him.*

Vivi answered, voice soft and worried, "I will. It's just so much nicer to distract the whole world with something shiny and stupid than it is to give them you. And then, the minute they find out about you, they'll want *our* breakup song instead of the love letter I want to write about being with you. It's a loop. But this moment, this in-between time, it's like the whole loop just freezes."

Remy nodded at the countertop but said, "It doesn't freeze, though, Vivi. This tour—it'll end. It won't be like this forever."

"Right," she said, so quietly, he nearly missed it. She was still for a few long moments. "When it's over, Remy—what happens?"

"I don't know," Remy admitted.

Vivi nodded, and even though she smiled, it was broken. "It wouldn't be easy. I'm not in LA. You are. If the world knows about us, your house is going to get staked out. They'll know when you're there. They'll know everything that happens with your brother. They'll go to your gigs, and people will hire you to mine you about me."

"I won't tell them anything—"

"That's not what I mean," Vivi said, shaking her head. "It's not that I don't believe in *this*, Remy. It's just that *this*, crazy as it is sometimes, is easier than real life. Even more so when the world thinks I'm really with Noel—"

She inhaled, like she'd been about to say more, but the oven timer dinged, signaling that the final batch of cookies was complete. Vivi retrieved them then washed her hands and surveyed the kitchen, silently counting the perfectly symmetrical rows, stalling as long as she could.

"Come on," Remy said, meeting her eyes. "Let's go to sleep."

Vivi's face lit up in sorrow and hope and relief, and she let her hand slide into his. They walked to the hotel bedroom together; Remy stripped off his shirt and fell into the enormous bed. Vivi took the time to wash her face and complete her complex nighttime beauty routine, which meant she smelled like lotion and honeysuckle when she curled up beside him fifteen minutes later. Her fingers and toes were freezing; Remy pressed her hands against his chest to warm them.

"Thank you," she murmured, turning her hands over to warm the backs and nestling closer to him. He responded by kissing her lightly on the head, inhaling the scent of her, and wondered why in the world he'd advocated for unfreezing this particular loop.

Chapter Twenty-Six

They planned to pull out of Amsterdam before noon the following day, after Remy helped Vivi pack the dozens upon dozens of cookies in bags individually labeled with the upcoming cities. One of the tour assistants, she said, would freeze them all to keep them fresh then unfreeze them bag by bag as they arrived at each tour stop. Next was Riga, in Latvia, followed by Helsinki and a handful of other comparatively smaller countries and arenas, all of which they'd be driving to. After that, Tokyo, Shanghai, and the final show in Sydney.

"Where's Parish?" Remy asked as he boarded the bus with the other musicians.

"Walter pulled him out of the hotel lobby this morning," David said, looking wary.

"Walter? Like, Walter himself? Not his assistant?" Remy asked.

David was mid-nod when the question was better answered by Parish himself. He shoved onto the bus with the threatening weight of a thunderhead. His features were lines—eyes, mouth, brows, even his flared nostrils and locked hands.

"Dude," David said.

"Some motherfucker told Walter about us going out last night, and even though doing *legal* motherfucking drugs isn't mentioned anywhere in the contract, apparently I've violated some clause and reflected poorly on the princess of pop and am fucking fired," Parish said, voice hissing, fingers shaking. He stomped past them and wrecked his bunk, grabbing bags and papers and a handful of clothes he'd apparently made up in the blankets.

"Wait, are you serious? You're fired?" David said.

"Why the fuck would I joke about that?" Parish asked without looking at him.

"What about Laurel? Did she get caught too?" Remy asked. "What about me and Michael?" How would he explain this to Vivi? Did she even know Parish was fired, or was this beneath her pay grade? And it wasn't as if Vivi could save his, Remy's, job, and not Parish's—it would arouse too much suspicion. But then, Remy hadn't really done anything wrong—

"I don't know. I don't think so. Maybe," Parish said. "I'm guessing one of the Vivi superfan freaks got a photo or something. They wouldn't even tell me who turned me in—they said they weren't required to reveal the source. I can't believe this shit. This is why I shouldn't tour with women. The stuff Nick Maddon did on his tour would make Vivi's little virginal heart break."

"Can you fight it? Is there anything—" Remy began but stopped when Parish glowered.

"Independent contractors. That's all we are in the end. Fuck this whole fucking industry, man. I wanted to be a musician, not a prop," Parish said. He lifted his hand; David and Michael shook it vigorously, pulling him in for quick bro-hugs. When Parish got to Remy, he gave him a serious, intense look. "Get yourself a contract, man, if you're going to keep working with her. She did this to me *with* a contract, all because some vague 'morality' clause means she can. You get everything in writing, or don't produce another note for her."

"Right. Yeah, right," Remy said, nodding, licking his lips nervously. Parish shook his hand then shouldered down the steps and toward a waiting cab.

"That's bullshit, right there. He parties, but he's here on time. He does the job. Damn," David said with a big breath.

"I can't see how she could justify firing the two of us," Michael said, glancing Remy's way. "I had an eye out for photos last night too and didn't see anyone give us a second look."

"How'd they get a photo of just Parish and not Laurel, though?" David asked. "It's gotta be a report, not a photo. Someone turned you guys in—*the fucking spy turned you guys in!* Who saw you come back into the hotel last night?"

"No one from the tour, I don't think. Just the staff at the desk," Remy said. His stomach was beginning to turn faster, faster, a ball rolling down a hill.

"I doubt a guy tripping on mushrooms would be anything worth commenting on to the staff at an Amsterdam hotel," Michael said. "And the dancers are in the other hotel, so it's not like anyone in touch with Walter could've, like…spied through a peephole or something."

"Police state. Jesus Christ," David said. "Think you can do a little digging, Remy, next time you do a producing session? Because I want to know who ratted Parish out, and then I want to make sure every contact I have in the industry hears about what a jackass that person is."

Michael nodded. "Yeah, do that. And, kid? Parish is right. Get a fucking contract with her *now*. And make sure it's void of a morality clause."

Remy went to his bunk as soon as the bus started off and texted Celeste so quickly, he dropped his phone twice.

Remy Young: Weird question: are there any photos of Vivi's band circulating from last night?

Celeste Yi: I can check, why?

Remy Young: Parish got fired last night and trying to figure out how he got caught

Celeste Yi: Nothing that I see but it's possible Vivi's people stopped the release. I'd ask her

Celeste Yi: can I write about it

Remy Young: I don't see why not

Telling Celeste she could write about Parish being fired was a cruel sort of freedom—a door slam, a retaliation, bitterness in action. Because, yes, perhaps Vivi's people stopped photos. But Remy was nearly certain it had nothing to do with photos, or dancers, or hotel concierges. *He'd* told Vivi that Parish was high. He'd mentioned Parish but not Laurel.

He was the spy after all.

***

"We need to talk," Remy said during move-in for the Arena Riga—a bright-blue glass building that, if the banners hanging from the ceiling were accurate, was used primarily for European hockey games (something Remy didn't even know existed).

"Is everything okay?" Vivi asked, sitting up straight on the couch in her dressing room. Vivi's dressing room looked the same as it always did. White couch. Craft table with health food. Navy-blue mugs and cream-colored fabric draping the walls.

Remy shook his head, leaned against the door he'd just closed. He'd been watching the dressing room with near-stalker-brand attention, waiting for the stylists and assistants and glam squad members to clear out for the alone time Vivi took before the show. If he hadn't been so angry over Parish, he might have smiled at having the right to punch in the door code and let himself in despite the sanctity of that alone time.

"Parish got fired."

"I know," Vivi said, frowning, as if she couldn't understand why Remy was bringing this up.

"Is it because of me?"

"No, it's because he broke his contract and got high in Amsterdam," Vivi said.

"And did you know about that because I told you?"

Vivi's lips parted in a sort of realization. "Remy, it wasn't really like that. You weren't tattling on him."

Remy exhaled, found he didn't know where to put his hands or eyes or thoughts. "So it was me."

"I couldn't pretend not to know once you'd told me! You said he was crazy high. There's a morality clause—"

"Vivi," Remy groaned and grabbed the back of his neck.

"He got a warning early in the tour when he got super drunk. This was his second chance. I can't just let people do stuff like that, not when they're performing with me. It looks like I condone it." Vivi rose, holding her palms out, a pained expression on her face. Not apologetic, not guilty, but rather like a teacher explaining something to a small child. It spiked Remy's adrenaline; he forced his hands down to his sides.

"I'm not saying you weren't justified in firing him. I'm saying you used information I gave you to do it."

"Well…I mean…like I said, I can't just unknow something once I've been told," she said.

"That was information I gave you not as your employee, but as your…" Remy closed his eyes for a beat. *Boyfriend? No.* She had a boyfriend.

"Oh," Vivi said, voice low.

Remy dropped onto the ridiculous Muppet-fuzz chair. Vivi walked over and sat on the floor near his feet, smoothing her skirt out. Remy felt both a pull to take her hand and a pull to rise and walk away from her at the same instant. He resisted both, instead saying, "You can't have it both ways, Vivi."

"What?" Vivi asked, voice crushed.

"If you want me to be with you, if you want me to be able to talk to you and keep your secrets and for us to be *together*, then I can't be your employee whenever it's useful for you."

Vivi looked like he was speaking a different language, one she could only barely comprehend. "Do you want me to hire him back?" Vivi asked when neither had spoken for a few long moments.

"I'm not sure how you could without someone suspecting something's up. But that's not the issue right now: I need to know you can keep my secrets as well as I can keep yours. You baited me with that other tattoo story to see if it leaked, right? And you'd have ended things if it had. Well, I unintentionally baited you with Parish. And it leaked."

Vivi nodded and, for the first time in the conversation, looked guilty. It was some small consolation to Remy and gave him a haunting feeling of hope, one that bounced around his chest and knocked against his heart.

"I'm sorry," Vivi said in a small voice. She reached a hand up to him, and Remy took it, kissing her knuckles lightly, forcing forgiveness into the action.

"Okay," he said, breathing against the back of her hand.

"Really?"

"No. But it will be," he said. She climbed to sit on the arm of the chair, and slowly, slowly, slowly, the rigidity between them began to break to pieces. It didn't vanish entirely; bits and pieces still prodded at Remy's corners, but he reached over to pull Vivi into his lap. When she tilted her head back, he lowered his lips toward hers and kissed her, kissed her, kissed her, until he forgot she was Vivi Swan and remembered only that now, in this moment, she was his.

Vivi Swan Guitarist Leaves Tour
With only a few stops left, Parish Wilcox is out and on to greener pastures

Yep, there *are* pastures even greener than the Vivi Swan Sweethearts tour. The "Better Than" singer allowed her second guitarist (slash banjoist, slash fiddler) to leave her tour in the eleventh hour to pursue a recording opportunity with her label, Blue Robot.

"Vivi knew he'd been hoping to record his own music for a while now, so she hooked him up with some guys at Blue Robot. They wanted him in *now*, but she didn't want to get between him and his dreams, so she allowed him to leave before the contract was up," a tour insider says.

Wilcox will supposedly be recording a few rock-inspired jazz tunes for the label, with a planned release late this year.

Comments: 261

Author: Bianca Treble

Chapter Twenty-Seven

Finland, a country of vowels and gold-and-turquoise-capped buildings. Remy had expected far more snow on the ground and was almost disappointed to see just a scattering of the stuff across the streets. The lingering Floridian in him longed to see big mounds of snow, kids making snowmen, reindeer nosing through holly bushes, polar bears, and ice-skating.

"Have you been here before?" he asked Vivi, looking out her hotel window. They were mending their argument slowly, carefully, each word a stitch pulling tight between them. Working on "Maybe It's Me" was doubly helpful—like working on that song shored up the foundation songwriting had laid for them back on the bus out of Portland.

"A few times," Vivi said, lifting her guitar, warm compared to the cool Finland skyline, off her lap. She walked up beside him, arms folded, then tilted her head to lay it against his shoulder, sighing gently when he reached for one of her hands and wound his fingers with hers. "So I was thinking that maybe we could go to one of the saunas tonight? After the show?" she said.

Remy turned, almost causing her to fall off-balance. "A sauna?"

"It's like their thing, here. The press isn't bad at all, and it's a super private sauna. Is that okay?" Vivi asked, looking apologetic, like she was nervous. "We can just go for a walk if you'd rather, but it'll be cold—"

"Of course that's okay," Remy said. "That's fantastic. I mean, I have no idea what one does in a super private sauna, but still."

"I think you more or less sweat and pretend to be Scandinavian," Vivi said, smiling and taking his other hand in hers. "But I've heard it's fun, and I've never gone to one before. I've never had anyone to go with before. I'm excited."

"I am too," Remy said, and smiled at her, then leaned in to kiss between her eyes gently. She turned and went back to the guitar, strumming through the first chords of a song Remy didn't know.

"Is that something new?" he asked.

"Just something I'm playing around with," she said with a shrug before opening her notebook and making a few lines with her pencil. "Nothing serious."

"You're just trying to keep me from asking to hear it," Remy said in half play.

Vivi smiled at him. "Maybe it's about you."

"Maybe that's what I'm afraid of," Remy said, and this time, despite the smile on his face, he wasn't playing at all.

The Helsinki show was tiny, compared to the rest of the tour—a twelve-thousand-person arena, when they'd been playing ones four or five times that big. Vivi did the show as big and powerfully and confidently as she ever had; the band, jittery from cup after cup of Finnish coffee, played along to a recorded version of the second guitar parts that Parish used to play. Remy didn't realize how accustomed he'd become to looking at Parish during certain points in the show. Despite the fact Vivi had set him up nicely as penance, Remy still found he missed the guy, bro-factor and all. Parish's firing meant the rest of Bus Three was on high alert, eager to prove they were doing everything right, that nothing was wrong, that they were models of the Vivi Swan Morality Clause. It made it easier—much easier—for Remy to slip away after the show for his and Vivi's sauna date, because everyone more or less went straight to bed, hoping to get eight hours before the flight to Asia the following afternoon.

He knocked on Vivi's hotel room door; when she didn't answer, he knocked louder then louder still, until he finally lifted his phone to send her a curious text.

Remy Young: Are you in your room

Vivi Swan: already in the sauna. Come on. You're slow. Leave your phone.

Remy frowned, dropped his phone in his room, then went down to the lobby. He made his way through a series of doors, struggled to explain himself to a series of Finnish people with rocky English, and finally found himself at an enormous sapphire-blue door guarded by a small woman with ice-blond hair.

"Hi, I'm meeting a friend," he said.

"Miss Swan? Are you Mr. Young?" she asked. He nodded. "Excellent. She requested no additional services, but please let us know if you would be interested in seeing our menu."

Remy had no idea what this meant, but he accepted a white towel and fluffy bathrobe from the woman. He was let into a large locker room, which was immaculate and smelled like tea tree oil. Remy slid into the robe, tied it tightly, then opened the door to the sauna itself, a place of hissing and herbs and air so full of steam, it nearly felt like he was drowning.

"Vivi?" he called out. The sauna room wasn't big, perhaps the size of a large family room back in Florida—but it was layered with mist and steam, making it impossible to see much. He could, however, make out two large dipping pools, teak benches, and what looked like smooth slabs of rock.

"Finally," he heard her say. She sat up—just enough that the top of her head poked through the mist above one of the rock slabs.

"Finally?" he said, making his way to her. He sidestepped one of the pools and shuddered when he could feel just how icy the water was even from a few feet away.

"I'm being impatient, that's all," she said. "Also, apparently Finnish people do this every day. So they've clearly figured out the secret to life."

"Oh, yeah?" Remy said, approaching the slab. Vivi's hair was slicked across her head, and he was fairly certain her face was free of makeup—though her cheeks and lips were so bright, bright pink from the heat that it looked like they'd been stained by her cherry-red lipstick.

"Yep," she said and then sat up a bit farther, enough that Remy saw—not to his surprise, exactly, but to his pleasure—she was naked. Her skin was shimmering with moisture, and the angle she was at made her torso curve in not the most flattering but in the most *human* way he'd ever seen. He smiled.

"The idea is you take the robe off, you know," she said with a clever smile.

"See, if you'd waited for me, I'd already know that," Remy said, but he untied his robe and let it fall to the floor. She reached for his hand and pulled him toward the slab, which, now that he was next to it, he read on a placard was made of crystal, "for healing." She curled against the side of his body, letting one leg drape over his thigh, and he felt the tension in his eyes, his temples, his jaw, fall away. *Healing*, indeed.

"Okay," Vivi murmured, her lips so close to his ear that he could feel their movement. "So I did something today."

"What?"

"I should have done it a long while ago," she said, softer, lifting to one elbow. Remy couldn't help but notice something gentle but worried in her eyes. He frowned, but then she smiled slightly and said, "I broke up with Noel. This afternoon. Officially. I mean, you know it wasn't…it wasn't a real thing, but now…"

He looked up at her, studied the way beads of water were pooling on her brow and cheekbones, making her sparkle. "You broke up with Noel," he repeated and smiled.

Vivi laughed a little and dropped back beside him, pressing her bare body against his. "Yes. It isn't becoming tabloid official for a few weeks, but yes. I don't want any part of me to be with Noel instead of you. I just—I want to be with you. Only you."

Hurt, and fear, and worry crumbled; he felt pieces of them fall away, chunks dissolve into warmth in his chest, and he lowered his lips to her forehead and held them there, breathing against her.

"Say something," she said.

"I'm trying," he answered, mouth still pressed to her. He wrapped his arms around her and pulled her on top of him, the steam and her body making his skin almost uncomfortably hot—but he knew he wouldn't let go anyhow. He really was trying to say something, but he wasn't sure what, exactly, the appropriate response was. Relief? Excitement? Gratitude? Exhilaration?

Her leaving Noel wasn't a cure for all the doubt in his heart, but it was something. It was something good, and it was something that hadn't come without a cost for Vivi. He knew what would happen on the blogs—on Celeste's blog, no doubt. Vivi being touted as the heartbreak queen. Questions as to what unreasonable action of hers had sparked the breakup. Accusations, slurs, laughter, pointed fingers. Leaving men they didn't love hadn't been easy for the women of Lake City Assembly of God, and it wasn't any easier for Vivi Swan, no matter how different their lives, no matter how reasonable the leaving might be.

He kissed her and spoke against her lips the purest, simplest, perhaps the stupidest of the many thoughts sweeping through his head. "I love you."

She pulled back, sitting on him, legs on either side of his hips and her hands pressed lightly against his chest. "Are you sure?"

"I am."

She smiled then leaned back down to kiss him, sliding her body against his, bringing her lips to his ear. When she spoke, her voice was whispered—no, scared.

"I love you too," she said, and something in Remy's chest unlocked. He turned her mouth to his and kissed her, drinking in the moment, the feeling of being alone in the mist, exposed and vulnerable and absolutely flawless.

Then

"Here's the plan," the exec, whose first or last name was Miller, said to Val and Remy. The label's offices were sprawling, taking up two floors of an old warehouse that, according to the signs up by the front, used to be where thousands and thousands of guitars were made in the 1950s. They were cheap things, which was what made them great— they were the guitars all the greats had learned to play on, had saved up their allowances to buy and strum on porches during the South's heavy, heatstroke summer days.

Now, the walls were covered in gold and platinum records by artists so famous, they seemed impossible. There were remnants of the factory—conveyor belt wires and old switches—which had been polished bright bronze. The modern lighting fixtures were made to match, so it was almost impossible to tell the old from the new. Miller's desk was one of those ancient metal tankers, the same sort some of the church elders had, but rather than beaten and scratched, it was pristine. Even the Formica top had been replaced with sleek, smooth wood. It all spoke to a time that moved much slower than the speed at which this whole "record deal" thing was moving.

"First, we release 'Everything but the World.' We want our producers to take a look at it, maybe make some adjustments to make it more accessible. We've already done some soft releases to station heads. We're also thinking we'll get you guys on with our summer tour series. There're some groups you'll pair well with. Sound good?" Miller said. He never stopped smiling.

"Sounds fantastic," Val said, nodding. "What do we need to do?"

"You just need to be ready to come into the studio and do a cleaner recording—the one you have is great, I mean, it got my attention, but we can probably do one that's a little higher-end. We'll plan on you guys joining up with the first leg of the tour next week. We're out of bus space, though—do you have travel means?"

"We have a van," Val said, glancing at Remy.

"It's a pretty shitty van," Remy added. This was the first time he'd spoken at the meeting. He was somehow afraid that if he said the wrong thing, the whole deal would go wrong. Val seemed equally afraid, but his fear translated into a nervous, excitable energy. He was afraid it could go wrong, but he was more elated that it could go *right*.

"Okay, okay, we'll see if we can get you a splitter—think the van can make it to the first few stops? They're Charlotte, Raleigh, and Richmond. Monday, Tuesday, Wednesday of next week."

"Next week?" Remy asked, eyes widening.

"We have to move, Remy. The numbers are hot right now—this industry changes faster than you'd believe. So we'll get a splitter van to you in Richmond and go from there."

"What do we do with our van once it's in Richmond?" Val asked.

Miller grinned—no, wait, he still hadn't stopped smiling; he was just grinning *bigger*, like a Cheshire cat. "You can leave that piece of shit there, because Quiet Coyote is about to be a household name. Household names don't drive Chevy Luminas."

"How did you know it was a Lumina?" Remy asked.

"It's always a Lumina," Miller answered. "Okay, we've got your signatures on everything we need. We'll see you here tomorrow, to rerecord. I'm traveling, but you'll be in good hands. One of our house producers will be working with you—he's got forty-seven number ones to his name, and we're still sorting out who we should set up as your manager, but that'll happen soon enough. I'll swing by to see you two perform in Richmond, okay?"

"Okay," the brothers said in unison. They wove out of the guitar-factory-turned-label-office, past antique office doors and vintage microphones behind glass. The secretary at the front smiled at them politely and waved them out. Outside, the Nashville sun was blistering and bright, making the world seem white and concrete and entirely unlike the warm woods of the label office.

"Did that just happen?" Remy finally asked, looking at his brother. It was a real question, because suddenly, it all felt very much like a fever dream.

"That just happened. We're rerecording. We're going on a tour. We're fucking Quiet Coyote," Val said, shaking his head. He glowed brighter than one would've thought his eyeliner would allow. "This is happening, brother. People want to hear us. People who don't even *know* they want to hear us want to hear us. Even if nothing comes from this—even if we're back to being broke as fuck in a month—people will have heard us."

Now Remy grinned back. "Should we call Mom and Dad?"

"Don't be stupid, Remy," Val said, shoving his brother's shoulder, though not even the mention of their parents could bring him down at the moment. "We're living the story everyone wants to tell. They won't want to hear about it."

Chapter Twenty-Eight

Plans were made with Aspen, the publicist, on when to announce Vivi and Noel's breakup. Remy didn't know the details but watched Vivi pace her expansive Tokyo hotel room like she was planning an invasion rather than a press release. It involved stages—first, the news that she and Noel were broken up. Before his new album came out but not so close to the release that it looked like sabotage. Next, a few months later—*if things are going well*, Aspen kept saying before Vivi took her off speaker—the fact that she was seeing someone new coupled with a few fluff pieces. Aspen didn't firm up any plans after that, no grand reveal that Remy was the someone new, but he didn't fault her for that. She was a professional, like he used to be.

Given the option, Remy would have preferred to spend all his time in Tokyo with Vivi, but the rest of the band made it clear that if he didn't join them for karaoke, he'd never work in music again. They went to the closest karaoke bar and ordered too many drinks, then Ro and Laurel served as judges while the rest of the band tried and failed to sing pop songs from the nineties. Joshua, the guy who'd replaced Parish, put the rest of them to shame. Remy was a serviceable singer but was better at harmonies than solos. The night dissolved after Ro and Laurel did a few power ballads; everyone bowed down then shambled back to their hotel rooms.

He could have texted Vivi, he suspected—he'd learned she was a light sleeper when it came to the sound of her phone chime. He owed Val a call, though, so he pushed the curtains open and collapsed onto the bed then tapped his brother's name. It rang once, twice, then—

"Hello? Hello? Dude, the connection is shit. Where are you?"

"Tokyo," Remy said, turning to look out the window. His hotel room still had a decent enough view of the Tokyo skyline, and though it was nothing compared to Vivi's penthouse, it felt somehow cheerful and sleek. Being alone in a hotel room was a heady sort of feeling, though. It'd been a few countries since he actually spent time in his own room rather than hers.

"Tokyo's connection is shit," Val said. Remy adjusted the phone—it likely wasn't Tokyo's fault, but rather the fact he was lying on his hotel room bed, the phone propped up on his chest. It was a position way too pathetic to explain to Val.

"What time is it there?" Remy asked.

"Nine o'clock in the morning."

"You're awake at nine o'clock?"

"Celeste made me," Val griped, though he didn't sound as exasperated about it as Remy might have expected. "What time is it in Tokyo?"

"Two in the morning. But I'm a day ahead of you. Or behind? I can't remember. But it's two o'clock," Remy said.

"Time traveler," Val said, and it sounded poetic despite the fact Remy was certain Val hadn't meant it to. "You're going to have jet lag for months when you get back."

"No kidding," Remy said, closing his eyes. They burned. He was exhausted, but he couldn't sleep—he'd crossed over tired and gone into that sort of mania that made him feel like he'd left a stove on or forgotten a gig, even though he'd done neither.

"So what's up?" Val asked through a yawn.

"Nothing much. Just checking in," Remy said. "How are things there?"

Val sighed, which on him sounded more like a groan. "Nothing to report."

"The song?"

Now Val went quiet, which on him sounded more like a sigh. "I'm done. Almost done. You know what I mean—I'm at that spot with it that I can see the song underneath the dust but can't get through it."

Remy nodded. He wanted to hear it but knew he shouldn't ask.

"What about there? How's the song? And the illicit affair with your boss?" Val asked with a snort.

Remy laughed, but even he could hear the way it sounded softer when Vivi was the topic of conversation. "It's good. It's very good. She broke up with Noel."

"With who?"

"She was still technically with this guy named Noel, but it was more of a fame thing. But they're done. She left him."

"Should I be pissed that she was technically cheating on you with him or him with you or whatever that is?" Val asked hesitantly.

"No. I knew. It was complicated. But they're done, now and…it's good." His voice was still doing that soft thing, but he couldn't stop it.

Val made a humming sound in his throat. He started a sentence twice, which was categorically unlike him and made Remy tense, until Val said, "Let me ask you something, though—and it's a real question. Not just hypothetical. What happens when the tour ends *now*?"

"Same thing as before, I guess. We'll figure it out—"

"Nah, man. That was the answer before, when it was new and you guys were like a summer camp couple—"

"You've never even been to summer camp—"

"Not the point," Val said, and Remy could picture him waving his hand to shut him up. "This is different. I can hear it. So what's the plan? You go with her? She comes to LA?"

"I don't know. I don't think she knows. Why do we have to know?" Remy said, wondering when, exactly, Val had become the type who wanted to know the plan while Remy was justifying spontaneity.

"You don't, man. You don't have to know anything. But look at her life—she's here, she's there, she's on the cover of a magazine schlepping lotion—"

"I know that. I know who she is. It doesn't bother—"

"Fuck, shut up and listen. I'm giving sage advice, and I don't think it's ever happened before," Val said, banging his hand on what sounded like the patio table. "I know you know who she is—that's what I'm saying. Make sure she knows you're on board. Make sure she knows you're all in. You're always on eggshells, brother, and this is the time not to be. She left her boyfriend for you, and even though it sounds like it was a stupid-ass relationship anyway, I know that means shit in famous people world."

Remy squinted at the Tokyo skyline. "Your sage advice is I should tell her that I'll go wherever she goes. Okay. I mean, I did just go to Europe with her, so—"

"That was a job. This one is personal."

"Well, yeah, but if I—"

"Me, fuckwad, I'm talking about me. I'm your boyfriend, in this scenario, which is a gold mine for a therapist somewhere, I'm sure. Listen: she left Neil or Noel or Nule for you. Does she know you'll leave me for her? Because, as it is, she had to fly to California and make out with you in a club office to get your attention."

Remy froze. Tokyo sparkled.

"She's not asking me to do that," Remy said slowly.

"She's not gonna," Val said, voice smooth. He took another drag off his cigarette; Remy could somehow smell the smoke through the phone. "But tell her you will."

"I…" Remy didn't know what he could say, what he should say. It was one thing to think about balancing Vivi and Val after the tour; it was another for Val himself to say he didn't need balancing.

"I'm okay, brother," Val said, voice lower. "So, if this is what you want, you've got to make it work."

"You act like I'm signing up for a space mission," Remy said, trying to brush off whatever this new sound was in Val's throat.

"Hell, it's Vivi Swan. For all you know, she'll do her next album on the moon as a marketing gimmick for NASA," Val said, and Remy laughed. Val coughed, took another drag. "Girl's made a career off breakup songs, brother. I'm just saying that if you're in, make sure she knows you've got no plans to be the next one."

Chapter Twenty-Nine

Of all the tour stops, Australia felt the most foreign to Remy. The birdcalls rising from the trees outside the hotel were different, the air smelled golden and cheerful, and everyone, from the shuttle driver to the hotel desk clerk, warned him to avoid "drop bears." He had to resort to Google to figure out if they were real or not (not) and what that golden scent was (a flower called the golden wattle).

Vivi Swan: Come to the opera house with me?

Remy Young: Now?

Vivi Swan: Yes, only have two hours before radio calls but Ive never been

Vivi Swan: Im bringing a guitar, Ive heard the acoustics are crazy

Remy Young: Sure, be there in a second

Vivi Swan: Go to the employee parking deck and security will meet you, the paps here are nuts

Whoever had told Vivi the Australian paparazzi were nuts wasn't wrong. They were pressed against the glass front of the hotel doors like a zombie horde when Remy exited the elevators. Camera shutters clicked a thousand times when he appeared, but he simply nodded politely, went to the front desk, then followed their directions to get to the employee parking deck as covertly as possible. Vivi was already in the back seat of a black-windowed car, writing quickly in her notebook, when he slid into the seat next to her.

"Hey," she said. She stashed the notebook away then looked up at him. Her eyes softened, and he smiled immediately.

"Hi," he answered and let his hand swing across the seats. They linked fingers for just a moment, too quick for the driver to see but too long for Remy not to feel the full effect of the lift in his heart. They hadn't seen each other since the morning after the Tokyo concert, and the few hours had hardly been enough time together.

"Ready, Miss Swan?" the driver asked in a thick Australian accent.

"Let's do it," she answered then grabbed at a blanket on the floor. She ducked into the floorboards and motioned for Remy to do the same.

"Seriously?"

"They're the worst here. They followed Figgy Blushing to the beach a year ago, yelling about her dead dog, trying to get her to cry for a picture," Vivi said, rolling her eyes. Remy ducked onto the floorboards with her and allowed her to pull the blanket over his head. The car eased forward, swirling to the left as it wound out of the parking deck. It launched Vivi against Remy, and he seized the opportunity, putting one arm around her and pulling her mouth to his.

"Look at us in middle school, kissing under a blanket." Vivi laughed against his lips.

"I didn't go to middle school. Making up for lost time," Remy answered, and she kissed him again. He could barely see her, but then the car broke out into the daylight, and she was illuminated in blue light from the blanket's color. It was hot and stuffy, and her hair was ruffled against the fabric, but he nuzzled her neck until she sighed the smallest bit—

"Why did I suggest going somewhere public?" she mumbled.

"Terrible decision," Remy answered then let his fingertips trace the small of her back, sliding under her shirt—until the driver took a surprise turn and they fell into a heap of elbows and knocked heads.

"Sorry, Miss Swan! Some hoon just cut me off," the driver shouted back then unleashed a stream of obscenities at whomever the hoon was.

"No problem!" Vivi yelled back as she and Remy untangled themselves.

When they were eventually released from their blanket prison then the car, they were led through a staff entrance to the opera house. Remy had always thought it was a single stage, almost arena-sized, though he didn't know why this was the case. It was actually a half dozen or so venues, according to the woman who met them at the door—the head of PR, she said by way of introducing herself.

"I wanted to see the concert hall and maybe play a little in it, if you don't mind," Vivi said pleasantly, lifting her guitar as proof of her intentions.

"Of course! We'd be honored," the woman said, leading them through a series of balconies and hallways. Groups were passing by underneath them on various tours, oblivious to Vivi's presence above. Outside, the white tiles of the opera house shined like opalescent fish scales.

The concert hall was warm-toned and beautiful, all curves and reds and teaks. The head of PR told them about the space and the designer, until Vivi expertly asked her for a few moments to play the guitar alone on the stage, promising she'd share a photo of the session and tag the opera house on social media in exchange for the favor.

"An opera house for a post," Remy said, smiling at Vivi as they made their way down the red-carpeted steps to the stage. With the head of PR gone, they let their hands clasp together; she spun in, and he bent his head to kiss the top of her head.

"Should I have tried to get them to bring in a drum set for you as a bonus?" Vivi said then nudged him with her elbow as she walked away. She set her guitar case down on the stage and retrieved the instrument, while Remy sat on the stage's edge.

"What do you want to play?" he asked as she tuned, standing before him.

"Our opus," she said, smiling at him. "We started the tour with 'Maybe It's Me,' so I want to end it like that. Just you and me and this song. But hey, I'll take requests if you want to hear one of my standards."

"No offense, Miss Swan, but I don't need to hear anything from your set again for the next year or so," Remy answered, and she nodded in complete agreement. She picked through the first part of "Maybe It's Me" a few times.

"We should write something else when we're done with the tour," Remy said, leaning back and looking up at the red-cloaked ceiling.

She kept playing but looked up at him. Her body curved around the guitar like she was protecting it, or perhaps it was the one shielding her. "Already over this song?"

"Not at all. I just want to do more. We're good together," he said.

Vivi's fingers trailed down the strings, and she looked at him, eyes sparkling and cheeks pink. "We are. I'm usually so ready for the tour to be over, but this time I just…" She rocked back a little then played the opening chords again.

"It's better with the drum intro, obviously," Remy said, and she rolled her eyes but kept smiling, never stopped smiling. "When it's over, Vivi—"

"Ugh, can we talk about something else? Please? It just depresses me." She shook her head and played a little faster, let her feet wander a little as she did.

"Hey," he said and waited; finally she lifted her eyes to his, and the music stopped. "I'm trying to tell you that when it's over, I'll go where you go. I'm in, Viv. Not just when we're stuck together on tour. I'm in even once we're done and are back to whatever regular life is."

Vivi swayed a little, like she was still playing the song in her head. "It's not regular, though."

"I know."

"I'm in Nashville—"

"I know," Remy said, more sternly this time.

Vivi shook her head, smiled. "Why are you telling me this?"

"Honestly? My brother told me to. Or, more specifically, that I should tell you I've got no intention of being a breakup song—since I don't," Remy said, shrugging with exaggerated nonchalance. "I don't know. Want me to call him, double-check the script?"

Vivi grinned. She swung the guitar over her shoulder, walked toward him, then extended a neon-yellow-manicured hand to help him up. Remy took it and stood, her head coming just to the tip of his nose, and looked into her eyes. He'd known her eyes were blue before, but suddenly they seemed even more so. Everything about her seemed even more so.

"Remy, are you telling me that your brother, the infamous Val Young, told you to keep hooking up with a...*pop star*?" Vivi whispered, faux serious.

"No," Remy whispered back, grimacing. "I'm telling you my brother threw me out, so I've *literally* got to go where you go or live on the streets of LA. I won't make it out there, Vivi."

She laughed, finally, and lifted her hands around his neck, letting him support her weight as she twirled her fingers against the nape of his neck. He slid his hands between her body and the guitar then kissed her forehead.

"I still don't want this part to be over, though," she said.

"Doesn't matter," Remy said. "The important parts aren't over."

Chapter Thirty

The article appeared two hours before the Sydney show, while Vivi was at radio interviews and Remy was taking a nap. He might have not found out about it until, say, thirty minutes to curtain—like most of the band did—had it not been for Walter's assistant pounding on his hotel room door at the two-hour mark.

"Remy! You're needed!" Walter's assistant whisper-shouted through the doorjamb. "Check your phone!"

Remy blinked himself awake, had that moment where he didn't know if it was eight o'clock in the evening or morning. He blearily rose and stumbled, sock-footed, to the door, trying to calm his hair with a swipe of his arm. He swung the door open to reveal Walter's assistant looking shiny from the film of sweat covering his face.

"What?" Remy asked. The look on Walter's assistant's face made him sure something insane had happened—he'd missed the van to the arena, or they'd dropped his drum set and needed him to work on a replacement, or the arena was actually constructed entirely of black mold so they'd be performing in a public park instead.

"There's a *crisis* happening, and you're not answering your phone, that's what," Walter's assistant said, looking particularly harried with Remy's existence. "Let's move."

Remy gathered his room key and phone then stumbled down the hall behind Walter's assistant, waking up with each step down the taupe-carpeted space, toward the enormous windows of the elevator lobby. Remy woke more fully on the walk, finally feeling with it by the time they reached the elevator.

"What's going on?" he asked, rubbing his eyes. The fact they weren't sprinting anywhere made Remy certain that the "crisis" wasn't as bad as the missed bus/drum set/black mold scenarios, as did the fact that Walter's assistant didn't seem to be holding any more clip-boards than usual.

"It's not my place to say," Walter's assistant said with a Schadenfreude-esque sort of frown.

"Can you…say if I need to bring my show bag?" Remy asked.

"I don't think you'll need it," Walter's assistant said. They stepped onto the elevator, and Walter's assistant inserted a key that allowed him to press the top button—the penthouse.

"Is Vivi okay?" Remy asked suddenly, his heart jumping. She was fine, she had to be—*We're not running, he's only got the three clipboards, she's fine*. He grabbed his phone from his pocket before Walter's assistant could answer—which he didn't, anyway—to see if she'd sent him anything.

He had eleven missed calls from Walter's assistant. One from Vivi. No texts, nothing from Val or Celeste.

"Oh," he said, relieved. It couldn't be that bad. Unless… "Is my brother okay?"

Walter's assistant answered that one. "I surely have no idea."

"So this isn't about Val?"

"Definitely not."

Then, surely, Remy thought as they reached the penthouse, it wasn't anything bad at all—a set list change, or a surprise opening act, new music to learn, something like that. The elevator doors opened into the penthouse breezeway; Walter's assistant walked toward the door to Vivi's room with trepidation that nearly made Remy want to laugh at him.

When the door swung open though, Remy swallowed the urge.

Vivi was sitting on the couch, legs neatly crossed. The concert director was at the kitchen table, as was a man Remy had never seen. A man he *had* seen, only in photos, was at the other end of the couch—Vivi's manager. A young woman, whose appearance— cat eyeliner, neat hair, cute clothes—screamed *publicist*, was on a computer screen—Aspen, Remy was sure. Finally, there was a cell phone on speaker sitting on the coffee table. Whomever was speaking through it stopped abruptly when Remy and Walter's assistant brushed into the room.

"Thanks, Eddie," the man at the table said. "Stay on your phone, please."

"No problem," Walter's assistant—Eddie—said. When he turned to go, Remy saw a look of disappointment in his eyes that he hadn't been allowed to stay.

"Remy, come on, have a seat," the man at the table said.

"Sure," Remy said, wishing he'd changed into a button-down. If he'd known it was this sort of crisis, he wouldn't have worn one of his old Quiet Coyote T-shirts. He tried to glance Vivi's way as he moved to take one of the straight-backed chairs on the far end of the coffee table. She stayed focused on her phone.

Which was how Remy knew without even seeing the article what the crisis was.

Another One Bites the Dust
Vivi Swan and Noel Reid are no more

Stars—they're just like us! Except when they break up, they do it in Helsinki, while in the middle of a massive world arena tour, over the phone. Despite insisting just a few weeks ago that the two were making vacation plans for the summer, Vivi Swan and Noel Reid called it quits a few hours after America's Sweetheart took the Finnish stage for her Sweethearts tour last week. It's unconfirmed, but rumor has it that Vivi's the one who called it off—and it might be because she's been getting awfully cozy with tour drummer and producer Remy Young. Call us crazy, but we always figured Noel would be the cheater, not Vivi—though this is certainly one way to shed that America's Sweetheart image.

Comments: 1147
Author: Bianca Treble

Chapter Thirty-One

"So it's happened. It's out there. We're talking damage control," Aspen said over the screen.

"Okay," Remy said, rubbing his now-sweaty palms against his jeans.

"I think we should move forward with pulling him from the show tonight," Vivi's manager said.

"That's stupid," Aspen responded immediately and without a shred of emotion. "First off, the fans who paid to come to the show aren't going to villainize her. Secondly, it's an admission of guilt. We don't need to add any fuel to this cheating fire."

"They're going to assume guilt no matter what—everyone is," Vivi said in a cool, professional voice. "But yeah, I don't want the headlines to be that I fired him or pulled him from the show because of a lover's quarrel or something."

"Right now, the headlines are going to be photos of the two of you onstage together," the large man at the table said.

"I know, Walter, but they've got plenty of us together in Spain and whatnot and a lot of him coming to the hotel in Cologne, so they have some pretty damning photos no matter what," Vivi said. "They just didn't have a headline to go with them before."

Holy shit, that's Walter, Remy thought and almost, *almost* smiled at this—the guy was far bigger and far more Italian than Remy had pictured. Walter's face, however, was pinched and angry, and when the man's eyes flicked over to Remy, it was clear smiling was not welcome at this meeting.

"What if you just pull the whole band from the show, then?" someone—Remy didn't even know who it was at this point—suggested.

"I can't do that—there's no time to get it all right, and we're filming the concert...no," Vivi said, shaking her head, pursing her bloodred lips.

"Alright, listen," Aspen said, holding up her hands, commanding the room through a nine-inch screen. "How about you go on as scheduled tonight, everything in place. Remy wears sunglasses so no one can get any shot of him looking at you that's particularly good. Vivi, just *don't look at him* throughout the show, okay? That'll fix that issue, at least. Let's move on to next moves."

"Has Noel released a statement?" Vivi asked.

"Not a statement, but he did just tweet the thumbs-up emoji," a young guy in a snappy suit said, scrolling through his phone frantically. "It might have been before the story released, though. People are interpreting it as passive-aggressive."

"He's not smart enough to be passive-aggressive." Vivi sighed.

"What about Tuesday Rivers? Here's an idea—can we get Tuesday out to Australia tomorrow?" Aspen asked. "She's not doing anything really, is she? Get her here, the two of you go out for a girls' day tomorrow. We don't address the issue with Noel for two weeks, minimum."

"Okay. When are we doing the perfume launch again?" Vivi asked.

"August—wait, no, Tuesday won't work. She just had another thing pop with Nick Maddon. It'll look like you're commiserating."

"What if we schedule something between now and the Billboards—just a commercial shoot or something? It doesn't need to be real, just something that shows me out and working," Vivi said wisely.

"I'll call Porch to let him know," Walter said. "And any new security concerns for tonight? Big Steve is asking."

Aspen said, "I think we should be fine. Two hours to curtain… let's all just be grateful Noel Reid isn't an Australian darling. Now, Vivi, monologues—do you want to say anything in them about all this? Nothing direct, of course, but maybe something small? I think no, but let's play with the idea—"

Remy stopped listening. No, that wasn't true—he was listening, but he stopped processing it. He looked down at his phone screen, at the article, reading through it over and over again. He counted—one hundred thirteen words, and they would change everything. If nothing else, he certainly wasn't moving to Nashville now.

"What are you doing?" Walter said brusquely. It took a beat of silence for Remy to realize the words were directed at him—that someone else had even realized he was in the room.

"Just rereading the article," Remy said as casually as possible.

"Don't say anything. Don't tweet anything, don't do anything. You've already violated the nondisclosure. Don't make this worse," the concert director said, not like a threat but rather like a warning. Like Remy was on a cliff, and it was the director sent to talk him out of jumping.

"I've never tweeted, period. I'm not doing anything," Remy said, offended, turning to Vivi and holding his arms up. "I didn't do this either, so no, I'm not violating the nondisclosure." He expected her to talk the crowd down, to remind them that he was a mere mortal in a room with fame robots and gods.

Instead, she gave him a stern look, heavy and intense and not at all like the girl who held her lashes close to his cheeks to feel them flash against his skin. "You said you talked to Val about us after the tour. That's the only leak we can find," Vivi said.

"Wait, are you serious? Vivi, Val has kept us a secret for *months*," Remy said, nearly rising with frustration—it was only her gaze, eyes blue and sharp, that kept him firmly in his seat.

"Then who? It's either him, or the opera house was bugged," Vivi said. Her voice hitched, went broken, and Remy's frustration morphed into concern, into fear. She was hurt, and she thought it was his doing, and no, no, no, it wasn't—

"Then the opera house was bugged—it's an *opera house*, you know they've got recording stuff there. It wasn't Val," he said through hard-gnashed teeth. "He wouldn't do this—I wouldn't do this, Viv."

Her shortened name hung like an ornament between them, something for the rest of the room to observe and gawk at. Remy was suddenly aware that everyone here knew about the two of them. How long had they known? No one seemed surprised, not even Walter. Remy felt himself shrinking, growing smaller and stupider under their eyes.

"Regardless, you need to stay with security and the tour all night tonight and tomorrow so we can get you prepped for answering questions," Aspen said through the pen she'd stuck in her mouth. "And I need your brother's number—"

"No," Remy said firmly. "He didn't do this, and he will absolutely lose his shit if you people start calling him and hassling him about it."

"They're trying to fix it, Remy," Vivi snapped. "Let them fix it."

"How can this be fixed? It's the truth. You can't undo it—let's just—what if we just admit it, Vivi. What if we go out and let them see—"

"Absolutely not," Aspen and everyone else in the room seemed to say at once.

"I was talking to Vivi," Remy said coolly, now staring only at her. He wanted to go to her, to take her hand, but everything about Vivi looked cold and icy, a girl carved instead of breathing. She looked the way he'd imagined her looking back before he met her. "Vivi, I'm sorry. I'm sorry this happened. But we're in this, so let's be in it. Come on."

Vivi looked at him, and for a moment, he thought she was going to nod. She took a breath, though, and put a hand to her head. "I need to think."

"Any chance the site will reveal their source?" Aspen asked. Remy wasn't sure who the question was directed at but then realized Aspen was talking to someone off camera in her own office. "Uh-huh. Okay—Vivi, do you want to do an interview with the site that first posted this in exchange for a six month right-of-approval on stories?"

"Yes, yes, absolutely," Vivi said, nodding through a sharp breath.

"Deal with the devil," Walter muttered, to which the others nodded in glum agreement.

"We actually have her information—let's move on this now, before anything else can get posted. Just a phone call, no video, okay? Can we get the room cleared, please, so Vivi can take this?"

"Yeah, yeah—where is Remy going?" Walter asked.

"He can go back to his hotel room, I guess," Vivi said with a dismissive hand as she sat up taller, primmed herself up a bit.

"Vivi, we need to talk about this," Remy said under his breath, knowing it was impossible for the others not to hear him—but being unable to care. He rose and took a few steps toward her before her gaze stopped him once again.

At this distance, though, Remy could see that what he'd thought was coldness in her eyes wasn't exactly coldness—it was shivering, and suffering, and trembling, and sadness. If she was cold, it wasn't coming from within; it was coming from him, from what she thought he'd done. He'd been asleep. He'd literally been asleep, he hadn't done this, she had to know—

"Please, Remy. Later," she said in a broken sort of whisper.

"Viv—"

"I have an interview to do right now," she said and turned to the phone on the table. It rang; Walter placed a heavy hand on Remy's shoulder, urging him gently toward the door. Other than that, the others from the room avoided him as they filed out and into the penthouse lobby. The door shut just as a secretary could be heard over Vivi's speakerphone, talking first to Aspen, then Vivi. The elevator chimed; Remy stepped on just in time to catch the caller's voice.

"Hello? Is this working?"

"Hi, this is Vivi Swan," Vivi said in a cheerful voice.

"Hi, Vivi! This is Bianca Treble from Outsourced. Great to speak with you."

Remy shut his eyes in time with the elevator doors and took a long, steadying breath. Bianca Treble—the woman who scooped the story about Remy and Vivi's song. The woman who knew about Remy getting the tour job before Remy himself knew he'd be offered the gig. The woman Vivi had said was very, very good at her job. Remy recognized her voice.

"Bianca Treble" was Celeste.

Then

Miller was right—household names did not drive Chevy Luminas. Household names, in fact, didn't drive anything; people drove them. Limo chauffeurs and pilots and car service guys from Uganda. The van was left in a friend-of-a-friend's yard in Richmond, along with all the amps, cords, and secondhand speakers Remy and Val had acquired over the years. They took their instruments—Val's guitar and Remy's drum set—even though neither were really as nice as they could afford now.

Now. Now that "Everything but the World" was killing it in the eighteen-to-twenty-four demographic and enjoying a tidy success on the demographics on either side of that one. They had a music video with a pretty redheaded girl playing the song's titular character, even though it'd actually been written about Val. They had a live concert series on a streaming video station. They had interviews at stations in every major radio region, and they even approved a cleaned-up version of the song to be used on some sort of kids-singing album.

The label was working on a "second song," a term whispered in the industry like a prayer or a curse. They couldn't simply release what they considered Quiet Coyote's second-best piece, nor could they just write something new themselves. Weekly, Remy and Val were sequestered in a room with people whose names they never bothered to learn, because it'd be different people the following week anyhow. They'd write one song, or five, hours broken up only when the runner returned with whatever ridiculous grocery list of supplies they'd sent for. A pack of Easy Mac, a bottle of Seagram's, a pint of ice cream, whatever goes into a Bloody Mary, sushi, and three ounces of weed.

Val wrote like he'd cracked open his soul, like he always did, only now he dug in deeper than ever before, hungry to show the label what he could do. Song after song poured from him; Remy would polish it up, careful to make it sound like his changes were actually someone else's idea—like the paid songwriters who filled those rooms with them, or the executives, or the more experienced producers who tended to make everything sound the exact same, no matter the artist. The room would celebrate, finish off the weed, send the song to the label.

The label was never "feeling it." Or they just didn't think it was "the one." Or it just didn't "have it." Or, on one occasion, they felt like "this is *it*, but just isn't really *it*, you know?"

"I don't get why the fuck they signed us if they're not at all interested in hearing us in our music," Val said one night, after they finished playing a local radio show. They were on their way back to a hotel, where they'd overorder room service as the most pathetic form of revenge they could access.

Remy shrugged. "I don't know. Once we find a second song though, we'll probably be able to do more of our own stuff, since they'll believe we can do it."

"Yeah," Val said, but it wasn't clear if he believed Remy. It wasn't even clear if he'd heard Remy, not really, as he was in the last throes of the day's high which, combined with Val's tendency to slide in and out of attention, meant he was more often zoned out than zoned in. "What was that thing we were working on today even about?" he asked after a few long minutes spent staring out the limo window.

"When we started, or when we finished?" Remy asked. Val made a face, so Remy went on, "I think they were still trying to make it about falling in love with a girl's ass when we left. They were into it."

"Waste of a fucking day."

"It'll be a good song for someone."

"Someone else. Can't believe I gave them that opening set for it. Were they still using that?" Val asked.

"I think so. I made the hook decent too. Or it was, before they put the word *assets* in it like fifty times."

"Fuck all this, man," Val said, exhaling. "I knew it'd be hard work, but I didn't think it'd be like this. I figured hard work would mean something, not that we'd bust our asses—"

"You mean *assets*," Remy joked, but Val breezed on without pausing.

"—to write every other artist at the label a decent song."

They'd written sixteen songs that the label liked, and every one had been handed off to another artist. Remy and Val were paid for the work, but it was beginning to grate on Val, watching something he once loved get chewed and mashed and bastardized before seeing it handed off to a sleeker, more polished star.

It was beginning to appeal to Remy. Which he would never say, of course, but there was something freeing about helping to poke and prod at a song then walk away. When songwriting with just Val, Remy was always aware of his limitations—how unpoetic and boring he felt by comparison. But when he was just coloring in someone else's lines? He could do that. He could do that, and cash the check, and use the money to prove to himself and Val that there was no need to worry about going back to Florida. They could do this, they could make it, and Remy was enough just the unpoetic and boring way he was.

"They're going to drop us," Val muttered under his breath as they arrived at the hotel. "We either keep writing for them, or they're going to drop us."

"That's not true," Remy said.

Which was the first time he really, truly lied to his brother. He couldn't tell his brother what he knew to be true: that they'd given the music industry their whole hearts, and now they had no choice but to stay in the relationship, for their own safety. You couldn't just walk away from someone who held your heart, after all, no matter how dangerous they were.

"Yeah. Maybe you're right," Val said, nodding. Trying.

Failing, but trying.

Chapter Thirty-Two

Motherfucker. It was Celeste.

Remy's stomach went fishbowl, his mouth tacky. The others shuffled aside when they arrived at his floor; he nodded faintly when Walter's assistant said, "See you at the van in thirty." He had thirty minutes before the show, and Celeste was the source, and if Celeste was the source, then it meant that Remy *was* the leak after all. He'd told Val about Nashville. Val must have told Celeste, and now...

A string of whispered curse words rushed from his mouth as he hurried into his bedroom and dialed Celeste's number. She didn't answer, and he badly wanted to leave a tirading voicemail but worried he'd accidentally leak something else, given that he was apparently a sieve. He called Val, but his brother didn't answer either. Of course—it was ten p.m. there; he was probably in the middle of a show.

"Val, call me. We need to talk about—we just need to talk," Remy snarled into the phone before dropping it down on the bed. This was insane—it was an accident. Vivi had to know it was an accident— that made a difference, didn't it? Even if it didn't make a difference to the Vivi Swan Machine, Vivi the girl had to know he hadn't meant to leak this.

Of course, confirming that it was him by way of Val by way of Celeste meant telling her what Celeste did for a living. The plausible deniability so carefully built into her anonymity wasn't so plausible now that it was a factor in a relationship, not a contract. *I should have told her about Celeste ages ago. I should have said something. I should have warned her. I shouldn't have—*

Well, if he was being entirely honest with himself, he shouldn't have gotten involved with a girl with a boyfriend, much less a girl with a boyfriend and six platinum albums who was his boss.

There was nothing to do, no one to yell at or call, so he paced his hotel room until it came time for him to meet the rest of the band to drive over to the arena. They'd heard about the story by now and were quiet and snickery around Remy. David, at least, had the decency to clap him on the back in a "we're not laughing *at* you—not exactly" sort of way. Laurel and Ro looked absolutely giddy with the shock, though even they didn't break the tension that festered throughout the van for the drive.

He isolated himself in the green room after changing into his show clothes, staring at his phone, trying to calm his stomach with crackers from the spread and failing. Even the roadies buzzing around him when he made his way onto the lift treated him like a leper, especially the one who hurried over with a pair of vintage sunglasses that still had the price tag on them from the thrift store.

"Here you go. Someone said you needed these," the young woman said with a shrug.

"Right. Thanks," Remy said blandly, plucking them from her fingers. He turned them over a few times in his hands then slid them over his eyes. They weren't particularly dark, but the backstage area wasn't particularly bright either, so they spun him into near blackness. He turned his stool to face the drum set and adjusted the monitors' brightness so he could still see them through the shades.

"Remy, standby," the roadie to the left called, and Remy nodded curtly. As his platform began to ascend, he instinctively looked to his right. He looked to Vivi.

She'd slid into her spot with little fanfare, and in the sunglasses-induced darkness, he couldn't see the roadies surrounding her, readying her on the lift. He could, however, still see her—easily. She glowed, sparkles and light and glitter in the darkness, from her hair to her shoes to the brilliant white dress she was wearing. The roadies and camera crew filming this show stepped back, and Vivi's cheek turned—

And she looked at him. For a millisecond, a glimpse of a moment he'd have missed had he blinked. But her eyes found his through the darkness and sunglasses and tension and air and world—

Then the look was gone, because Remy's lift had ascended too far. Vivi's gaze was sliced away by the stage, then the lights, then the cameras, the crowd of seventy-five thousand people.

When they were young and living at home, Val was the one who always turned the music up too loud. He was the one their parents scolded for destroying his hearing, he was the one that discovered the bass setting. He blasted choir music, then gospel, then classics when their parents were home, and music as offensive as possible when they weren't.

"You can't even hear it that way," Remy had griped once.

"I can't hear anything else this way," Val had answered—well, shouted, since he'd turned up Black Sabbath until the old speaker hissed and crackled angrily on the beat.

It'd taken years for Remy to understand exactly what Val meant, because it'd taken years for Remy to badly need to drown out the world. But when Val started using, Remy began listening to music loud, louder, loudest, until his ears rang.

Now, in the arena, Remy was grateful for the crowd's roar, for the drum set, for the millions in amps and speakers, for the way the sunglasses lifted his ear protection just enough so the chaos of it all flooded his eardrums and silenced his thoughts. He played as hard as he ever had, his eyes flashing between the monitors and David and Michael, keeping the beat, keeping the show on tempo as flawlessly as he always had.

The lights flared as the first half of the show ended, startling him back to a world without music to drown out all that had happened. Vivi's platform descended first, as per usual; by the time Remy's was back below the stage, she was gone, whisked away to her dressing room. He hooked the sunglasses around the cymbal stand and, hands slung in pockets, made his way back to the band's room. His hands hurt—he couldn't believe he'd played hard enough to make *his* hands hurt, given how long he'd been doing this. They vibrated and burned against his jeans.

"One more half and we're all free!" David said when Remy shoved into the dressing room.

"Huh? Yeah. Yep. Nine more songs," Remy said absently.

"You okay?" David asked.

"Yeah."

"Man, I'm asking. Are you okay?"

Remy paused then nodded again.

"It'll be over soon, kid," Michael said. "Go home, get away from all this bullshit."

"Yeah," Remy said. Then he looked up.

It'd be over soon. Nine songs, and everything was going to

change—that'd have been true regardless of the story about them leaking. This was the last, last, last bit of the tour, the final countdown, and his life was going to become something entirely different.

It'd be over soon, so he might as well.

He inhaled, sharp and deep, then turned and pushed through the dressing room door. He cut past the dancers in the hall, the camera crews interviewing them, the roadies and crew and security guards. Vivi's dressing room was ahead, the keypad lock on the door a give-away as to who was inside. He walked up to it without hesitation and punched in the code. The lock turned, and he stepped inside.

Vivi gasped—he didn't see it, but he heard it as the door swung open and he stepped inside. She was on the couch, eyes closed, wear-ing a silky white robe. He'd rarely visited her during intermissions and thus had no idea how long he had to say whatever it was he'd come here to say—when did she get dressed for act two? When did hair and makeup descend? When did—

"Remy, what the hell are you doing? Did anyone see you come in here? Did the film crews get it?" Vivi asked, panic in her eyes.

"No. I don't think they—Vivi, we've got to talk about this."

"We can, after the show—" she began. Her words shook.

"Please. Please, talk to me about this now, before it's all over," Remy said, voice hard and firm.

Vivi's lip quivered, her eyes went watery. She pulled her knees to her chest and shook her head. "I don't know what to say, Remy. I thought you understood, is the thing. I thought you understood that with me, there's no room for an accident. From the day we started… being together…from that day, you knew how much I wanted to get rid of this heartbreaker reputation. Now I'm in deeper than ever before."

"I know. I get that. We wrote a whole song about it," Remy said and managed a half laugh that was a particularly sad attempt at humor.

"We did—and I can't release 'Maybe It's Me' now, because everyone's going to say, 'Yeah, it is, because you're a cheater,'" she said, throwing her hands in the air. "It's all ruined."

"It will die down, Vivi."

"It will die down, but Remy, it'll get stirred right back up again. This story is going to be linked, and filed away, and on websites for the rest of my life. When Noel dates someone new, I'll get brought up. When he releases new songs, people will wonder if they're about me. When I release new songs, they're going to assume they're about him. When *you* leave the house, people are going to ask you about me. Everything we are now is dirty and wrong and scandalous, forever." There was still hurt in her voice, yes, but suddenly it'd gone combative and blaming, and Remy felt a shift somewhere in his abdomen.

"I know," Remy said, pressing his lips together. "I know. I understand. But it's done. Your career is not over because you broke up with Noel Reid and got with me. You've had relationships end before."

"Not like this. Not where everyone can point and say I was cheating. *And* I'm your boss, which is going to make it look even worse. I just...I trusted you when you trusted Val, and that was stupid of me. I should have said you couldn't tell him—"

"He literally saw us kissing, Vivi. I think he would've figured it out."

"Then I should have made him sign a nondisclosure. I'd have doubled whatever they paid him for the story to keep it quiet."

Remy ran his tongue along the inside of his cheek then gave in—she had to know. He had to be the one to tell her. "He didn't sell the story."

"Remy, I know you want to think your brother wouldn't do this, but come on. Bianca Treble just *happened* to be hanging out with your brother, and he just *happened* to mention—"

"It's Celeste," Remy said, closing his eyes. "Bianca Treble is Celeste." Silence, silence, until finally Remy dared to look.

Vivi looked like she'd been slapped. Her mouth was open, her eyes darting around the room like she might find the words she needed scrawled across a chair or on the top of the curtain rods.

"Your sister-in-law is Bianca Treble, and you didn't tell me?" she finally said. Her voice was fragile like a bomb.

Remy's heart was pounding loud as any song. "I didn't know. I knew she had websites, but she's always kept them a secret from us. She keeps that world separate so her sources—"

"Sources like you," Vivi said breathlessly. Her makeup was running, her tears too much for even the waterproof stage stuff to handle. Her lipstick was smudged, and her robe was slightly open, and had it been any other moment, any other place, any other time, he'd have thought about how beautiful she was.

"I guess," Remy finally answered, defeated. "Sources like me."

Vivi nodded, and when she spoke, her voice was hard. "Maybe this whole thing was a mistake. Maybe it was too much to ask of either of us."

Remy jolted backward a little on her stupid peach stool. The word twisted in his gut, first painful, then infuriating in a way he'd never felt. "I'm sorry—a *mistake*?"

"I just—this is why people like me don't date people outside the industry. Outside my...part of the industry. It never ends well." She wiped her eyes with her hand, and her fingers drew away smudged black and cream. She wouldn't look at him, and he couldn't stop looking at her.

Remy swallowed hard. "We're breaking up, aren't we? During intermission of the last show. We're breaking up."

"Look, I need to start getting changed and get this fixed," she said, looking up and waving a hand over her face. "Let's just talk later, okay? Please, we can just figure it out—"

"No."

"Remy—"

"No," Remy said, shaking his head. "If it's a mistake, like you said, then we should let it be done."

"Can we just—"

"You already know it's coming, Vivi. Like you said: Dating regular people like me never ends well. We're a mistake. We're too complicated." He took a breath, put his hands to his head and tried to press the headache from his temples. "I was a breakup song waiting to happen, and the worst thing is, I knew it. I think I knew it all along, but I wanted to stay anyway, I wanted to believe the love letter bullshit. What the hell is wrong with me?"

He stood up, and for a moment, it looked like Vivi might stop him. She didn't, so he turned around and walked toward the door. He heard her inhale right when his hand hit the knob, and he froze—

In an instant, he decided to give her five seconds. Five seconds to say something, to stop him, to talk to him, to do something other than let him leave. He counted.

Five.

Four.

Three—she made a noise in her throat, a gentle one that sounded like a cry, but said nothing.

Two.

One.

He left.

Then

Val became a walking conflict of interests.

He'd used drugs ever since they left Florida—various things, more out of experimentation and the desire to finally, finally do something wildly unsafe. It never concerned Remy in a significant way; it was never a habit, but rather, a hobby, and besides, Remy was fairly certain that trying to order Val around would only result in Val taking the opposite action. Tell him to write a ballad, he wrote a rock anthem. Tell him to sit quietly and pray, he ran away from home with a guitar. Tell him to feel bad, he felt proud.

So the drugs were just another thing Remy shook his head at, hoping Val would grow bored of them sooner rather than later. But then, almost unexpectedly, they became part of Val. When he wrote, he used them. When he played, he used them. They became a highway directly into his creativity, the only way he could push pass the frustration of writing song after song for other people— with a little cocaine in his body, he could find the inspiration without having to muddle through the anger and disappointment of it all.

And there was the conflict of interests—because Remy saw Val light up again when he wrote a new song, even if that light was fueled by schedule-one narcotics. Seeing him look excited, look happy, glow from the beauty of creating music after watching that light be slowly stamped out by executives and contracts and managers was wonderful. But seeing his brother's face grow even more gaunt, seeing the marks on his arm go from indistinguishable to bright red, seeing his hair become brittle…

"I'm just worried you're going to forget how to write stuff without help," Remy said. *Help* was what Val called the substances. He needed a little "help" today. He could go get some "help" to finish the song the label was interested in for a new pop diva. Was there anything in the house to "help" out at the show tonight?

"You don't just forget how to create music," Val said, rolling his eyes and taking a long drag from a bong. He held the breath for a moment then let out the cloud of bright-white smoke.

"Yeah, but this is becoming expensive, and you're an even bigger pain in the ass to work with when you're on something," Remy said, trying to keep the conversation light. "I'm just saying, maybe it can be like a Monday-Wednesday-Friday thing."

Val set the bong down and looked at Remy hard—or rather, as hard as he could with his mind significantly dampened. "Too bad I don't just sell out on Mondays, Wednesdays, and Fridays, huh?"

Which was true—the label wanted them in more and more often for songwriting sessions, for producing sessions, for "consultations" that were really just producing sessions the label wasn't contractually obligated to pay them for. One day, almost a year after they arrived in LA, and six months since "Everything but the World" dropped off the charts, Miller called Remy and asked him to come to the label offices. Alone.

"We're just not seeing the progression we want in order to keep Quiet Coyote on as an artist," Miller said bluntly, with the sort of cool detachment that let Remy know he'd said this sort of thing a thousand times to a thousand different industry hopefuls.

Remy's lips parted; he frowned. "But you literally emailed us yesterday and said you felt like we were on the verge of something."

"Yeah, yeah. And I did, but now that I've slept on it, I just don't think that's the case."

"So, like…we just stop? What happens to our songs? The second album? We've been writing it for months."

"We never really found the mix of music we wanted to use on it, though, so we won't be releasing it."

Remy felt shot, the force of all this pushing him into the back of the expensive leather chair he was sitting in. Miller had his hands steepled, his elbows spread wide; between this and the massive executive desk, he looked a dozen times bigger and more formidable than his body really was.

"Val should be here for this. Quiet Coyote is his band before it's mine," Remy said.

"Well, yes, but I actually needed to talk to you alone about an additional business proposition."

Remy's eyes widened, and the *What?* he intended to say was lost somewhere in his throat.

Miller went on, "You've got real producing chops, Remy. We'd like to keep you here so you can continue helping our artists. You're able to understand what people are trying to say and just capture it so perfectly. It's a gift."

"The last song I produced for was about sending nude selfies," Remy said, stunned.

Miller shrugged. "And you made it sound sexy instead of sleazy. You make the love songs more romantic and the party anthems more epic. You magnify the songs, and we need that. We need you. We can get you on contract and really let you loose with some of our new talent."

Miller already had the contracts drawn up, of course. He pulled them from a folder like a wizard tugging a rabbit from a hat then rose and walked around the desk. He took the seat beside Remy and placed the contracts on Remy's lap, tapping them twice with a pen before depositing that as well.

"Let's do it, kid. You've got talent. We've got means. We can make this happen," Miller said.

Remy looked down at the papers but didn't touch them, like they might bite. "I need to talk to Val about this first."

"Why?"

"He's my brother."

"But this is about your career. It involves him, sure, in the way that everything involves family one way or another, but you don't need his permission."

"Before I sign with the label that literally just dropped us on our asses?" Remy said, a flare of anger peeking out from the professionalism he usually exuded.

Miller looked a little surprised but then nodded, sat back. "I get it. It sucks. Dropping artists is never fun, for what it's worth. It's not something I enjoy. But you can still play in Quiet Coyote. We're not taking anything from you and Val—you'll still have your music and your band and your brother. We're just trying to give *you* something extra. A chance to help people tell their stories."

"About nude selfies."

"About everything," Miller corrected.

"I need to talk to Val," Remy said more firmly. He rose, clutching the contracts so tightly, they bent in his grip.

"Okay," Miller said. "But keep in mind, our figures are *very* current. We can't guarantee that offer will stay on the table for long."

"Of course," Remy said and reached forward to shake Miller's hand. When he did, Miller smiled, and Remy couldn't help but notice it was a carbon copy of the smile he'd given Remy and Val ages ago, when they'd eagerly scribbled their names on the Quiet Coyote contracts. Before they'd given away their hearts.

No, not *their* hearts. Val had given his heart, and Remy had kept his guarded the entire time. He'd held back. He'd encouraged Val to push on. And now, Val was a broken thing, and it was Remy's fault.

When Remy returned to the apartment that evening, it smelled of malt liquor and smoke. Val was on the tiny balcony, surrounded by bits of tinfoil and red Solo cups. He was grinning.

"Finally! The fuck have you been?" Val asked excitedly. Before Remy could stumble onto an answer, he went on, "Remy, man, I've got it."

"What?"

"A second song. No way the label won't want this shit. It just hit me while I was in the shower, and it was like, I had to run out here and start immediately before I lost it."

"That explains why you're wearing a towel," Remy noted.

"I wasn't, but then the lady in 4B complained," Val said darkly. "Anyway, listen."

Val played through a song, loud, angry, as powerful as he'd play it if he were at an arena concert. There was a howling chorus, a chant, a B-section that paused in all the right places. Remy's mind immediately began clicking, whirring, working, thinking of the ways he could improve it, of the ways he could make an already great song greater by highlighting the theme of it: Creation. Singing loudly, writing loudly, living loudly in the faces of those who want to stop you.

It wasn't a new theme, by any means—but it was executed with the rage of a childhood spent in Florida, an adulthood spent writing songs for others, an existence spent being told that despite Val's passion, he wasn't marketable enough or quick enough or famous enough to be worthwhile. Remy felt himself molding it into something amazing, the same feeling he'd had when he'd first heard Val play through "Everything but the World."

This was, perhaps, Quiet Coyote's second song.

But Quiet Coyote didn't need a second song anymore.

"Yeah?" Val said brightly when he finished.

"It's great," Remy said, and he tried to smile but failed.

"Not that great, huh?" Val said, eyeing Remy's expression.

"They're dropping us. The label is dropping us," Remy said

quickly, before he could second-guess himself, before he could justify a way to delay the news.

Val narrowed his eyes, and Remy found himself wanting Val to have the answers, like they were children again and he'd come to his big brother with bad news. Then Val sat back, holding his guitar, looking across the apartment complex's desert of a parking lot.

"Finally," Val said.

"Huh?"

"Finally. We're free of those motherfuckers," Val said. "We're out. Now we can go back to doing what we want to do instead of being their little slave musicians. It's a good thing, Remy. Don't worry so much. We were Quiet Coyote in spite of them, not because of them. Fuck them all."

"Right," Remy said. They stared at the parking lot together for a while.

"Are you going back out?" Val asked, looking up at Remy.

"I can. Why?"

"It's a day for celebrating, brother. I want some help to get excited," Val said, grinning.

Chapter Thirty-Three

At LAX, Val came to pick him up, which was both a blessing and a curse—a blessing because it meant there was someone to share the burden of the media's sea of flashbulbs and shouts. A curse—well, a curse for Vivi's team, probably—because Val ruined every photo opportunity by flipping off the cameraman, the finger held right by Remy's face, therefore making the photos unusable on tabloid covers.

"Nice," Remy said, impressed.

"Celeste told me to do it," Val shouted—he had to shout to be heard over the press mob—and despite a crest of anger that rose in him at Celeste's name, Remy was grateful. It'd been nearly eighteen hours of travel back from Sydney, and frankly, he was beyond exhausted by all things paparazzi.

They made it out of the airport and into the van with far less drama than Remy expected, and as they drew closer to their home, he dared to crack the window and let in the salty, sharp smell of Venice Beach.

"You glad to be back?" Val asked.

"You have no idea," Remy answered, closing his eyes, breathing in the citrus-laced air. It hit him in the chest, just how hard it smelled like home, even though he'd have never thought he could be nostalgic about a place like LA.

Things weren't quite as he left them, of course. Houses had been repainted. Tiny shops had closed, and new tiny shops had opened, and the grocery store had changed names. There were new buildings going up, whose future purposes Val tried to explain as they zipped past them, back toward the fig-and-lemon house.

Celeste was at the door when they pulled into the driveway, tending to flowers she'd planted in crumbly pots by the entry. She looked up at Remy, and her eyes were hesitant, wary.

"Hey, Remy," she said as he climbed out of the car.

Val went still, waiting to see Remy's reaction.

Remy nodded.

"Remy, look—" Celeste started.

"Not right now, Celeste, okay?" Remy said, sighing, and walked toward the door. "I just—not right now."

"Give her a chance, brother," Val said.

"Not right now, from either of you, alright? I just can't right now," Remy said. He meant it—he couldn't fight with them on the heels of fighting and breaking up with Vivi. He wanted to, of course; he wanted to shout, to make Val apologize for telling Celeste, to make Celeste apologize for publishing the story, to make sure they knew it was their fault he and Vivi were done.

Except…honestly? He wasn't sure it was their fault. They were the catalyst, but the more he replayed his and Vivi's fight and the months preceding it, the more he thought they weren't the actual cause. A spark, not the powder keg.

"Alright," Celeste said, stepping aside so Remy could enter the house. "I just—I have to say one thing, okay?"

"Fine," Remy said, sloughing his bag off in the entryway. The house, like the neighborhood, had changed. Val and Celeste hadn't just moved into Remy's room; they'd made the house their own. There was a new couch, they'd painted the kitchen, the trees outside had been pruned. It felt like the two of them, not the three of them.

"Before you left, you told me to do my job the best I could and that you'd do your job the best you could. I didn't know that'd changed. I didn't even know anything about you and Vivi, really, until Val told me, and it sounded like it was...I don't know. Too big to break."

"And I only mentioned it to her because I thought it meant you'd be moving," Val jumped in. "I wasn't just...uh...gossiping."

They were both behind him, now, watching him stare at the house. Had the floors been refinished? No, no—they were just clean, mopped and waxed. There was a picture on the wall that said *I love this town* over an artsy rendition of the LA skyline.

"Remy?" Val asked.

"I didn't know it would do all this," Celeste said, her normally bold voice strangely small. Remy turned to look at her and saw that Celeste looked truly crushed—her eyes, her mouth, her cheeks were all pinched and worried. "It was just a story about another star," she finished. "I didn't know—"

"It was a story about a girl," Remy corrected. "And it was a story about me. People, not stars."

She took a breath. "I was just doing my job," she said.

Remy firmed his mouth but nodded. "It wasn't—there were other issues, okay? You didn't break us up, it just...that isn't how I wanted it to end." He exhaled. "Don't write about that."

"I won't. I promise. Nothing else about you or Vivi. I'll stick to crotch shots," Celeste said with a weak smile.

Remy tried to smile back, though he wondered if it had occurred to Celeste that those crotches also belonged to people, not stars.

"Well, hey, different subject," Val said, jumping in, either because he wanted to diffuse the tension or because he was Val and didn't notice there was tension to begin with. "I got a new tattoo. Want to see it?"

"I thought you were done with tattoos," Remy said, looking to Celeste, who was actually the one who had said Val was done with tattoos.

"I told him he could get one for his two-year sober date, since that would really be a new musical milestone," Celeste said, rolling her eyes. "I didn't know he was going to get something so stupid."

"What'd you get?" Remy asked.

Val grinned broadly and pulled his pants down so his hip bones jutted out. Across his right hip was an enormous, full-color tattoo of a burrito, with the words *Burrito Armageddon* written across the top in sour cream and guacamole.

"Oh my god," Remy said.

"Musical milestones," Val protested, looking pleased at Remy's horror. "I'm writing again, I'm clean, I'm getting shit done."

"And all that's best symbolized with Burrito Armageddon?"

Val gave Remy a wry smile. "It's the end. The end of me rolling up all my shit and trying to hide it in my pale white exterior."

Remy rolled his eyes. "That's stretching it."

Val laughed loud and hard, in a way bigger than that pale white exterior looked capable of. "I'm so fucking glad you're back, brother."

It was only a few days before Remy realized the rumors were true—you can't just go home again. The house was too different now, too *them* for him to come in and crash on the floor, to wedge his life back into theirs.

He was different too—he missed Vivi, even though he didn't want to, and it made him want to be alone in a way he had never wanted to be before. It was hard, seeing Val and Celeste together; watching them wordlessly duck around each other in the tiny kitchen, seeing them do each other's laundry and know just what could go in the dryer and what couldn't, listening in on Val's list when Celeste called from the grocery store, asking him if he needed anything. Val and Celeste's lives intersected so beautifully, and it made him distressingly aware of just how much his and Vivi's lives had not.

Moreover, Val and Celeste's lives intersected in a way that didn't leave much room for Remy now.

"It's just that this is your house. I don't belong here anymore," Remy told them after making up the couch a few weeks later—this couch wasn't a sleeper like the old one, which meant he had to tuck blankets and sheets around the cushions to make it bed-like. Celeste and Val glanced at each other then back to Remy.

"We didn't think about all this, man. We were just at the store and got sort of weirdly excited about a couch—I know, like I said, it was weird. We can get a sleeper sofa instead," Val said.

Remy shook his head. "The second I left, it became your house— the two of you. I don't think I should stay here. Besides, I can afford my own place now, and you guys can afford this place on your own."

Celeste looked stricken, perhaps because the reason she and Val could afford the carriage house was because of the popularity of her Vivi and Remy story. "Are you leaving because of me?" she asked.

"It's not because of you," Remy said, and he was surprised to realize just how much he meant it given that he and Celeste had been tiptoeing around each other, routing messages through Val and making conversation about frustration-free topics such as brick pavers, the mailman's schedule, and if that new conveyor-belt sushi place had finally opened or been sold yet again. But it wasn't about Celeste, not really. Even the breakup hadn't been about Celeste, when it came right down to it.

"Where are you going to move to? Not like…somewhere far…" Val said cautiously.

"No way. I've got too much producing work lined up in LA. I'll rent something in the neighborhood. And you'll help me move."

"The fuck I will. Hire movers. You're a producer now. Producers are too rich to let their brothers haul boxes around," Val said, but he was grinning.

The apartment Remy ended up renting was indeed in the neighborhood—a few blocks away, a third-floor studio walk-up with a view of the ocean and, in the distance, the Santa Monica pier. It was tiny and bright and cool, and it was more than enough space for Remy. He didn't have much to move, and Val helped him; they spent the afternoon hooking up speakers and cable and the internet. That evening, they sat on the balcony in dingy folding chairs left by the previous tenant, staring at the golden Ferris wheel lights as it spun in circles.

"Do you need me anytime soon, by the way? At SALT, I mean. I want to get my schedule together," Remy said, trying to make his words boring and uneventful. The truth was, his schedule was packed. For all the heartbreak it'd caused, people were interested in him now that he had a Vivi Swan producing credit, even if the song had never been released. Sure, Remy had to take time to sort out the legitimate production asks from the gossip seekers, but still—he was getting work as a producer, and that was something.

"I haven't really booked anything at SALT. If you want to play a little, I'm sure they can fit us in," Val answered, as aggressively bored as Remy.

Remy fought the surprise that twisted in his stomach at Val's words—SALT was the only place that regularly booked them. It was like hearing Val had quit his job. Too much time had gone by without Remy responding, so he finally said, "Nah, I don't need to play a little yet. I just spent months playing."

"Okay."

"Are you booking another venue or something?"

Val smiled a little and took a sip of his soda, some locally made fruity stuff that smelled so strongly of strawberries, it made Remy's breath short. "I'm not booking anywhere. I'm just focusing on writing," Val said. "You're focusing on producing."

Remy exhaled. "Yeah. Definitely."

"Remy Young, producer."

"Yep."

"Val Young, druggie. Celeste Yi, homewrecker." Val flashed a bright smile. "Vivi Swan, pop star."

Remy narrowed his eyes at Val. They'd rarely spoken of Vivi since Remy got back—and Remy was eager to keep it that way. He already thought about her all the time; he didn't need Val to turn thinking about her all the time into talking about her all the time.

"You keep trying to break people into parts, brother," Val said, shaking his head at Remy's expression. "You've always done that. There was me, the musician, then me, the addict. There's our parents, the religious psychos. We change titles, sometimes—there was you, the drummer, then the caretaker, now the producer—but you always want to narrow people down to a single thing. Shit, that's why you're a great producer—you're good at boiling a song down into a simple, single thing and driving that point home hard as fuck. But that's not what life is. That's not what people are."

Remy narrowed his eyes. "What's your point, brother?"

"That I'm an addict and a musician and your brother and a really good lay, is my point. *I am large. I contain multitudes.*"

"You said that before. Did you write it?" Remy asked.

"Nah, Walt Whitman," Val said, grinning. "I'd have said, *I contain a fuckton of multitudes.*"

"Deep."

"I know. But I do, indeed, contain a fuckton of multitudes, brother. And don't forget that you do too—and so does she."

Chapter Thirty-Four

Celeste's—well, *Bianca's*, since she was still incognito for most of the world—interview with Vivi, post-scandal, was one of the most popular things she'd ever written. Remy managed to avoid reading it, though the questions he got from friends, other musicians, and the paparazzi more or less gave him the gist of the article. Work, once again, became a beautiful distraction; producing required enough brainpower that it didn't allow his thoughts to drift to Vivi for more than a few scattered moments each hour.

He wasn't particularly surprised but was still struck by how different being a producer was than being a session drummer. There wasn't a daily routine, a single right way to play the notes, a system for each and every artist he worked with. No—as a producer, there was more ambiguity. There was looking at the artist and discerning what made him grin, or made her laugh, or made them look astounded and delighted and bob their heads to the beat. Producing was a puzzle, only he had to draw the final pieces himself.

But he was good at it—better at it than he'd been before the tour. He'd always known how to mold a song into something made of heartstrings and fist pumps, but now he knew how to look into the artist, to draw out what *they* wanted the song to be. To ask the questions that told him what direction to take it, even when he didn't know the artist all that well. Remy knew he wouldn't be the last producer to touch the songs he worked on, of course—he was still too new for labels to let him put a bow on anything—but he did his part, polished them up, sent them on their way.

In two months, he had a fair amount of work, most of it based on his proximity to Vivi. In three, more and more people sought him out for his credit rather than his role in the tabloids. In five, the already-scant paparazzi outside various studios barely lifted their heads to snap photos of him, and it was rare an artist asked him about his Sweethearts days. He was almost, almost able to get through a morning without thinking about Vivi. Each day he timed himself, noting the first moment she sprang into his head.

At the month six mark exactly, he didn't make it past ten o'clock in the morning—because that's when Celeste called with Vivi Swan news.

"What's the number?" he asked Celeste. They had an agreement—if there was Vivi Swan news that involved him, she would give it a number before sharing it. A one meant he was mentioned in passing—he usually passed on hearing news that ranked a one. A ten was *holy shit, this article is totally about you and will come up, so you need to know what it says ASAP so you don't look like an ass when someone asks you about it.*

"It's…uh…I guess an eight?" Celeste said.

"Fine, go," Remy said with a heavy sigh.

Celeste launched forward. "Okay, so Vivi just released the titles of the tracks for her upcoming album. Good news is that I don't think there are any songs *about* you. Which is a win, with her, right? Most of the songs are about Noel, I think, based on the titles. I'll text you the list—"

"Bad news?" Remy asked.

"She put 'Maybe It's Me' on the album. It's the last song."

Remy meant to respond, but the words didn't make it to his mouth. She was using the song? Their song? After all that had happened. Without so much as letting him know.

"Remy? Still there? Did you guys ever get a contract on it?" Celeste asked impatiently.

"Yeah, I'm here, sorry. No, we didn't. I just never got around to getting a contract," Remy said, voice trailing in and out. He remembered thinking he should get a contract. Everyone had even told him to get a contract. But then, he also remembered how precious and special writing with Vivi had felt. How the very idea of bringing a contract into it would have felt cold and stiff.

"Ugh," Celeste said, groaning. "Look—you still have the file from when you recorded a demo, right? We can get that to a lawyer friend of mine, if you want. She'll pay you royalties before she screws you over, I'm sure. No artist wants people to think she steals songs, not when they're trying to rehab their image like Vivi is."

Remy took a long breath, trying to give Celeste's words and his own professionalism room in his brain, which was currently flooded with hurt and memories of Vivi. "Uh, I'll think on it. I don't know—you're not writing about my response to hearing this, are you?" Remy asked.

"No, I promise," Celeste said solemnly. She didn't sound offended by the question; Celeste seemed to understand this was a question Remy would always ask for the foreseeable future.

"Cool. Thanks for letting me know," Remy said and hung up a little more abruptly than he'd intended.

He stared at the empty recording studio in front of him, Oriental rugs and rich teak-colored walls, all warmer and gentler than the microphones and diffusers and cords and stands. The artist he was working with today would be in within the next half hour; he had plenty of work to do before she arrived. He had plenty to focus on. Plenty to worry about.

Vivi was using "Maybe It's Me." She was using their song, their love song, without asking him. No, without telling him. He was going to hear it on the radio, he was going to hear his music and her voice and a song that he'd cultivated while he loved her. She hadn't even thought to tell him. It wasn't something Celeste's lawyer friend could fix, because the hurt wasn't about the money. It'd be easier, in fact, if it were about the money.

Remy's eyes blurred the microphone stands into pencil-thin lines, the rugs into blobs of red paint, his hurt into anger. He pulled out his phone, pulled up his messages, typed furiously and stupidly and ignored the fact he knew he'd regret this sooner rather than later.

Remy Young: Saw you're releasing Maybe It's Me.

He waited. She didn't respond, but the message was read—was this even her number anymore, though? It wasn't like they'd communicated since Sydney. Maybe she'd changed her number to ensure he disappeared from her life completely.

Remy Young: you could have at least told me

No response. He felt his heart beating fast and angry in a way it rarely had. She could at least respond. She could at least say something. She could at least send him an emoji, for fuck's sake.

The message was read. Still no response.

Remy Young: I can't believe you'd release a song we wrote together without even telling me. This is ridiculous.

Nothing.

Remy closed his eyes, tried to cool the heat growing behind them. He took a deep breath, another, another, trying to slow his heart and failing. Of course there wasn't a response, he told himself as he tossed his phone on the table like it'd bit him. She was Vivi Swan, and he was just another ex-boyfriend now. Why would she message him?

Multitudes, my ass.

Chapter Thirty-Five

The package was delivered four days after his fruitless texts to Vivi.

It was delivered in the middle of the day to his new apartment's office, shoved into his hands so casually by the manager there that he had no reason to expect it was anything special. When he opened it at his kitchen counter, however, his mouth went sticky and dry. It was a notebook—black, leather-bound. A Moleskine with worn edges and well-loved pages.

It was Vivi's.

Remy stared at it, looking for signs he was mistaken—but knowing he wasn't. It even smelled like her: vanilla and hair product and light, wafting up at him to break his heart. He laid it down on the counter for a few moments, like it needed to cool off before he could handle it again. It watched him. He watched it.

There was no explanation, no note, no card explaining why she'd sent it. Remy found himself balancing reason and emotions ineffectually; was it a reminder intended to hurt him for hurting her? Was it something she was throwing away and thought she'd toss unceremoniously at him? Was it supposed to be meaningful, something to tug his heart along as he fought to free it from her ropes? Some kind of test, to see if he'd violate her trust and read it?

Finally, he lifted it again and walked to his couch, sat back, and set the book on his lap. He opened it using the tips of his fingers only, like whatever was between the pages might poison him. She wouldn't have sent it to him if she didn't intend him to read it, right? And even if this was some sort of twisted trustworthiness test, he didn't owe it to her to pass. He could read it. He *should* read it.

He flipped open to the first page. Vivi's tiny, perfect print screamed at him, right there at the start.

"Untitled (Favorite???) (They Said No???)"

It was an incomplete song about Noel—clearly, a song about Noel, one that had been scribbled out in multiple pens, probably over multiple days. It was little more than a few opening lines and a rocky chorus she'd crossed out and rewritten a handful of times. He read it over and turned the page.

"Make It Work"

Noel again, a song about how she and Noel would make their relationship happen, how it wouldn't be easy, but they'd figure it out. No music—just lyrics. He turned the page again, again, song after song about Noel for the first third of the book. Some of the song titles he recognized—they were on her upcoming album. Others were so incomplete, he doubted they'd ever even made it to contender status, relegated to be ugly baby songs for the rest of their lives.

And then there it was, almost exactly a third of the way through— the golden song. The page she'd opened when they were on the bus out of Portland, graph lines and number charts. The song that eventually, slowly, cautiously became "Maybe It's Me." It was like looking at an old school picture. The notes were wrong, the words different, how had they possibly thought that chord progression made sense?

His eyes picked through each pen mark individually. She'd started the song on her own, but he'd been able to join in so easily. It'd felt like this song was waiting for him.

Golden.

He turned the page. There was a revision of what would become "Maybe It's Me" then a different song entirely called "That Night." It was incomplete, but it was about…well, it was about that bus ride out of Portland. Remy saw himself in it, saw himself in the way she described sitting and talking and sharing and discussing and having no option but to find common ground. Saw Noel in it too—in the guilt over knowing there's someone else out there waiting on you.

Next song—no title. It was about falling asleep on the bus, about falling asleep in front of someone for the first time. It was about Remy. So was the one that followed, and the one after that, and after that, and after that. There were bits and pieces of songs he'd heard her playing, he realized, some clever insults and some stinging accusations launched at her exes. Songs with descriptions of the garden in London and the Eiffel Tower and memories of the time they'd held hands on the bus and the first time she fell asleep curled against him. Songs about him and Vivi coaxing music from each other, about hiding from the world, songs about the space between heartbeats where no one could ever find them. About beautiful things being secrets, and about secrets being precious.

They weren't breakup songs. They were love letters in song form, sappy and sweet and poetic and prowling along heartbeats. He felt himself growing weary and heavy with loss as he read through them, as he carefully hummed tunes and sang lyrics under his breath. He turned page after page, swimming through a musical diary of what felt like each day that they'd been together. Every few pages there was a new version of "Maybe It's Me," a chronicle of how the song had changed meaning so many times. First, the version that served as a clapback at the press. Then the version about worrying it was you that hurt your family, your friend, your brother. Then the version they'd recorded in Spain, when it'd become a song about hoping you were the one. *Maybe it's me, maybe I'm it, maybe we're the ones that are going to be different.* Six versions of the song, all together. Six letters about the way they'd fallen for one another.

He remembered how she'd looked singing that last version, the one from Spain. The way her eyes fell on him, the way he believed it with all his heart. The memory was a desperate sharpness, pain he didn't want to be rid of but wasn't sure he could manage. How had that look morphed into one of betrayal? Into a meeting with managers, into arrangements for them to avoid each other, into him wearing sunglasses so there was no chance anyone would see them make eye contact onstage?

It was her fault. She'd forgotten he was a mere mortal. That he couldn't lock himself away with her and never make a mistake.

It was his fault. He'd walked away from her when he should have fought. He'd been annoyed when she was hurt by the very thing he'd always known would hurt her.

He turned the page. He had to turn the page, or else it would devour him.

There were more songs—songs about Paris and Cologne and arguing and waking up together and imagining what it'd be like to be together without eyes on them. Love letter after love letter. This was proof—she'd sent him *proof* that he hadn't been another breakup song waiting to happen; he'd never been a breakup song at all.

His stomach spun as he ran his fingers across the lyrics of their song, fingerprints sliding across the indentations of the pen marks.

The book wasn't totally full—he came to the last song with a few blank pages to go. It was a sixth iteration of "Maybe It's Me." His eyes danced across the number charts first. It was still the same song, for the most part, only minor changes here and there. He realized it was meant to be played slower, like a ballad almost, rather than like the upbeat, cheerful version they'd recorded in Spain. He frowned and began to scan the lyrics.

They were different—totally different. It wasn't a clapback to the press, or a song about fear, or a song about being the one. It was an apology. A song about knowing that it's your fault, a plea. *Maybe it's me that broke us in pieces, maybe we could just go back in time, maybe I could find a way to tell you*—

He looked away.

If she wanted to apologize, she could have called. She could have answered his texts. She could have written a letter, rather than sending the book. This was nice, but it was still their breakup song. It was still over. They were still done. An apology song—and apology, period—didn't make them any more feasible, after all. She was still Vivi Swan.

She was still Vivi.

She was still the girl who loved him long before he realized he loved her.

She was still the girl he loved.

Motherfucker.

Chapter Thirty-Six

"There was a contract too, in the back. For a royalty percentage. A good one, honestly, given how much of the song has changed for the album version," Remy said flatly. "I guess she figured that's what I wanted. Or something."

"Well, I mean, that's great. Awesome," Val said stiffly.

"Pretty decent of her, considering," Celeste added, nodding. "I mean, would've been nice for her to get that to you *before* announcing the release of a song you cowrote without your permission…"

Remy leaned his head against the crumbling brick, inhaling air full of figs and lemons and salt. It was late afternoon, the warmest part of the day, and the sun was low enough that it was blurry and flickering through the leaves of the neighbors' orange trees. Celeste and Val were sitting in metal patio chairs—they'd only bought two for the little bistro table, and despite Val's attempts to give up his seat, Remy had slumped against the wall of the house.

"I guess I should just sign the contract and send it back to her," Remy said.

"The book? Or just the contract?" Val asked.

"Both. The contract. I don't know," Remy said, sighing. "I don't want to keep the book. I don't want to know it's there because I don't think I'll be able to just stop looking at it, you know?"

"We could burn it," Val said, frowning.

"What the fuck is wrong with you?" Celeste snapped and shoved him on the arm hard enough that Val winced.

"What? He won't be able to read it then! I was just saying," Val griped, rubbing his arm.

"You don't torch a book of love songs, idiot. And you of all people should know better than to torch someone else's music," Celeste said.

Val looked ashamed—clearly, he hadn't thought about the music-murder aspect of lighting the book on fire. This didn't surprise Remy but rather comforted him. His older brother, threatening to beat up the book that was hurting his sibling.

But no. "I can't just burn it. But I don't know what to do with it. I don't know what to do with any of it," Remy said. "I wish she hadn't sent it."

Celeste gave him a hopeful look. "But then you wouldn't know. I mean, you'd just go on thinking it hadn't been real. So that's sort of great, right? That you know...well...that you know it was real... and..."

"And that it's over? Thanks," Remy said, rolling his eyes.

"Well, it's still nice to know she loved you," Celeste said, folding her arms. "But fine, whatever, burn the book, then."

Val reached over and, before Remy could think to stop him, grabbed the Moleskine from where it'd been lying on the patio table between the three of them, like a poisonous snake or forbidden idol. It took Remy a beat to realize what his brother was doing—Val reached into his pocket and produced a vintage silver lighter, flicked it open, and—

"The fuck?" Remy said and scrambled to his feet. Celeste yelped. Val froze with the flame beside the pages—

"What?" Val asked, startled. "What?"

"Don't!" Remy and Celeste both screeched in a harmony they'd never be able to duplicate on a record.

The flame from the lighter swished in the breeze. Val's eyes opened a bit wider. "You want to keep this?"

"I don't want to burn it! Put the lighter down, asshole," Remy snapped.

"You literally just said you don't want to look at it—"

"I don't want to look at pictures of people's newborns either, but that doesn't mean I want them destroyed!"

"The pictures or the newborns? That's dark," Val said thoughtfully.

Celeste swooped in and knocked the lighter from Val's hand; he whined at her, giving Remy a moment to snatch the book from his other hand. Remy glowered.

Val grinned. "Calm down, I wasn't going to actually burn the book," he said. "I was trying to make a point."

"That Remy doesn't actually want it destroyed? We'd already made that point," Celeste said. She looked eager to make Val pay for all this later.

"No—that you, brother, don't destroy the things you love. Even when they're hurting you, you find a way to hang on to them in some tiny little way. When they're me, or our parents, or our sister, or Celeste, or even when they're Vivi Swan. You're not going to burn this book up because you still love her. I'm no expert in romance or anything—"

"Truth," Celeste said.

"Thanks, babe—I'm no expert in romance or anything, but the *book full of excruciatingly romantic love songs* makes me think she still loves you too."

"That doesn't mean it'll work out. That's the whole point I'm trying to make here, Val—that yeah, the book is nice and all, but she's *still* Vivi Swan and I—"

"Still contain multitudes," Val said. "You can love her and be angry with her at once, you know. You did it to me."

Remy closed his eyes. *Breathe, breathe, just breathe.* He felt the decision swelling in him, needing to be made before it burst and broke forever. There was no time to weigh pros and cons, no time to make a list, no time to dwell on it. In so many ways, it was just like the decision he'd made to go on the Sweethearts tour all those months ago.

And so, he trusted his gut, just as he'd done then.

"What do I do?" he said in a near whisper.

"You give it another chance. One more chance," Celeste said.

"No," Remy said, opening his eyes to look at the two of them. "What do I do? Do I call her? Do I write her a letter? What do I do to tell her I'm not giving up on us after all?"

Celeste made a squealing noise, and Val grinned cockily then clapped his hands together. "Oh, man, okay, let's do this shit. She's all into romance, right? What if you write her a love letter and get some jackass in a cupid costume to deliver it? Send like a flower a day for every day you were together?"

"No, no, bigger," Celeste said, flapping her hands.

Val nodded then gave Remy a dire look. "Okay, okay—show up at her house at midnight with a boom box held over your head. From the movie. What movie is that?"

"*Say Anything*," Celeste answered, right as Remy said, "No way, she's got security guards."

Val scowled like this was a stupid response. "Punch them in the balls, leap over them, run to her window shouting her name."

"That's literally the kind of thing a stalker would do," Remy said, but he was smiling now, his heart was racing; he felt like he'd OD'd on caffeine or sunlight.

Val rolled his eyes. "A stalker she's in love with! I swear to God, I can have that boom box here in, like, an *hour*, man, tops."

Remy groaned and held a hand over his face when he answered. "No, no—I need to…okay. Let me think. Where is Vivi's next show or performance or whatever?"

"On it!" Celeste said. "I know this one! Or, at least, I know when she'll be performing *soon*. She has an exhibit at the Grammy Museum, and she's doing an acoustic set at the opening."

"There's a Grammy Museum?" Val and Remy asked in unison.

Celeste rolled her eyes. "And it's in LA. But her concert isn't ticketed—it's just Grammy officials and their guests. I'm only going because…" She trailed off then bit her lip. "Well. They offered me a press pass. Ages ago, Remy, I swear—"

"Can you get me in with you?" Remy asked.

Celeste shook her head. "No. It's just for one, and I'm sure they'll check the name on it at the door to keep people from selling theirs, so I can't just give it to you."

Remy hadn't thought to ask, really, but something in his chest softened that she might have offered. He took a breath. "Okay, then I guess that show's out—"

"Oh, for fuck's sake," Val said then dropped his head into a hand.

Remy and Celeste exchanged a glance; neither knew what Val meant.

"Are you saying a definite no on the boombox?" Val continued, giving Remy a hopeful look.

"It's a definite no," Remy confirmed.

"Right. Okay. Well, shit, then," Val said and stood.

"At some point, Val, you're going to have to share with the rest of the class," Celeste demanded.

"Remy, I'll get you a guest pass to the Grammy show. Let me make a call." Val sounded like he was arranging his own execution. He sighed and explained further, "The tennis party gig. I'll play the tennis party gig in exchange for tickets. The husband's a recording academy executive, remember?"

"Oh, sweet Jesus," Celeste said, eyes wide.

"You're going to play the tennis party? The one where they wanted you to change the words—"

"I'll be playing Quiet Coyote's hit, 'Everything but Colleen.' Just shut up and let me call him, fucking hell goddammit fucker," he said and stormed into the house.

But a half hour later, he emerged, looking beaten but triumphant all the same. "They'll have a ticket for you at will call, brother."

Then

Even after being dropped, Remy wasn't terribly worried about money. They still had plenty from their hit, plus a nice stream of royalties from the songs they'd written for others during their time at the label. For a while, it seemed almost like *this* was "making it," rather than sitting in a room trying to come up with a second song. They slept late in the day. They played at clubs and bars. They were free, free, free, and stretched their wings to lengths they'd forgotten about entirely during their time as label darlings.

Then two things happened, at nearly the same time: they ran out of money, and they met Celeste.

The first was inevitable, though it still came as a shock to Remy. He anticipated opening their bank account—technically Val's bank account, though they shared it—and seeing a five-figure number, maybe even a low six-figure number. It was a four-figure number. The account was riddled with cash withdrawals, sixty here, forty there, a hundred nearly every other day.

"We're basically broke," Remy said, panicking, waiting for Val to return his tone.

"We are not, Remy. We left Florida with basically nothing. We made it. This isn't broke. You've just gotten spoiled," Val said, dismissing Remy with a wave.

"We don't have an income right now! We barely get anything for gigs, the royalties aren't producing as much as they were. Val, this is serious," Remy said, slapping a printout of the account down on the table. Val was writing music—or rather, Val was staring at paper, drawing notes and then erasing them.

He didn't answer.

That night, they had a gig at a local bar called the Manhattan, a place for rich people dressed up as a dive bar—dark enough to feel scandalous but with clean bathrooms and bottle service. They arrived at the loading docks with the van and eventually made their way to the bar, where Remy scoured his phone for additional industry jobs and Val struck up a conversation with the bartender. She was a pretty woman, of indistinct ethnicity—black hair, brown eyes, a smattering of freckles across her nose, full lips. She was wearing a sleek dress and neon fuchsia lipstick that somehow worked, despite the unnatural shade.

"Quiet Coyote?" she asked, reading the band logo off Val's exposed chest. He'd gotten the tattoo to celebrate signing their deal. Two days before they left Nashville. Three weeks before they recorded a new, sleek cut of "Everything but the World," the one that climbed the charts and made them famous.

Val buttoned his shirt back up and said, "You know our song," then hummed a few bars of the hit until the girl nodded in acknowledgment. Val leaned over the bar and nursed his drink in a way that somehow convinced girls he was worth their time. It was the closest Remy had ever seen to actual witchcraft.

"I know it," the girl said, drying a glass. "You wrote it?"

"Yeah, and my brother down there produced it. It's my heart song. Piece of my soul, even after all this time," Val said, swirling his drink.

"You're playing it tonight?"

"Yep."

The girl frowned then leaned over the bar and looked closely at Val's eyes. Val looked pleased—like he was proud of how quickly he'd won this girl's affections. But then she snorted and leaned away. "You're high as fuck."

Val looked appalled but then laughed, loud enough that the sound carried through the empty bar. "What's it to you?"

She shrugged, put the glass away, then began cutting Meyer lemons into perfectly even wedges. "You don't play a piece of your soul when you're high as fuck."

Val's laughter faded, and his face went blank. "Who the hell do you think you are? You don't know shit about me."

The girl gave him a tired look. "I live in LA, and I run a gossip blog. I remember Quiet Coyote. I covered one of your concerts, when you were hooking up with that girl from your opening band."

Val scowled, like he'd forgotten the opening band girl ever existed and was displeased to be reminded. These things were likely true.

"That concert was amazing because the music was amazing. You played it like you cared about it, not like the overproduced bullshit reality stars that Steve hires to play this bar and *forces me to endure*," she shouted loud enough that Steve, who was on the second-floor balcony, could hear. Steve flipped her off without looking in her direction.

"And because I like to have a little fun, it's not going to be good anymore? It's gonna offend your delicate LA sensibilities?" Val asked.

"I'm sure it'll be fine," the girl said, shrugging. "Whatever."

"What's your name?" Val asked.

"Celeste," she said and reached across the bar to shake his hand, even though Remy could see hers was covered in lemon juice.

Months later, the intervention would be Celeste's idea. Well, that wasn't entirely true—Remy had wanted to do it for ages, but the prospect of giving his brother an ultimatum was laughable. Celeste, however, found it anything but. She'd done the research, she'd found rehab centers, she'd priced it all out and verified with Remy that they could afford sending Val there for a solid two months.

They sat down with Val in the living room apartment and told him the drugs had to stop.

Val laughed.

Then he shouted.

Then he punched a hole in the wall.

Remy tried to backpedal, but Celeste put a hand on his arm and charged forward.

"You're done, Val. It's not an option. You're done, or you're dead, and frankly, I'm uninterested in being with someone who is essentially a walking corpse," Celeste said flatly.

"You're saying you'll leave me if I don't go do this thing?" Val snapped.

"I'm saying we're not really in a relationship anyhow, if you keep using. I'm just the mistress to a substance. Why would I hang around knowing you and cocaine are going to be the things buried together?" Celeste said. She spoke the same way she wrote—direct, clear, a touch haughty. She wasn't crying. Celeste was too in control to cry.

Remy was, though he was trying not to. Val looked at him and found some form of ammunition. "Whatever, Celeste. Remy and I don't need you."

Celeste gave Remy a hard look, one that told him to just say it.

"Val, she's right. It has to stop," Remy said, forcing the words out. "I can't do it anymore either. When it was just, like…a hobby, okay. And then it was an expensive habit, and that was worse, and then it was an addiction, and now I think you're going to kill yourself if you keep it up."

"I can't just *stop*, Remy. You know how sick I get," Val said, rolling his eyes, like Remy was being entirely impractical.

"The rehab place will help with that," Remy said. "They'll give you medicine to make detox easier."

Val snorted. "Sure, yeah. They'll give me more drugs to undo this drug. Everyone in LA does some kind of drug, Remy."

"Then maybe we should get out of LA."

"And go where?"

"I don't know. Nashville. Maybe back to Florida," Remy said, grasping at straws.

He hadn't meant to play such a powerful card—he didn't even know he had such a powerful card. But Val suddenly went very, very still, his lips parted.

"Florida? Fucking *Florida*?" Val asked. "Are you crazy? After we finally got out?"

Celeste tensed, spying the opening, willing to take it even as Remy doubted doing so. While Remy fumbled for words, she spoke. "If LA is the problem, maybe Florida is the answer. If LA isn't the real problem, then rehab is the answer."

Val made a strangled noise. His eyes went wide, he fought for words, he ran a hand over his chin repeatedly, stroking a nonexistent beard. He looked panicked now, rather than angry, and when Val sat, Remy saw that his knees were trembling.

"You can't go back, brother. They'll get you. They'll pull you back in. We escaped together. We can't go back," Val said, locking on Remy's eyes.

"Then go to rehab, Val. Go get clean, and we'll stay here and be amazing musicians and create our own label, and it'll be amazing," Remy answered just as quietly. Celeste had faded into the background, probably very intentionally. She'd possessed the power to start this conversation, but it was clear Remy was the only one who could get results.

"Promise me you won't go back," Val said, shaking his head.

"Go to rehab."

"Remy, I'm serious. You can't. They'll kill you," Val said.

"Rehab. I'll stay here while you're in rehab, and then, when you're out, we'll be fine," Remy repeated, and his jaw shook so hard, his teeth knocked together. Val looked crushed, offended, and sat back, put his head in his hands. While his brother's eyes were averted, Remy glanced at Celeste. They were manipulating him, playing him like he played audience members. He wouldn't leave Val, not now, not ever, and it crushed Remy to make Val think otherwise.

"Fine," Val said, snorting back tears. "Whatever. I'll go. But I want to go right now. Right fucking now."

"Deal," Celeste said and leapt up, grabbing for her car keys, pleased to have won despite the cost.

"And Remy—" Val said, rising, "I'm only doing this for you."

The Vivi Swan Experience
The Grammy Museum's most popular exhibit yet—and it hasn't even opened!

The Vivi Swan Experience opens this weekend, and tickets are already sold out for the next three weeks! The new exhibit will be at LA's Grammy Museum for two months, before moving across the country for two years. Features include Vivi Swan's first tour bus, a collection of dresses and costumes she's worn to awards shows, performances, and in music videos, as well as a smattering of childhood photos, videos, and even a few never-before-seen diary entries! Vivi Swan herself is performing at the museum to kick the whole thing off, but don't bother trying to buy tickets—it's by invitation only. Good news, though—the mostly acoustic performance will be filmed and played as part of the exhibit.

Supposedly, the room will only hold five hundred for the performance—a far cry from her record-setting Sweethearts tour crowds.

Comments: 792

Author: Bianca Treble

Chapter Thirty-Seven

In the movies, Remy would have immediately dashed to Vivi's side. Instead, he had to wait three long, horrible weeks, during which he doubted himself into actual nausea more than once. He called David and Michael to make arrangements, along with the new drummer— who, incidentally, was the old drummer whose elbow was now totally healed and who had sworn off skateboards forever. Remy paced. He swore. He listened to Val complain about having to play "Everything but Colleen" for a few hours each day.

And then it was the day of.

The Grammy Museum was wedged between two other buildings, though the glass front made it feel more special than the spaces on either side. Escalators climbed up several flights inside, and red and violet lights hinted at the exhibits tucked just out of sight. There were security guys at the front; he approached them with more calm than he'd have had before the Sweethearts tour. They scanned the ticket in his hand then waved him through the doors.

The scent of makeup and suit fabric hit him with just as much force as the frigid air-conditioning. The room was filled with all of the above—people who weren't glossy enough to be celebrities yet were wealthy enough to be wearing designer clothing from head to toe. A few eyes turned toward him, and as if from nowhere, a waiter arrived with a tray of champagne glasses.

"Thanks," Remy said, plucking one from the tray. He edged around the side of the crowd, trying to blend into the walls—something he'd always been fairly good at. Occasionally people gave him a friendly nod and a toothpaste-commercial-white smile, as if they recognized him, but Remy knew it was professional, not personal. Finally, a chime sounded, and everyone made their way from the lobby into the theater.

The space was tiny—a few hundred seats, maybe, all decked in red velvet, and heavy golden curtains. Remy lingered in the darkness of the back row as the rest of the room filled in; when a particularly tall man sat in front of him, he nearly sighed in relief. This wouldn't work if she spotted him in the crowd.

And then her voice—her voice *there*, not in a recording or on a video, but coming from the stage, greeting the audience. The room erupted in applause as Vivi appeared in a fitted black turtleneck. Every hair in place, lipstick drawn on by skilled hands, high-heeled boots that made her tower over the musicians filing into place behind her—David, Michael, and Jason on the drums.

Remy had prepared plenty about this day but not about what it would feel like to watch her play music with someone else. It twisted at him, not quite jealousy, but some relative. Longing, maybe. Nostalgia. It occurred to him that he'd never seen her perform from this direction, and as she launched into her first song, he found his lips curled into a smile. She was wonderful.

They played through a collection of her old and new hits, most of which Remy had performed on the tour. As they started to edge toward the end of the set, Remy rose and quietly slipped back into the lobby. Museum staff lifted their eyebrows—why would anyone leave so close to the finish? But he just nodded and started in the direction of the bathrooms before diverting down the hallway, down another. He used the sound of the music to guide him—it was on his left now, so the door to the backstage area had to be just ahead somewhere. He shouldered through an EMPLOYEES ONLY door, kept an eye on the signs, then saw what he needed—TO STAGE RIGHT.

The song Vivi was playing ended; she was talking to the crowd now, her words muffled by walls but still bell-like, a cadence he knew by heart. He put his hand on the door, pulled it open, and darkness flooded over him as he stepped through—

"Close it, close it!" someone hissed. He pulled it shut quickly, unsure who the speaker was. He saw the sides of the curtains ahead, Vivi in profile, the band members arranging themselves for the next song, and the silhouettes of people watching, like him, from the dark.

"I need to see your pass," the hissing person—a woman with her hair in a perfectly sleek bun—whispered.

"Sorry—" Remy said and pulled out his ticket.

The woman shook her head. "This area is for press only. If you've got a ticket, you should be—"

"Hey!" a new voice whisper-called. Even in the dim of backstage, Remy recognized the silhouette coming toward him. It was Celeste, wearing a black jumpsuit that gave her the presence of a Disney villain with the shine of a princess. Celeste smiled at the bun-haired woman. "He's with my site, sorry." Celeste held up her neon-green press pass with the breezy confidence of someone used to getting what she wanted.

The woman shook her head. "Do you have his badge?"

Celeste didn't miss a beat. "No—wait, did you not bring yours?"

"Nope," Remy answered, having to speak up—Vivi had just begun a new song, which, if memory of the set list David sent him ahead of time was to be believed, was the second to last.

Celeste rolled her eyes then looked at the bun-woman. "He's the new photographer, sorry."

"He needs a pass to be back here, unfortunately," the woman said unflinchingly. "It's policy."

Remy swallowed, mind racing for a solution. What would Val do? That was a stupid question, actually—no one ever stopped Val. If David or Michael saw him, they'd probably get him through, but they were mid-set.

"Sir, if you don't have a press pass—"

"Here," Celeste said, yanking the lanyard off her neck. She pushed the pass into Remy's hands. "That's fine, right?" Celeste asked, looking at the bun-woman. "He can just take mine if I go?"

The woman shrugged. "As long as everyone in here has a pass, sure."

"Celeste—" Remy started.

"Don't worry about it. I did my job, now do yours," Celeste said with a meaningful look.

"Right. I'll get lots of…great pictures," Remy answered and smiled at her.

"No flash, please—do you even have a camera?" the woman asked, shaking her head at them, but Celeste was already gone, and Remy was headed toward the back of the press mob, to the curtain's edge. Vivi was right there, closer than she'd been in months.

The song ended; the tiny audience applauded. Vivi began to speak again, to introduce the next piece. *The* piece. Remy tried to collect his thoughts and failed.

Her voice was clear and bright. "This song changed a lot, over the course of writing it. It started as just a little sketch I was working on, and then I met someone who helped me turn it into something more powerful. Something better," she said. Behind her, Michael was changing guitars, David was switching from one keyboard to a baby grand piano. Now. It was time.

Remy slipped onstage without ceremony; Jason looked up at him with a quick smile. He rose without a word and gave Remy the seat at the drum set—like they'd discussed via messages in the weeks before. It was a risky move on Jason's part, and Remy silently thanked David and Michael for encouraging him to make it.

Remy's heart lurched as he sat in the seat that felt so familiar, despite the fact it was a different setup than the one he'd toured with. Still—being there, behind Vivi, listening to her talk…his stomach twisted, hard enough that he bent over a little from the nerves.

"Hang in there, kid," David whispered and grinned at him. Remy nodded weakly.

Vivi kept talking in her slow, thought-out voice, the audience clinging to each and every word. "It's what I've always called a golden song—because no matter how we changed it, what we turned it into, it always seemed to work. So the real trouble with this piece was figuring out *which* story to tell with it. Something about a boy?" The audience tittered; Vivi paused to let them finish. "Or something about a friend? Something about falling in love with the perfect person? In the end, it ended up being about all those things. It ended up being about *losing* all those things."

Breathe. Breathe. Breathe. He went over the music in his head— he'd never once in his life been so nervous for a performance and wasn't prepared for what would happen if he forgot something.

"So, anyway," Vivi said, reaching to take hold of a new, differently tuned guitar from the assistant standing just off to her left. "This is from my upcoming album, and it's called 'Maybe It's Me.'"

Remy let his sticks hover over the drum set and took a long, deep breath—he had to start, or she'd turn around and see him before the song began. Michael looked over at him, waiting for the cue, waiting for the intro—for the intro to the old version of the song. The version of the song that wasn't about losing anything.

The version he and Vivi had recorded in Spain, when they were in love but didn't know it, when the song was about finding *the one*. When the song was just as golden but far more perfect.

Remy clicked his sticks together to count off, a tempo far too fast for the newest version of the song. His eyes slid over for a millisec-ond to Celeste and Val, standing just off the stage, both grinning like fools, with confidence Remy didn't have. One, two, three clicks, and he launched into the song.

Vivi spun around, alarmed, hair whipping around her face like a halo, blue eyes landing on Michael. In slow motion, they continued across the stage, to David, to—

To Remy.

Her eyes fell on him as he played the opening lick over and over, David and Michael following his lead. Vivi's lips parted, her eyebrows knitted, her chest wobbled with a sharp breath.

She didn't look away. Neither did he. His hands kept moving, playing the lick, kept drumming like he'd been trained to do. He barely realized it, though; he was too busy watching her, waiting to see what she'd do, watching her eyes go watery and her lips curve into the smallest, quivering smile.

She'd smiled. She was smiling.

He exhaled and nearly missed the beat when he smiled back. Vivi pressed her lips together, spun back around, and brought her pick down to the guitar, sliding right into the song like they'd rehearsed it this way. Vivi sang loud, confident, certain, despite the fact her voice shook on the big notes, despite the fact her breath control was all over the place, despite the fact Remy could feel her fighting not to rush the song. The audience lit up, the room lit up, the world lit up golden.

They soared through the bridge, David and Michael looking delighted with themselves, Remy desperate to hold himself together, Vivi glowing. When they ran into the last few moments of the song, Remy found himself fighting the urge to rise, to go to her, unsure what he should do—he'd prepared for playing the music but for nothing beyond that. Vivi held the last note long, let the guitar fade out, let the audience rise in applause—

Remy dropped the drumsticks and stood, because if he sat at the drum stool a moment longer, he might dissolve. He didn't go to her, though—he wasn't sure if he could step toward her, if he could move, what he should do—

Vivi turned around. Her cheeks were still wet, her lips pressed together, her eyes apologetic and hopeful, forcing Remy to smile. She pushed the guitar over her shoulder and walked toward him, heels clicking along the stage, louder than the applause, louder than Remy's heart. He scooted around the drum set, waiting for her to reach him, trying to anticipate what she might say—that she'd talk to him after the show, that she was happy to see him, that she needed to finish this set—

Vivi grabbed his hand, and it felt like she was grabbing his heart. "Hi," he said.

"Hi," she answered, voice shaky. "I can't believe you did that."

"I don't know if you mean that as a good or bad thing," he said, trying not to hold her hand back too tightly, trying not to relish the way it felt to have her so close to him again. The audience was still applauding, the lights felt hotter than before, Remy could feel everyone staring at them.

Vivi didn't look back. She was facing him and the black curtain behind him, like the crowd wasn't there at all. She swallowed and stepped closer, and before Remy prepared himself for it, she slid her hand up his arm and pulled his face closer to hers.

He thought of so many things to say. *I love you. I've missed you. Can we try this again? One more time? Can we—*

She kissed him. She did it like no one was watching—and there, under the lights and cameras and gazes, he kissed her back like everyone in the world was.

Both were true.

Neither mattered.

Yes, it's me. It's you. It's us.

Vivi Swan > Remy Young
Sort: Oldest to Newest, Most Popular

>*Vivi's New Man*

Vivi's got a secret weapon on her tour—producer-slash-drummer Remy Young, formerly of indie band Quiet Coyote. Rumor is that the two have been spending a lot of time on Vivi's tour bus lately, but there's no need...

>*Vivi Swan and Producer in the House*

Vivi Swan and new producer-slash-tour-drummer Remy Young (of Quiet Coyote fame) stopped by Casa Oro studios in Madrid yesterday morning. Sources say they were inside for approximately four hours, and recorded a single...

>*Another One Bites the Dust*

Stars—they're just like us! Except when they break up, they do it in Helsinki, while in the middle of a massive world arena tour. Despite insisting just a few weeks ago that the two were making vacation plans for the summer...

>*Romance Isn't So Dead*

Remy Young surprised Vivi Swan by playing drums for her Grammy Museum performance of their cowritten tune, "Maybe It's Me." Rumors—some not so sweet ones—have swirled about these two, but now it's pretty clear: Vivi Swan and Remy Young are an item, and an adorable one at that...

>*Vivi Sporting New Bling*

Is that an engagement ring!? Vivi Swan wouldn't say, but given the smile our cameras caught, we're going to guess that the answer is YES—it looks like Vivi Swan and Remy Young are engaged! The two met while...

Acknowledgments

This has been a book of my heart for many, many years; a book written when I needed something fresh and new and precious in my writing soul. I'm so grateful I get to share it with you. It wouldn't have happened if it weren't for a bunch of amazing people. Namely—

Christa Désir, who believed in a weird romantic musical book and championed it with her whole heart, and the whole team at Sourcebooks for their enthusiasm and energy.

Josh Adams, my extraordinary agent, who didn't flinch when I waded outside the kidlit waters for the first time.

Lauren Morrill, who listened to me talk and talk and talk and talk for years about this book, and pop music, and celebrity culture, and the joys and woes of writing.

Kyle Jones, who had all sorts of up-and-coming musician knowledge, and his brother/bandmate, Michael, who I'm sorry I never got the chance to meet.

Arlan Hamilton, Janine Foster, and her band, who let me be a kinda subpar merch girl, but also let me pepper them with questions about the music industry—I learned more in that single night than I had in many hours of online research.

I love this book so much. I love you guys so much. I love writing so much—and I think I'd forgotten that. Thanks for helping me remember.

About the Author

Jackson Pearce is an unapologetic lover of pop music, an avid gossip-site reader, and a frequent watcher/rewatcher/binge-watcher of romantic comedies. She lives in Atlanta, Georgia, where she has been involved in music and arts education for high schoolers for over a decade.

THE STAND-IN

A hilarious and heartwarming story
of fame, family, and love

Gracie Reed is doing just fine. Sure, she was fired by her overly "friendly" boss, and no, she still hasn't gotten her mother into the nursing home of their dreams, but she's healthy, she's (somewhat) happy, and she's (mostly) holding it all together.

But when a mysterious SUV pulls up beside her, revealing Chinese cinema's golden couple Wei Fangli and Sam Yao, Gracie's world is turned on its head. The famous actress has a proposition: due to their uncanny resemblance, Fangli wants Gracie to be her stand-in. The catch? Gracie will have to be escorted by Sam, the most attractive—and infuriating—man Gracie's ever met…

"A sparkly, cinematic adventure that combines emotional drama with hilarious and relatable moments."
—Talia Hibbert, *USA Today* bestselling author

For more info about Sourcebooks's books and authors, visit:
sourcebooks.com

THE GIRL WITH STARS IN HER EYES

Her name's Antonia Bennette, and
she's not (yet) a rock star...

Growing up, Antonia "Toni" Bennette's guitar was her only companion...until she met Sebastian Quick. Seb was a little older, a lot wiser, and he became Toni's way out, promising they'd escape their small town together. Then Seb turned eighteen and split without looking back.

Now, Toni B is all grown up and making a name for herself in Philadelphia's indie scene. When a friend suggests she try out for the hottest new band in the country, she decides to take a chance...not realizing that this opportunity will bring her face-to-face with the boy who broke her heart and nearly stole her dreams.

"A brilliant standout."
—Christina Lauren, *New York Times* bestselling author

For more info about Sourcebooks's books and authors, visit:
sourcebooks.com

I HATE YOU MORE

"Romance that blends heat, humor and heart," (*Booklist*) from author Lucy Gilmore. She'll show him who's best in show...

Ruby Taylor gave up pageant life the day she turned eighteen and figured she'd never look back. But when an old friend begs her to show her beloved Golden Retriever at the upcoming West Coast Canine Classic, Ruby reluctantly straps on her heels and gets to work.

If only she knew exactly what the adorably lazy lump of a dog was getting her into.

"Romance that blends heat, humor, and heart."
—*Booklist*

"As appealing as a puppy."
—*Publishers Weekly*, Starred Review, for *Puppy Christmas*

For more info about Sourcebooks's books and authors, visit:
sourcebooks.com